THE BLISSFULLY
DEAD

OTHER TITLES BY LOUISE VOSS AND MARK EDWARDS

Killing Cupid

Catch Your Death

All Fall Down

Forward Slash

From the Cradle

OTHER TITLES BY MARK EDWARDS

The Magpies

What You Wish For

Because She Loves Me

Follow You Home

OTHER TITLES BY LOUISE VOSS

To Be Someone

Are You My Mother?

Lifesaver

Games People Play

The Venus Trap

LOUISE VOSS & MARK EDWARDS

THE BLISSFULLY DEAD

THOMAS & MERCER

This is a work of fiction. Names, characters, organisations, places, events, and incidents are either products of the author's imagination or are used fictitiously.

Published by Thomas & Mercer, Seattle

www.apub.com

Amazon, the Amazon logo, and Thomas & Mercer are trademarks of Amazon.com, Inc., or its affiliates.

ISBN-13: 978-1503947474
ISBN-10: 1503947475

Cover design by bürosüd° Munich, www.buerosued.de

Printed in the United States of America

*This one is for Louise's fiancé, Nick Laughland,
and for Mark's wife, Sara Edwards.*

Prologue

Rose looked up at the hotel, wishing she'd been allowed to save the image on her phone, that it wasn't against the rules. This was definitely the place – although, as with everything in her life, she retained a niggle of doubt. She was surprised that he would stay in a Travel Inn. That was the kind of lame place her dad stayed in when he went away on business. But she guessed that was the point. He was being clever. He had arranged the rendezvous – the word sending a little *frisson* of excitement through her insides – here because it was exactly the kind of crap-hole where nobody would expect him to hang out.

She was wearing her new pants – pink with the word 'LUCKY' stamped across the front. She'd flushed the same shade of pink as the knickers when she'd put them on the counter in Primark, though the woman who served her didn't even smile as she stuffed them in the paper bag. If only that woman knew who Rose was meeting, she would be sick with jealousy, and she would see – like everyone would see, soon enough, when the whole world found out about their love – that she, Rose Emily Sharp, was special.

Not *different*, as Dad said, thinking it was a compliment. Not *weird*, like the girls at school sneered.

Special.

The first photo had been of this hotel, taken from this very spot, with the caption '*11 p.m.*'. She stood and fiddled with her phone, drizzle spotting its shiny surface. There was hardly anyone about, probably because of the weather, and the streetlamps struggled to cut through the gloom. A couple of young blokes in hoodies strolled past. Her whole body clenched, but they ignored her, not even bothering to give her the once-over. Not that she cared, anymore, if boys noticed her.

It was 10.59, and as the time on her phone rolled over to eleven o'clock, she received another photo, dead on time. She stared at it, her heart pounding, knowing that she only had ten seconds before it would disappear. The picture showed a pair of grey doors, with one of those big wheelie bins in front. She looked up at the hotel, confused for a moment, then got it.

He wanted her to go round to the back entrance. Of course. This was a secret rendezvous. He didn't want anyone at the front desk to see her or, worse, try to stop her. He wanted to make sure that nothing stood in their way.

She smiled. He was so thoughtful, even more so than she'd gathered from his interviews and tweets.

Rose waited for the green man and crossed the road on shaky legs. She felt as she had that time when she'd been sent to see the head teacher after screaming at that slut Bethany Douglas in class, who had spread a rumour that Rose had wet the bed on the school trip. Bethany also said that OnTarget were a band for tweenies and toddlers, and had made up her own lyrics to their biggest hit, 'Forever Together', replacing 'together' with 'bed-wetter'. The head teacher, Mrs Morpurgo, had sighed and said, 'What are we going to do with you, eh, Rose?'

Rose ground her teeth together at the memory. Mrs Morpurgo would regret it when Rose was famous and spent some of her an interview once – actually, she'd read it a hundred times – in which he said that he liked girls to be natural. And he'd also said, in a Q&A with an American website, that his favourite smell was fresh rain.

The lift door pinged open. The corridor was empty. As she walked down towards room 365, she felt light, like she was full of helium, and as she knocked on the hotel door she experienced a great sensation of warmth, of peace, a feeling that she could describe only as *coming home*. Like this was where she was meant to be. It was her destiny.

The door was pulled open and she stepped into the room. She could smell air freshener, the same one her mum used at home, but she couldn't see anyone in the room. Just a bed, with – what was that lying on the sheets? Something metal, glinting in the harsh light.

He was, she realised, standing behind her, but before she could turn she felt a sudden, sharp pain in her head, and then she was being dragged, with blood in her eyes, across the room. All she could hear was breathing, and all she could think about was Mum, her lovely mum, knocking on her door at home with a steaming mug of tea.

PART ONE

Chapter 1
Day 1 – Patrick

D I Patrick Lennon was in a foul mood as he drove around the one-way system of Kingston-upon-Thames's town centre with the unmarked pool car's blues and twos on. He was trying hard not to let it show, out of respect for his passenger, his colleague DS Carmella Masiello, but she knew him all too well.

'Come on, Pat, spit it out. You look like a bulldog chewing a wasp.' She chuckled. 'Don't you love that expression? I think it's my favourite, with "a face like a slapped backside" coming a close second.'

He didn't smile, although her deep voice and soft Irish accent usually helped lift his spirits when he was in a funk. They'd been working together for three years now and increasingly he thought that he couldn't imagine anyone else as his partner. The traumatic events of their last case had served only to strengthen their bond.

'Are you thinking about the girl?' she prompted, then paused, her chatter halted by the grim awareness of what awaited them in the hotel at the end of their car journey.

There was a long silence that Patrick finally broke, his voice barely audible above the wail of the siren.

'No. I probably should be, but I'm not.'

'What is it, then?'

Patrick took a corner too sharply and a corkscrew of auburn hair fell loose from Carmella's long ponytail. She blew a sharp puff of air from her mouth to get it off her face, then tucked it reflexively behind her ear. It was that habitual gesture that finally made Patrick crack a small smile.

'Sorry, Carmella, ignore me. I've just had it up to here with living with my mum and dad. It was a necessary evil when Gill was . . . not around . . . but now she's out, it just seems crazy that me and Bonnie are still cooped up in my old tiny bedroom, while Gill has our whole house to herself! I can't moan about it at home because my mother already thinks Gill is the Antichrist. And she's been so helpful – Mum, I mean. I couldn't have managed without her and Dad, but they're clearly knackered as well. It's been eighteen months! Imagine, living with your parents at my age for eighteen months! Sharing a bedroom with a toddler! My street cred is in tatters, and let's not even mention my sodding sex life . . .'

He was joking – sort of – but somehow couldn't raise another smile. Carmella was his friend as well as his partner, but he suddenly wished she hadn't wormed it out of him. The words had gushed out involuntarily, but now, far from being cathartic, it felt emasculating. He accelerated around a line of stationary cars and zoomed past a red light, on the wrong side of the road, as if the speed could shake off some of his frustration. Frustration, and humiliation, that everyone at the station by now knew his situation. DI Winkler, the perennial thorn in his side, had asked if 'his mummy tucks him in at night' just the other day, and it had been all Patrick could do not to sock him one.

He shifted gear up to fifth and took off down the long straight road.

'Slow down, boss,' Carmella said. 'The girl's still going to be dead when we get there. So, tell me to mind my own business, but when do you think you'll be able to go home? Doesn't seem right, somehow, when you're not the one who can't be trusted with Bonnie . . .'

Patrick shot a sidelong glance at her – his instinct to tell her, yes, mind your own business – but he knew she was only concerned. And the truth was, he'd bottled it all up for so long that it would be a relief to talk about it. Doing so while driving at seventy in a 40 mph zone seemed as good a time as any.

'It's been six months since Gill was released. She seems absolutely fine, and Bonnie sees her most days – unsupervised now. But her doctor recommended that she shouldn't feel she has total responsibility for Bonnie until she's completely ready, and I don't want to push her in case . . . you know . . .'

He still couldn't say the words out loud: *in case my wife tries to kill our child again.* He didn't think it could ever happen again – Gill had suffered a huge mental breakdown – but, on the other hand, he'd never had any indication that it could happen in the first place, and the risks just seemed too great. Sleeping in his single bedroom at his folks' house with Bonnie in a toddler bed next to him – which meant actually in bed with him at some point every night – had been a small price to pay for the knowledge that she was safe. But he still had to go out to work every day, so his mum and dad had taken over the childcare. There had been no other options – at least, not affordable ones.

'Does she want you both to come home?'

Patrick saw the distinctive red and white lettering of the hotel's sign in the distance and slowed down, killing the blues and twos. He turned and gave Carmella a rueful smile.

'She does, but she's scared. I'm not sure she trusts herself around Bonnie anymore, however well she feels now.'

Carmella opened her mouth to ask another question and Patrick would have put money on what it was: *What about you and her?* But thankfully she chose not to ask.

Because that was one question Patrick really couldn't answer.

He pulled into the hotel's car park and parked in a space next to the three squad cars and one police van already present.

'Right.' They got out and strode purposefully towards the hotel entrance. 'Let's see what we've got.'

Chapter 2
Day 1 – Patrick

C rime tape was strung across the third-floor corridor, the rooms in this stretch vacated, the guests moved to other rooms. In the lobby, Patrick had spoken briefly to the manager, a woman with a Brummie accent who looked like she'd applied her eyebrows with a child's black crayon, and told her that they would need a list of all the guests, including anyone who had checked out. He had expected the usual tedious complaint about privacy and the bloody Data Protection Act, but the manager, whose name was Heidi Shillingham, had said, 'Yes, of course. Anything we – anything I – can do to help.'

She smiled obsequiously and, in the lift, Carmella had winked at Patrick and said, 'She wants you.'

Patrick ducked under the yellow tape just as DS Gareth Batey emerged from the room, his face white with a hint of green. His jaw clenched and he swallowed, like he was trying to stop himself from throwing up. A bad sign. Gareth was a valuable member of MIT9, a young detective who was definitely going places – though with every day, with every grim case, the sheen of his enthusiasm and earnestness was rubbed off a little more. *One day he'll be as hard-bitten and resigned as the rest of us*, Patrick thought. *Poor sod.*

'All right, Gareth,' he said.

'Boss.' Batey swallowed again, blew air from his cheeks.

'Feeling OK?'

Gareth nodded, but his eyes showed that he was feeling far from OK. There was a rich smell creeping out of the room – the coppery odour of blood and something else. Cheap perfume or aftershave that stung Patrick's nostrils and made him want to sneeze.

'The SOCOs here yet?' Patrick asked.

'On their way.'

'Good. So tell me what we know so far.' He knew that as the first senior officer on the scene this case would almost certainly be his. He took out his pocket-sized Moleskine notepad and looked at Gareth, daring him to smirk. But the younger cop was too nauseated, and too used to Patrick's little quirks, to be amused.

'The chambermaid entered the room this morning just after 10 a.m. and found her. She was very cool about it, apparently. No screaming. No panic. She made sure she didn't touch anything, locked the door behind her and calmly went downstairs to tell them what she'd found.'

'OK. Is she still around? I'll want to talk to her.'

'Yes. She's downstairs in the manager's office.'

'Good.' He nodded for Gareth to continue.

'I already asked Ms Shillingham for details of who was staying in the room. But nobody was checked in. The room was supposed to be empty.'

Bang went the chance of this being an easy case, a nice stat to make the clear-up rate look better.

Gareth fell quiet, as if he had nothing more to say – not till Patrick had looked in the room, witnessed the scene. He was aware that he was stalling, delaying the moment when he would have to see the body, the source of that bloody smell. Recently he'd begun to wonder if he was losing the stomach for this job, if he should quit, do something different. But what else would he do? The only other job he'd wanted was to be a rock star, to go on tour supporting his heroes, The Cure. That was one dream that would never come true.

He motioned to Carmella. 'Come on, then. Let's take a look.'

Being careful not to touch anything, he entered the hotel room. Immediately, the chemical sting of perfume made him sneeze, and as he opened his watering eyes he saw her. The victim. He heard Carmella catch her breath behind him.

She was laid out on the bed, naked and spread-eagled in an X-shape, each limb pointing towards a corner of the bed. She had light brown hair; pale, freckly skin; downy hairs on her arms. A strip of pubic hair, shaved legs and armpits. Patrick felt his breathing deepen and the anger that fuelled him, that kept him doing this damn job, bubbled and simmered as he realised how young she was. Somewhere between thirteen and fifteen. A child, though doubtless she would have recoiled to hear herself described as one.

Her eyes were open, staring at a future that would never come. What had this girl's dreams been? To travel the world or have a family? Be a doctor or pilot or footballer's wife? However modest her ambitions, they were over. She would never go to university, get her first job, give birth, grow old. This was it. A life truncated. A full stop.

Patrick stepped closer, trying to ignore, for the moment, the injuries, the mortal wounds, his eyes refusing to focus on them. He wanted to see the victim, to get to know her for a moment. To make this personal.

The girl was fleshy, with large breasts and a soft stomach, wide thighs. He guessed she had a BMI of about 26 or 27. It was a body that hundreds of years ago would have been considered perfect, the ideal of womanhood, but not now, in the days when emaciation was the look most young women craved. He studied her face. She wasn't pretty, not in a conventional way, anyway. Her nose was a little too large, her eyes too close together. It crossed his mind that this would make the media less interested, that her face wouldn't sell many newspapers, which could be both positive and negative for the investigation. The last big case he'd worked, the so-called Child Catcher case, had been a media shit storm from the off. Unlike his colleague DI Winkler, Patrick wasn't the kind of cop who craved attention. In fact, despite his youthful desire to be a singer in a band, he abhorred it.

He closed his eyes for a second and made this young woman a silent promise. He would do everything he could to find the person who had done this. The man – in this case, it surely had to be a man – who had ended her young life.

There were marks on her throat that made it evident she had been strangled. But that was far from the most striking thing. There were cuts, short and shallow, all over her body, including her breasts and inner thighs, tiny trickles of blood patterning her skin. One of her outstretched hands was twisted and bloody, as if it had been stamped on. Her lips were puffy and smeared with dried blood too, like they had been punched or, perhaps, bitten. As he stepped closer he noticed that her skin was shiny in patches around the welts, and also around her vagina. The smell of perfume coming off her was intense.

'I think he sprayed her with perfume – in the cuts.'

Carmella stared as he pointed.

'He cut her, then sprayed perfume into the open wounds.' He kept his voice even. 'He tortured her.'

Patrick noticed a patch of blood on the pillow beneath her head and stepped around the bed. The hair at the back of her scalp was matted with blood, where she had apparently been struck with a heavy object, or banged against a wall.

He caught Carmella's eye. Her own shock was morphing now into something else. Determination. He nodded and they left the room, just as the scene of crime officers – the SOCOs – arrived. Patrick and Carmella headed back down the corridor, Gareth following. They would leave the SOCOs to do their job.

———

Thirty minutes later Patrick and Carmella sat in a conference room on the ground floor, the cleaner who had found the body sitting across from them. The room was dry and hot and smelled of Shake 'N' Vac. Patrick was sweating, his white shirt sticking to him, but the cleaner, whose name was Mosope Adeyemi, was cool, leaning back in her chair like she was about to interview them for a job. She was an attractive woman, with large, bright eyes and long limbs that Patrick fleetingly imagined wrapped around him.

'Where are you from?' Carmella asked. Patrick had asked her to conduct this interview while he made notes.

'I live in Teddington.'

Carmella smiled. 'I meant originally.'

'Abuja, Nigeria. I was a teacher over there, you know. Now I clean rooms, make beds.'

'For how long?'

Mosope twisted her lips. 'Hmmm, a year. Just over.' She leaned forwards conspiratorially. 'The people who come to this hotel, they are disgusting. Animals. And they never leave tips.'

'Can you walk us through what happened this morning?' Carmella said.

The woman sighed. 'I'd already cleaned half the rooms on that floor, apart from the ones where the guests were still in their rooms, like lazy pigs.'

'This was, what, just after ten?'

11

'Ten fifteen. I checked the time after I found the girl, because I knew you'd ask.'

'That's very thoughtful of you. Why did you go into room 365 if it was unoccupied?'

'Because I smelled the perfume.' She screwed up her nose. 'Terrible. Cheap. It was coming under the door, the smell. I was curious, so I went in, saw the girl on the bed and came straight out again. That's it.'

'Did you see anything strange in the room? Anything different?'

She tipped her head. 'You mean apart from the dead white girl on the bed?'

Patrick liked this woman, wanted to engage with her. But he stayed silent, letting Carmella continue. 'I mean . . . You clean these rooms every day. You know how they look. Apart from the body, did you notice anything unusual, anything that struck you?'

Mosope thought about it, then shook her head. 'Apart from the smell, no.'

'You didn't move or remove anything?'

'No, of course not.'

'Did you see anyone in the vicinity of the room this morning?'

'Just guests coming in and out of some of the other rooms.' She paused. 'There were no clothes on the floor of room 365. You noticed that? I guess he took them with him.' Her eyes widened. 'Like a souvenir.'

Chapter 3
Day 1 – Patrick

At the beginning of a murder case, Patrick's first job was to consider the obvious. A woman beaten to death at home – look at the husband or boyfriend. A youth knifed in the street – check out gang affiliations. So here was a young girl murdered in a hotel room. Less straightforward, but the obvious first action was to check the list of guests and staff. Find out who was in the hotel at the time of the murder.

DS Gareth Batey was waiting in reception, chatting to one of the security guards, a black man with a belly like a department store Santa. As Patrick and Carmella entered the lobby, Gareth came over and said, 'I've asked about CCTV. They have it down here, in the lobby, but nowhere else in the hotel. I've told them we'll need the tapes.'

'OK.'

'That's the security guard who was on duty till midnight last night. Derek Childs. After that, a colleague' – he consulted his notes – 'Stavros Demetriou took over. Mr Childs says he didn't see anything suspicious last night. No-one lurking around, nothing. I don't have a picture of the deceased, but as soon as we get one I'll check if he or Mr Demetriou saw her.'

Patrick nodded for him to continue.

'What else? I've spoken to the station. They're checking reports of missing persons, seeing if we can get an ID on the girl.'

'Good.'

Heidi Shillingham, the manager, was waiting behind the reception desk. He walked over to her, trying not to think about Carmella's observation from earlier. Heidi had just put the phone down and was wringing her hands, her face creased with anxiety.

A smile flickered on her lips as he approached.

'Detective.'

'Mrs Shillingham . . .'

'Miss. No-one's managed to catch me yet.'

Well, don't expect me to chase you, thought Patrick. 'I need that list of guests. Also, a full list of staff – everybody who works here, whether they were on shift yesterday or not.'

'Yes, no problem.' She hesitated.

'What is it?'

'Oh . . . I've just been on the phone to head office. We – they were wondering how long it would be before the body is removed and we can have the room back?' She squirmed. 'The hotel is fully booked tonight.'

Patrick sympathised. Heidi was no doubt getting shit from someone higher up. But it irritated him too, like the hotel wanted to check somebody into the dead girl's grave.

'I'm afraid it's going to be a day or two before we can let anyone access the room.'

'Oh dear. What about the floor? We can't afford to have the whole floor cordoned off . . .'

He shrugged. 'Get me that list and hopefully we can get this resolved today. Then you can go back to business as usual.'

He walked past Derek, the security guard, and pushed out through the front doors into the bright but chilly morning. He took his e-cigarette out of his pocket and took a deep drag. The light flashed, indicating that it was out of charge, and he cursed it, wishing he could have a real cigarette. There was a newsagent over the road and the temptation to go and buy a pack of Marlboro Lights was dangerously strong. *Go on*, a devilish voice whispered. *You could get hit by a bus tomorrow.*

You could be murdered by a maniac tomorrow.

He resisted, checking his phone to distract himself. There was a text from Gill: *I need to talk to you x.* He sighed and put the phone back in his pocket. He would reply later, when he got a moment. He knew exactly what she would want to talk about. Them. Bonnie. Their situation. And at the heart of it were the red-hot questions: did he forgive her? Did they have a future? Or had any possible future died the night Gill had tried to kill their daughter?

The thing was, he would happily talk about it – if he knew the answers. If he knew what he wanted, if his heart and mind didn't vacillate so much. And to make things worse, he knew he was under pressure, that there was a time limit. Gill, quite understandably, wanted to know where she stood. He was going to have to make a decision very soon. Make a decision and stick with it.

And every time he thought about that, he sought a new distraction, because he didn't want to make that decision.

As soon as he got back inside, Gareth hurried over, phone in hand. Carmella was upstairs, talking to the SOCOs. It crossed Patrick's mind that Gareth saw Carmella as a rival, that he wanted to win brownie points with his superior officer. *He* wanted to be the one to make the breakthroughs, deliver the news. Patrick looked Gareth up and down as he approached, thinking how different they were. At school, Gareth would have been one of the popular kids, the football team captain, head boy material, the kind of guy that Patrick avoided, hanging out with his Goth mates, going out with girls who only chose him because they knew their parents would disapprove. There was something of the Peter Perfects about Gareth Batey and Patrick didn't know if he wanted to protect him or encourage him to stop being such a . . . swot and get himself an attitude.

'Boss. I think we've got an ID,' he said in his crisp Scottish accent. 'A teenager whose mum reported her missing this morning.'

He held up his iPhone. On the screen was a picture of a frowning girl. A selfie, as they called it. He thought the frown was meant to be a pout but had gone wrong.

'Once I got the name I looked her up. I couldn't find her on Facebook, but she's on Twitter and Tumblr. Calls herself MissTargetHeart.'

She had a soft face, dotted with freckles, and light brown hair. The photo looked like it had been taken in her bedroom, sitting on her bed with a teddy bear propped on the pillow behind her. She had drawn a crude target on her cheek in eyeliner, three concentric circles, with an arrow through. It was definitely her – the girl upstairs in room 365.

'Her name's Rose Sharp and she lives about ten minutes from here.'

Patrick looked at him.

Gareth's cheeks coloured faintly. 'Lived, I mean. Lived.'

Rose Sharp's mum, Mrs Sally Sharp, lived in a terraced house in a backstreet of Teddington, the kind of place that a decade ago would have been considered moderately desirable but was now worth the kind of money that would make anyone north of the M25 gasp and shake their head. Close to a good school, low crime, a couple of organic delis nearby. A whole generation of Londoners had become property millionaires simply by buying at the right time. Patrick knew he could sell his house and move to Thailand and live like a prince. Sometimes, when confronted with this kind of task, he was tempted to pack up and go.

Patrick rang the bell, Carmella standing beside him. Gareth had wanted to come, but Patrick had instructed him to go back to the station and start checking the list that the hotel had finally produced. They were looking for known offenders, anyone with a record of violence or sexual offences. Even though they didn't know yet if Rose had been raped, the fact that she was underage and had been found naked meant there was almost certainly a sexual element to the crime.

'Call me the second you find anyone who looks like a good hit. Don't go off on your own, OK? It won't impress me,' Patrick had told Gareth.

Sally Sharp opened the door almost instantly, and it was clear that she had been hoping to see her daughter standing there.

Sally looked over Patrick's shoulder, peered around Carmella. Realisation entered her eyes then, and her face crumpled. But there was still hope – for a few more moments.

'Mrs Sharp?' Patrick said. 'Rose Sharp's mother?'

She nodded, inspecting Patrick's badge as he introduced himself and Carmella. Her hands were trembling visibly as she held on to the front door.

'Can we come in, please?'

She led them into the living room. It was an ordinary room: medium-sized TV, saggy sofa, a bookcase filled with DVDs and framed photographs. There they were – the pictures of Rose as she grew up, from a bald-headed baby with dribble on her chin to a teenager in a school blazer. There was a framed photo on the wall of Sally, Rose and a man Patrick assumed was Rose's dad. Sally was blonde with green eyes, and in the family portrait she sparkled with life and happiness. Now, standing before them, she looked squashed, as if a giant boot had stamped on her.

'Are you here on your own?' Carmella asked.

Sally's eyes followed the two detectives' towards the portrait.

'Yes.' She sounded like she had no saliva in her mouth.

'Is your husband at work?'

'I expect he's at work, yes. But he's not my husband anymore. He left us a year ago, so it's just me and Rose now.' She had a string of beads round her neck that she fiddled with. 'Have you found her?'

Patrick braced himself. 'I think you should sit down, Mrs Sharp.'

And before he'd even managed to tell her that they'd found the body of someone who matched the description of their daughter, that they would need her to identify the body, that her life would never be as happy or bright or hopeful again, she started wailing.

Patrick went into the kitchen to put the kettle on, while Carmella attempted to comfort Mrs Sharp. He called the station to check that the body had been removed from the hotel and taken to the mortuary so they could organise the identification. Sally had instantly said that she needed to call her sister, and that she would need to tell Rose's dad, Martin, which had prompted a fresh wail.

While Patrick was waiting for the kettle to boil, he slipped into the hall and looked up the stairs. Looking over his shoulder to check Sally Sharp wasn't watching, he went up onto the landing. The first door he opened was the bathroom; the second was the master bedroom. That left Rose's bedroom.

He pushed the door open gently and stepped inside. His eyes widened.

Four male faces stared at him from every surface: three white, one Asian. Every inch of wall was covered with posters and pages carefully torn from magazines or printed off the Internet. The screensaver on the computer showed the four boys with their arms around each other's shoulders. A T-shirt bearing their logo lay on the unmade bed and a life-size cardboard cut-out of Shawn, the most popular member, stood at the foot of the bed.

Patrick was in his mid-thirties. He liked indie and rock music. He didn't watch much TV apart from CBeebies with Bonnie. He didn't read a tabloid paper or any glossy magazines. But even he knew who this lot were. Rose was an OnTarget fanatic. Now, he thought, the media were going to have one hell of an angle.

Chapter 4
Day 2 – Patrick

The MIT9 incident room at Sutton station smelled of machine coffee and bacon sandwiches, making Patrick's stomach growl and clench simultaneously as he took his place at the front of the room beneath the blown-up photo of Rose Sharp. In the picture, she was smiling, revealing a gap between her front teeth, though there was a far-off look in her eyes. He wondered if she'd been happy and, if not, how far she had been from finding joy in her life. Growing up had been the best thing that ever happened to him, Patrick thought. Getting away. Reinventing himself.

He mentally glossed over the fact that he was back living with his parents now.

Half a dozen officers, including Carmella and Gareth, perched on tables or stood, and Patrick found himself appraising them as his eyes passed over them. DC Preet Gupta was leaning against the wall at the back – competent and affable, she was a straight-down-the-line, trustworthy young woman Patrick was always pleased to see on his team. DC Martin Hale, a tall man with thinning hair who reminded Patrick of Kevin Spacey, was older and seemingly happy to stay at his rank forever. He had teenage daughters, and Patrick noticed how Hale's jaw clenched as he surveyed the picture of Rose. He was sitting at the front of the room, so close to Rose's photo that he could count the few freckles on her nose – and indeed probably was. That summed him up – keen, with an admirable attention to detail.

The next member of the team, Wendy Franklin, another detective constable, was a newcomer, having transferred in from Wolverhampton in the West Midlands, and an unknown quantity. Patrick's initial impression was that – as his mum would say – she looked like a stiff breeze would blow her away. She was skinny and appeared to be about Rose Sharp's age, though he knew she was actually twenty-five. She was one of the desk-perchers, fidgeting and shuffling about with nervous energy, twiddling a biro between her fingers, looking like she was dying to get stuck in.

There was one notable and very welcome absence: DI Adrian Winkler, a man to whom Patrick had barely spoken since they came to blows, literally, on the Child Catcher case. He knew that Winkler was working on another murder at the moment, had seen him parading around the station self-importantly, flicking back his shoulder-length hair and puffing out his chest like a mating pigeon. Hearing that he wouldn't have to work with Winkler on this one was the one good thing that had happened in the last forty-eight hours.

'OK,' Patrick began, all eyes focusing on him. 'Welcome to the first briefing for Operation Urchin.' This was the name the computer had generated. 'Here's what we know so far. Rose Sharp, fifteen years old, resident of Teddington. Rose's parents are divorced and she lives with her mother. The father isn't a suspect, before you wonder. He was away on business in Germany and is on his way back now.'

He went on to describe the scene where they'd found Rose, consulting his notepad, writing down several points on the whiteboard as he spoke.

'The main points to consider about the crime scene are: One – the room was supposedly vacant, no key cards had been given out, so how did Rose and her murderer get in? Two – how did they get into the hotel room without being seen? We are checking lists of guests and staff, but so far there have been no hits. There was no CCTV in the hotel corridor, so we can't tell if she went into the room willingly or not. Three – did she know her killer? If not, what persuaded her to go to a hotel room with him? Four – Rose's clothes were missing from the scene. Where are they, and why did the killer take them? Rose's mum has been through her daughter's clothes and given us a description of what she thinks Rose was wearing. This information is on your printouts.'

Sally Sharp hadn't seen Rose leave the house, but by checking her daughter's wardrobe and the washing baskets she believed Rose had been wearing her new Top Shop jeans and a long-sleeved pink and white cotton top. 'She always wears earrings too,' Sally had said, her voice catching. 'And a necklace that her dad gave her. It's a locket. She keeps a photo of *him* inside it.' She pointed to a poster on the wall. 'Shawn.'

Then Sally Sharp had paused.

'She was wearing her new underwear too.' Avoiding Patrick's eye, she went on. 'She came home yesterday with a bag from Primark and I had a peek inside when she was in the loo.' Sally had described the knickers: pink with the word 'LUCKY' printed across the front. 'They're not in her room.'

Patrick handed out jobs to the gathered officers. Wendy was instructed to help Gareth continue interviewing the guests and hotel staff. Martin was given the responsibility of checking Rose's communications: social media, email and phone. Had she left any clues there?

'Her phone was missing too,' he pointed out. 'She had a contract with O2, paid for by her mum. Martin, I need you to chase up getting the records. Preet, I want you to start talking to Rose's friends.

Had she said she was going to meet someone? Any boyfriends her mum didn't know about?'

'What secrets did she have?' Wendy asked in her Black Country accent, as if she were thinking aloud. Seeing the look Patrick gave her, she said, 'All teenage girls have secrets. If my mum and dad had known half the things me and my mates got up to . . .'

'Yes, very true. But, according to her mum, Rose was a bit of an introvert. Spent most of her life in her bedroom.'

Wendy nodded. 'Probably an online predator, then. Some guy pretending to be a fifteen-year-old arranges to meet her at a hotel; she freaks out when she sees he's fat, bald and fifty; he knocks her over the head.' She shrugged. 'Simple.'

Patrick suppressed a laugh, seeing the daggers Carmella was shooting towards Wendy.

'Yes, well, let's not jump to any conclusions, eh?'

Wendy shrugged again. 'All right. But I bet'cha that's what it was.'

As Patrick was about to start talking again, the door opened and Detective Chief Inspector Suzanne Laughland, Patrick's boss, slipped through.

'Pretend I'm not here,' she mouthed.

What with Wendy's interruption and now Suzanne's appearance, Patrick had lost the thread of what he wanted to say. He turned back to the whiteboard. He could feel Suzanne's eyes on his back and all of a sudden felt hot, sweat breaking out beneath his white shirt.

He turned back around, trying not to be distracted by the sight of Suzanne tucking a strand of long blonde hair behind her ear.

'The other thing to note about Rose Sharp is that she was a massive fan of OnTarget.'

'Ooh, I love them,' said Wendy.

'Manufactured shit,' muttered Martin.

'All right,' Patrick said. 'This isn't the time for a *Culture Show* debate about the merits of boy bands. I don't think you're the target audience, anyway, Martin.'

'The *On*Target audience!' Wendy almost shouted, laughing at her own joke and looking around in the hope that the others would join in.

Give me strength, thought Patrick.

'The point is,' he said, embarrassed at this display in front of Suzanne, 'Rose was a fan. According to her mum, she was obsessed. She spent all her money on them, most of her time chatting about them online . . .' He shook his head. 'Talked about little else, apparently. OnTarget were her life. This fact is going to give the media an angle, make them more interested than they might have been otherwise. We need to be aware of that.'

'They're playing tonight,' Wendy piped up.

'OnTarget?'

'Yeah. At Twickenham Stadium. I was thinking about going but couldn't find anyone to come with me.'

'What a surprise,' Carmella said, eliciting laughter from everyone else. Wendy, though, looked hurt and Patrick felt sorry for her. It was unusual for Carmella to be bitchy, so he wondered what about Wendy had antagonised her.

'Maybe I should go,' Patrick said, enjoying the shocked expressions on the faces of his colleagues.

'I thought you were more of a Cure fan?' Carmella said.

Out of the corner of his eye, Patrick could see that Suzanne's lip was twitching.

'I am. But if Rose was a prominent member of the OnTarget community, this could be a good chance to meet some of them.' He pointed at Carmella.

'Oh no, please . . .'

'And you can come too.'

Chapter 5
Day 2 – Jess and Chloe

Oh my God, that was just so amazing, wasn't it? Wasn't that incredible? Did you see the way Shawn winked at me? I'm on such a high right now. He winked right at me, it was definitely me, wasn't it, do you think he recognised me from my profile picture?'

'Oh shut up, how thick are you, Jess? He's got fucking fifteen million Twitter followers; do you really think he'd recognise *you* from the stage forty feet away? . . . So where do we go, then, for this vigil thing?'

The two girls exited the stadium, borne along on a wave of identical over-excited girls in OnTarget merchandise, with identical long ironed hair limp with sweat, most with mascara running down their hot red faces. Chloe consulted her phone, where she had saved a screenshot of the directions that had been posted on Twitter. Jess couldn't stand still. She was jumping from foot to foot, bursting with adrenalin from the gig.

'What happens at a vigil anyway? We don't have to, like, say prayers or anything, do we? Or sing? I'm not singing.'

'It's not church, Jess, so I doubt it. But I don't know either. We'll just have to see, won't we?'

'Wonder who'll be there?'

Chloe pointed in the direction of the hot dog concession. 'Dunno. Loads of people from the forum, I think. I reckon it's that way. Exit P, by Gate 12. There.'

They managed with difficulty to fight their way sideways across the tide of girls streaming straight ahead to the gates, to a small static enclave of sheepish-looking fans standing awkwardly around. Jess and Chloe joined the group and stood at the back, staring curiously at the huge blown-up photograph of one of their own – a dumpy, freckled girl in her school uniform, staring into the camera with a fake smile on her face.

'So that's what she looked like,' breathed Jess.

The canvas was propped on a folding trestle table covered with an Indian throw and a cardboard sign saying '*RIP – ROSE EMILY SHARP. VIGIL 10 p.m.*'. An older woman was passing through the group, picking small candles on circles of tinfoil-covered cardboard out of a large crate carried by a sad-looking man behind her and handing them out to the assembled girls.

Jess still couldn't stop fidgeting. She hitched up her errant bra strap and adjusted her OnTarget crop top so that it covered half an inch more midriff. 'My ears are ringing. Are your ears ringing? That was the best one yet, don't you think? Eight concerts and that was definitely the best. You never know, he might've been winking at me. I tweet him so much. He might've recognised me!'

Chloe rolled her eyes. If it weren't for their mutual adoration of OnTarget, they would never have been mates, she thought. Jess had only contacted her on the forum last year after she, Chloe, had posted the photo of Shawn Barrett visiting her in hospital, when she'd had leukaemia, right before the bone marrow transplant that saved her life. They'd met up and Chloe could tell straight away that Jess was 'one sandwich short of a picnic', or 'away with the fairies', as her mum would say – but she could be a right laugh too. It was always Jess who made them get up at 4 a.m. to queue for the in-store performances or to be the first in line for when the ticket office opened. Jess was the one who organised them to get to whichever hotel the band were rumoured to be staying in, and who spent the longest on the forums trying to get the band members' attention. Any of them would do, but they both loved Shawn the most. He was the hottest by a long shot with his olive eyes and tan muscled chest; more man than boy.

'You and all the other fifteen million . . . anyway, shhh, settle down – we're here for MissTargetHeart.'

'She's so lucky. All these people here for her.'

'Jess, MissTargetHeart isn't lucky, for fuck's sake, she's *dead*.'

'Yeah, sorry . . . I don't see why we have to stand around with candles. These candles are shit, like the ones we had at infants' school in the carol concerts. It's embarrassing. It's not like we knew her anyway.'

'We kind of knew her,' Chloe said quietly.

Both girls fell silent for a moment.

'Do you know anyone who ever actually met her?' Chloe asked.

'Jade and Kai did, I think.'

'Jade? Don't mention that girl's name to me.'

As always, the thought of Jade sent a deep and uncomfortable *frisson* through Chloe, a shiver of guilt and shame. Fear, too. She had seen how vicious Jade could be; worse, the other girl was proud of it. 'I'm a proper Scorpio,' Jade had said once. 'Cross me and I'll sting you.'

Jess's eyes widened as Chloe said this. 'Shit, speak of the devil – she's, like, right over there.'

Chloe, panicking, looked in the direction of Jess's pointing finger until she saw the couple snogging disrespectfully to their right. It was hard to miss Jade, with her badly dyed long blonde hair. It seemed to swamp her boyfriend, Kai, as if she was swallowing him alive. Chloe had known, of course, that Jade would likely be at the gig, but she'd hoped that the massive crowd would mean their paths wouldn't cross. No such luck, it seemed.

Chloe and Jess slipped into the crowd before Jade saw them, just as the woman who had handed round the candles picked up a microphone, switched it on and tapped it. The main stadium audience had mostly dispersed now, and the small crowd assembled for the vigil turned its attention to the woman.

'Er . . . hi . . . and thank you so much for coming. As you know, we're here to pay our respects for a fellow OnTarget fan – my beautiful niece Rose who was tragically murdered two days ago in Kingston . . .'

The woman's voice faltered and she blinked hard behind large red-framed glasses. A middle-aged couple next to her was clinging together, openly sobbing.

Jess nudged Chloe and pointed at the crying woman. 'That's MissTargetHeart's mum and dad. I saw their photo on the news.'

Rose's aunt gulped and contained herself. 'Sorry, girls and' – she looked around and identified one or two males present – 'boys. I promised I wouldn't get all emotional, but it's hard. Anyway, so, what we'd thought we'd do shortly is all light our candles and stand still for two minutes thinking of our Rose and praying that she's in a better place now. But first, we have a policeman who wants a quick word with you all. This is Detective Inspector Lennon.'

Everyone present, including Chloe and Jess, perked up at the sight of the rangy man who stepped forwards. He was quite fit for an old bloke, thought Chloe, although she didn't usually find men in their thirties attractive. He was wearing proper jeans, not the shapeless dad-jeans her father favoured, and a well-cool battered leather jacket. She imagined him rugby-tackling a burglar to the floor and found it gave her a little thrill of excitement.

The detective took hold of the microphone and spoke, his expression grave as he scanned their faces. A woman stood beside him, quite old but fit-looking, her hair in long auburn corkscrew curls. His side-kick, Chloe guessed. She wondered if the curls were natural.

'I won't keep you for long. I'm hoping that you might be able to help us in our search for Rose's killer. I gather that you all heard about this vigil from either Twitter or the OnTarget forum on their website, and, under the name MissTargetHeart, Rose was an extremely active participant on both sites.'

'Extremely *annoying* participant more like,' whispered Jess to Chloe, who cringed again, wishing Jess would shut up. 'Smug cow. Acted like she was gonna, like, marry Shawn when she totally didn't stand a chance.'

'Shh, Jess. Stop it. I can't hear him.'

'I'm bored,' Jess said. 'And I need the loo.' She stalked away, pushing through the crowd towards the Ladies, leaving Chloe to listen to the hot detective without any more distractions. He talked for a few more minutes, telling them to report anything at all that seemed unusual or in any way worrying, and Chloe briefly pondered this. *Many* of the things said on the forums could be described as unusual and/or worrying, she thought.

When Jess came back she seemed totally spaced-out, a look of stunned joy on her face.

'What's up with you?' Chloe hissed. 'Did you meet Jesus in the toilet or something?'

Jess smiled mysteriously. 'It's nothing. What did I miss?'

'It's clearly not nothing!'

'Shhh,' Jess said primly, as though she had been the attentive one from the start. Several Bic lighters were going around the crowd and they were all lighting their candles. OnTarget's song 'Forever Together' came on and the girls all immediately joined in, their thin reedy voices swelling together as the tiny candles flickered and steadied. Rose's parents and her aunt now too all cried, as did many of the girls, even though hardly any of them could have known her.

The next time Chloe glanced across at Jess she was gazing contemplatively at the large tattoo of Shawn Barrett that covered most of her left forearm. Her mum had apparently gone nuts when she'd got it done at the age of fifteen, threatened to report the tattoo parlour, but Jess hadn't cared.

Now, Jess was biting the inside of her top lip to stop herself smiling and, with her right forefinger, she stroked the smudgy cheek of Shawn's tattoo.

If Chloe had had to describe her friend's appearance, she would have said it was ecstatic.

'Are you on drugs?' Chloe asked. 'Did you get some E?'

'Don't be daft. Drugs are for losers. Now be quiet, all right?' And she started to sing, belting out the words like her life depended on it.

Chapter 6
Day 3 – Patrick

'Mummy, you put the triangle in there.'

Gill beamed and slotted the triangle through the triangular hole in the apparatus. 'Here, Bonnie, do the circle.'

Bonnie took the proffered plastic ball, scrutinised it for a moment, then handed it back to her mother, shaking her head so vigorously that her pink cheeks wobbled. 'Mummy.'

Gill posted the circle, then handed a square one to Patrick. 'Daddy do the square?' she asked Bonnie.

Bonnie pointedly turned her back on him, as though he had just made some devastatingly insulting personal comment to her. 'No. I want Mummy to do it.'

Patrick shrugged, feeling ridiculously slighted. Bonnie seemed more than fine, playing with Gill as if nothing had ever happened – although of course she wouldn't remember it; how could she, she'd only been five months old, and that was as it should be. It would be terrible if she recoiled at Gill's touch.

Patrick remembered it, though.

He knew he would never, ever forget it. The sight of Gill's purple fingermarks on their baby's neck would accompany him to the grave, her tiny limp body within seconds of eternal lifelessness . . .

As if she could read his thoughts, Gill looked up at him from where she was crouching on the rug next to Bonnie and her toys. She gave him a slow, tentative smile, the neediness of which made Patrick's teeth clench. *This is all so screwed up*, he thought. She had recovered; they had the chance for a fresh start. He knew deep down she would never try to hurt Bonnie again, she'd never wanted to in the first place, she'd been in the grip of a devastating bout of postnatal psychosis. As long as they resigned themselves to being a one-child family, there was no reason to be fearful. Bonnie was now a happy, normal two-and-a-half-year-old. Gill was his beloved wife, and they were a family again. He and Bonnie could move back in here with Gill tomorrow – the social worker had already signed Gill off and she could be left alone with Bonnie all day if she wanted now, after a few months of supervised visits.

But the problem was, he wasn't sure that he felt anything at all for his wife, bar a deep sense of sorrow and pity. How could he go back to sharing his bed, his life, his heart with someone he wasn't sure he even loved anymore?

Their house was immaculate, far better than it had been in all the months it was rented out on short-term lets. Patrick looked around the room.

'New picture? It's nice.' He gestured towards a large canvas on the wall – abstract artily out-of-focus petals. Privately he thought Gill's tastes must have changed. The old Gill would have dismissed that as anodyne or too predictable. Perhaps that was a consequence of being incarcerated in a secure mental unit for over a year . . .

Gill actually blushed. 'I got some new scatter cushions too,' she said, pointing at the sofa. The cushions were the exact same shade of crimson as the petals in the picture.

'Yes, I noticed,' said Patrick, although he hadn't. 'Lovely.'

'The kitchen was really dirty,' Gill said, helping Bonnie slot jigsaw pieces into place. 'Those tenants were supposed to have had it professionally cleaned when they left, but they clearly didn't. We should complain to the letting agent. Who *was* the agent?'

She hated this, Patrick realised. She hated the fact that he'd had to do all the work involved in the temporary lets of their house, negotiating with the letting agents when she didn't even know who they were because she'd been locked in a mental unit, having daily therapy while he was approving the inventory, checking references, having to live with his mum and dad, parent Bonnie *and* work full-time . . . It was as though she felt she could never make it up to him.

Often, Patrick also thought that she never would be able to. 'Does it matter now?' he said, more testily than he had intended. 'We've got the house back.'

Gill sat back and held her arms wide for Bonnie to sit in the V-shape made by her outstretched legs. She gazed at him thought-fully. 'Yes. But we aren't all living in it, are we?' Bonnie snuggled into her lap, sucking her thumb, and Patrick regarded the two pairs of identical hazel eyes scrutinising him.

He stood up and walked away, cursing his cowardice.

'I'm still not ready, Gill,' he said, without looking at her. When he glanced back from the kitchen, she was hugging Bonnie silently, dropping her lips to Bonnie's soft brown hair. Patrick felt like a heel. She must know how hard it was for him to live with his mum and dad and have to share a room with Bonnie, and yet he still didn't want to come home. That must be making her feel terrible, he thought.

He put the kettle on, for something to do, and stood at the kitchen counter listening to the water heat up as Bonnie chatted obliviously to Gill in the next room. She seemed to be telling her about some penguins she knew. Patrick smiled, then the smile dropped away as he realised that every day he prevaricated was another day Bonnie was being deprived of her mother's continuous and stabilising presence.

It was doing his head in. Why could he not just go for it? Fling himself back into the marriage, for Bonnie's sake if no-one else's?

Throwing tea bags into two mugs, he did what he always did when his thoughts reached this impasse: he thought about something else instead.

He remembered the vigil last night. All those big versions of what Bonnie would become all too soon – little girls in almost-adult bodies and scaled-down adult clothes – well, *prostitutes'* clothes, in many cases. He grinned briefly, thinking that he sounded just like his mother.

The girls last night had been torn between simmering post-gig euphoria – bordering on hysteria – and the pressure to be hushed and respectful. Patrick suspected that the murder of one of their own was making these girls feel even more excited, blood and hormones at boiling point, than they would at the end of a normal OnTarget gig. At least he and Carmella hadn't had to sit through the gig themselves. When he'd found out that the vigil was taking place, he'd decided that their attendance at the actual concert wasn't necessary. The vigil had been an unexpected bonus – a great chance to talk to the girls in his official capacity.

Many of them had got so hot from dancing and screaming inside the stadium that they had stripped down to tiny crop tops and removed the tights that they'd probably sported at the start of the evening in the chill February air. Half-naked, flushed girls holding lit candles was definitely at odds with the funereal atmosphere and Rose's poor crying parents. He had looked around him at the thirty or forty girls who were all gaping at him as though he'd been beamed down from Mars, trying to spot anyone who seemed particularly uncomfortable or as if they had something to say. But even when he'd exhorted them to come forward, none of them had appeared flustered or anything other than curious, or ghoulishly fascinated by the whole affair.

Surely one of them must know something. Why had Rose gone to that hotel? Had she been dating an older man – the sort of man who would invite her up to a hotel room? He'd asked her mum, but Sally Sharp had been utterly convinced that Rose had no time for boys her own age, let alone older men. Rose had been a young fifteen who had never had a boyfriend and who had only had four, virtual, loves in her unformed and now unfinished life – the members of OnTarget. The girl had apparently slept, eaten, breathed OnTarget. Her whole life revolved around them – trying to get their attention online, buying CDs and downloads, concert tickets and merchandise with whatever birthday or babysitting money she happened to have. Her only friends were other OnTarget fans – Patrick had taken the names of all the ones that Sally Sharp knew of, and obviously he or Carmella would be talking to them as soon as they could – but he wondered if Wendy was right, and this was a simple case of an online predator. So far, the investigations of her online history and phone records had shown nothing interesting, just endless meaningless chit-chat with other fans.

There had been one interesting thing – apparently she had used a good chunk of data in the hours before her death, showing that she had been online on her phone. But there was no way for the phone company to track what she'd been doing.

'*Pat!*' Gill's voice from the living room had taken on a familiar edge of exasperation, one that he hadn't heard since before . . . well, since they all lived together. Patrick didn't like to refer to the incident, even in his thoughts, if he could possibly avoid it.

'Yes?'

'Bonnie's been calling you. Could you bring her some juice please?'

'Dooce, Daddy!' Bonnie echoed, in a matching tone of exasperation.

Hm, thought Patrick, *she's perfectly willing to talk to me when she wants something. That's probably not likely to change for the next sixteen years or so.*

'Coming, darling,' he said – and then immediately felt guilty because he hoped that Gill hadn't thought the 'darling' had been addressed to her.

Solving murders was easier than this, he thought. At that moment he wished he was back in the incident room, a place where he didn't have to make any emotional decisions further than what sort of biscuit to have with his coffee.

As he carried the juice in to Bonnie, his mobile began to vibrate in his pocket. Groping for it, he trod on a stray piece from the shape sorter, lurched and spilled the juice down his leg.

'Ow, shit, f—'

He just managed to stop himself from saying more naughty words.

As Bonnie made a beeline for the remains of her drink, he answered the phone. 'Lennon.'

It was Carmella. 'Hey, Patrick. We just got the call from Daniel Hamlet.' The pathologist who had been assigned to this case. 'He says he's ready to see you. He sounded excited.'

Chapter 7
Day 3 – Patrick

Of all the many people Patrick came into contact with through his work, Daniel Hamlet was probably the man he most admired and respected. The forensic pathologist was deadly serious about his professional responsibilities, Patrick thought, wincing at the involuntary pun. A black man in his mid-forties, with hair that was greying around the temples, Hamlet had shown rare emotion the last time they had worked together. But today he was back to his earnest, serious self, no sign of the excitement Carmella had mentioned on the phone.

'I hear you have something interesting to share?' Patrick asked as they walked towards the lab where the autopsy had been carried out.

'That's right. But first I want to show you something.'

Rose was laid out ready on a metal table, covered with a sheet. Even though Patrick had seen her body already, it still caused him to gulp down air as he approached. She looked even paler now, but more serene, removed from the bloody scene of her death.

'So,' Hamlet began. 'The cause of death is clear – she was strangled. The murderer used a two-handed grip, suggesting that they may not be particularly strong. Of average strength, I would guess.'

'He used his hands?'

'Yes. Assuming it is a he.'

Patrick nodded. He had erroneously made that assumption before.

'There is no sign of sexual assault, which is surprising. No semen. No sign of Rose taking part in any sexual activity at all, consensual or otherwise.'

'Was she a virgin?'

Hamlet kept his eyes on the corpse. 'It's difficult to tell. I would say very possibly. But she definitely wasn't raped. Of course, when I say no sexual assault, I mean nothing vaginal. Stripping her, touching her body . . . that is assault, of course. But there is no evidence that the murderer derived sexual gratification.'

'I understand.'

'She was in good health, a little overweight but nothing wrong with her at all. She ate a burger and fries an hour or two before her death, so it might be worth seeing if anyone spotted her in McDonald's or similar that evening.'

Patrick made a note.

'Now, the really interesting thing . . .'

'The little cuts.'

'Yes. The cuts are all so small that, though each one bled a little, they weren't enough for her to bleed to death, even if the murderer waited a long time. The purpose of the cuts was undoubtedly to cause pain. Especially as perfume was sprayed into each one.'

The smell of the perfume had faded, but the scent came back to Lennon now – the way it had filled the hotel room, stinging his eyes and nose.

'It would have hurt like hell,' Hamlet said. 'Like a hundred little wasp stings. Worst would have been these, on the softer and more sensitive parts of her flesh – her thighs, the soles of her feet. Unless it was part of some strange ritual I've never heard of, it seems clear this was done to cause her pain. A very unusual form of torture. Slow, painstaking and not too intense, but the cumulative effect would be quite awful.'

They both stared at the body, concentrating on the miniscule marks.

'The murderer used a very sharp knife. Small, with a blade around four inches long. A pocket knife, but too sharp to be a penknife or Swiss army knife.'

'Have you ever seen anything like this before?' Patrick asked.

Hamlet nodded. 'That's what I wanted to tell you. The interesting thing is that yes, I have.'

Patrick felt it then: that tingle; the fizz in his bloodstream that acted like a narcotic; the rush that made him addicted to this job. He waited for Hamlet to go on, the pathologist seeming to enjoy the build-up of anticipation, like he was announcing the winner of the latest series of *Britain's Got Talent*.

'There were marks like these on a body I examined three months ago.'

He produced a file, which he'd clearly dug out earlier, and opened it. Immediately, Patrick felt confused. He had expected to see details of an autopsy on another teenage girl. But the date of birth of this victim was 1931. Her name was Nancy Marr, and she had lived in Wimbledon. Patrick vaguely remembered the case. He flicked through the autopsy report. Her body had been found in her flat, killed by strangulation. No sign of sexual assault.

'Here,' Daniel said, sliding a photograph from the file. It was a close-up of the woman's torso, showing her collarbone and upper chest. There were around twenty little cuts on the skin, just like the ones on Rose's flesh.

'Shit,' Patrick said, his voice hushed. 'Was she naked like Rose?'

'No.' Hamlet pointed to the relevant text in the report. 'Her top had been ripped just below the neck, seemingly as the result of a struggle, possibly the assailant grabbing hold of her before strangling her.'

Patrick leafed through the report. 'Is it the same knife?'

'Hmm. It's impossible to say for certain, but it's the same size.'

Patrick flicked to the back page. 'Whose case is it?'

'One of your colleagues',' Hamlet said. 'I called and left a message for him too, earlier today.'

Patrick's heart sank when he saw who it was: Winkler.

Chapter 8
Day 3 – Kai

H ey, bae.'

Silence, apart from the background sounds of OnTarget's latest album on Spotify shuffle.

Kai tried again. 'Hey, sexy. Wanna get pizza?'

'Shut it, Kai, I'm busy.'

'What'ya doing, babe?'

From her bed, where she was lying on her stomach, tapping away at her laptop, Jade turned and pulled a face. 'Duh! I'm roller-blading naked round the park.'

'*Are* yer?' Kai actually looked puzzled, as if he had somehow missed this. He noticed that she'd turned her Shawn Barrett duvet cover the wrong way up, so it looked like she was lying on top of him while he gave her head.

'Oh for fuck's sake. No – what does it look like? I'm on the forums, aren't I?'

'Anything good?'

Jade made a frustrated sort of noise. 'I mean, look at this, I'm only being realistic and I'm getting a load of abuse!'

Kai came and lay on top of Jade, grinding his pelvis into the small of her back as he looked over her shoulder at her screen.

F-U-Cancer: *I'm still totally cut up about Miss TargetHeart.*

Jade had responded: *You need to get over that, seriously. Not like you two were BFFs, FFS!*

F-U-Cancer: *How can you be so heartless, Jade? I knew I shouldn't have started talking to you again.*

'How can you be so heartless, Jade?' mimicked Jade in a high-pitched, whiny voice. 'God, she's *such* a sap. Posh cow.'

Kai fixed his gaze on one of the dozens of Shawn Barrett posters on Jade's bedroom wall. 'I'd be proper gutted if you got throttled.'

Jade ignored him. A new message had made her stiffen with outrage. 'WHAT. THE. ACTUAL. *FUCK?*'

'Sup, bae?' Kai tried to playfully straddle her on the bed so he could massage her tense shoulders, but she slapped him away as though he was a particularly irritating bluebottle.

'I don't believe it,' she muttered, scanning the computer screen. 'She's bang out of order. No, no. I ain't having that, no way.'

'Who – Miss TargetHeart?' Kai was puzzled. Rose Sharp, a.k.a. Miss TargetHeart, was in a mortuary somewhere, so it was hard to believe that she could have done anything recently to incur the wrath of Jade – hard to believe, but not impossible. Jade was very easily offended, as he well knew.

'No, you twat, YOLOSWAG. How dare she?'

'What's she said?'

Jade stabbed impatiently at her screen with a long fingernail – each of her gel nails was decorated with a different OnTarget logo.

'*YOLOSWAG – 5 minutes ago – 11,987 times?!*'

'What's she on about, bae?'

Jade jumped off the bed and paced around the room, furious. 'Who does she fucking think she is? She's just jealous, innit, that she didn't do it, and now I'm getting all the props and she thinks she can have a pop at me? She's got another think coming.'

'The tweets?' Kai asked nervously.

'Yeah, the tweets!'

Jade was inordinately proud of the fact that the OnTarget website had recently featured her in an article about how she'd tweeted Shawn Barrett 11,897 times in an attempt to get him to follow her back. It called her 'Shawn's Biggest Fan?' She'd printed out the article and it was sellotaped to the wall next to a life-size poster of Shawn:

Of course, we're all massive Targeters here, but there's someone out there who's dedicated weeks to repeatedly spamming Shawn Barrett with almost 12,000 tweets. Now, that's *slightly* excessive, but the girl behind the tweets, Jade, insists she has a very good reason for doing so. And that reason is that she's truly, madly, deeply in love with him.

According to BuzzFeed, Jade began tweeting Shawn telling him how her day was going, but she thought that was 'useless', so instead decided to write *'Before I met you @ShawnBarrett I never knew what it was like to be able to look at someone and smile for no reason, follow me, ily.'*

She told the website: *'I only tweet Shawn, I don't need anything but his follow.'* Unfortunately for Jade, Shawn Barrett is still yet to follow her on Twitter, but we're sure she won't stop there.

'I love them more than my own life, but Shawn is the one who I love the most,' Jade told BuzzFeed. *'I actually love him more than I love my boyfriend.'*

Kai scowled at the last sentence, as he did every time he looked at the printout or Jade mentioned it – which was about as many times as she'd tweeted Shawn. But he never let Jade see him scowl.

'Haters gonna hate, babe, she's totally jealous.'

Why, Kai thought, couldn't he have thick blond hair and a strong jaw like Shawn's? Perhaps Jade would be nicer to him if he didn't have spots on his forehead, skinny legs and wiry black hair that looked like pubes. Secretly he hated Shawn Barrett with a passion and, with his limited imagination, spent a great deal of time planning all sorts of lurid misfortunes for him, preferably humiliating and public ones. Jade was so fit, with her unbelievable boobs and long blonde hair, that he did seriously worry whether all her millions of tweets would eventually attract Shawn's attention – and then what chance did he, Kai, have? Jade wouldn't give him a second look.

Now, though, Jade rolled onto her side on the bed and twined her arms around his neck. He breathed in her scent – Friendship perfume, hairspray and the sickly smell of her thick brown foundation. She had a tidemark on her jaw contrasting with the white skin of her neck and throat.

'Yeah, but what are we gonna do about it?' she whispered, her words tickling his ear. 'YOLOSWAG has, like, really upset me.' She flapped her fingers in front of her eyes – the gesture that meant she was trying to hold back tears.

Kai couldn't bear the prospect of Jade crying. He wrapped his arms around her waist and hugged her tightly. 'I'll do whatever you want, bae. I mean it. Whatever you want.'

She nuzzled into his neck and he felt her cheeks curve up into a sly smile.

'People who dare diss me don't deserve—' She sniffed.

'To live?' Kai asked.

She guided his hands to her boobs and Kai thought, just like the last little bitch who dared to mess with Jade, that he'd died and gone to heaven.

Chapter 9
Day 3 – Patrick

DCI Suzanne Laughland stuck her head through the door of her partitioned office and called across to him. 'A word, please, Pat?'

Heads bent over desks immediately popped up in curiosity, reminding Patrick of meerkats – meerkats in cheap nylon shirts and poorly fitting jackets. Why did so many of his colleagues dress like teenage cashiers in a building society? He pondered this conundrum as he wove around the rows of desks towards Suzanne's office, mostly to try to quash the tiny lift of excitement he felt whenever she spoke his name.

Patrick could see through the open slats of the blinds that there was someone else sitting in with her, but couldn't tell who it was until he was almost at her desk. Then he swore softly, although it came as no surprise. Sitting with his back to the door, cleaning under his fingernails with an unfolded paper clip, was Adrian Winkler.

He nodded curtly at them both and Suzanne gestured for him to take a seat next to Winkler. Unfortunately, because her office was quite small, they ended up sitting next to one another opposite

Suzanne as if they were naughty schoolboys receiving a telling-off from the Head for fighting. Pat made a conscious effort to relax. He sat back in his seat and tried to stretch out his legs, but the walls of the solid desk were in the way, so he couldn't. Winkler noticed and smirked. Then he shifted in his chair slightly so that he turned his body away from Patrick, cold-shouldering him.

He's a cock, thought Pat. *Don't let him make you act like one too.*

'Good afternoon, Patrick. Adrian and I were just discussing Hamlet's autopsy findings, specifically the new development regarding the cuts on the body of Nancy Marr matching those on Rose Sharp's. Have you had a chance to read up on the Nancy Marr case yet?'

'Not in detail, I'm afraid,' Patrick said.

Winkler tutted and Patrick glared at him.

'I've been going over the interviews Carmella and I did with the Travel Inn personnel, and Rose Sharp's parents. As I'm sure you appreciate, that's a lot of material to get through.' He managed to stop himself adding 'I've been here since 6 a.m.', because it would sound like a defensive whine. 'Has Hamlet confirmed that it could have been the same knife?'

Suzanne nodded. 'He just rang Adrian to say that he's sure it was the same kind—'

She was going to continue, but Winkler jumped in and interrupted. Patrick was childishly glad to see an expression of irritation flicker across Suzanne's features.

'So we need to figure out what could possibly be the link between an eighty-three-year-old widow in Wimbledon and a fifteen-year-old boy-band fan in Kingston. If indeed there is one. Just because it's the same *sort* of knife doesn't mean it's the same perp. Lots of lowlifes will have the same *sort* of knife.'

He wondered, why was it that everything coming out of Winkler's mouth made Pat want to punch him?

Suzanne put a hand up before Patrick could respond. 'Pat, Adrian is already up to speed with Rose Sharp's murder. So I want you two to sit down together and work through the similarities, see if there's any other connection. You can jointly head up the operation.'

Both men gaped at her.

'You're kidding,' Patrick managed, furious with himself that he was unable to prevent his voice momentarily turning into an adolescent squeak. He was furious with her too. She knew there was no love lost between him and Winkler – what was she thinking?

Adrian had gathered himself and was now nodding sagely, as if him being involved with the case would give it the only possible chance of getting solved. Patrick jumped to his feet.

'I'm sorry, but I have to object. As Adrian here so rightly says' – at this he bared his teeth in a fake grin to indicate that he was being sarcastic rather than deferential – 'any old scumbag could be carrying a knife like that used on both of these victims. It's worth investigating, of course, but surely it won't mean both of us have to run the case?'

'That's as may be, regarding the knife,' said Suzanne. 'But you know we're low on numbers at the moment, what with Connolly still on sick leave and Regan retiring, and Adrian never got a perp for the Marr case, so if you work together you could end up killing two birds with one stone. I'm relying on you both to put aside any personal differences. You're big boys, so don't behave like kids in the playground. Sit down, Patrick.'

Chastened, Patrick thought how ironic it was for her to say that, after his earlier image of them in front of the Head. She was right, though. At all costs, he must not allow himself to sink to Winkler's level. They were professionals, with a job to do.

He believed his face would confirm this, but instead Suzanne looked concerned. She turned to Winkler. 'That's all for now, Adrian. I just want a quick word with Patrick.'

Winkler left the office without a backwards glance at Pat. Suzanne took a sip of her coffee and grimaced.

'What's the problem, Suzanne?'

'This coffee is not only disgusting, it's stone cold.'

'I didn't mean with the coffee. You look worried.'

Suzanne leaned towards him over the desk, as if she wanted to take his hand. 'Yes. Well, I have to say, I *am* quite worried. I know you and Adrian don't particularly see eye to eye' – Patrick just about managed to prevent a snort – 'but I need you two to pull together on this one. Unless . . . and forgive me, Pat, but I know things are tough for you at the moment, what with getting ready to move back home . . . and I'm trusting you here to be honest with me – would you like to take a bit of leave, get yourself settled again and have some time with Gill and Bonnie? It can't be easy juggling all those logistics, let alone the emotions, alongside a high-pressure case like this . . . I could let Winkler lead the investigation.'

'No way!' Patrick leapt to his feet again. He was livid. 'Are you serious?'

'Oh for God's sake, Patrick, you're like a bloody jack-in-a-box! This is precisely why I'm worried about you! It's just not like you to be so sensitive. You can handle Winkler. He's an arse and we all know it.'

Patrick couldn't resist a grin. He knew she would never have said that to anybody else in the station. He saluted her in sardonic acquiescence and took his seat again, glad that Suzanne had twisted the blinds closed when he'd first come in, so that the rest of the open-plan office hadn't been privy to him jumping up and down like a maniac.

'You're right. And not just about the bit where you said Winkler's an arse. I'm sorry, Suzanne. Not that it's any excuse, but I had a toddler sleeping on my head all night, so I'm not exactly raring to go today. But I swear to you I'm going to crack this investigation, and although it would be so much easier to do it without Winkler's opinions, you're the boss. If you think it's the right thing to do, then I will work with him, and I promise I will do my utmost not to let him rile me. Bonnie and I are moving back in tomorrow, so that's absolutely going to help – Gill will be able to take over the childcare full-time since she's not going back to work for another few months at least – and Bonnie will be back in her own room again. Plus, I won't be living with my folks anymore. It will all be a massive improvement.'

'Good man,' said Suzanne, and for a moment their eyes met. 'If you're sure you can take the pressure.'

Patrick laughed drily. 'I handled it during the Child Catcher operation, didn't I? And that was even more of a nightmare, domestically.'

'True. OK. Don't let me down.' She swivelled in her chair to face her computer screen, indicating that the meeting was over. Patrick caught the faintest whiff of her scent as she turned.

As he left the office, he caught sight of Winkler at his desk, smirking at him. He marched straight past him, unable to face him at the moment, and headed over to Carmella.

'Come on,' he said, loudly enough for Winkler to hear, wanting to make him paranoid about what Suzanne had said and not caring if he was being childish. 'Let's go. We've got two murders to solve now.'

Chapter 10
Day 3 – Patrick

Patrick and Carmella sat in the McDonald's round the corner from the Travel Inn, a pair of steaming coffees between them. Patrick had resisted the urge to buy a Big Mac and Carmella had surveyed the menu as if it listed a variety of poisons. Just across from them a toddler was munching chicken dippers and rattling the toy from her Happy Meal. So far, Bonnie was barely aware that McDonald's existed, but he knew this place drew children like a mermaid luring sailors to the rocks. It wouldn't be long, he suspected, before he was feeding her chicken McNuggets and fries.

The manager hadn't recognised Rose from the photograph they'd shown him, nor did any of the almost exclusively teenage staff, though their eyes had widened and a whisper of excitement had whipped through the restaurant. The girl who was murdered! They all so desperately wanted to recognise her, to have something to tell their friends. But it looked like the burger Rose had enjoyed as her last meal had come from somewhere else.

'Going round every fast-food place in Kingston,' Carmella said, wincing at her coffee. 'We should have given this job to Gareth. He'd love it.'

'Maybe I will,' Patrick said. 'Or Winkler.'

'Uh-uh. He doesn't eat junk food, does he? Only the finest organic produce passes his lips.'

Hearing this made Patrick reconsider ordering that Big Mac.

They walked round to the Travel Inn, dodging puddles and warily eyeing the sky, with its battalion of black rain clouds. Before leaving the station, Patrick had spoken to the senior SOCO on the investigation, Marie Branson, who had confirmed what he already knew. The killer had left no DNA at the scene – no stray hairs, blood or semen. No fingerprints. All the hotel staff had been interviewed, CCTV tapes had been reviewed, including those from the streets surrounding the hotel, and the names of all the guests had been run through the system. Nobody had seen anything. The cameras had captured nothing. And no-one who'd been staying in the hotel had anything more on their record than a parking ticket or some other minor misdemeanour.

Somebody must have seen the murderer entering or leaving the hotel. He wasn't a phantom. The problem was that nobody who'd seen him would know they had been looking at a killer. After all, he wouldn't have been cackling and carrying a knife dripping with blood. That was the thing about murderers: they usually look just like everyone else.

Heidi Shillingham, the hotel manager, was waiting for them in the same conference room where they'd interviewed the cleaner a couple of days before. Heidi had grey smudges under her eyes and Lennon noticed her bite down on a yawn as she greeted them.

'Ms Shillingham,' he said.

'Oh, call me Miss, please,' she replied with a tired smile. 'I can't be doing with any of that feminist nonsense. In fact, call me Heidi.'

Carmella raised an eyebrow.

Patrick said, 'We want to talk to you about room 365. Specifically, how the perpetrator and the victim got inside. We don't know which one of them entered the room first, or if they arrived together. But we need to know how they got in.'

Heidi nodded. 'OK. Well, all of our rooms are controlled with these key cards.' She produced a white credit-card-sized key, the type Patrick had seen and used many times before. 'It's pretty standard. The magnetic strip on the back controls which room you can access. When a guest checks in, we give them a key card and set it to their room using the central computer system.'

'I understand all that. What if someone kept their key after they checked out? Could they come back the next day, or a week later, and use it again?'

As Patrick predicted, Heidi shook her head. 'No. The card – or, rather, the link between the card and the room – is cancelled when the guest checks out. Then the next time the card is used, it will almost certainly be set to a different room.'

'Had anyone reported losing a key on the day in question?' Carmella asked.

'Yes, I checked this. One person. But that was room 218. The system clearly shows that no cards were set to room 365 last Wednesday.'

'What about master keys?' Patrick asked. 'Staff always seem to be able to get into any room. Like the cleaners. I guess they have a master key to all the rooms?'

'Only for the rooms they are cleaning.'

'So only Mosope Adeyemi had a key for room 365 that day?'

'Yes. And the day before too. The day of the . . . unfortunate incident.'

That's one way of putting it, Patrick thought. 'And what about you, Ms – Miss – Shillingham, er, Heidi?' He was gratified to see Carmella's lips twitch at the same time that Heidi pursed hers. 'Do you have a master key to all the rooms?'

She hesitated. 'Yes, I do. Several of the staff have them. But they are on our person all the time we're in the hotel, and they're deactivated when we go off shift.'

Patrick drummed his fingers on the table. 'Have you ever had any issues with people accessing rooms that they shouldn't? Any thefts? Guests going into the wrong room?'

Heidi squirmed in her seat. 'No . . . Well, sometimes staff accidentally allocate a room twice, so we've had incidents of guests walking into a room that's already occupied. Which can be highly embarrassing.'

'I can imagine.'

'And there was one incident . . . But not at this hotel.' The way her eyes jumped around the room made it clear that Heidi was worried about getting into trouble.

'Go on.'

'A couple of years ago, someone got into a few rooms at one of the hotels in Essex and stole valuables – a laptop, an iPad, some jewellery, cash. It turned out that they had – how did they put it? – reverse-engineered a master key so it was able to open any door.'

'Hang on – you mean they basically created their own master key, waltzed into the hotel and opened whatever door they fancied?'

'That's how I understood it. It was this young lad, a hacker. But he got caught after boasting about it on his website. Stupid prat. I know we made some changes to the security system after that and we were all told it wouldn't happen again. But . . .'

'But?'

'Well, you know what these hackers are like. It's a challenge, isn't it? Maybe that's what happened here.'

Patrick and Carmella took the lift back to the third floor. Patrick wanted to see the room again, not because he expected to find any useful information there but because being at the scene of the crime helped him focus, allowed him to imagine the scene. He used the key Heidi had given them to open the door, which was still sealed off with yellow tape.

'So our murderer is also a hacker who knows how to reverse-engineer hotel keys?' Carmella said.

Patrick sighed. 'It seems unlikely, doesn't it? Let's talk to the tech guys, but I'm guessing it isn't easy to do.'

'But maybe our murderer acquired a hacked key from someone. Bought it online, or paid someone to create one.'

'That's exactly what I was thinking.' He tapped the key against the palm of his hand. 'Which means we might finally have a lead.'

Patrick ducked under the tape and entered the room, Carmella following. The smell of perfume had faded now and been replaced with the musty smell of closed rooms and dust. The Travel Inn had asked the police not to release the room number to the press, fearful that no-one would ever want to stay here again. Patrick wanted to tell them not to worry. There were probably a lot of people out there who would get a kick out of staying in a room where a girl was murdered.

The perfume that had been sprayed into Rose's wounds was being analysed at the lab and results were expected back soon. Patrick didn't expect to learn much from this. What difference would it make if the killer used Chanel No.5 or CK1? Maybe it would tell them whether he could afford expensive perfume, but that was about it. All the wheelie bins and patches of wasteland within a mile radius had been searched, but there was no sign of Rose's clothes. They were probably on a dump somewhere, Patrick thought.

'Let's get back to the station,' he said. 'We need to find out if there are any hackers for hire out there selling hotel key cards.'

As they left the hotel, his mobile rang. It was Gareth.

'Ah, Gareth, I've got a job for—'

Gareth interrupted. 'Sorry, boss, but something's happened.'

Patrick stopped walking and gestured for Carmella to wait. The rain pummelled the pavement, soaking the two detectives as Patrick bent almost double, protecting his phone from the downpour. He couldn't hear what Gareth was saying.

'Can you repeat that?'

'I said, we've found another body. Another girl.'

Chapter 11
Day 3 – Chloe

Chloe Hedges sat on the edge of her bed and checked her phone for the twentieth time in the space of five minutes. She had been caught on the horns of this particular dilemma for the last few hours – Jess had not returned her calls or texts since they'd parted after last night's vigil. This in itself wasn't unusual – Jess was the touchiest of all Chloe's friends and could be offended at the drop of a hat, leading to a period of cold-shouldering for perhaps three or four days. And they had argued after the vigil – Chloe had got annoyed with Jess's bizarre and irreverent behaviour. After the singing ended, Jess had got the giggles during the two minutes' silence for Rose, when Chloe had suddenly found that tears were pouring down her own face, even though she hadn't known Rose in real life. It was the sight of Rose's poor parents that had set her off. She imagined it was her who'd been brutally murdered, and that it was *her* mum and dad up there at the front of the small gathering, looking as though their lives were over too. Already annoyed because Jess wouldn't tell her why she was acting so weird, she'd snapped at her friend, who had then stormed off, leaving Chloe to get the bus home in tears on her own.

But before that, they'd made an arrangement to meet this afternoon, to go to the Rotunda – mainly because there was this boy who always hung out there that Jess had the hots for. Jess had been a no-show. Chloe waited for ages, trying to call her friend, before giving up. In the couple of hours since then she had sent a series of increasingly worried messages, apologising for the row and begging Jess to let her know she was all right. Silence.

She tried to take her mind off it by returning to the story she'd been working on for over a week – it was her best yet, much better than anything she'd written before, she thought. Miss Jameson, her English teacher, told Chloe she needed to write from the heart, and Chloe was finally doing that, now she felt brave enough to write about the C-word. But she found that her thoughts kept drifting anxiously back to Jess, and after ten minutes' staring at the screen without adding a single word, she gave up. She decided to check the forums instead, but only got as far as inputting her login – F-U-Cancer – when her mum yelled up the stairs.

'Supper, Chloe!'

Chloe grimaced, closed her laptop and bade a silent farewell to the poster of Shawn from OnTarget sellotaped to the back of her bedroom door. She trudged downstairs. 'What is it?'

'Quorn fillets in tomato sauce,' said her mother, sliding three empty plates out of the top oven where they had been warming.

'The ones in breadcrumbs? What kind of tomato sauce?'

Her mother sighed. 'No. Not the ones in breadcrumbs. Normal tomato sauce, like pasta sauce.'

'*Eurgh*. I only like the ones in breadcrumbs. Where's Dad?'

'He's not back from the match yet. Probably gone to the pub.'

They sat down at the table. Chloe's little brother, Brandon, was already seated, quietly tinkering with a Transformer. He looked up when he saw his mum dishing up the food. 'Oh no, not broccoli.'

Chloe's mum slammed a plate down in front of him and glared at them both.

'For heaven's sake, can we not have *just one meal* where you two don't complain about everything?'

After that they ate in silence. Chloe wanted to ask her mum's advice but was afraid she would get on the phone to Jess's mum, and it would be really embarrassing, especially as they didn't even know one another. She imagined her mother doing her posh phone voice and squirmed. Also, Chloe might then have to admit that she had got the bus home by herself after the OnTarget concert, which was strictly *verboten*. They only lived three miles away from Twickenham Stadium, but her dad would go mad if he knew she'd got the bus by herself after nine o'clock at night. Not to mention getting Jess into trouble too, for leaving her after the vigil. Jess might never talk to her again.

But what if Jess was in danger? Rose Sharp's face flashed into her head. No – if she'd gone missing like Rose Sharp, they'd know about it by now. It would be on the news and everything – appeals circulating on Twitter and Facebook. Jess was probably just still in a strop with her.

Then why did Chloe feel so anxious? She glanced at her mum, who was still looking cross, then opened her mouth to say something. 'Mum—'

Brandon interrupted her. 'Can I get down, Mummy? I'm full.'

'Eat your broccoli first.'

Chloe had *so* known her mum would say that. It was as predictable as being told to put her iPhone outside the bedroom door every night at 10 p.m. She decided to wait until Brandon had left the table.

Her phone beeped with an incoming text and she snatched it out of her back pocket as Brandon gingerly poked a stem of broccoli into his mouth, making disgusted faces throughout.

'No phones at dinner, Chloe!' admonished her mother.

'It's urgent!'

'I don't care. Put it away.'

But Chloe had seen that the text wasn't from Jess. She must have looked upset because her mum gave her a long searching look, and let Brandon get down without clearing his plate. He scampered off immediately with his Transformer, thumping up the stairs to his bedroom before she changed her mind again and made him sit there until the broccoli was cold and limp and even less appealing.

'Everything all right, Rog?'

'Don't call me that!'

Her mum smiled. Chloe's dad had a habit of adapting everyone's names, so Chloe had, as a baby, become Chlo, which he had lengthened into Clodagh Rogers – who had apparently been some sort of ancient singer – and then shortened again to Rog. She hadn't minded it when she was little, but now she loathed it.

'Sorry. Is everything all right? You seem a bit on edge.'

Chloe swallowed hard, still undecided about whether or not to unleash this potential shit storm. Her mother pressed her advantage, knowing that it must be something major if Chloe hadn't immediately bitten off her head and told her to mind her own business.

'Are you still upset about that poor girl who was killed, honey? You know, I thought it was really sweet of you and Jessica to go to the vigil last night.'

At the sound of Jess's name, Chloe knew she couldn't dither anymore. Worst case scenario, Jess never spoke to her again – well, she could deal with that. There were plenty of other OnTarget fans she could hang out with and chat to. Jess didn't go to her school, so she wouldn't have to face her ire in person if she really got her into trouble. And sometimes she was a bit of a pain anyway.

'It's just that me and Jess were meant to meet up today and she didn't turn up,' she blurted. 'And now I can't get hold of her.'

'You haven't fallen out, have you?'

'No. We did sort of have a fight – but, like, it wasn't a real fight . . .'

Her mother looked thoughtful. Chloe knew that her mum didn't much care for Jess. On the couple of occasions that Jess had been to her house, she hadn't made much of an effort to be polite to her mum, and hadn't even thanked her for the flapjacks that she had made specially for them one day when they'd come back to hang out in her room and watch the new OnTarget movie.

'I wouldn't normally be worried,' Chloe said. 'But after what happened to MissTargetHeart . . . Rose.'

'Do you know her home phone number?'

'Oh. Yeah, I do actually.'

'Why don't you call it, then?'

Chloe pulled a face, she was a bit scared of Jess's mum. Jess's mum was vague and a bit of a hippie, but not a mellow one – a sort of bitter, neurotic one who drank too much and didn't tell Jess off when she said 'fuck' and 'shit'.

Her mum smiled softly. 'OK, I'll do it.'

Chloe stood in the kitchen doorway, biting her thumbnail as she listened to her mum call Jess's mum.

'Hello? This is Rebecca Hedges, Chloe's mum . . . No . . . Sorry, I think we're talking at cross-purposes. Jess isn't here.'

She looked across the hallway at Chloe and Chloe felt her heart drop into her stomach.

'No, she hasn't been here at all today. She told you she was coming here?'

As Chloe's mum continued to talk to Mrs McMasters, Chloe sat on the bottom stair and hugged herself.

'Please God,' she whispered. 'Please let Jess have gone off to meet a boy. Please don't let it be anything more than that.'

By the time her mum said, 'Perhaps you should call the police,' Chloe was convinced. Something terrible had happened to her friend.

Chapter 12
Day 4 – Patrick

The Rocket Man Film and Photography Studio was hidden away on a grim industrial estate at Sunbury Cross, close to the top of the M3, between a food-packing warehouse and a factory that manufactured sex toys.

'For all your Rampant Rabbit needs,' Carmella deadpanned as Patrick took in the run-down buildings, shivering as a frigid wind whipped across the estate. In the distance, he could hear the roar of cars and lorries heading west, but apart from that, all was silent. This whole place looked a long way from sharing in the bounty of economic recovery.

The SOCOs' vans were parked on the wide driveway of the studio, several officers milling about in the entrance. Above their heads, a window was smashed and Patrick mentally marked this as a possible entry point. But it was more likely to be the work of bored local kids or squatters.

On the way over, Carmella had looked up the studio on Google while Patrick drove.

'So . . . Rocket Man . . . opened in the early eighties and was used mostly by the music business for photo shoots and pop videos.

It shut down a year ago. Their website is gone too, but there's a news story about it closing here . . . The owner said that they were a casualty of the music biz tightening its belt, most of the music magazines and papers going bust, et cetera.'

'Seems a weird place for a studio,' Patrick said.

'I guess the rent was cheap. And it was out of the way. Less chance of the pop stars being papped as they came in and out. Oh, listen to this, from the news story last year: "New boy-band sensation OnTarget shot the video for their debut single 'Our Little Secret' at Rocket Man, one of the last promo films to be made at the studio." I'm starting to feel haunted by that band. You know, I popped to the shops yesterday and the amount of OnTarget merchandise I saw was unbelievable. Soft drinks, lunch boxes, loom bands, socks, pyjamas, dolls, mouse mats, sweatshirts – and their perfume, Friendship. If I'd known then that Friendship was the perfume that had been sprayed into Rose's wounds, I'd have bought a bottle.'

Patrick had steered the car onto the estate. 'I think Rose was carrying the Friendship perfume with her. Women do that sort of thing, don't they?'

Carmella smiled.

'And the killer used Rose's own perfume on her.'

'Rather than bring his own?'

'That seems the most likely scenario. And he removed it along with all her other stuff. I'm hoping he's kept it all as souvenirs, so when we find him . . .'

Carmella scrolled down on her phone. 'There's one more thing. Allegedly, the studio was also used recently to shoot porn movies.'

'I'd have thought that would keep them going.'

'You're behind the times, Patrick. No-one's willing to pay for porn anymore. It's all freely available online.'

'Oh yeah. So I've heard.'

Now, the two detectives approached the building. Patrick exchanged a few words with the SOCOs, who handed them full protective gear and told them where the body was located. They suited up and headed straight into the reception area, where a corridor led past another empty room to a single studio.

The building smelled musty and unpleasant – pigeon shit and rat piss – a cloying smell Patrick had encountered before, in the abandoned flats on the Kennedy Estate a couple of miles up the road. As they opened the door of the studio, though, another odour reached Patrick's nose and he exchanged a look with Carmella.

Friendship.

Patrick quickened his pace, his natural reluctance to see the body overridden by the need to see if he was right, and the smell was indeed the OnTarget perfume that he and Carmella had just been talking about. They did not speak, and the shuffling of their blue paper overshoes in the dusty corridor sounded loud in the silence.

The SOCOs were gathered, in their protective gear, in a cluster at the far end of the surprisingly large studio, in front of a torn white screen that remained from when this place had played host to glamorous pop stars. There was no longer any whiff of glamour, just the stink of decay and neglect. And, now, death. There were no windows in the studio, and the lights had been removed, but the SOCOs had brought lamps that cast shadows around them like crosses. Without the police lights, this place would be dark even during the day. Jessica McMasters must have died in the shadows.

The chief SOCO, Neil Maslen, whom Patrick knew reasonably well, came up to them.

'Who found her?' Patrick asked, after they'd exchanged greetings.

'A security guard,' Neil said. 'He comes round once a day to make sure squatters haven't broken in, apparently. He said he noticed that a window had been forced open round the back and came in to investigate.'

'Where is he now?'

'In the back of the van – we're waiting for him to stop puking before we take him in for questioning. He's already splattered the crime scene once and I don't want any more of last night's chicken tikka masala ruining the evidence, so we put him in there with a placky bag, a bottle of water and some wet wipes.'

'OK. I'll talk to him later,' Patrick said.

Jessica had been reported missing at 7.35 p.m. the previous evening, after not being seen all day. Her mother had thought she was out with her friend Chloe, since it was a Saturday. So the last person to see her alive was the mother, who'd looked in on her when she was still asleep at 8.15 a.m. that morning, and now the body had been found at 8 a.m. the following day? That meant Jess could have been killed at any time during that twenty-four-hour period.

'I'm not imagining the smell of perfume, am I?' Patrick asked, and Neil shook his head. In this large space, the smell was less concentrated and eye-stinging than in the hotel room at the Travel Inn, but it was unquestionably the same. And as the SOCOs parted and gave Patrick his first look at the body, he knew without doubt that, regardless of the connection or lack thereof to the murder of Nancy Marr, this was the work of a serial killer.

Jessica lay on her back on the hard floor in front of the tattered screen. Her eyes were open, staring sightlessly at the dead strip lights. Her body had a curious orange sheen that, Patrick realised after a moment of confusion, was fake tan, streaked in places. She was naked, much skinnier than Rose had been – not anorexic but definitely underweight, her ribs sharp beneath her skin.

Patrick felt the low stirring of rage deep in his belly. He moved closer, Carmella at his side, and took in the worst of it: the bruising on her throat, showing that she'd been strangled, and the cuts. Hundreds of tiny cuts across her body. Just like Rose, except many of these cuts were deeper, longer, as if the killer had found it harder to maintain control. There were marks on her face too: her lower lip cut and puffy; a mark on her cheekbone. A clump of hair had been pulled out. And most sickening of all: the tips of several of her fingers were bloody and raw. He had pulled four of her fingernails out.

Patrick turned away, the white, cold anger pulsing inside him.

He forced himself to stand still on one of the metal stepping stones protecting the scene, taking it all in. Her left forearm was adorned with a huge, smudged tattoo of a person – Patrick couldn't tell whether it was meant to be male or female until he read the name underneath it: *Shawn*. It looked nothing like the lead singer of the band, as far as he could tell, but it was clearly meant to represent him. *Silly girl*, he thought. How would that have looked when she was in her forties?

But now she would never even see her twenties.

Noticing something else, he stooped low and examined the underside of Jess's other wrist. She had a small red tattoo there: a love heart with a pair of crosshairs through it – the OnTarget logo.

Patrick looked around. As with Rose, there was no sign of the clothes the killer had removed from Jess. None of her possessions were to be seen anywhere. He approached one of the SOCOs.

'Her fingernails . . . Have you already picked them up?'

'No, sir. We did a sweep of the floor, but there was no sign of them. They might turn up, but . . .'

Patrick clenched his teeth. The murderer had taken them. But why? Why leave the bodies where they were so easy to find, but remove everything else? Was it because he wanted souvenirs? Or did he have some other purpose for the girls' belongings?

He took a final look at Jess's body and thought, 'We're going to find him, sweetheart. And when we do, I'm going to make him wish he'd never been born.'

It was only when he saw the way Carmella was staring at him, mouth agape, that he realised he'd spoken his thoughts aloud.

Chapter 13
Day 4 – Patrick

Patrick paced the incident room, the rest of the team gathered nervously around the edges – all except Winkler, who was perched on the edge of a desk, arms folded, wearing his omnipresent smirk.

Patrick had asked Gareth to print a map of the area, on which they'd marked the murder scenes of the teenage girls in red, their homes in green. Jess and Rose lived less than a mile apart but went to different schools – Jess attending the grammar school, Rose the local comprehensive. Patrick paused by the map and drew a circle that encompassed the four points.

'Two girls, both fifteen, living close to one another. White, middle-class, though Jess's family appear to be better off than Rose's – much bigger house, nicer car, et cetera. Rose's parents are divorced; Jess's are still together. We know that both girls were massive fans of OnTarget. According to Jess's mother, she attended the vigil for Rose at Twickenham Stadium.'

This fact made him shiver. He and Carmella had been in the same small crowd as the second victim-fan. He had no recollection of seeing her. But it made him wonder – had the killer been there too?

And had the murderer's *next* target – because he had no doubt this was not the end, the killer wasn't going to stop now – been at the vigil as well?

'Jessica was at the vigil with her best friend, one Chloe Hedges. Jess told her mum that she was going round to Chloe's house, but she didn't turn up. Gareth is going to interview Chloe later.'

Patrick went on to describe the similarities between the two murders: the cuts; the perfume; the fact that their clothes had been taken.

'Was this one wearing lucky knickers too?' Winkler asked.

Patrick looked at him with disgust. Trust Winkler to seize on the girls' underwear. 'What?'

Winkler shrugged. 'I noticed on the info sheet about Rose – she was wearing knickers with "LUCKY" written on them, wasn't she? Thought it was pretty ironic.'

'Yes. Well, we have a full description of Jess's clothes on your new sheets, but it appears she was wearing new, black underwear.'

Winkler nodded and made a note.

Patrick moved on. 'We know from the mothers that both girls were extremely active on the band's forums and talked about them endlessly on social media. We've looked at their Twitter accounts – Rose was tweeting about OnTarget up to a hundred times a day; Jess even more. Jess's mum says that her daughter lived and breathed the band, that she became obsessed with them from the moment they were put together on that talent show. She got those tattoos last month despite being underage.'

'Crazy,' Winkler muttered.

Patrick counted to three, not wanting to lose his temper. But before he could speak, Wendy, the young-looking DC who had transferred from Wolverhampton and had admitted to being a fan of OnTarget, spoke up.

'Why is it crazy? Ill-advised, yes, but this is what a lot of teenage girls do – they form an intense interest in a band, or a pop star, or an actor. It's a normal part of growing up. It's only because of social media and the Internet that it becomes more visible, more . . . amplified.' Her confidence visibly grew as she went on. 'Because now they have a channel, a way of broadcasting their love for these boys. When I was a teenager I was a massive Blue fan. But I didn't go on Twitter to talk about it – I wrote endless declarations of love in my diary.'

'You probably still do,' Winkler said.

Patrick was amazed and impressed by Wendy's outburst, partly because he too understood how it felt to be a huge fan of someone. When he was a teenager he had been . . . well, he hesitated to use the word 'obsessed', but he had spent a huge amount of time and energy thinking and talking about his favourite band, The Cure. He spent all his money on their records, collecting rare vinyl and posters, wearing their T-shirts, going to gigs and connecting with like-minded fans who spent many hours sitting around analysing Robert Smith's lyrics.

'Thank you—' he began to say, but Wendy spoke over him.

'The point I'm trying to make,' she said, a pink flush creeping across her throat, 'is that we shouldn't dismiss or judge these young girls. We mustn't call them crazy.'

The whole room, including Winkler, was silent in the aftermath of Wendy's words, everybody following her gaze towards the photos of Rose and Jess that were pinned to the board beside the map.

'Thank you, Wendy,' Patrick said, finally, smiling at her. She looked at her feet.

Winkler said, 'Yeah. Sorry.'

Patrick pointed at the map again, drawing a line with his finger between the two houses. 'We need to find out every connection between these two, apart from their love of OnTarget. Did they know each other online? Had they met? Mutual friends and acquaintances – they must have some. Is there any connection between their families? Places they both frequented – somewhere the killer might have spotted them. I also want to know about boyfriends. Again, according to their mothers, neither girl had a boyfriend. Mrs Sharp says that, to her knowledge, Rose never had a boyfriend, though of course she might have had one her mum didn't know about.'

'Or she could have been gay,' Carmella said.

Winkler rolled his eyes.

Patrick didn't think that fitted with Rose's boy-band obsession but said, 'Of course we should keep an open mind. Jess's mum says that her daughter was very popular, that boys were always asking her out, but – and I quote – "Jess was saving herself for Shawn".'

'Deluded,' said Winkler.

'A bit like you,' Carmella said. 'Thinking any woman would be interested in you . . .'

'As a matter of fact—' Winkler began.

Patrick cut him off. 'All right. Let's focus. Wendy, I want you to find out everything about these girls. And I mean everything.'

'So are we assuming that my case isn't connected to the girls now?' Winkler asked, sounding hopeful. 'Can I get on with my investigation without you interfering?'

Patrick stared at him. He didn't want Winkler involved; he didn't want the Nancy Marr murder tied to this one. Apart from wanting to jettison Winkler, the elderly woman's murder didn't fit. It confused things. But they couldn't dismiss it, not after what Daniel Hamlet had said. And Suzanne wanted them to consider every possibility.

'No,' he said. 'We have to do what the DCI asked, until we find evidence that Mrs Marr's death isn't connected to the other two.'

'It's a bloody joke.'

Patrick ignored him, biting his tongue again, and turned to the map, drawing a question mark on Nancy Marr's home, which was also the scene of the crime.

'I want to go over your case notes with you,' Patrick said, and Winkler reacted as if Patrick had told him he wanted to have sex with his mother.

'No fucking way.'

Patrick was aware of everyone else in the room watching them. 'Let's talk about this afterwards,' he said.

Winkler gave him a Medusa-like stare and folded his arms, glowering at Patrick. *Less Medusa, more feral cat*, Patrick thought.

'For fuck's sake,' Patrick said under his breath. He took a moment to gather himself and turned again to the photos of Rose and Jess, emotionally anchoring himself, reminding himself of what needed to be done and why. He needed to ignore Winkler, not let the little twat get to him – though he was going to get a look at those case notes if it killed him.

'Any joy with the hotel key card?' Patrick addressed Gareth, who shook his head apologetically.

'But I'm talking to Cyber-Crime later, boss. Peter Bell reckons he could have some leads for us.'

'OK, good.' Again, Patrick pulled the lid off a marker pen and wrote a heading on the whiteboard beside the map.

SUSPECTS/TARGETS

'All right. We don't have any named suspects yet. But let's think about our line of inquiry. Who is doing this, and why? Until we know more, let's assume that the strongest things that connect Rose and Jessica are, first, their interest in OnTarget and, second, their consequent use of the band's social media.' He wrote these two points on the whiteboard. 'Martin, can you share what you've found out about the girls' Internet use so far?'

Martin Hale hauled himself to his feet, wincing slightly – Patrick wasn't sure whether this was from an injury or at the thought of speaking to the assembled group.

Hale didn't need to refer to his notepad – the details of this case were etched on his mind, Patrick knew. As he spoke, Patrick added notes to the board.

'I haven't had much time at all to look into Rose's Internet history, but here's what I've got so far. Both girls used the official OnTarget forum, which is hosted on the band's website.' He shook his head. 'There are girls on there who write a hundred posts about Shawn every single day . . . Apart from that, they both used Twitter extensively and have unprotected accounts. They had Facebook accounts but barely used them. They were both on StoryPad, which is a site where teenagers write short stories and poems. Um . . . what else? Rose had a Tumblr account where she posted about the band, as well as numerous Pinterest boards where she pinned endless pictures of Shawn and his bandmates.'

Winkler muttered, 'Give me strength.'

'I've found something that could be useful regarding Rose's phone,' Martin said. 'I've been through her phone records and there are no unknown numbers – just lots of calls to her mum and dad, texts between her and her friends. Between leaving her house and going to the hotel, she didn't make any calls or send any texts. However, she did use a fair amount of 3G bandwidth during the hours before her death.'

'You mean she was online?' Patrick asked.

'Exactly. She might have been on the Internet on her phone or using apps that connect online. Unfortunately, the mobile provider can't tell us what she was doing. I've checked her social media and she didn't tweet or update any of the other sites she uses regularly.'

'But perhaps she was communicating with somebody?'

'That's what I think. She might have been using one of those messaging apps. From the amount of bandwidth she used, it's possible she was sending or downloading photos, or even a video.'

'Good stuff, Martin. See what else you can find out. We need to talk to her friends and her online, er, buddies and see if she shared anything with them.'

'And I'll see if there was similar activity on Jess's phone.'

Patrick popped the lid back onto the marker pen and looked around at the, mostly, eager faces. The one bored face belonged to Winkler, which was hardly a surprise. Winkler's attachment to Operation Urchin felt like a pebble in Patrick's shoe.

Catching Patrick watching him, Winkler looked up and raised his eyebrows. 'What are you staring at?'

It took all Patrick's inner strength to stop himself from regressing to the primary school playground and saying, 'I dunno – it hasn't got a label on it.'

Most of the assembled officers filed out of the room, leaving Patrick gazing at the whiteboard. He sensed a presence behind him.

'Boss?'

It was Wendy. She fidgeted, knotting her fingers together in front of her, shuffling one foot.

'I hope you didn't think I spoke out of turn,' she said in her lilting Black Country accent.

'No, not at all. I was impressed, Wendy. It's refreshing to hear somebody speak up for these girls. To talk about them like they're real people. You showed empathy. I like that.'

Two bright spots of pink glowed on her cheeks. 'I've got an idea,' she said, her eyes focusing on the photos of Rose and Jess.

'Go on.'

'You said you want me to find out everything I can about these girls.'

Patrick noticed that she didn't refer to them as the victims.

'Well, what if I were to, you know, covertly go on the OnT forums and social media and pose as a fan? Get to know members of that community and try to connect with other people who knew Rose and Jess?'

'I don't know. It's not a bad idea, but it's a specialist skill. Martin has had the training.'

She stopped fidgeting. 'But, boss, with all due respect to Martin, he's . . . well, he doesn't know how to think like one of these girls.' Before Patrick could interrupt she said, 'I understand them. I know that world. I can chat about OnTarget without sounding fake. I really think I'm best placed to do this.'

'I know what you're saying, but—'

'Please. Let me do this. Give me a day or two and if I don't make any progress, I'll hold my hands up and hand it over. At least let me set up the profiles, reach out. I'd only have to give Martin a crash course in OnTarget fandom anyway.'

She grinned and Patrick found the smile infectious.

'I won't let you down.'

He sighed. 'All right. But keep me fully informed. And if it doesn't seem like you're making swift progress . . .'

'Thanks, boss. I'll get on it straight away.'

She strode from the room before he could change his mind. Why, he wondered, as he faced the pictures of Rose and Jess, a wave of tiredness crashing over him, did he feel like he'd just been steamrollered?

Chapter 14
Day 4 – Winkler

DI Adrian Winkler strolled out of the gym with his bag slung over his shoulder, catching sight of his reflection in the glass doors as he emerged into the cool air. His black, shoulder-length hair was still damp and his veins snaked around his freshly pumped biceps. He felt good, calm, the endorphins from his workout blowing away all the negative energy that had been fucking with his flow since the meeting with DCI Laughland and her pet weirdo.

He'd already posted details of his workout on Facebook, which he knew his friends would find fascinating, and he felt proud. He might call Francesca later, ask her if she wanted to come round and worship at the Temple of Winkler. That woman, whom he'd met on a case, had a thing about detectives. She liked being handcuffed to the bed, told she was a bad girl and all that crap. She was a bit of a ming-troll, with a face like a pug with piles, but hey, you don't look at the mantelpiece, as his dad used to say when asked why he'd married Winkler's mum. Francesca thought Winkler was the best thing since Idris Elba, and he knew she'd *ooh* and *aah* later when he flexed his pecs and let her run her hands over his granite-hard glutes.

Yeah, he was in a good place, his chakras lined up as neatly as the martial art DVDs on his bookcase at home.

But then he felt a gurgle in his stomach and a noxious fart hissed from his body, just as a blonde hottie strolled by, giving him a look of disgust as the smell assaulted her nostrils. He scowled. Why had he glugged that kale and gooseberry smoothie in the gym café? He felt another one brewing and, clenching those rock-like glutes, walked away as naturally as he could, aware of the blonde's contemptuous glare on his back.

Now his chakras were fucked again.

Two minutes later he got into his car and pressed play on his *Rainforest Dawn* CD. The sounds of the jungle waking up, the chattering monkeys and squawking parrots, usually made him feel like Tarzan, but it was too late: his good mood was ruined. All he could think about was Patrick motherfucking Lennon and the fact that he was the DCI's darling, the golden boy of the MIT who got all the juiciest cases, despite being a wet ex-Goth weirdo with a baby-battering fruitcake for a missus. It was unjust, that's what it was. It went against the laws of nature.

Lennon had humiliated Winkler at the end of the Child Catcher case, and Winkler deeply regretted that he hadn't taken the opportunity to bash Patrick's head in with a heavy object. He probably could have made an official complaint too, maybe even got Lennon suspended. But, at the time, Lennon was a hero and Winkler was pretty sure he was slipping one to the guv behind his banged-up wife's back. It would have been, what was the word? *Impolitic.* Better to bide his time and wait for Lennon to slip up. When he did, Winkler would be there to provide a hard landing.

Even better, maybe he would be the one to cause the slip.

Winkler couldn't see how the three murders – the teen girls and his old woman, Nancy Marr – could be related. OK, so there were the cuts, but he was convinced Daniel Hamlet had made a mistake there. It was a coincidence, that was all. Nancy's case was dissimilar in every other way. Two victims were young and nubile while the other was well past her sell-by date. Unlike the other two, Nancy's murder was in her home. They were in different areas of south London, the girls miles apart from Nancy. There was nothing at all to connect Nancy to the other two victims except that they'd all been female and had met with a nasty end. Winkler was grudgingly pleased that Lennon didn't seem to think there was much of a connection between the murders either, but he didn't trust him. He was likely to steal the case from under Winkler's nose – or steal the credit if they did turn out to be connected.

The best thing to do, Winkler decided, was to pretend to go along with Suzanne's plea for cooperation while doing two things. First, solve the Marr case, or at least find a credible suspect, in order to stop Lennon muscling in. Second, use the 'in' the guv had given him to get involved in the more glamorous and exciting teen murders. Winkler had been a whisker away from cracking the Child Catcher case, had put in a lot of the important legwork, and received absolutely zero credit or thanks. That wasn't going to happen this time.

He started the car and headed over to Wimbledon, thinking how sweet it would be when he got one over on Lennon.

Winkler stood outside the house where Nancy Marr had been murdered, wishing the building would give up its secrets, that a shaft of light would fall from the sky and reveal some devastating clue. He sighed as the sky remained grey and unhelpful. He was going to have to rely on his brains rather than miracles.

Being honest with himself, he hadn't put an enormous deal of effort into solving this murder. Nancy Marr had no good friends and only one close relative: a son in his late fifties who lived in Yorkshire, whose main concern appeared to be how quickly he'd be able to sell the house and pocket the money. There was a 'For Sale' sign outside now, but, as the scene of a brutal murder, this property hadn't shifted, despite the property boom that was going on at the minute.

His emotional indifference and unconcealed interest in his mother's money had made the son, George Marr, the initial suspect. But he had a rock-solid alibi. He'd been in Majorca with his partner and a couple of friends and there was nothing that pointed towards George hiring a hitman to bump off his mum.

Winkler's next line of inquiry had focused on known burglars in the locality – he'd got the team to check out a dozen other known names, but none of them appeared guilty. They'd done the usual, going door to door, interviewing the neighbours, with no joy. No-one had heard the old woman scream. And there was no useful forensic evidence.

So, with no relatives or friends to pressure the police and no great media interest in the case – after an initial cry of outrage and a leader article about 'the sickness in our society', the local paper had soon lost interest – Winkler had been able to put this investigation on the back-burner. It hurt, though, that his clearance rate, which was excellent, was affected. Winkler didn't *do* failure. So he was pleased now that he had the motivation to reignite it. Somebody around here must have seen something. It was time to start knocking on doors again.

Chapter 15
Day 4 – Patrick

Patrick and Gill regarded one another warily from opposite sofas. It was ten o'clock on Sunday evening, his and Bonnie's first night back in their own house, and Bonnie had only just settled back in her bedroom. She'd grizzled and fussed for hours and they had taken it in turns to read to her and stroke her until eventually she passed out from sheer exhaustion, her bum in the air and her grubby knitted Peppa Pig under her armpit. Patrick couldn't shift the uneasy feeling that maybe she remembered something bad had happened to her in that little room. He wished they had a third bedroom they could have redecorated so she could have had a fresh start in there, but they didn't. The house was too small.

Patrick guiltily upended the almost finished bottle of Merlot into his wine glass. He'd downed most of it in between his Bonnie-shifts, although he was technically still on duty. There was so much going on in his head, after finding Jessica's body and all the subsequent interviews he'd done, that now all he wanted to do was to block it all out so he could focus on this new chapter in their lives. He just prayed that he wouldn't be called back to the station; not tonight.

Gill was sipping cautiously at half a glass – she'd never been a big drinker, but said that now she drank even less. He almost wished she would – perhaps it would make the atmosphere more relaxed, had they both been half-cut. But her counsellor strongly recommended against it, for obvious reasons.

'So,' Gill said shyly, staring intently into her glass. 'This is awkward, isn't it?'

'It's like a weird sort of first date.' He laughed mirthlessly and then, when he saw how crushed she looked, backtracked. 'No, I mean, it's not really, of course, it's you and me, and how many dates have we been on? I just meant in terms of feeling . . . strange.'

She nodded, but he could see he'd upset her. Was this how it was going to be from now on? Him having to tread on eggshells around her, terrified of saying the wrong thing, constantly worrying that she would lose it again? He forced himself to stand up and walk across the room to her. He sat down close to her and put his arm around her shoulders. It still felt weird. *This is my wife*, he had to keep reminding himself, glancing down at her wedding ring, trying to feel an echo of the happiness that had consumed him the day he'd slipped it onto her finger.

'It's great to be home,' he whispered into her ear, gazing at the side of her face, unable to prevent himself noticing how much of a toll the last two years had taken on her appearance. Her skin had a permanent greyish tinge that never used to be there, and her dark brown hair, once so shiny and buoyant, was flat and dull.

They needed a holiday, he thought. All three of them.

He felt her shoulder relax a little under his hand and saw the side of her cheek curve up into a smile. 'This is our new start, right?'

She nodded again, but she didn't seem overly enthusiastic either.

'How do you feel about it, Gill?' he ventured. 'Are we OK?' He realised he was asking himself that question as much as her.

In reply, she turned to kiss him. It was the first time they had properly kissed for two years, and initially it was clumsy, teeth clashing, tongues out of synch. Patrick felt like he was fourteen again. That thought in turn led him to have an unwelcome flash of Jessica McMasters' disfigured body spread-eagled on the dustsheet of the makeshift studio floor earlier that day, with the trappings of a real photo shoot around her, lights and reflectors, making a mockery of a studio portrait. *Stupid girl,* he thought. How could she have been taken in like that? He would make sure he brought Bonnie up to be far more street-smart.

He banished the thoughts immediately and pulled Gill's warm body closer to him. She responded, pressing her breasts into his side, and gradually the kiss became more comfortable and erotic. For the first time, Patrick felt that he had his wife back.

'I've missed this so much,' he mumbled. 'I've missed you.'

Gill put her hands on either side of his face and kissed him again. 'I've missed you too, Pat.'

After a few minutes, Gill's hand slid down his torso and inside his jeans. He groaned with pleasure. He was so turned on that he thought he would come then and there, as soon as Gill's probing fingers touched his flesh.

'Let's go to bed,' he whispered, standing up with difficulty and holding out his hand to her.

She smiled properly at him then and he was reminded again how beautiful she was. He had forgotten how her nose crinkled when she smiled; how her eyes magnetised him when she looked at him like this. He hadn't looked at her properly for two years, had averted his gaze since that terrible day when he came home and found her sobbing – here on the stairs.

He froze, plunged back in time for a moment, his ardour ebbing away.

'What's wrong?' Gill whispered, but he shook his head, unable to answer. He led her up the narrow stairs, stepping over the step where she'd sat, shoving away the memories. As they reached the landing, Gill stumbled and ricocheted off Bonnie's bedroom door. They both froze as they heard Bonnie stir and mumble in her toddler bed, but after a few moments all fell silent again and they tiptoed into their bedroom.

Patrick was glad it was dark. It felt too weird being back in this intimate space together. Trying to bring himself back to the moment, he gently pushed Gill onto the bed on her back, and lay down on top of her, pressing himself into her as they kissed again. He relaxed again, lost in the moment, trying not to think about how long it had been since he'd had sex, fighting back the urge to crack a joke about having forgotten what to do.

He worked Gill's skirt and knickers down over her hips and, as she unbuttoned her shirt, breathing hard, he kissed her there, between her legs, the smell and taste of her and the way she gasped so familiar but so strange. He moved back up the bed, trailing kisses across her belly. She pushed him onto his back and straddled his thighs, unbuckling his belt and helping him pull his T-shirt over his head, tracing his tattoos with trembling fingers.

'Oh God, Pat, you don't know how much I thought about this when I was . . . away . . . I used to construct this fantasy about what you'd do to me in bed; it was all that would keep me going. I dreamed about you all the time. Shall I tell you what my fantasy was?'

Her voice snapped him out of the zone. No. He didn't want to hear it. He didn't want to talk, to listen to the desperate, strained note in Gill's voice, like she was only saying all this to please him. He shook his head, said, 'Just kiss me,' and she did, leaning forwards, bare breasts pressing against his chest. It felt good; she felt good; so why couldn't he fully relax?

Because when she ran her hands over his torso, he saw them shaking Bonnie.

When she wrapped her fingers around him, he pictured those fingers encircling their daughter's throat.

He must have made a noise in his throat because Gill stopped kissing him and sat up, staring at him. 'What is it?' she asked.

He tried to smile, to say, 'Nothing.' He was still hard, his body so starved of this, so desperate for fulfilment that nothing, no images, no doubts, could stop him. He rolled Gill over onto her back and, with eyes closed, entered her, concentrating on the feeling, the pleasure. Pushing away the pictures in his head.

'I love you,' Gill said, and he was sure he said it in return. Because he did. He still did. And this had to get easier, didn't it? They just needed time.

Chapter 16
Day 4 – Wendy

Wendy sat at her desk in the half-deserted office, one of the strip lights flickering in a way that made her glad she wasn't epileptic, and wondered what DI Lennon was doing right now. Snuggling up on the sofa with his wife, probably. Or reading his little girl a bedtime story. She knew all about Lennon's wife and her heart went out to the poor cow. She hoped he was kind to her . . . Actually, she couldn't imagine him being anything but. Despite the tattoos, the hair that needed cutting and that serious face, he was, well, he was *lovely*.

Lovely and gorgeous. The kind of man who was sensitive and empathetic but strong enough to be protective and sexy.

Jesus, listen to her! Sexy? She laughed, drawing a curious look from Martin two desks down, and reminded herself that it was a bad idea – a bloody terrible idea – to have a crush on her superior officer. Especially one who was married. Wendy's dad left them after a younger woman he worked with tempted him away, moving to the other side of Wolverhampton, and Wendy would never, ever be a homewrecker. Never be like that scutter who made her mum bawl her eyes out for months. Not that she was the type that men left their wives for. She hadn't even had a boyfriend for three years. Not for the first time, she cursed the fact that she had the body of a teenage gymnast – flat as a pancake, straight up and down, like an ironing board, and only five foot two. Twenty-five years old and she still got ID'd any time she tried to get into a club, and pretty much every time she bought drinks in a pub. It was deeply irritating. Unless she wore a ton of make-up – and often even then – she looked younger than her fourteen-year-old sister, Lucy.

Her latest attempt to appear her age was to have all her dark hair chopped into the shortest of pixie cuts because most teenage girls had the obligatory long, artificially straightened curtain of hair, but it hadn't made a lot of difference. Pat – as she'd heard Carmella call him, not that Wendy would dare to herself – hadn't appeared to even notice that anything was different about her.

Wendy really wanted to impress him, and the best way she could possibly do that, she thought, would be to find the bastard who had killed those two poor girls.

She gazed again at the photo of Rose Sharp on the whiteboard across the office. Even if it wasn't about gaining Pat's admiration and respect, she'd do anything to get the scumbag murderer off the streets. This was her chance!

Rose reminded Wendy of her little sister, Lucy, who still lived at home. Lucy actually thought OnTarget were a bunch of twats, preferring Jake Bugg and cooler indie music, spending her weekends hanging around the horse statue in the city centre with the alternative kids. Lucy thought that her older sister was 'well sad' for being into pop music, though she would happily join in with a game of *Just Dance* if none of her friends knew about it. Lucy would laugh her socks off if she saw what Wendy was doing now: signing up to the official OnT forum. She had chosen a picture of Shawn looking dreamy as her profile picture, with an animated GIF of the band on stage as her signature, and she decided on the username ShawnsCupcake.

As well as signing up to the forums she had also set up a new Twitter account, and had joined Tumblr and StoryPad. She didn't bother with Facebook because OnT fans didn't congregate on there, mainly because Facebook was seen by teenagers as a place for mums and grans.

Then she had spent an hour catching up with the latest OnT news and gossip, searching for the OnT hashtag on Twitter and seeing what the fans were talking about at the moment. Predictably, the deaths of MissTargetHeart and YOLOSWAG were hot topics, but so was Blake's new tattoo and rumours that Zubin was seeing Trixie from Love Bomb. There was a disturbing amount of vitriol aimed at Trixie, which reminded Wendy of how much she'd hated any girl who was linked with Lee from Blue. For two years she had been convinced she was going to grow up to marry Lee, had longingly stroked the posters of him on her wall, sketched his face a thousand times, though his nose always came out wonky and his lips not quite kissable. She closed her eyes and remembered how that had felt – the rushing hormones, the deluded certainty that if the object of her rampant affections met her, he would see she was special. That she was The One. She recalled, too, the pain she'd experienced when Mandy Briggs told her she didn't like Blue anymore and was switching her allegiance to McFly.

She plugged her headphones into her PC and opened Spotify, streaming the latest OnT album. She stared at photos of the band, trying to convince herself that they were not just fanciable but godlike. It crossed her mind that maybe she should pretend Shawn looked like DI Lennon, instantly chiding herself. She closed her eyes, inhaled deeply, and entered the zone. She was an OnTarget fan now. She loved them more than she loved her parents, her dog, her friends. They were her Everything.

It was time to join the fray.

She soon noticed that there were half a dozen 'super users' on the forum, girls – she assumed they were female, anyway – whose threads got the most views and comments, and who responded to nearly every thread started by another user. It was ridiculously cliquey. These half-dozen fans dominated discussions and opinion, with a second, larger group of acolytes who agreed with their opinions and acted as cheerleaders. Anyone who dared voice a different opinion, who wrote anything deemed to be in any way negative or stupid or 'sad', was instantly shot down. Sometimes arguments broke out between new users and the forum elite, page after page of passionate back and forth, which went on until the new user surrendered or a moderator stepped in. It was an intimidating place.

Wendy realised that her best bet was to ingratiate herself with these super users. If, as it seemed, they spent their entire waking lives on here, they would surely know Jess and Rose, if not in real life – or 'meatspace' as it was called – then online.

The most fanatical user of all, the queen of this microcosmic world, called herself, quite simply, Jade. Her real name, or a reference to the gemstone? There was a line in one of OnT's songs, Wendy remembered – something about a girl with jade-green eyes. This was the kind of fact she needed to know, so she looked it up. Yes, it was from 'Green, Green Eyes', their song about a jealous girlfriend.

Anyway, this Jade had the most powerful voice on the forum and anyone who dared question her or voice an opinion that deviated from hers in the slightest was throwing themselves into a pit of flame. Jade had just started a thread headed 'WHY SHAWN MAKES ME FEEL LIKE CHOCOLATE!!!'

Just watched the 'You're So Amazing' video for like the billionth time and decided that Shawn makes me feel like chocolate on a hot day. I MELT!!!!

This was followed by numerous posts full of OMGs and multicoloured dancing smileys, all the girls agreeing and discussing what chocolate bar they would be.

Wendy's fingers hovered over the keyboard. She needed to get this first response right. Inside, she was that thirteen-year-old girl, desperate to be liked, to be part of the gang.

She typed: *Shawn makes me feel like a Haribo on a hot day – all sticky* ☺ *!!!*

She hit enter and waited for the response. Would the girls find it too gross? Unfunny? Would they ignore her or, worse, attack her?

She hit refresh. To her enormous relief, two users had already posted responses full of rolling, laughing smileys. The first of these called herself F-U-Cancer – another of the site's super users – and then the rest were off, discussing what confectionary Shawn made them feel like, and why. Wendy waited, but Jade didn't post in this thread again. Instead, she started a new one, and soon all the girls were chatting about how long they had been OnT fans, as if it was a competition, and then they were all laughing about 'noobs' who thought they had the right to call themselves proper fans. Jade was the most scathing about noobs, as if anyone who hadn't got into OnT from the moment they formed was an inferior being. Wendy contemplated joining in with this thread, either defending new fans or claiming she'd been into them since day one. She decided to leave it. She didn't want to rile this Jade person further.

Wendy was going to have to work hard to show Lennon the progress he demanded. She got up and went to the coffee machine in the corridor. She had a feeling she was going to be pulling an all-nighter.

Chapter 17
Day 5 – Patrick

Patrick's teenage self had endlessly fantasised about the thing he was doing at this very moment: pushing his way through glass revolving doors into the cavernous atrium of a multinational music corporation. He quashed the thought immediately, castigating himself for such shallow egotistical whimsy when two teenage girls had so recently lost their lives. Besides, in his fantasy he was there because his Cure-rip-off band had just been signed for a six-figure sum and was being paraded around the offices as the Next Big Thing. *That* was never going to happen.

'Posh, innit?' said Carmella under her breath, looking around the mirrored foyer. Global Sounds Music – GSM – had, over recent years, taken over several other major record labels and was now the biggest multinational player in the market. Ten-foot-high glossy photos of the various labels' most successful artists interspersed the mirrored panels, and the vast expanses of perfectly toned flesh, male and female, made Patrick subconsciously suck in his stomach and push back his shoulders. The music industry was meant to be in trouble, battered by free downloads and streaming, but there was little sign of a tightening of belts here.

'I don't recognise any of these artists,' he commented in reply. 'Do you?'

Carmella inspected the pictures. 'Hmm. That's – thingy, you know, that R&B guy who got done for doing 150 mph on the A3 in his Aston Martin last week. And that's Selina Whatsername. Married to the Liverpool footballer.'

'Helpful, Carmella.'

Patrick felt quite disgruntled at his lack of current pop knowledge. How had he got so old? He had always prided himself on his musical trivia skills, but now he realised he'd be stuck in any pop quiz question post about 1990. Still, it wasn't the same these days. Whenever he heard snippets of chart music, he turned into his father – the words 'tuneless racket' sprang immediately into his head.

'Well, you must recognise these boys,' Carmella said, jerking her head towards the larger-than-life photograph of OnTarget. The four members were dressed in matching but different coloured suits, standing with their arms folded and self-important scowls on their faces. Patrick thought they looked like junior school kids – if junior school kids had tattoos, thousand-pound suits and artfully sculpted facial hair.

'Ridiculous,' he muttered, and Carmella poked him in the ribs.

'Come on, you old fart,' she said. 'I mean, you old fart, *boss.*'

They approached a smiley young receptionist in a crop top with a bird's nest of fake blonde and pink dreadlocks piled in a massive bundle on top of her head. Through her glass desk, Patrick could see a diamond belly bar winking at him, drawing attention to her flat midriff.

'Morning,' he said, holding out his badge. 'I'm DI Lennon and this is DS Masiello. We need to talk to someone connected to the band OnTarget, the A&R director or a publicity director perhaps.'

The receptionist gaped at him, then snapped into action, swivelling on her chair to a computer monitor on the desk's return, scrolling busily down a list of names and extension numbers, muttering as she did so, an expression of intense concentration on her round, babyish face. Patrick wasn't sure whether she was talking to herself or to him. It was kind of sweet how seriously she clearly took her job, though. He felt foolish for requesting someone in A&R because of course in no way had OnTarget been 'nurtured' or 'discovered'. They were as manufactured as a tin of biscuits, selected from the most addictive ingredients of competitors on a TV talent show.

The girl slapped her forehead. 'Duh, why am I looking through the address book? They're all upstairs in the first-floor meeting room – not the band, of course, but everyone involved in their campaign. Their manager's here as well. And Mervyn Hammond.'

'Excellent,' said Patrick briskly. 'What time did the meeting start? Wait – did you say Mervyn Hammond, the PR guy?'

Everyone knew who Mervyn Hammond was, the celebrity publicist who had made a name for himself that was almost as big as that of his biggest clients. He graced the tabloids and TV chat shows on an almost monotonously regular basis.

The girl peered at her computer, and Patrick noticed how she wrapped her arms protectively around her body when talking about Hammond. 'Yes, the one and only. Um . . . it started at nine thirty. Mervyn and Reggie, the manager, haven't come out yet, so it's probably still going on. Would you like to wait and I'll let them know you're here? That's Kerry, Mervyn's security guy, over there; do you want me to ask him . . . ?' She gestured towards a belligerent-looking brick shithouse in a cheap suit loitering near the leather sofas.

Patrick glanced over at the man, noting the aggressive way his enormous thumbs were stabbing at the tiny buttons of a BlackBerry. 'No, that's fine. We'll find our way up, thank you. You've been most helpful.'

She blushed and fiddled with a dreadlock until her phone flashed to indicate a call, at which she swivelled back towards her screen. 'GoodmorningGlobalSoundsMusicLottiespeakinghowcanIhelpyou?'

As Pat and Carmella walked up the stairs, they exchanged small grins. Some people just made you smile, thought Patrick. He could see the shaven, wrinkled scalp of the security guard's head, and that the man was playing Candy Crush on his phone.

'Why does Mervyn Hammond need security?' he mused out loud.

'Perhaps the guy's really just a driver,' said Carmella as they pushed open the fire door through to the first floor.

'Could be . . . That's OnTarget's label,' said Patrick, nodding at the brass plaque on the door etched with the words 'GIDEON RECORDS'.

Carmella looked confused. 'I thought Global Sounds was their label?'

'That's the company. It used to be a label, but now it's the parent company. It bought out a load of smaller labels including Gideon.'

'Oh,' she said, none the wiser.

The office inside was huge and open-plan, not unlike a swanky version of their own office at the station, with half a dozen people seated at desks in the centre, and smaller meeting rooms and offices around the edges. Dance music blared out from wall-mounted speakers and Patrick made a face. 'Couldn't work with all this noise,' he said to Carmella.

'Ever thought of going on that TV show *Grumpy Old Men?*' she replied.

Patrick laughed at her blatant lack of respect for him, then arranged his features into a sombre expression as a rake-thin woman in her thirties approached them. She had black wiry hair scraped back into a Croydon facelift and half a dozen chunky bead necklaces that looked as though their purpose was to weight her down and prevent her from floating away.

'Can I help you?'

They showed their police badges again and Patrick explained why they were there. The woman glanced over at a roomful of people behind another glass wall who were chatting worriedly. They reminded Patrick of lizards in a tank. 'And you are?' he asked.

'I'm Hattie Parsons, PA to the MD. They're all in there,' she said, pointing a bony finger.

'What's the meeting about, could I ask?' Patrick thought he could tell already, by the expressions on their faces. He was right.

'Er . . . it's a sort of PR crisis meeting for OnTarget – they're our biggest band. They'd probably welcome your feedback in there, actually. *The Sun* is about to run a big article about those girls who were killed being OnTarget fans. Obviously this could be a bit of a nightmare for the band, PR-wise.'

Patrick sighed heavily. 'Bit of a "nightmare" for the girls and their families too, don't you think?'

Carmella frowned at him, an expression that said *it's not her fault*. Hattie was blushing as though it *was* her fault and her hand flew to her neck to fiddle with the beads.

'OK. We'll pop in, then. Thanks for your help.'

'Would you like coffees?' Hattie asked nervously. Carmella declined on both their behalf, although Patrick could have mainlined an espresso. He had barely slept last night after the less-than-ideal sex with Gill. They had lain like corpses next to one another for hours, both of them knowing the other was awake and yet neither acknowledging it.

Patrick pushed open the meeting room door and ushered Carmella in. Hattie Parsons followed. Six surprised faces looked up at them, conversation immediately stilled.

'Sorry to interrupt. I'm DI Patrick Lennon and this is DS Carmella Masiello. We're investigating the murders of two girls and I understand that you're discussing this at the moment? We'd like to join you.'

Without waiting for an answer, he pulled out a chair for Carmella and took the remaining spare one next to her. The five men and one woman around the huge walnut table looked at them as though they had just beamed down from outer space.

'Carry on,' said Patrick mildly. 'Don't mind us.' He took out his Moleskine notebook and a pen.

Mervyn Hammond – instantly recognisable with his shock of curly dyed black hair, like a clown's wig – placed both his palms flat on the table. A small bag of nuts lay opened before him. 'I'm sorry,' he began, belligerently. 'But this is a private internal meeting. This is most irregular. Of course we're happy to help you with your enquiries, but we're discussing publicity damage limitation here; it's not going to be of the slightest interest to you types . . .'

'That's for us to decide, Mr Hammond,' said Patrick, noticing a flicker of smug pleasure at being recognised cross the man's florid face.

'It's fine, Mervyn,' said the blond, hearty-looking man next to him, reaching across the table to give Patrick's and Carmella's hands a bone-squeezing shake. 'Let me introduce you to everyone. I'm Tris Kent, managing director of Gideon Records.

'Mervyn Hammond you obviously know already. That's Reggie Rickard, OnTarget's manager.'

Reggie Rickard gave a brief nod in Patrick's direction without meeting his eyes. He was a small weedy man with thin brown hair who looked as though he needed a good wash. Patrick thought you'd never guess that he represented the biggest band on the planet. He more resembled someone who you would call to get rid of a wasp's nest in the attic.

Tris Kent pointed across to the other side of the table. 'Lauren Greene, senior publicity manager for Gideon, Graham Burns, OnTarget's social media manager, and Kazuo Yamada, head of A&R.'

Carmella had discreetly taken Patrick's Moleskine and was writing all this down as Patrick nodded at them all.

Lauren was a stocky woman dressed in flowing layers of the sort of cotton that Patrick thought was probably labelled 'organic', and Graham Burns looked exactly like all the hipster guys who frequented Shoreditch and Brick Lane these days. Carmella said that they were called D.H. Lawrences because they all sported bushy beards, slicked-back hair, and wore baggy cords and checked shirts. Burns even had a tweed waistcoat on and although his hair was dark brown, his beard had a distinctly gingerish hue. Patrick mentally labelled him The Fashion Victim. Kazuo Yamada was a tubby Japanese man of indeterminate age in a too-tight T-shirt.

'How can we help you, then, Detectives, er . . . ?'

'Lennon and Masiello. We want to talk to you about OnTarget's online community.' The room fell silent, all eyes on him. 'You're already aware that Rose Sharp and Jessica McMasters were both fans, but that alone isn't what interests us. I understand nearly every girl under sixteen in the world is a fan. What interests us is that both were keen users of OnTarget forums and social channels.'

'Like, as you say, a large proportion of teenage girls around the world.'

Patrick wished he could tell them about the perfume sprayed into the girls' wounds, along with the fact that they now knew, thanks to Martin's continued investigations, that both girls had been using apps or the Internet on their phones shortly before their deaths. Martin had worked out that both girls spent 82 per cent of their time online engaged in 'OnTarget-related activities'. If they had met their murderer on the Internet, the chances were they had encountered him – or he had found them – somewhere in the OnTarget universe.

But all he could say was, 'There are other details that I'm unable to reveal at this time that make us believe the two girls' interest in OnTarget was almost definitely a factor in their deaths.'

Mouths dropped open around the desk and Graham Burns shook his head with what could have been sadness or frustration.

Patrick addressed Mervyn Hammond. 'I'm concerned about this *Sun* article. If there's any way at all you can use your influence to prevent it from being published, we would greatly appreciate it. The last thing we want is to engender a sense of panic among OnTarget fans and their parents. We'll release a statement to the press when the time's right, but for the moment, the less the public knows, the better. It brings out all the copycats and attention-seeking weirdos.'

Tris looked pained. 'Believe me, that's the last thing we want too. It's what we've been discussing for the last hour. It's hardly good for the band's reputation, is it?'

Mervyn still appeared very put out. 'I'm afraid there's nothing I can do about the article. The editor thinks this OnT story is juicier than anything else I can offer at the moment.'

'Who would be in charge of monitoring the OnTarget forums and the social media activity?' Patrick glanced at Carmella's notes. 'I assume that would be you, Mr Burns?'

Graham Burns leaned forwards earnestly, brushing his foppishly floppy hair behind one ear. 'That's in my remit, yes. The official forum is hosted on a site that we own, though we use a specialist agency to monitor and track all the social activity and online mentions, of which there are many. And I mean *many*. Somebody tweets about OnTarget every second. Add to that all of the stuff going on across Facebook, YouTube, Tumblr, et cetera, and the noise is . . . intense. We're talking about a community of many millions globally. Last time a new video was released, the servers almost melted and it was viewed on YouTube 600 million—'

Patrick held up a hand, fearing he was about to be buried beneath a landslide of stats.

'Let's talk about the official forum first. Is there a private messaging system within it?'

'Yes, of course. But we can't access PMs.'

'You must be able to.'

Burns pulled a face. 'I'm afraid not. Privacy is a big thing among teenage girls.'

'Except when they're sharing semi-naked photos on Instagram,' Mervyn said, guffawing. Patrick noticed Lauren Greene shifting uneasily from one chunky buttock to the other.

'I could check if the two girls ever communicated privately on the forum,' Graham said. 'I just won't be able to access the content of the messages.'

'That would be useful, thanks.'

Burns left the room, smiling obsequiously at Mervyn Hammond on his way out. He looked like a right lick-arse, thought Patrick.

'So, OnTarget are pretty . . . massive, then?'

Reggie, the band's manager, cleared his throat and recited a long and boring list of statistics about sales figures and chart-topped territories. He had a strange way of emphasising random words.

Carmella was scribbling frantically and looked relieved when Reggie ended with, 'Tour of the US and Canada planned for *summer*. You could say *massive*, yeah.'

Mervyn Hammond had said nothing since confirming that he couldn't do anything about the *Sun* article. 'Are you sure there's nothing you can do to help us with the newspaper, Mr Hammond?' Patrick asked him.

He shrugged and re-crossed his legs, showing a flash of red silk sock. 'Sorry, Detective. Don't the police have any powers?'

'If only, Mr Hammond. If only.'

Mervyn smiled his oily smile. 'They might be interested in a profile of the cop who's out to catch the killer. Could be useful . . .'

He slid an embossed card across to Patrick who stood up, ignoring the card and turning away from the PR man. He had finally encountered someone he liked even less than Winkler.

Patrick and Carmella left the room, both glad to escape the curt silence. Hattie was typing furiously at a desk on the other side of the room, looking up at her screen and pausing, as if something there had grabbed her attention. Her fingers fluttered over the keyboard.

Patrick wandered over to her desk. 'Where can we find Graham Burns?'

Hattie jumped like Patrick had sneaked up behind her and popped a balloon in her ear.

'Shit. Sorry . . . Graham? Oh, he's right behind you.'

Patrick turned to see the social media manager coming towards him across the lobby.

'Any joy?' Patrick asked. 'Did Rose Sharp and Jessica McMasters ever message each other?'

'Yes.' Graham had that excited air people get when they think they are helping the police solve a tricky puzzle. 'They exchanged several messages last year.'

'But you really can't access those messages? That's incredibly frustrating, Mr Burns.'

Graham looked over his shoulder and said quietly, 'Well, it's possible that, if I dig deep, I could find something . . . It goes against policy, but . . .'

'That would be extremely helpful.'

'No problem, Detective.'

Yep, he really was an arse-kisser, Patrick thought.

Patrick handed him a business card. 'Here's my number. If I'm not around, you can talk to any member of my team. I'll need your contact details too.'

Graham delved in the back pocket of his cords and pulled out an antique engraved cardholder that looked as if it was made of ivory. He flipped it open and gave Patrick a card from it. 'Certainly,' he said. 'Anything I can do to help.'

As they left the building Patrick heard footsteps tapping hurriedly up behind them. It was Hattie Parsons, the PA, her beads bouncing against her flat chest as she broke into a run to catch them up. She was looking behind her as though she was being chased by a pack of wolves.

'I can't let Kerry see me talk to you.'

Patrick and Carmella exchanged glances. 'Kerry? Mervyn Hammond's security guy?'

Hattie nodded and Carmella smiled reassuringly at her. 'I wouldn't worry about that. He's far too engrossed in Candy Crush. What is it?'

Hattie actually wrung her hands together. 'I shouldn't tell you. It's probably nothing.'

'Go on,' said Patrick.

'I could lose my job . . .'

'You won't,' said Carmella soothingly. 'Not if you're just helping us with our investigation. That would be unfair dismissal.'

Tears sprang into the woman's eyes. 'Mervyn would definitely have me fired. So would Reggie. If the press got hold of it . . .'

They waited expectantly. Eventually Hattie leaned forwards and spoke so quietly that they had to strain to hear her over the noise of the Knightsbridge traffic.

'It's Shawn Barrett. Nobody knows outside of Gideon, but . . .'
She hesitated again.

'Please tell us, Miss Parsons.'

The words came out in a panicked blurt. 'There are things about Shawn that nobody knows. Put it this way: if I had a teenage daughter, I wouldn't let her within a million miles of him.'

'And why's that?'

She looked over her shoulder, then handed him a business card. 'Call me later,' she said, and turned and ran back to the office.

Chapter 18
Day 5 – Kai

Kai looked up from his position on the carpet where he was lying on his front, surrounded by used make-up wipes, empty Pringles tubes, dirty knickers, screwed-up bits of A4 paper from uncompleted school assignments and Haribo packets. The same litter had lain in the same place on the carpet ever since he'd first got it on with Jade, almost six months ago now.

He unscrewed the little pot of nail polish and began painstakingly sweeping brushfuls of silver glittery varnish onto Jade's toenails, having already squeezed her toes into the pink foam toe separators.

Jade scowled down at him over the top of her laptop. 'You didn't shake it! All the sparkles will be at the bottom if you don't shake it!'

Kai obediently shook the bottle – but he'd forgotten to put the brush back in it first, which prompted more howls of outrage from his girlfriend.

'Oi, you NOB!' she shouted.

'It's OK, bae, look, it ain't spilled anywhere,' he placated her.

'It had better not. It'll ruin me carpet if it gets on it and me mum'll kill me!'

Kai thought it best not to point out that he couldn't even *see* the carpet, under all the trash, that Jade's mum – who looked like she might one day need to be winched out of this house – had given up long ago. He decided it would be safer to change the subject on to something happier. 'What date's the OnT book signing, babe?'

'The thirteenth. The day before Valentine's Day.' She paused. 'Lol! Friday thirteenth! Can't wait to go to that posh restaurant you booked us.'

Kai looked up again, worried. 'I didn't book no posh restaurant, bae, was I meant to?'

Jade slapped the side of his head, a little harder than necessary. 'Duh! I was joking! You'd better get me a lush pressie, though. So, right, we'll get a night bus over there, yeah? If we get there for 3 a.m. I reckon we got a good chance of being first in line. Or should we make it earlier, like the night before?'

Kai didn't answer, as he was concentrating too hard on the toenails. He suspected, correctly, that Jade wasn't interested in his opinion anyway and that she was just thinking out loud.

'I wonder when the others'll get there. We gotta make sure we get in that queue before them chavs like Chloe and ShawnsCupcake.'

'ShawnsCupcake? Who's she?'

'I dunno, she's a noob. Tell you what, though, she's a right know-all and I bet she's a right little chav. She just comments on everything I post, like, straight away, chatting shit 'n' shit. It's not respectful to us lot who've been on the forums for, like, ever. You can't just barge in and take over. I bet you she'll try to jump the queue at the signing, well, *that* ain't happening, no way!'

'No way,' echoed Kai from her feet.

'She's acting like she's Shawn's biggest fan when everyone knows that *I* am. She's been commenting on StoryPad too – she, like, had the nerve to say that Shawn and Blake wouldn't go that way round, that Blake would be on top? I mean, I wrote the fucking thing! How dare she? If I see her, I'm gonna have a word or two!'

'How dare she? Blake would never be on top!' Kai protested, although he hadn't read Jade's latest shipping story or any of her stories for that matter. He found it a struggle to read anything longer than a tweet. *Hashtag Boring*, he thought, but would never admit it. *Actions speak better than words,* was his motto. Besides, he really didn't want to read about two blokes getting it on. But writing her stories kept Jade off his back for hours at a time, plus it made her horny as hell, and so was an activity to be encouraged.

'More than a word or two, I reckon,' he said, running a thumbnail around a smudge on Jade's toe. 'If she's that much out of line, we need to let her know she can't go around acting like that. I'll sort her for you.'

'Gettin' good at that now, ain't ya, bae?' Jade smiled at him and their eyes met in a moment of sly complicity before hers flicked back down to her feet. 'Don't forget to do another coat. And shake it first this time!'

Chapter 19
Day 6 – Patrick

Patrick fondly remembered the days when pubs were filled with the aroma of cigarette smoke, the blue-tinged cloud that hung over the tables, just as he recalled with a pang of nostalgia a time when he was young and foolish enough to puff his way through a pack of Marlboro Lights every day. Now, there were a couple of blokes sucking on e-cigarettes and the first smell he noticed when he entered the pub was the sickly sweet odour of the toilets.

He ordered a lime and soda and looked around for Hattie Parsons. The Prince Regent in Kentish Town was almost empty at this time of day. It seemed the kind of place that would always be empty and the barman wore the thousand-yard stare of a man who has seen terrible things. But Hattie insisted they meet here as it was a long way from her office and her colleagues would rather have their eardrums ripped out than visit a place like this. Patrick smiled. He'd rather have his eardrums ripped out than listen to the new OnTarget album again. Carmella had forced him to play it in the car yesterday, after picking a copy up from the record company office. It was so anodyne that the moment it ended he'd forgotten every note – though later, to his intense disgust, he'd found himself humming OnTarget's latest hit, 'Lonely Girl' ('You are a lonely girl/ But you are the only girl/For meeeeee'), in the shower.

Hattie was in the corner, wearing dark glasses, which she raised when she spotted him, which made him laugh.

'It is I, Leclerc,' he said as he sat down.

'Huh?'

'Never mind. You obviously don't share my love of corny sitcoms. Lovely place.'

She leaned across the table. She had a glass of wine in front of her, lipstick smudges on the edge. 'Ghastly, isn't it? And the wine . . .' She pulled a face. 'Wise to choose a gin and lime.'

'It's lime and soda. I'm on duty.'

'Oh. Shame. Never as much fun, drinking alone. Sure you can't have just one?'

He noticed her eyes flicking up and down his torso, sizing him up and apparently liking what she saw. Carmella was right – he must be giving off some kind of heavy pheromone at the moment – which was ironic, given the situation at home. If he was free and single . . . Hattie was a few years older than him but still a very attractive woman, with appealing laughter lines that showed she wasn't always as wound-up as she was right now.

'Thank you for agreeing to talk to me,' he said, ignoring her question.

She had taken the sunglasses off now and glanced left and right. Her eyes were slightly glazed and Patrick thought that, despite her complaint about the wine, she had downed at least a couple of glasses while waiting for him. That was fine. In fact, he had been deliberately ten minutes late, thinking this might encourage her to have a drink, which would help relax her and loosen her tongue.

'You know, if I'm caught talking to you, it will be the end of my career. Not just at GSM but the whole music business. And although I'm just a PA, and could probably be a PA anywhere, I like working there, you know? It's a hell of a lot more glamorous than being a PA in a bank.' She sipped her wine and winced. 'You look like you're into music. Let me guess . . .'

He was keen to move on to the point, so curtailed her guessing game. 'I'm a big Cure fan.'

'The Cure! I *love* them. They were my favourite band when I was younger. Saw them at this fantastic outdoor gig at Crystal Palace in, ooh, 1990? Actually, this is a big secret, but OnT are planning to record a cover of "Boys Don't Cry" for their next album.'

Patrick spat his lime and soda across the table.

'Or possibly "Love Cats" . . .'

Attempting to recover from this awful news – for Patrick, it was akin to being told his mother had started a new career as a stripper – he said, 'I have to warn you, Hattie, that if what you tell us leads to a prosecution, you might be required to testify in court.'

She blanched. 'Oh God. Really? Can't you blame an anonymous source?'

'I'm not a journalist.'

Another big gulp of wine. 'Maybe I should have gone to the press instead. Then you would have found out that way.'

'Found out what? Listen, Hattie, I will respect your need for privacy as far as I can, but if you know anything, you *have* to tell us.'

Hattie shuddered, but then said, 'OK, OK. I understand. Oh God . . . I've got teenage nieces, and when I imagine them . . .' She trailed off.

'Do you want another drink?'

'I shouldn't. Oh, yes please. White wine.'

He returned from the bar and she immediately raised the glass and swallowed half its contents. Then he waited.

'OK, so, the thing is . . .' Her voice dropped so he had to lean forwards. 'There have been rumours about Shawn Barrett for a long time. Since the band went on their first world tour.' She paused. 'Actually, that was only two years ago, but it feels like a lifetime, like they've been around forever. OnTarget are so huge. You know, without the cash they've generated over the last couple of years, GSM would be in deep shit. The company will do anything to protect them. There was an exposé last year when Blake and Zubin were caught smoking a joint on the tour bus, but no-one really cares about that sort of stuff anymore, do they?'

'Well, it is illegal.'

'Yes, but the media can barely be bothered to act outraged by a bit of ganja these days. It's hardly in Ian Watkins territory, is it?'

Ian Watkins had been the singer with the rock band Lostprophets, who had been convicted of sexually assaulting a one-year-old baby, a case that had made Patrick wish, in his most furious moments, that he could spend an hour alone in a cell with Watkins.

'And you're saying that the rumours about Shawn are in Watkins territory?'

'Well, not *that* bad. But . . . OK, you know pop bands get a lot of groupies, obviously. With rock bands – grown-up bands – it's quite straightforward. Women throw themselves at them and, in most cases, the bands act like Augustus Gloop let loose in Willy Wonka's factory. I'm sure there's a lot of weird, blurred-lines stuff that goes on, but on the whole it's consenting adults. With a boy band like OnTarget, though, where most of the fans are very young, underage, we have to build a protective wall around them.'

'When you say "we", you mean the record company?'

'Yes. The record company and their management. It would be an absolute disaster – some fourteen-year-old girl, who probably looks seventeen, going to the press revealing she had sex with one of OnTarget. Nightmare. We basically have to ensure that any girl who goes near the band is ID'd and isn't a nutter. Anyway, it's not such a big issue now as most of the band have girlfriends and are good boys. Carl is engaged to Alexa Woolf from The Shenanigans, and Blake is going out with wotsername from the *Harry Potter* films. Zubin is in between girlfriends. Shawn, though, has never had one, which has led to loads of rumours that he's gay, especially as he's the best-looking and most popular member, the one that everyone assumes will eventually go solo.'

'But he's not gay?'

'Uh-uh.' Her voice dropped another notch. 'He's definitely not gay. What I've heard is that he likes young girls. Fourteen, fifteen. I mean, he's only twenty himself, but that five-, six-year gap is massive. And that's not the worst of it.'

Patrick looked up from his notebook, where he'd been scribbling notes. 'What is the worst of it, Hattie?'

A man walked past the table and Hattie jumped, but it was just a guy on his way to the Gents.

'The rumour is that he . . . hurt a girl while they were on tour in Ireland.'

'What do you mean, hurt?'

Her voice was so quiet now that he had to lean right across the table, and she did the same. To observers, they must have looked like a couple having an affair, whispering secrets and plans. 'The rumour is that he's into bondage and . . . role-play. He likes to tie girls up and whack them with a riding crop.'

'Hm. Influenced by *Fifty Shades of Grey*?'

'Probably. Listen, this came from a guy who was looking after Shawn on tour. Shawn would ask him to take him to local sex shops where he would buy handcuffs and rope and, you know, kinky underwear. The guy thought it was a bit weird, but this is the music industry – everyone sees extreme behaviour all the time. Anyway, apparently, they were at the hotel in Dublin after a gig there and it was mayhem, as it always is – the place surrounded by fans and press – and the guy who was looking after Shawn let this girl go up to

Shawn's room. Two hours later she's in the hotel corridor, sobbing, and Shawn's minder manages to get her into an empty room where she tells him that Shawn tied her to the bed and then he laid into her with a crop. He gagged her so she couldn't scream . . . She was in a dreadful state, apparently, and then she drops the bombshell – she's only fourteen.'

'I thought they were meant to ID all the girls?'

'Yes. They are, but this guy fucked up. The girl had fake ID, he said she looked about nineteen, was determined to get into a room with her idol.' She shook her head sadly. 'Anyway, the minder called GSM and they managed to persuade her not to tell anyone. They paid her off. That's how I know about it – I saw my boss's emails.'

Patrick stared at her. 'So he committed at the very least statutory rape . . .'

'Hang on, no. He didn't have sex with her. This girl apparently said afterwards that although Shawn was excited through the whole thing, he didn't actually, you know . . .'

'Penetrate her?'

She nodded, a hint of pink blossoming on her cheeks.

'How can you be sure this girl in Ireland won't talk?' Patrick asked.

'She was paid extremely well and . . . Mervyn Hammond got involved. I believe he made certain threats, explained to her, in a very nice way, of course, how the media works, how her life would be over if this ever came out. And I think he made promises too, that he would help her if she ever got into one of the talent industries. Do some positive PR for her. Vile man.'

From what he'd seen of Hammond, Patrick had to agree with her assessment.

'This could be extremely helpful,' he said, glancing down at his notebook, which he angled so Hattie couldn't see it. The key words he'd written down, which tallied with Rose's and Jessica's murders, were *underage, crop, hotel room* and, underlined, *no sex.*

Suddenly, they had a prime suspect. A prime suspect who just happened to be one of the most famous men, not just in Britain but in the whole world.

'I need to talk to this girl,' he said.

'What?'

'I need her name, Hattie.'

'Oh God, it's all going to come out that I've talked to you.' She put her hands over her face. 'I didn't mean to say so much.'

Patrick looked wryly at the empty wine glasses on the table.

'You can't talk to the girl, Detective. It's impossible.'

'Nothing's impossible, Hattie,' he said.

Chapter 20
Day 6 – Patrick

O n the way back to the incident room, Patrick had a moment of brain-panic – the realisation that there were so many layers of thought going through his head that they all swirled together like tutti-frutti ice cream, and separating them out into a cogent to-do list seemed as impossible as restoring the ice cream back to its original ingredients. He parked in the staff car park and pulled out his Moleskine and a pen, balancing the notepad on the steering wheel so he could try to get it all down before he forgot:

Get update from Peter Bell re key card
"   "   " Gareth
Brief Suzanne
Get Mervyn Hammond in
Find out name of girl Shawn attacked – MH should know
Check on Gill
Chicken fillets/washing powder/binliners
Winkler – what's he up to??

He paused after this last one and underlined Winkler's name again. Although they were meant to be working together on this case, it occurred to Pat that he hadn't seen anything of his 'colleague' – how that word stuck in his craw – since the last team briefing. During the Child Catcher case, Winkler had gone off on his own and almost screwed up the whole operation. He was pretty sure Winkler's apparent lack of interest in this case would prevent that happening again, but he couldn't help but feel a tickle of anxiety.

Even though the list needed to be four times longer, Pat decided it was enough to be going on with. Most of those things were doable that afternoon. He toyed with the idea of ringing Gill first, having just had a sudden grim vision of her and Bonnie, stuck in front of the TV on this cold wintery day, Bonnie chatting to her Barbies and Gill ignoring her, staring with unseeing eyes at the screen . . . He shuddered. No, it wouldn't be like that. Gill wasn't like that anymore.

Yet he could never quite shake the worry that she might be, that she was just hiding it well when he was around.

He got out of the car and pulled out his phone to call her, but then saw Peter Bell heading towards his own car, remote key in his hand.

'Cyber-Crime office only open mornings these days?' Patrick enquired. He hadn't meant to sound snippy, but it came out that way, and Bell's fleshy face folded into a brief scowl that he immediately covered up with an obsequious smile.

'Ha ha, Guv, no, far from it, actually. I'm back off to the Travel Inn to check out something I've unearthed about their room key system. Just a theory I'm going to test. If it works, I think we'll have our answer as to how the perp managed to get in.'

Patrick nodded with surprise and pleasure. 'That's excellent! I was about to come and ask if you were getting anywhere. Nice work, Bell.'

The man's smile was genuine this time, displaying yellowy teeth crossed slightly at the front. He wasn't a looker, poor guy, thought Patrick.

'Well, as I said, it's just a theory at the moment, but I'm reasonably confident . . .'

'Keep me posted. That would be a big step forwards.'

Bell gave Patrick a mock salute, almost poking himself in the eye with his car key in the process, and Patrick swallowed a grin.

By the time he'd got into the incident room he decided he'd ring Gill later. Suzanne was standing by the water cooler with her back to him, and he couldn't help but take a moment to let his gaze sweep up and down her body. Her long blonde hair was in a loose, glossy sheet almost to her waist, emphasising her trim hourglass figure in a pencil skirt and tight white shirt . . .

Suddenly aware of someone hovering behind him, Patrick snapped out of his reverie and turned to find Gareth Batey by his right shoulder. The man did have a habit of lurking anxiously. He needed to be far more assertive, thought Patrick. He was a good solid cop, bright and efficient, but this slightly weird diffidence didn't do him any favours.

'Gareth,' he said. 'I was about to come and find you. Did you hear we've got a potential lead on the key card?'

Batey nodded. 'I was coming to tell you the same thing,' he said in his soft Scottish accent. He was wearing a fuzzy sort of woollen tie in heathery colours and Patrick wondered if it was a statement or a reminder of his Highland origins. 'I'll go with Bell back to the Travel Inn, if that's OK with you.'

'Good idea. Report back to me later,' Patrick replied, slightly distractedly, as Suzanne was walking back to her office, draining a paper cone of water on the way. She lobbed the empty cone with perfect accuracy into a waste paper bin five feet away. When she saw Patrick, he thought he saw her eyes light up. But perhaps he was deluded.

'I'm just back from interviewing Hattie Parsons from OnTarget's record company,' he said, catching up and falling in step with her. 'Very interesting. But potentially tricky – can I fill you in?'

She gestured him into her office. 'Tricky why?'

He explained what Hattie had said about Shawn Barrett and the underage girl in Dublin, and that Mervyn Hammond had gone to great lengths to cover up her complaint. 'Hattie says she can't remember the girl's name, but I reckon she could find it if Mervy-boy won't tell us. He definitely knows it.'

'Let's get him in, then,' Suzanne said. Patrick noticed she had slipped off her high shoes under the desk, and the sight of her stockinged toes had the usual effect on his groin.

'Who – Barrett or Hammond?'

'Hammond first, get the lie of the land.'

Patrick groaned. 'He's as slippery as a barrel of eels, but yes, I think you're right. I'll lean on him. Can you imagine the media shit storm we'll have on our hands if we have to haul in the singer from the world's biggest boy band?'

'Never a dull minute,' said Suzanne, smiling at him. 'But better we expose this now, if it's true, than have another Operation Yewtree in thirty years.'

Patrick agreed. Every day seemed to bring a new story about historic cases of rape or sexual assault by some former TV favourite or pop star.

'But don't go in on Hammond with all guns blazing – he's the sort who'd set his lawyers on us if you even look at him funny.'

'Credit me with some sensitivity!' Patrick pretended to be offended. 'I'm not a bull in a china shop . . . well, not usually . . .'

There was that smile again.

'I know you're not, Pat,' she said, holding his eyes for just a second too long.

Chapter 21
Day 6 – Wendy

The queue for the signing stretched all the way from the Waterstones bookshop on Piccadilly to the Costa Coffee on the corner of Church Place. Wendy had a friend from back home who was an obscure crime novelist. Wendy had been to one of his book signings once – three people had turned up, including her.

Now here was a boy band who probably hadn't read their own book, let alone written it, with hundreds of people desperate to get in to see them. Not that this had anything to do with the book itself, of course. It was a chance to actually meet OnTarget, to be a foot away from them, breathing the same air. Even Wendy felt a little excited at that prospect. The allure of celebrity. Wendy's mum had been almost overcome when she'd bumped into Dave from Slade in the supermarket, forty years after they were properly famous. In this secular society, celebs were the new gods.

She walked along the line, mostly made up of teen girls, and wondered if she was walking past Jade, F-U-Cancer or any of her other contacts – she wouldn't allow herself to call them friends – on the forum. Over the last couple of days she had spent every spare minute chatting, tweeting and posting on Tumblr, barely sleeping, her eyes scratchy from staring at screens. She had been friendly and bubbly, uncontroversial but witty and, she believed, had made quite an impression. Even the initially stand-offish Jade had responded to some of her posts and retweeted her a couple of times. This was partly because Wendy had written the most over-the-top gushing review of one of Jade's shipping stories on StoryPad, laughing to herself as she bashed out superlatives to praise what was actually the most appallingly written erotic dream sequence in the history of literature.

After she'd been doing this for a day, DI Lennon had asked Wendy how she was getting on. She had responded with a torrent of enthusiasm and a plea that she should be allowed to continue. And the lovely man had said yes, which had made her want to give him a hug.

Though, to be honest, everything Patrick did made her want to give him a hug. More than that, she wanted him to handcuff her to a bed and . . .

She refused to allow herself to think any further.

As soon as Wendy heard that Jade and a bunch of the other girls were heading to this book signing, Wendy knew she had to come along. This was her chance to observe them in the flesh, maybe chat to one or two of them. She didn't know what any of these young women looked like, but if she kept her eyes and ears open, maybe she would be able to figure it out.

She also suspected that, maybe, the murderer would be here. If he was targeting girls like this, perhaps he would come along to observe his prey. The idea stoked the flames of anger that burned inside her. The determination to catch him before he struck again. There weren't many men here. A few teenagers, standing sheepishly beside their star-struck girlfriends, clearly hoping their mates didn't see them. A number of dads too, accompanying younger girls who bounced up and down in the queue, eager for the doors of the bookshop to open. Apart from that, there were just security staff and, of course, the band and their entourage who would be inside in the warm, doubtless bracing themselves for the snowstorm of female hormones.

Wendy reached the front of the queue and wondered what to do next. There was a small group of teenage girls right at the front, chatting excitedly, clutching their phones and grabbing each other whenever there was a sign of movement behind the doors of the shop. One of the girls, a blonde in a fake fur, leopard-print coat, shivered like a smack addict locked in a freezer; another girl with black hair couldn't stop thumbing her phone. Just in front of them, at the very start of the queue, was a girl of about fifteen with orange fake tan and big boobs, her forehead already lined from too much frowning. Beside her stood a boy about her age who kept trying to put his arm around her. He was about her height but with ridiculously short legs. As Wendy watched, the girl with the tan said something to him and he trotted off up the road on his little legs, coming back ten minutes later with two cups from Costa.

'Thanks, babe,' the girl said, cream bubbling up through the lid in the cup as she slurped at it.

'Anyfink for you, bae,' said the boy.

Wendy tried not to smirk. Was one of these girls Jade? She knew from Twitter that Jade had been planning on coming here in the middle of the night, with her boyfriend, whose name Wendy didn't know. She took her phone out and opened Twitter, to see if Jade had updated recently. Sure enough, she had tweeted a boast about being the first in line.

OMG I'm going to meet Shawn!! #OnT #booksigning

In fact, Wendy remembered now, Jade had an Instagram account that was full of selfies. She navigated to it and found Jade straight away. There she was, pouting at the camera. This was definitely her. There was even a shot of her with her boyfriend.

Wendy hesitated. Should she approach Jade and her friends? She was worried about whether she would actually pass for a fourteen-year-old. She'd been to New Look to buy a new outfit, had applied her make-up in the way she thought her younger self would, and on the way here had gone into a supermarket and attempted to buy cigarettes, though she didn't smoke. The twenty-something woman behind the counter had asked for ID and Wendy had grinned and immediately walked away. To an adult, she could pass for a mature-looking fourteen-year-old, she was sure – but would she fool Jade and her mates?

As she summoned her inner teenager, trying to think of a good reason for approaching Jade that wouldn't make her look like a stalker, the doors opened. Jade and her gang squealed, the line surged a little, but then the doors were immediately shut. It was just a few guys coming out, smiling at the sight of the queue. Wendy recognised one of them: Mervyn Hammond. A shifty-looking bloke stood next to him, a Staffordshire terrier in human form, and just behind was a beardy guy in his early thirties with a bland, pleasant look.

'Amazing turnout,' Wendy heard Mervyn Hammond say, and the bland man nodded and smiled.

Right, Wendy thought. *Time to see if I can fake it as a teenager.* She prepared to head over to Jade's group when someone put their hand on her shoulder.

'Wendy?'

She turned. It was DS Masiello.

'What the hell are you doing here?' Wendy asked.

Carmella raised her eyebrows. 'That's a nice greeting! Thought I'd come down here, take another look at our OnTarget fans. See if there's anyone hanging around.' She spoke in a hushed voice. 'What about you?'

'I was just passing by, actually.'

She squirmed. DI Lennon hadn't given her permission to do this. She was supposed to be conducting her investigation solely online, not putting her face out there. She knew if she got a result he would forgive her, would be impressed and pleased, she hoped. But Masiello turning up like this ruined it!

She groped for something else to say and was saved by movement behind her as the doors opened again and a pair of security staff beckoned the crowd forwards, two at a time, while Mervyn Hammond and his companions looked on.

'Makes you wish you were young again,' Wendy said, gesturing at the expressions of anticipation on the faces of the girls in the line.

'I don't know about that.'

'Well, anyway, I'd better be getting on,' Wendy said.

Carmella was looking at her suspiciously now. Oh God, she was going to run back to Patrick and tell him.

'See you at the station,' she said, softly, and as she walked away she became aware that someone was watching her. She turned. Jade's boyfriend frowned at her before Jade grabbed his wrist and tugged him through the doors into the shop, the crowd surging forwards behind them. Wendy walked on, towards the Costa, wishing she'd had a chance to introduce herself to Jade and the other girls. When she looked back, Carmella was talking to Mervyn Hammond.

Oh shit, please don't let Patrick be angry, she thought. But now she had an even greater reason to make this work. She was going to have to push things forwards. She knew exactly what she needed to do.

Chapter 22
Day 6 – Chloe

Chloe was gutted. Her mum had made her wait because she had to take an important call from a client, and then Brandon had announced that he needed the loo just as they were about to leave, and the traffic had been predictably horrific, and they had to stop for petrol and there was a long line at the garage. By the time she got to Waterstones, having run the last hundred yards, her stress levels were off the scale and, as she feared, the queue was already so long that the chances of getting in were less than zero.

She joined the line anyway, behind a group of shrill twelve-year-old girls and tried to figure out if there was some way of getting farther ahead without getting her hair pulled out. Security staff walked up and down the line, presumably to stop queue-jumping and fighting among fans, or to drag out any girls who fainted with excitement.

If only Jess were here. She'd know how to get them in. The thought was followed immediately by a rush of sadness. Jess *wasn't* here. Tears welled up in Chloe's eyes and she remembered the dream she'd had a few nights ago. She'd been waiting down at the Rotunda to meet up with Jess, but her friend hadn't turned up and Chloe felt increasingly panicked. Just before she woke up, her pillow damp beneath her face, Chloe realised: Jess wasn't coming. Not ever.

She inhaled deeply, aware that the twelve-year-olds were gawping at her. Maybe she shouldn't have come . . . It was too soon after Jess's death, too painful to think how much Jess would have loved this. MissTargetHeart – Rose – too. Brandon kept going on about it, how it was 'mad' that Chloe knew two girls who'd been killed, till she'd been forced to smack him around the head and tell him to shut up, which made him cry and go running to Mum. It wasn't 'mad'. It was tragic. Although she hadn't really known Rose, not properly.

The twelve-year-olds were whispering and giggling now and, irritated and embarrassed, Chloe left the line, stalking down towards the store. She could see Mervyn Hammond up ahead, talking to a woman with auburn hair. The woman turned and Chloe realised she was that cop, the one who'd stood next to the detective at the vigil when he made his appeal for information. And just beyond the female cop, Chloe saw Jade and Kai, right at the front of the queue.

Her knees wobbled and all of a sudden the wintry sun seemed too bright. She staggered away, almost colliding with a security guy, and sat down on the kerb, sucking in deep breaths. It all came rushing back to her, the reason why she didn't talk to Jade anymore; what had happened to that girl; the things that she hadn't told the police about . . .

She forced herself to her feet, praying that Jade and Kai hadn't seen her, and walked briskly away. She needed to be far away. To be anywhere but here.

Chapter 23
Day 7 – Patrick

P atrick cracked his knuckles and checked his reflection in the
mirror, making sure he didn't have anything caught in his
teeth and that his hair wasn't sticking up. He knew that
Mervyn Hammond was the kind of person who placed high importance on image and Patrick needed Hammond to take him seriously,
even if the PR man had a faintly ridiculous air about him – an older
man with dyed black hair and a smooth Botoxed face, a permatan
and bling on his wrist in the form of a diamond-studded Rolex.
As Carmella had pointed out, Hammond probably wore control
pants to keep his stomach sucked in. But despite all these ludicrous
foibles, Hammond had power, friends in the press and other high
places, and the means to afford teams of expensive lawyers. Patrick
needed to tread carefully with him.

He cracked his knuckles again, gave his reflection a final
once-over, and left the Gents. Careful or not, he was looking
forward to this.

Mervyn Hammond was waiting in interview room one,
Carmella sitting opposite him. Hammond had brought his own
large coffee from Starbucks, along with a bag of mixed nuts, which

sat open on the table. When Patrick had spoken to Hammond on the phone he had explained that the PR man was not under suspicion of the murder of Rose or Jessica, but that information had come to light that they needed to ask him about. Patrick had expected Hammond to protest, to come in flanked by an entourage of lawyers, but he had been surprisingly willing and had come alone, driving his own limited-edition F-type Jag Coupé, at which several cops had gone into the car park to gawp. Maybe, Patrick thought, Hammond found this kind of thing exciting, interesting.

'I'm diabetic,' Hammond explained, catching Patrick eyeing the bag of nuts. 'I need to snack regularly or my blood sugar goes . . .' He pointed his thumb downwards like a Roman emperor ordering an execution. 'That is all right, I assume, Detective Lennon?' He chuckled. 'I met your namesake a few times, you know. Up himself, he was. Paul was always the talented one . . . though they both shared the same dodgy taste in women.'

'Yes, that's fine,' Patrick said, referring to the nuts. He took the seat opposite Hammond, who was wearing a suit that was slightly too tight, his fake tan glowing orange in the badly lit interview room where the body odour of the youth who'd been questioned here last still lingered. 'I should point out that you are here voluntarily, that you are not under caution and that you can leave at any time.'

'Well, that's a relief. I wouldn't want to be locked up. Unless it was a women's prison.' He winked at Carmella. 'Enjoy the book signing, Detective?'

Patrick was eager to get started. 'Thank you for coming to talk to us, Mr Hammond.'

'Call me Mervyn.'

'Mr Hammond, we want to ask you some questions about one of your clients. Like I said on the phone, some information has come to light that is connected to a case we're working on, and we are hoping to get some information from you to help clear it up.'

'It's not Bruce, is it? I warned him about those small boys.' He guffawed and said, 'I'm only kidding. It's obviously about OnTarget and the murders of those two teenagers. It's all over the papers this morning. Both massive OnT fans; the boys sending their condolences to the families; planning a minute's silence at tonight's gig. That was my idea, by the way. Though the boys really do care, you know. They love their fans.'

Patrick studied Hammond's face, trying to work out if he was taking the piss. Before he could ask the next question, Hammond scooped up the bag of snacks and leaned across the table towards Carmella.

'Nut?'

'No thank you,' she said coolly.

His eyes flicked up and down her upper body. 'Yeah, you don't look like the type of woman who likes nuts.' He turned his attention to Patrick. 'Ever thought about a TV career, Detective? I reckon you'd do well with those rugged, alternative looks. Plus you've got a good backstory – wife trying to kill your nipper. You could probably get a book deal. The cop who arrested his own wife. *The Mirror* would serialise that, no question.'

Patrick blinked, then took a deep breath. Of course, it would be easy for Hammond to find that out – it had been in the papers at the time, although the detail about Patrick arresting Gill himself had been omitted. He was disconcerted by the fact that Hammond had made the effort to research him, though. But he couldn't let that show.

'Mr Hammond, the allegations we've heard concern Shawn Barrett.'

Hammond's eyebrows rose, his forehead remaining immaculately smooth. 'Allegations? A minute ago, you said "information".'

He popped a brazil nut into his mouth, displaying his brilliant white teeth.

Patrick cursed himself, but it didn't really matter. The allegations were going to come up anyway.

'Information has come to light that, while on tour in Ireland, Shawn Barrett assaulted a girl at his hotel. According to our source, he tied this girl up and beat her.'

Hammond stayed immobile and silent for a moment. Patrick could almost hear his brain ticking. According to Wikipedia (*You're not the only one who can do research, mate*, Patrick thought) Mervyn Hammond had an IQ of 160. Not that Patrick placed much faith in IQ scores. Some of the people he knew with high IQ scores had common sense scores of zero.

'Who's this source?' Hammond asked, his voice flat.

'We can't reveal that.'

Hammond barked a laugh. 'Ever thought about working in PR, Detective? Or journalism? This is the first I've ever heard about such an allegation, and I can tell you that Shawn Barrett is a sweet, normal lad who has no interest in S&M or tying little girls up.'

'Who said she was a little girl?' Carmella asked.

'Huh?'

'We didn't mention anything about her being underage.'

Hammond snorted. 'Well, you said girl instead of woman. You police are trained to be politically correct now, aren't you? You probably have to say *person of a female persuasion* in public, don't you? I was simply extrapolating from the vocab you used.'

Patrick resisted the urge to roll his eyes. 'We want the name and contact details of this young woman – and yes, she was underage.'

'Did he have sex with her?'

'What?'

'Well, you talk about her being underage. I assume you mean the age of consent, though I don't even know what it is in Ireland.'

Patrick had checked – it was seventeen.

'Listen, Detective, Shawn Barrett and the other members of OnTarget have *persons of a female persuasion* literally jumping on them and begging them to fuck them, if you'll excuse my Anglo-Saxon. Maybe one or two of these chicks asked Shawn to tie them up after showing him a dodgy birth certificate. I know for a fact that Shawn is not a psychopathic rapist who gets his kicks from attacking his fans. He's a normal red-blooded bloke who is taking advantage of the goodies being served up to him on a plate.'

He sat back and folded his arms.

'How do you know "for a fact" he's not a psychopath?' Carmella asked.

Hammond looked at her. 'Because the management company had them all tested.'

'Tested?'

'Yes. The whole band underwent extensive psychometric testing and assessment by a psychologist before being allowed through to the final stages of *Face the Music*.' That was the talent show on which the band had been put together. 'They are all normal, healthy, young heterosexual men with conventional tastes in the bedroom. They are ambitious but lack aggression. In other words, they failed the psychopath test with flying colours.'

Patrick sat up straight. This interview was threatening to skid out of control. 'Mr Hammond, regardless of that, we need to take this information seriously. I want to talk to this young woman.'

'And what makes you think I can help you?'

'Because our source told us that you helped cover it up.'

Hammond stood, snatching up his half-empty packet of nuts. 'I'm exercising my right to leave of my own free will.'

'Please sit down, Mr Hammond.'

'Why should I?'

'Because I'm sure you don't want anyone to know that you allegedly covered this up. It won't help Shawn Barrett's reputation, and it certainly won't help yours.'

Hammond dropped into his seat, his lip curling. 'No-one in the press will print anything negative about me.'

'Who said anything about the press? There's this thing now called the Internet. You might have heard of it.'

Hammond's mouth opened, then closed, then opened again. 'So . . . you're threatening me?'

'We are merely asking for your cooperation.'

Hammond took several deep breaths, then tipped a handful of nuts into his palm, inserting them into his mouth one by one and chewing thoughtfully. 'You think Shawn Barrett's a murderer.'

'What makes you say that?'

'Come on, Detective. If you want me to be straight with you, I need to ask for some *quid pro quo* here. Two days ago you were at Gideon Records' office, asking about OnTarget in relation to those two dead girls. And now you're asking me about this. It isn't a coincidence. You think that because Shawn allegedly engaged in some light bondage on tour it makes him a killer.' He shook his head. 'So unimaginative, you plods.'

Patrick clenched his fists.

'OK, so maybe Shawn did get a little carried away. But he didn't know that girl was underage, and he didn't do anything she didn't want to do. It was all consensual.'

'He hurt her, Mr Hammond.'

'That's what S&M is all about, isn't it? Pleasure and pain. Except this girl says yes, gives her consent, and then when it actually hurts she's all *boo hoo hoo, I want my mummy, you hurt me, you brute.*'

Patrick sighed. 'I don't want to get into a big debate about this. But I need the contact details of this young woman.'

'You're wasting your time. Detective Lennon, you're going down the wrong avenue, I assure you. If you want to catch whoever murdered those OnTarget fans, you should stop messing about pursuing Shawn Barrett. The person who murdered those girls has to be a psychopath – and, like I said, Shawn Barrett can't be one of those.'

'Just give us the details.'

'Or you'll leak?'

Patrick didn't respond. He reached across the desk, took one of Hammond's nuts from the bag and put it in his mouth, maintaining eye contact throughout.

Hammond stood up. 'I will need to look up the details at my office and get back to you. I guarantee you won't find anything worthwhile.'

'We'll see.'

'I'll send the details over later.' He gave Patrick a final sneer. 'If this does leak, if I find my name on a website related to this story, you might just regret it. Your wife is back home now, isn't she? That would make an interesting story. *Baby-Battering Wife on the Loose . . .*' He wiggled his fingers into speech marks.

Patrick leapt to his feet and grabbed hold of the front of Hammond's jacket. 'If one word is published about my wife . . .'

Hammond pulled away, dusting himself off.

'Then we have an understanding,' he said. 'Nothing appears about me, nothing appears about your wife.' He stood before the door. 'I'll send that information over later.'

Chapter 24
Day 8 – Carmella

As the plane climbed above the bank of thick cloud, the seatbelt sign light went out with a ping, and an answering echo of unclicking buckles rattled around the cabin. Carmella switched on her iPad and swiped to the Notes section to double-check where she'd be going once she landed. The witness was called Roisin McGreevy and she lived in the roughest part of Tallaght, an already-rough area in South Dublin that used to be known as Knackeragua among Carmella and her school friends. Land of 'knacker-wash' denim – their name for stone-washed – blond mullets and petty crime. Carmella hadn't been there for years, but by all accounts it was still fairly grim.

The flight was bumpy, as it so often was across the Irish Sea, but they landed without too much drama, and Carmella made good time through customs. She was striding out of arrivals towards the bus stop twenty minutes ahead of her planned ETA, taking a bus into the centre of town, and then another one out to Tallaght, arriving at her destination by half past eleven.

Roisin McGreevy was just sixteen now. She'd been fourteen when the 'incident' with Shawn Barrett occurred, according to

Mervyn Hammond's reluctant intel. Since it was before noon, the girl would likely still be in bed – if she was anything like Carmella herself had been as a teenager – assuming she didn't have a Saturday job. Carmella hadn't seen a photo of her but realised she was imagining her as a hard-faced skanger with piercings and dyed hair; the sort of girl who would jump into bed with a pop star without a second's hesitation for the glory of it, and who probably thought all her Christmases had come at once when said pop star was as good-looking and famous as Shawn Barrett . . .

When Carmella walked into the small cul-de-sac, situated in the roaring shadow of a flyover, she thought her fears about Roisin would probably be realised. Cars on bricks decorated several of the driveways; others exposed decaying crazy paving and rusty pushchair skeletons. Carmella adjusted the skirt waistband of her navy suit, feeling self-conscious and over-dressed, as several grubby kids playing on scooters and skateboards in the circle of road at the end of the cul-de-sac gawped at her. One pointed and laughed.

'Lookit the mad hair on yer one!' This set them all off, roaring and jeering. Carmella felt affronted. Her hair was tied up! If they thought her ponytail was 'mad', they should see it when it was loose and brushed out.

None of the houses seemed to have numbers on them.

'You,' she said, pointing at one of the kids. 'Where's number twenty-one?'

He gaped at her as though she'd asked him for a snog. One of his mates replied by jerking his thumb towards the neatest house in the street. It had the only square of lawn in sight, a lawn that looked as though someone had mowed it recently.

When she rang the bell, a short, stocky woman answered immediately. The woman wasn't much older than herself, but she had the sort of perm Carmella hadn't seen for years, at least not on anybody under the age of eighty – regimented rolls of tight, short curls all facing the same direction.

'Good morning,' Carmella said, just about managing not to greet her with the habitual 'howya'. 'Mrs McGreevy?'

The woman nodded, frowning. She was wearing some kind of nylon housecoat that, with the perm, made Carmella wonder if she'd fallen into some kind of seventies time slip black hole.

'My name is' – she dropped her voice so that the kids couldn't hear. They had all crowded closer, rigid with curiosity, and she didn't want to get out her police ID unless she had to – 'Detective Sergeant Masiello, from the London Metropolitan Police. I'm after speaking to your daughter, Roisin – if you're her mother?' She couldn't help noticing how much more Irish she sounded when she came home.

The woman stared at her, eyes wide with alarm, her hand frozen on the door.

'Please don't worry, nothing's happened to her, she's not in any trouble. It's concerning another investigation we're in the middle of over in London.'

'I think you must have the wrong girl,' Mrs McGreevy said cagily. 'Roisin's never been to London.'

'May I come in?'

Mrs McGreevy stepped aside to admit her but only, Carmella thought, to get her away from the prying eyes of the neighbourhood lads.

The interior of the house was as neat as the front garden, but utterly devoid of any style or flair. It was as seventies as Mrs McGreevy herself, although clearly not in any sort of retro or ironic way. Carmella half-expected to see a man with Brylcreemed hair and peg-top trousers smoking a pipe in an armchair in the front room. She blinked at the swirly carpets and flock wallpaper, and followed Mrs McGreevy through to the back of the house, to a slightly less eye-watering breakfast room.

'Sit down, now. I'm sure you've had a wasted journey, but can I get you a coffee at least before you go, Miss, er, I'm sorry, what do I call you?'

'Carmella is fine.' She smiled at the woman, who looked sick with worry. 'Thanks, I'd love a coffee, white, no sugar, please.' She sat down at the kitchen table.

'Are you sure Roisin's not in trouble?' Mrs McGreevy blurted, busying herself with the kettle.

'No. It's in connection with an incident a couple of years back.' Carmella hoped the woman already knew about it. It would be a hell of a shock to discover your fourteen-year-old had been engaged in non-consensual S&M with one of the planet's biggest pop stars.

'What's going on?' came a small high voice from the doorway. Carmella turned, expecting from the voice's pitch to see a young child, but was surprised to find a teenage girl in a blue uniform and baseball cap bearing an embroidered logo of Supermac's burger bar resting on top of brown curls.

'Who are you? Mam, who is this?'

'Roisin, love, don't be worrying. She's a police officer from London. She wants to ask you a few questions about something. I can't imagine what.'

Roisin couldn't have been further away from Carmella's mental image of her. She looked about twelve, and so wholesome that it was almost impossible to imagine her naked, indulging in all sorts with Barrett. The only hint that she might not always have looked this innocent were the empty pinpricks of holes in her ears, four or five in each.

'Oh God, really? Why?' Roisin's eyes immediately filled with tears, making her look even younger.

'Come and sit down, Roisin. I just need your help, that's all.'

'It was ages ago.'

Her mother's eyes opened wide. '*What* was ages ago, Roisin Marie McGreevy?'

'Mam! You know. That business with that man. The money.' Roisin was actually wringing her hands.

'Ach, *that* business. I might have known.'

'Well, what else would it be?' Roisin turned to Carmella. 'Amn't I right? Is that what it's about?'

Carmella smiled gravely at her. 'It depends what man you mean.'

'Mervyn Hammond . . . We weren't supposed to tell anyone about the money.'

Carmella nodded, although this was the first she'd heard about any money. So the sleazy bastard had actually paid Roisin's family off, to keep quiet?

'How much money did he pay you, Roisin? It's OK to tell me. He's the one that gave us your address, so he knows I'm talking to you.'

'Ten grand, he gave her,' said Mrs McGreevy contemptuously. 'Damages, he called it. Not nearly enough, in my book. You should've seen the bruise on her cheek! Still, it'll pay for her university.' She banged down a cup in front of Carmella, grains of undissolved coffee swirling in a greyish liquid on top.

A guilty look passed across Roisin's peachy face, unnoticed by her mother. *Ahah*, thought Carmella. *Mrs McGreevy clearly doesn't have* all *the facts.*

'I've to be in work in half an hour; my shift starts at noon,' Roisin said.

Carmella took a sip of the coffee and tried not to grimace. It would be better for her bladder for her not to drink it anyhow. 'Mrs McGreevy, would you mind ringing Supermac's for Roisin, to tell her boss that she'll be a bit late?'

'I'll get fired!' wailed the girl.

'Tell them that you're being interviewed as a police witness but you can't say why – I'll call them too if they give you any grief, OK? Please go ahead, Mrs McGreevy.'

As soon as Mrs McGreevy had left the room, Carmella pulled out the chair next to her, gesturing to Roisin to sit. 'Quick, now, if you want to tell me while your mum's out of the room. You've not told her the whole story, have you?'

Roisin bit her lip, her shoulders slumped. She was an exceptionally pretty girl, with pink, clear cheeks, a pointy little chin and bright blue eyes. 'Has he done it to someone else?'

She started picking at the skin around her fingernails, ripping shreds off them, worrying at them until she pulled a strip too far on her thumb and a bead of blood sprang to the surface. She stuck it into her mouth, then turned it sideways so that she didn't look like a toddler sucking its thumb. *Poor kid*, thought Carmella.

'I'm afraid I can't say what it's about. I know this won't be easy for you, dragging it all up when I'm sure you don't ever want to think about it again. Can you talk me through what happened? But before your mum gets back, tell me – was it just the bruise on your face that made Hammond give you that money? I'm guessing it wasn't.'

Roisin shot a panicked look towards the hall, where her mother was on the phone – they even had an old-fashioned telephone with a curly cable, on a little wooden table by the front door. 'Please don't tell her. It would kill her if she knew what he really did to me,' she whispered. 'They wanted to make sure I never told the papers.'

'What was it, Roisin? What did Shawn Barrett do to you?'

But at that moment they both heard the click of the receiver being replaced and Mrs McGreevy came back in. 'It's grand. Nicola will see you when she sees you, she says. I told her you'd been a witness to a road accident and the police were talking to you.'

'Oh, Mam! What if she asks me about it?'

Carmella glanced at her watch. 'I'm sure you'll think of something, Roisin. In the meantime, could you talk me through how you first met Shawn? Do you mind if I record this, just so I can write notes later?'

Roisin nodded. Her mother bustled around the already-clean kitchen, wiping down clean surfaces with a clean sponge, listening but pretending not to.

'I went to an OnTarget concert, their first big tour. It was the first time they'd played in Dublin. I'd never been to the O2 arena—'

'That's the place that used to be the Point, right?'

'Yeah. Think it's changed again now, to the 3Arena. Anyway, I'd never been there. Me and my mate Scarlett went together, queued for hours to get near the front, we did. Couldn't *believe* it when Shawn got me up out of the crowd.'

There was just a hint of pride in her voice, even after everything that happened that night.

'Go on.'

'It was during "Catch Me Falling", in the first encore. He just pointed at me and beckoned, and before I knew it these two massive bouncers dragged me up on the stage. Everyone was screaming and cheering. I sang a whole verse with him into his microphone! He kissed me . . .'

Her voice faltered.

'Then what? How did you end up at his hotel?'

'When I was up there, he put this little bit of paper in my hand without anyone noticing. It said "CALL ME AFTER THE SHOW", with a number on it.' She was starting to look slightly sick.

'And you did?' Carmella prompted.

Roisin looked at her mother's set shoulders in her flowery housecoat. 'I know it was wrong. I know it was asking for trouble, but I honestly thought it would be OK. I mean, he's so famous, surely he wouldn't risk doing anything mental . . .'

'What about your friend – Scarlett? Did she come with you when you went to meet him?'

Roisin shook her head. 'Her older sister was there, at the concert. We were meant to be going home with her after, but I told them that I'd bumped into my auntie and my cousins who live round the corner, and they'd take me. Shawn said on the phone not to worry about getting home, he'd get a car for me, but I wasn't to tell anyone and I was to come on my own.'

'Did anyone ask how old you were?'

Roisin looked sheepish. 'Yes. One of his bodyguards. But I . . . I—'

Her mother interrupted, a harsh edge to her voice. 'She had a fake ID saying she was eighteen. And she looked different then. You wouldn't believe the phase she was going through. Right little skank she looked – bleached hair, ridiculous heels and enough make-up it's a miracle she could even open her eyes. If her da and me had seen her before she went out dressed like that, we'd never have let her go. Never!'

'I've not worn a scrap of make-up since that night,' Roisin said quietly. 'Or heels, or short skirts.'

Poor girl, thought Carmella. The sort of rite of passage that no girl ever deserved.

'So that's one good thing that came out of the whole sorry business,' said Mrs McGreevy sanctimoniously, polishing the already-gleaming kettle. Carmella suddenly felt desperate to get Roisin on her own. She clearly wasn't going to say what really happened, not with her mum there being all judgemental.

Roisin looked up, anguished. 'If he has done it again, will I have to go to court? They'll kill me – if my name gets out, they will actually kill me, I'm not joking.'

Her mother's hand stilled on the disinfectant spray.

'Who will, Roisin?' asked Carmella gently, wondering who she meant. Hammond? The band? Shawn's family?

135

'OnT fans!' Roisin wailed. 'They'd hunt me down and kill me, I know they would! Some girl got glassed in the face by four fans just for getting her picture with Shawn – can you imagine what they'd do to me if I helped get him sent to *jail?*'

She was weeping now, so Carmella got up and fetched her the box of tissues – housed in some sort of hideous pastel knitted cosy thing – on the windowsill. Interestingly, Roisin's mum made no move to comfort her daughter.

'Listen,' Carmella said kindly, putting her hand on the girl's shoulder. 'Don't worry about that now. It's very unlikely, and if the worst happened and you did, your name would absolutely be kept out of the press, you have my word on that. Now, how about I walk you to work? If we go now, you won't even be very late, and we can talk on the way.'

Without your mother listening, she thought. *Then I can find out what really happened.*

Chapter 25
Day 8 – Patrick

P atrick hauled himself out of his bronze Prius and made his way through the station car park, passing Winkler's white Audi and noticing the gleam of the paintwork, the alloy hubcaps, the licence plate bragging that this car was brand new. Winkler had been banging on about his new motor for weeks, and Patrick couldn't help feeling a clench of envy, especially when he peered through the window and saw how immaculate it was. No crumbled Wotsits on the carpets; no half-chewed Haribo stuck to the seats; no discarded toys in the footwell. Bonnie had systematically wrecked the interior of Patrick's car and he needed to take it to one of those valet places, where silent Eastern European men would render it spick and span – until Bonnie got in it again. Still, it was all worth it, wasn't it? He'd rather have crisp crumbs mashed into his upholstery than live Winkler's shallow existence. Rather get a big goodnight hug from his daughter before settling in front of the TV for an evening of – albeit currently awkward – conversation with Gill, than live Winkler's life: pumping iron at the gym, then heading to bed with his latest desperate woman.

He sighed. He hadn't been to the gym in months, and when he tried to do press-ups at home Bonnie would invariably leap screeching onto his back. And going to bed with desperate women . . . well, there was 'exciting' desperate and there was the other kind. By the time Patrick reached the building, his mood had dropped from grumpy to foul.

Winkler was hanging about in the corridor, chatting up the custody sergeant, the two of them falling silent when Patrick walked past scowling, a fresh burst of laughter following him down the hall. He was in a good mind to go back there, ask them what was so fucking funny. But he was distracted by the beep of his phone. Carmella? He was eager for news from Ireland. But no, it was Gill, asking what he wanted for dinner, even though he'd only left her company an hour ago. He very much doubted he'd be home before midnight – she knew that – and he felt irritated, then felt bad for being irritated. He knew she was nervous today because she had a meeting with her chambers about going back to her previous job in a month or so. He badly wanted Gill to resume her work as a barrister, even though it would cause more nightmares with childcare, because he believed that if she returned to work, she would begin to regain her old self, and the nervy, anxious woman he lived with would become his strong and capable wife again. He knew it wouldn't be that simple, but surely it would be a start? Something had to give. Because at the moment he was happier at work, dealing with Winkler and dead teenagers, than he was at home.

He replied to Gill as he sat at his desk, saying he'd grab a takeaway later, not to worry, and wishing her good luck with the meeting. He ended the text with a single kiss (there were four kisses on Gill's message) and then sent a text to Carmella, asking her how it was going. He hated waiting around like this.

He also felt antsy because at the moment they only had this one line of inquiry, if you didn't count Winkler's strand of the operation – which he didn't. He knew from bitter experience how dangerous it was to focus on one suspect, to have tunnel vision in a case. In 90 per cent of investigations, the obvious solution was the right one. The prime suspect did it, the odds worked out. Human behaviour was depressingly but reassuringly predictable. But sometimes, as in the Child Catcher case, it was like trying to fathom a magic trick: misdirection, sleight of hand. Smoke and mirrors. Right now, all the evidence seemed to be pointing towards one person, but Patrick lived in fear of Plan A going tits up when you had no Plan B in place.

He opened his Moleskine notepad, plugged his headphones into his computer and opened Spotify. This morning, even The Cure couldn't lighten his mood. He needed something that would block out the chatter and ambient noise around him while not distracting him too much. Aural wallpaper. He clicked on an Elbow playlist and got to work.

At the top of the first page, he wrote 'ROSE', adding 'JESSICA' in the corresponding spot on the facing page. In a space in the middle he listed the similarities between the two murders.

On Target fans.

Users of social media/fan forums.

Caucasian, teenage (14/15 yo), lower m/c, state schools, average height/weight.

M.O. of perp: strangulation, no sexual penetration, torture – cuts, sprayed with perfume, clothes and possessions removed.

On Jessica's side, he wrote some extra details: her injuries were worse, displaying an escalation in violence. The cuts were deeper and, according to Daniel Hamlet, had been inflicted with more force. Jess had bruises on her face; some of her hair had been yanked out. Why was this? Had she fought, made him angry? Was it the kind of escalation sometimes seen in serial murders, where the killer got more extreme as he went along, more confident and frenzied, needing the greater violence to feel satisfied? Or had he hated Jessica more than he hated Rose?

Patrick pondered this last question. How had the killer chosen these two victims? Were the girls interchangeable or had they been targeted specifically?

He wrote this down too, with a thick question mark that made him itch with frustration. From what Wendy and Martin had found out so far, there was no sign of them interacting online except in the most superficial way. They had both tweeted and written about the same subjects, namely how much they loved Shawn, how amazing the last OnT video was, how much they despised a *Daily Mail* journalist who had interviewed the band and described them as 'vacuous puppies without the guts or gumption to say a single interesting thing'. The only thing that set them apart from a hundred thousand other OnT fans was the level of their online activity. They were – what did Wendy call them? – super users.

What were the other differences and similarities? Rose was found in a hotel; Jessica in a photo studio. They knew the studio had once been used by OnTarget, but there appeared to be no connection between the Travel Inn and the band. They had never stayed there, not in this or any other branch. No-one at the hotel had any connection to the band. So why had the killer chosen the photo studio, with its direct connection, and the hotel, which had none? The use of the perfume suggested deliberate symbolism. It seemed he wanted it to be known that their fandom had made them targets. Or was it, as Carmella had pointed out, just that both girls had been carrying the fragrance with them? Their mothers had confirmed that they both owned a bottle of Friendship. Maybe that was all it was.

Maybe, Patrick thought with a start, the fact that they were both OnTarget fans was a red herring. Could that be possible? After all, a large percentage of teenage girls in this country liked OnT.

He spotted Wendy at the other end of the office and called her over.

'All right?' she said. She seemed a little wary, like an office worker who's been summoned by their boss, but, more than that, she looked tired. Knowing her exhaustion was caused by the long hours she'd been putting in, Patrick felt more pleasure than sympathy, sure that Wendy was going to make an excellent officer when she got some more experience under her belt. With her youthful looks and Black Country accent, Wendy struggled to be taken seriously. Patrick, with his tattoos, could empathise with that.

'Wendy,' he said. 'I need to know if there's any connection between the Travel Inn and OnTarget.' He summarised what they knew so far. 'Any ideas?'

She pondered a moment and then asked, 'What room was Rose found in?'

'Three-six-five.'

She snapped her fingers in triumph. 'Thought it might be.'

'Eh?'

'"Room 365" is the title of an OnTarget song. It's on the first album. It's about wanting to lock yourself away with a girl 365 days of the year.' She sang a snatch of the song, her voice sweet and tuneful. *And my baby comes alive/In room three-sixty-five, three-sixty-five.*

Patrick stared at her. 'Why didn't anyone else know that?'

Wendy gave him a little shrug. 'You obviously didn't ask the right person.'

He grinned at her and she appeared delighted to have been so helpful.

'How are you getting on?' With the new focus on Shawn Barrett, Patrick had lost track of what Wendy was up to. 'I assume you haven't found any direct connections between Rose and Jessica online yet? Nothing on the forums? Or on their computers?'

'Nothing direct.' Her eyelashes fluttered nervously. 'But I am making good progress. I'm getting to know the girls who use the OnT forum, the other super users, gaining their trust. I'm pretty much ready to start a conversation about Rose and Jess now. I just need a couple more days.'

Patrick tapped his fingers on the desk. Was this a waste of time? Maybe it would be better to pull her off this task. Winkler kept going on about how he needed someone to help him with, as he put it, the donkey work. He would hate to bestow that fate upon her, but . . .

'Please, Patrick.'

He looked up sharply.

'Sorry, I meant, *sir.*'

'It's OK. You can call me Patrick when it's just the two of us around. Or "boss", if you prefer.'

She turned pink and met his eye and he realised his words had come out wrong.

Embarrassed, he said, 'OK, it's fine. If you're sure you're getting close. But if it seems like these young women don't know anything useful, I want you working on something else.'

'Of course. Thanks, er, Patrick.'

'Any decision I make is for the sake of the case, so you don't need to thank me.'

She deepened from pink to red, as bad as Gareth Batey, who was renowned for his blushes. Patrick sighed, wishing he could shake this prickly, irritated mood.

'Listen, you look shattered. When did you last go home?'

'Um. I can't remember. Yesterday?'

'Right. Well, take a few hours, go home, have a nap. I think you've earned a break.'

'But I want to stay here and—'

'Wendy, I'm ordering you to go home. OK?'

She opened her mouth to argue, but shut it again. 'Thanks, boss.'

After she'd gone, he returned to his notebook, adding in what Wendy had told him about the 'Room 365' song, which seemed to eradicate any last doubt that OnTarget was the link here. He checked his mobile again. Still nothing from Carmella, just two more texts from Gill, telling him she had decided not to go to the meeting with her old firm because she had a headache, and that she'd called Patrick's mum and asked her if she could drop off Bonnie for a couple of hours. For fuck's sake! He thumped the mobile down on the desk, just as Gareth Batey walked into the office.

'Boss,' said Gareth, hovering sheepishly at the edge of the room.

Patrick looked up at him, frustration and irritation scratching at his skin. 'Yes?'

'I've been round all the fast-food places near the Travel Inn, like you asked. There are dozens of them and they all have tons of staff, most of whom work shifts, half of them not officially on the books, so trying to talk to anyone has been a total—'

'Just cut to the chase. Does anyone remember seeing Rose that night?'

'Well, no, but one guy thought he remembered seeing a girl wearing an OnTarget hoodie . . .'

'Rose wasn't wearing a hoodie.'

'I know, but—'

'So why are you telling me this utterly useless piece of information? And what's going on with this key card? Has Peter Bell got back to you yet?'

'I haven't had a chance to chase him, boss, because I've been trudging round burger bars in Teddington.'

Patrick glared at him. His impatience with the case; waiting for Carmella to call; everything that was going on with Gill . . . It was rare for Patrick to lose his temper, but right now he felt like a bunch of toddlers were tugging on his nerve endings, shrieking, and it took every ounce of self-control not to point a finger at Gareth and yell, *'Haven't had a chance? I thought you took this job seriously? Get the fuck out of my sight and don't come back until Peter fucking Bell has told you everything he knows about hackers and fucking hotel key cards and . . .'*

But he still couldn't stop himself shouting something almost as unprofessional in Gareth's face. 'You'll be working in a burger bar in Teddington yourself if you don't get some sodding results soon! Go and see Peter Bell, now!'

He stopped dead. Winkler was standing at the far end of the room, a sickening grin on his face. Gareth, who had gone pale, turned to follow Patrick's gaze. Winkler walked off, waving, and Gareth hung his head.

'Actually, DI Winkler needs help. Why don't you go and talk to him? Find out what he needs?'

'Yes, boss.'

Gareth hurried away, just as Patrick's mobile started to vibrate. Carmella, at last. As he answered, he looked up and saw Winkler talking to Gareth through the window, resting a hand on the younger man's shoulder. Probably best, he thought, if Gareth did Winkler's donkey work for a day or two. Then Patrick would apologise to him for losing his temper.

He swivelled his chair away from them. He'd listen to Carmella's report, and then he was going to go home and take his daughter to the park, try to shift this funk.

Chapter 26
Day 8 – Patrick

Bonnie was ecstatic when she saw Patrick walk into his parents' front room, where she had been playing with his old Fuzzy Felt farm set. She flung aside the board and threw herself into his arms.

'Daddy! My daddy!' she cried, reminding him of the ending of the movie *The Railway Children,* as she grasped him tightly around his neck, still clutching a limp felt cow in her fist.

His mother, Mairead, looked pleased to see him too. 'Pat! We weren't expecting you for hours yet!'

He smiled at her. 'It's all getting a bit fraught at work. Needed a couple of hours away from it. Who fancies a trip to the swings?'

'Me!' shrieked Bonnie, struggling to get down. 'Gonna wear my wellies!'

'Coming, Mum? Or do you fancy putting your feet up for a bit?'

Mairead pursed her lips. 'I'll come, I think. I could do with some fresh pear.'

'Fresh *pear?*'

'Air, Patrick, I said. Air. And you look like you could yourself too; you're as white as a rice pudding.'

She had definitely said 'pear'. This wasn't the first time he'd noticed her randomly misusing words, but he had always put it down to her being tired. Now that Gill was going back to work and Mairead was resuming her duties as Bonnie's post-nursery nanny, he hoped it wouldn't all be too much for her. He felt the familiar stab of guilt at the burden he was placing on his parents – or, at least, his mum, he thought, regarding his dad, Jim, fast asleep with his mouth wide open on the sofa.

'Let's go, then,' he said, helping Bonnie push her feet into her spotty wellies. 'If I sit down, I won't get up again.'

It was such a cold day that the playground in Bushy Park was almost empty. Bonnie's cheeks turned bright red and her nose was running within moments of her leaping into the sandpit with both feet, where she raced around in circles cackling with excitement.

Patrick and Mairead sat together on a nearby bench.

'She makes me feel knackered just looking at her,' Patrick observed.

'She's a dote,' Mairead said fondly. 'So, how's work going?'

Patrick sighed and took out his e-cigarette. 'Tough. I feel like Bonnie's not the only one going round in circles. It's so frustrating when we get stuck like this, and terrifying to think that if we don't figure it out, another girl could die.'

'Ah, it's a responsible job all right,' his mother agreed, refusing to engage with the grimness of what he'd said. 'And how's the lovely Carmella?' She'd always had a soft spot for Carmella. They'd met once, and Mairead had been delighted to discover that she knew of Carmella's auntie from County Meath – which, in Mairead's book, made them friends for life.

'She's fine. She went over to Dublin today following a lead. She'll be back later.'

'Dublin?' His mother looked puzzled. 'That's an awful long flight!'

Patrick turned to look at her. 'What are you on about, Mum?'

'You can't be sending her over there for just a day, when it takes nine hours to get there on a plane!'

'*Nine* hours? Mum, are you winding me up? You know it only takes an hour to fly to Dublin!' Patrick experienced a new rush of all the irritation he'd felt earlier with Gareth Batey.

'Oh,' she said in a small voice. 'Does it now? I must be mistaken.'

'You are,' said Pat briskly, standing up to hide his worried expression. This was not normal. *Oh God*, he thought, *please don't let her be losing her marbles.* He took a deep drag of his e-cig and was about to join Bonnie in the sandpit when a familiar voice called his name. Looking up, he thought for a second he was hallucinating. Of all people, *Suzanne* was jogging down the path alongside the playground towards him. He laughed at the incongruity of it, and she did too, stopping on the other side of the low fence.

'Fancy seeing you here!' she said, panting loudly. He couldn't help noticing the way the skintight Lycra top and leggings hugged her figure. 'You wouldn't think we were in the middle of a case, would you?'

He looked sharply at her to see if this was a criticism, but she was still smiling at him.

'Needed to clear my head.'

'Yeah, me too,' she said. 'Don't worry, Pat, I know how many hours you've put in over the last week. Of course I don't begrudge you a couple off. Is that your Bonnie?'

Bonnie was now gawping up at an older boy, of five or six, who was studiously ignoring her as he made a sandcastle.

'It is,' he said proudly.

Suzanne gazed at her, her shoulders still heaving. 'She's absolutely beautiful.'

'And this is my mother, Mairead.' He turned to her. 'Mum, this is my boss, Suzanne. DCI Laughland.'

'You look awful glamorous for a detective,' Mairead said suspiciously.

'Well, thank you, Mrs Lennon,' she replied, wiping her forehead. 'Not that I feel it at the moment, after running three miles, I must be bright red . . . Pat, since we both find ourselves here, could we have a quick word?'

He vaulted over the fence to where Suzanne stood on the gravel path. 'Mum, keep an eye on Bonnie, would you?' he called back.

It was odd, being so near Suzanne when she was unkempt and sweaty, but Patrick couldn't help feeling turned on. It was the way her breasts were heaving, the flush at her collarbone, the scent of fresh sweat coming off her. He had a mental flash of her in a post-coital tangle of sheets, a cat-that-got-the-cream smile on her face, arms reaching out to him.

Their eyes met.

'So,' she said, briskly zipping up her jacket to cover her chest.

Why did she make him feel like a randy teenager? He suddenly smiled at her, unable to help himself, and she returned the smile. Neither of them spoke for a moment, but their chemistry puffed almost visibly around them in the chill February air, like Suzanne's hot breath.

'So,' he repeated softly, equally unable to stop himself reaching out and gently touching her hand.

The spell was broken by a screeching voice. '*Daddeee! Look at meeeee!*'

He and Suzanne both turned to see Bonnie lying on her back in the sandpit making sand angels, while Mairead tutted and tried to peel her onto her feet.

'Any news from Carmella in Dublin?' Suzanne asked abruptly, taking a swig from her water bottle.

'Not yet. She's about to visit the girl at home, says she'll call when she's done.'

'Hmm. Anything else?'

Patrick frowned. 'Not a lot. Batey's dicking around getting nowhere, says he's been to all the burger bars but nobody saw Rose. I got pissed off with him, actually – he should've been chasing up Peter Bell and the hotel key card. Oh, one bit of good news . . .'

'Yes?'

'Wendy's made an OnTarget connection to where Rose was found – "Room 365" is apparently the name of one of their songs. I'd never have figured that one out in a million years. Bright girl, that one.'

'Hmm, well, I wouldn't say that an encyclopedic knowledge of OnTarget's back catalogue would normally be an asset in a PC's skillset, but good on her.'

Patrick laughed. 'I meant that she's a bright girl, in general. I like her.'

'She likes you too,' Suzanne said, a trifle darkly, Patrick thought, puzzled. 'Anyway, I'd better be heading off; I'm getting cold. Are you back in this afternoon?'

He nodded. 'See you later, boss.'

'See you, Pat. Good to bump into you. Say goodbye to your mum and Bonnie.'

She smiled again and set off, her blonde ponytail swinging on her back and her long legs stretching gracefully as she ran. Patrick couldn't help but stare after her, watching the way her buttocks moved in the tight black Lycra. She had an amazing figure – she could pass for a teenager from behind, he thought.

'Patrick!' his mother called sharply.

'Yes?' He climbed slowly back over the fence into the play-ground and jumped into the sandpit with both feet, to make Bonnie laugh. She did laugh, but Mairead was fixing him with one of her Paddington stares.

'I'm not as green as I'm cabbage-looking, you know,' she said, *sotto voce* so that Bonnie couldn't hear. 'Would you care to tell me exactly what's going on with you and that one, now?'

It wasn't difficult for Patrick to arrange his features into an expression of horror and outrage – although what he was really horrified about was how easily his mother appeared to have read the situation.

'Nothing, Mum,' he said meekly. 'I swear. We're just work colleagues.'

'And the rest, Patrick Martin Lennon. You watch yourself with that one. You've enough on your plate.'

'I know I have,' he said, but he couldn't prevent a pang of misery stabbing him in the chest. So was that it, then? Having 'enough on his plate' meant that he was trapped in an unhappy marriage with Gill forever, with no hope of ever getting what *he* wanted out of a relationship?

The trouble was, he wasn't entirely sure what it even was that he wanted anymore, or with whom.

He and his mother both watched Suzanne jog away in between the trees, until she shrank to a blonde dot and vanished.

It was the first time since Gill's release that he had articulated, even to himself, that his marriage was unhappy.

———

As soon as Patrick got back to the station, the woman on reception said, 'There's a chap here to see you.' She gestured towards the waiting area, where a bearded man in a corduroy jacket sat thumbing a smartphone. Graham Burns, the social media manager from Global

Sounds. His trousers, Patrick noticed, were a few inches too short, displaying a pair of bright yellow socks.

Patrick strolled over. 'Mr Burns.'

Burns looked up, startled. He jumped to his feet. 'Detective. I think I've found something . . . interesting.'

Patrick led Burns to an interview room and asked him if he wanted a coffee.

'Flat white, please.'

Patrick gave him a look.

'Um . . . actually, don't worry. I'm good. Yeah.' He was carrying a mustard yellow satchel, which he rummaged inside, pulling out a sheaf of papers. 'You remember you asked me if I could access the private messages Rose and Jess exchanged?'

Patrick nodded, trying not to look too eager.

'Well . . . I could be fired for doing this, but . . . you're not going to tell anyone, are you?'

Patrick couldn't make that promise in case this evidence was ever needed in court, so said, 'What did you find?'

Graham handed over the sheets of A4 paper and spoke as Patrick cast his eye over them. 'These were sent last year, on the fifteenth of October.'

The first message was from Jess to Rose.

Hey, I saw you posting about Shawn, saying you didn't believe he'd ever go with a groupie . . . Well, a friend of mine got picked out of the crowd at Wembley and met Shawn at a hotel!!!

As Patrick read, Burns pulled a cotton handkerchief out of his inside pocket, blowing his nose loudly.

Rose wrote back: *OMG, no WAY!!! What happened? Did she have sex with him?! What was it like?*

Jess replied: *Get this: apparently, Shawn wanted to tie her up and smack her bum with a riding crop!!!*

Rose replied with a row of smiley faces in various states of shock and alarm. *Did she let him?!?!*

Yeah. She said she couldn't sit down for a week. But this is obvs TOP SECRET, OK?

Patrick looked up. 'Is that it? Did they exchange any more messages?'

'No, not that I could find. It's possible there were more, but if they deleted them, they wouldn't be stored anywhere. It's pretty worrying stuff, isn't it?'

'I assume you know about Shawn and the young woman in Dublin.'

'Yeah, I was aware of that . . . Part of my remit is to stop rumours spreading about the band on social media, to manage their reputation. So if any of this stuff ever got out . . .'

Patrick stood up and led Burns out past the reception area, thanking him and asking him not to talk to anyone about what he'd found.

'Don't worry, Detective. I won't tell a soul.'

Patrick watched him go, bright yellow socks and all. Now he was keener than ever to talk to Shawn Barrett.

Chapter 27
Day 8 – Carmella

Roisin McGreevy visibly relaxed once they left the house, despite the presence of the little gang of staring boys in the cul-de-sac. She obviously found them far less scary than her mother. Carmella waited until they were out onto the main road, hoping her phone would continue to record clearly enough.

'It must've been bad, to make you completely change the way you dress and look.'

Roisin's lip trembled. 'It was . . . I couldn't believe what he wanted to do to me. What he did.'

'Tell me. It's OK. I'm not going to judge. You had a terrible ordeal.'

She took a deep breath. 'His bodyguard came and got me after the show, then we – me and Shawn – got smuggled out into a limo with black windows. I was so excited at that point. He said we were going out to dinner. He was lovely. The car was lovely. We had drinks; it had a proper bar inside and everything. I couldn't believe my luck. He was talking to me all romantic, telling me how beautiful I was and that. Then he goes, "Let's just go back to my hotel so I can get my wallet." So we stop off at The Merrion, in the back door 'cos there were fans outside, and next thing we're in his room – some massive suite with a four-poster bed. I don't know what we were drinking 'cos I didn't really drink, even then – and I never drink now – but I started feeling woozy and kind of dreamy; the whole thing was like a dream. I wanted to take a photo of him, but he wouldn't let me. Then he goes, "Why don't we just lie down a little while before we go out? I'm pretty tired after that show. Let me jump in the shower."'

Roisin swerved to avoid a large pile of dog poo on the pavement. She glanced up at Carmella.

'You're doing great, Roisin. This is so helpful, really. Go on.'

'When he was in the shower I felt really tired, so I lay down on the bed. I think he must have given me something to make me sleepy. Next thing I know, he's sitting astride me, naked, kissing me. It was nice at first, once I got over the shock of him suddenly being . . . on me. Although I was a bit scared because I'd never been with a boy before, not . . . properly. And he . . . he . . . didn't look like a boy, you know what I mean? It was massive.'

She looked away, blushing scarlet.

'He tried to tie my hands together with a scarf. I didn't want him to, but he wasn't listening. He just kept saying, "This is fun, isn't it? Let's have some fun." But then he got out this riding crop thing, and—' She stopped, gulping.

'Did he hit you, Roisin?'

'I tried to ask when we were going out to dinner and he just laughed and said he wasn't hungry anymore. He got more and more . . . worked up. It was like he was in a proper frenzy, hitting me all over my body until he . . . you know . . .'

'Climaxed?'

'All over me,' she said, looking as though she was about to throw up. 'Not in me. I mean, we never actually, you know, did it.'

'No penetrative or oral sex at all?'

The girl shook her head, mortified. 'Just kissing, and . . . hitting me.'

'What happened then, Roisin?'

'Then he got his driver to take me home. I bashed my face on the door frame, I was in such a hurry to get out of there. I was in a right state, and so these two guys came in the car with me.'

'Which two guys?'

'One of them was Mervyn Hammond. He looked, like, completely stressed, and he kept saying "So, you're all right, aren't you?" like he was daring me to say I wasn't, even though I could barely sit down, Shawn hit me so hard. I couldn't believe it had happened to me. I couldn't stop crying. I was so humiliated . . .'

What an evil toad that Barrett was, thought Carmella angrily, and Hammond not much better, clearly trying to cover up for his protégé.

'Who was the other guy, Roisin?'

She shrugged. 'Someone from the record company. Gordon? Gary?'

Carmella didn't recall anyone with either of those names.

'From the Dublin office or the London one?'

'I don't know. I don't think I heard him say anything, so I'm not sure if he was English or Irish. He was nice. He put his arm round me in the car – not in a creepy way, just comforting me. . . . Then when the cheque arrived from Mervyn Hammond it was in a big package of OnTarget stuff, you know, CDs and T-shirts and what have you – I mean, like I *ever* wanted to see Shawn's face again? You must be kidding, I thought. I threw it all out. Except the cheque. I had to tell my folks about the cheque because I didn't have my own bank account then and I didn't know what to do with it. I told them that they'd paid me off 'cos Shawn got drunk and shoved me into the doorway, and they wanted to make sure I wouldn't tell the press or tweet about it or anything. I did have a big bruise on my cheek. Mam said it served me right for going into his room, and I was lucky nothing worse happened . . . I've never told her that it did. If she'd seen the bruises all over the rest of me, she'd have taken me straight to the police.'

Roisin was crying again. They were passing a scrubby little park, so Carmella steered her to a graffitied bench, sat her down and handed her another tissue.

'I've never told anyone this before.' Roisin sniffed.

'You're being really brave. And so helpful. Really. It's been totally worth me coming all the way over to speak to you – thank you. So you didn't even tell your friend Scarlett?'

Roisin shook her head and wiped her eyes. 'Never saw her again, or any of my other OnTarget friends. Couldn't hack it. They think I'm a weirdo, but I don't care. I don't think I've been out anywhere since; only school and work. If an OnTarget song comes on the radio, I have to switch it off, or leave the room. If I see Shawn on telly, I have to go and actually throw up.'

Carmella wanted to give her a massive hug. She felt unspeakably sorry for her – but then thought that Mrs McGreevy could well have been right: Roisin *was* lucky nothing worse had happened. She thought of the mutilated bodies of Jessica McMasters and Rose Sharp and wanted to tell the girl that she might well have had a very lucky escape.

'That Mervyn Hammond . . . he didn't need to pay me off. I was never going to tell anyone about it anyway.'

'You shouldn't feel ashamed—'

'No, it's not that. It's them – the fans. You know I said before, they can be vicious. If it was in the papers that I was accusing their hero of attacking me, they would kill me. Literally kill me. I'm not really scared of Shawn or Mervyn Hammond or anyone else – well, I am, but not nearly as scared as I am of the other OnT fans . . .' She shivered.

Carmella took a business card out of her bag and handed it to Roisin. 'Listen. I don't know if you've had any counselling or not, but you ought to. I understand you don't want your parents to be involved, but I know a few excellent counsellors in Dublin I could put you in touch with directly, now that you're sixteen.'

'You're super nice. I wish more Dublin cops were like you.' She blushed.

What a lovely kid, thought Carmella. She wanted to help her, make the bad memories go away as completely as the bruises Shawn had inflicted on her. 'Are they not?' she said lightly, smiling at her. 'Anyway, I need to get going back across the water. Don't want to miss my flight – and you don't want to be too late for work. Did you want me to talk to your boss so you don't need to lie about witnessing an accident?'

Roisin shook her head and balled the tissue up small, sticking it into her pocket. She stood up and tucked her hair underneath the Supermac's baseball cap. 'Na, you're all right, thanks. I can handle it.'

Carmella stood too, delving into her bag for a biro. 'If you're sure. Just call if you change your mind. Or if you remember anything else about that night, whether it's about Shawn or Mervyn Hammond, OK? Can you write your mobile number down for me in case I need to ask you any more questions later?'

'Sure,' the girl said, taking the biro and writing her number on the back of the second business card Carmella produced. 'Well. I'm glad I could help.' For a second she looked as if she was barely out of primary school. 'I don't think I'm ever going to . . . be with a boy again,' she said, her lip wobbling.

Carmella wondered if Roisin had somehow sensed that she, Carmella, was gay, and if she were tacitly asking for advice . . . but, much as she liked her, it just wasn't in her remit to give that sort of help.

'I meant what I said, about helping you find a counsellor,' she said instead. 'You've been through a major ordeal. It was lovely to meet you, although I'm sorry about the circumstances. I'll be in touch, OK?'

Roisin nodded, blushing again. 'Bye,' she said, and put her head down against the stiff breeze, striding away towards the burger bar, her sensible trainers making no sound on the pavement. Carmella watched her go, the dejected slope of her shoulders saying almost as much about her as their conversation had. *Poor kid,* she thought. She wondered if Shawn Barrett had any idea what he'd done to her. It was as if he'd taken the spark out of her and crushed it like a lit cigarette underfoot. Even if she had been a bold little trollop before, too much make-up and slutty clothes, this was surely worse, this awful despondency and world-weariness in a girl who wasn't yet seventeen.

Sighing, Carmella headed for the nearest bus stop back into O'Connell Street. At least she'd have something to tell Patrick. He'd want to get Barrett in for a chat, for sure – which would be a whole shit storm of media chaos and injunctions up the wazoo, if they weren't careful. Mervyn Hammond would see to that.

Suddenly, Carmella felt tired and almost as dispirited as Roisin had looked. All she wanted was to be home in Jenny's arms.

Chapter 28
Day 8 – Patrick

The cab dropped Patrick off outside Shawn Barrett's apartment block at the same time that a white van pulled up. The van's driver jumped out, sliding open the side door and emerging with a tower of brown boxes that came up to the bridge of his nose. He wobbled towards the door and was buzzed in, Patrick following, aware that the fifteen or sixteen paparazzi camped out across the street were watching them closely. The paps looked miserable, huddled together in the cold, smoking and sipping from Starbucks cups. What a life. Patrick bet that each of them would sell his or her grandmother to do what Patrick was about to do: ride the lift up to Shawn's home for an audience with the most famous – with the possible exception of princes William and Harry – young man in England.

'What do you mean, he can't come here?' Patrick had said to Suzanne after she'd got off the phone to the Met's press bureau, who had asked to be kept informed of all developments in the case.

She gave Patrick a calming smile. 'I've been told that if Shawn Barrett comes to the station, it will be on the front of every tabloid in the country tomorrow, every celebrity gossip site; there'll be fans blocking the doorways; photographers sticking their cameras in our faces . . . It will be mayhem. Until we get to the point where we're actually going to charge him, when we've got a rock-solid case against him, we need to go to him. Discreetly. He's agreed to meet you at his apartment in Chelsea Harbour.'

'*Agreed* . . . ?'

'Patrick, don't be grumpy. It really doesn't suit you.'

She came across the office, glancing through the window to check no-one was watching, and laid a hand on Patrick's arm. He felt the current run from the point where she touched him through his veins into his chest.

'We don't have any evidence to prove it's him,' she said.

'Yet.'

'And until then, I'm afraid we have to play by their rules. Do you really want to be on the front page of *The Sun* tomorrow?'

So here he was, standing behind the van driver and looking down at the grey, churning Thames through the wall-to-ceiling window outside Barrett's apartment, on the twelfth floor of a building that was home to a collection of Russian oligarchs, movie stars and bankers. Patrick had looked it up on the way over: a two-bedroom flat at this address cost upwards of £4 million. And this wasn't Barrett's only home. He also had places in Los Angeles, Ibiza and Stoke-on-Trent, where he had bought not just the ex-council house that he grew up in, where his mum still lived, but the entire street. According to the news story, Mrs Barrett didn't want to leave her beloved two-up two-down, so Shawn had bought all the houses around it and was paying for the street to be turned into a kind of country estate, with landscaped lawns, pools full of koi, a sauna house ('My mum loves her saunas') and a garage full of Bentleys, slap-bang in the middle of the city. You couldn't make it up.

The door opened and a man Patrick recognised took the tower of boxes from the van driver. Reggie Rickard, OnTarget's manager.

Rickard spotted Patrick, nodded at the driver and put his finger to his lips. Only when the other man was safely in the descending lift did he say, 'Lennon.'

'Detective Inspector Lennon.'

'Ooh, sorry.' He smirked. 'Did any of the paps try to talk to you, ask you why you're here?'

'Yes, and I told them that Shawn Barrett is a sex offender who I'm questioning in—'

'For God's sake, man. Come inside.' Rickard ushered Patrick in, flapping his arms and peering up and down the corridor. His eyes nearly popped out of his head, making Patrick think of a squeezed hamster. 'You didn't really . . . ?'

'Of course I didn't.'

Rickard pointed at him. 'Ah-hah! A cop with a sense of humour. I like that. Mervyn didn't mention that.'

I bet he didn't, Patrick thought.

'Anyway, come in. Shawn's looking forward to meeting you, showing you what a lot of nonsense this all is.'

Patrick followed the other man down a short hallway, which opened up into a cavernous living room, flooded with light from the windows that gave a spectacular view across Battersea Park. A huge canvas hung on the opposite wall – a cartoonish scene created by a famous Japanese artist whose name Patrick couldn't remember. The equally vast TV was on, the sound turned down, a PlayStation 4 plugged into it, with games piled up on the floor, spilling from their cases. And at the far end of the room, perched on a black leather sofa with his legs curled beneath him, sat Shawn Barrett, his floppy hair falling over his eyes, a bored expression on his face. He was staring at his iPhone.

'Shawn, this is Detective Inspector Lennon.'

The boy-band singer looked up. His eyes seemed glazed, not showing much sign of activity behind them. Was he drunk or stoned? Then Patrick remembered Barrett always looked like this, except on stage or in his videos, when he would adopt a cheeky grin and turn on the charm.

'I come alive when I'm performing,' he'd said in an interview Patrick had read online last night; an interview in which every line Barrett uttered came straight out of the Big Book of Pop Star Clichés. This guy was so media trained, Patrick suspected, that the chances of a journalist ever getting him to say anything interesting were somewhere between zero and none.

'Lennon,' Barrett muttered. 'Like that guy . . .'

'John Lennon,' Rickard said gently. 'From The Beatles.'

'Oh yeah! Love them.' He squinted at Patrick. 'Are you related?'

'I don't think so.'

'Oh.' Barrett turned his attention to his manager. 'Did my deliveries come?'

'Yeah, Shawn. Hang on a tick.' Rickard left the room and returned with the pile of boxes, which he set down on the floor in front of the sofa. Barrett began immediately tearing them open like a five-year-old on Christmas morning, scrutinising each video game, DVD or gadget before tossing it aside. Only once did he pause, exclaim 'Awesome!' over some PS4 game, before moving on to the next parcel. Soon, the floor was covered with brown cardboard.

'Do a lot of online shopping?' Patrick asked, halfway through this display.

Rickard answered. 'These are from Shawn's Amazon wish list. He lists whatever he wants and his fans compete to buy the stuff first.' He laughed. 'I've had to ask Shawn to restrict the amount of stuff he adds to the list. The delivery company can't cope.'

Patrick noticed that the pop star didn't bother to read the notes that came with each gift.

After Shawn had tossed aside the last item, he returned to staring at his phone. 'Tweeting,' he said. He thumbed the screen, concentrating hard. 'There you go.'

'What did it say?' Rickard said, checking his own phone. Patrick realised the manager was worried Barrett might have tweeted something about his own presence. A look of relief crossed the manager's face. '"Just chillin." Nice one.' He winked at Patrick. 'Bet that gets ten thousand retweets.'

Patrick tried hard not to roll his eyes. He scrutinised the young man before him. Could he really be a savage murderer? It seemed difficult imagining this spaced-out kid gathering the energy to make a sandwich, and it was equally hard to picture him persuading a girl to join him in a sadomasochistic sex session – let alone be powerful and cunning enough to do what the killer of Jess and Rose had done. But he knew for a fact that Barrett engaged in S&M. And Barrett had enough drive to achieve what millions of teenage boys only dreamt of. It couldn't purely be luck; surely Barrett wasn't a mere puppet? This slacker puppy act had to be just that: an act.

Patrick sat down in a leather armchair opposite Barrett, with Rickard hovering close by. 'Shawn, thank you for agreeing to talk to me. I need to—'

Barrett interrupted. 'What kind of music are you into?'

Patrick decided it wouldn't do any harm to act friendly. 'My favourite band are The Cure. Have you heard of them?'

To Patrick's surprise, Barrett's eyes lit up. 'The Cure? Oh yeah, my granddad likes them.'

'Your *granddad*?'

Rickard interjected. 'His grandfather's about your age. Shawn's mum had him when she was seventeen. And her parents were teenagers when they had her.'

'Yeah,' Shawn drawled. 'He's into all that eighties stuff. Depeche Mode, The Human League. That miserable bloke – what's his name? Morrissey, that's it.' To Patrick's even greater surprise, Barrett started singing one of The Smiths' songs, 'Panic'. So he really could sing: his voice was bland but tuneful, and Patrick could imagine how horrified Morrissey would be if he heard this rendition of his song.

'I met the guy from The Cure. He gave me a signed disc . . . Hang on.'

Barrett got up and crossed the room to a shelving unit, fishing out what Patrick knew to be one of the rarest Cure picture discs, an item Patrick had coveted for over twenty years. And it was signed! Barrett looked at it and then shoved it back between the other records on the shelf. 'I need to get a turntable so I can listen to it.'

It was only when Patrick saw how Rickard was grinning at him that he was able to gather himself and remember what he was there for. He cleared his throat.

'Shawn, do you know why I'm here?'

Barrett plonked himself down on the sofa again. He seemed more alert now, though he wouldn't meet Patrick's eye.

'Yeah, Mervyn told us. But that girl . . . I thought she was over sixteen. Actually, I thought she was nineteen. That's what she told me. And she was well up for everything we did.'

'And what exactly did you do?' Patrick wanted to see Shawn's face as he said it, to see if there was anything vicious or gleeful in his expression.

Shawn opened his mouth to speak, but his manager spoke up first. 'Shawn hasn't actually admitted to doing anything at all with this girl you're referring to.'

'It sounded to me like he just did.'

Rickard shook his head. 'It doesn't even come under your juris-diction. And we know why you really want to talk to Shawn. We know about this nutty idea you have.'

Patrick looked over to the young boy-band singer. He was staring at his phone again, probably flicking through his Twitter messages. As cool as any suspect Patrick had ever seen. He was either completely innocent, a brilliant actor . . . or a bona fide psychopath. Patrick certainly didn't trust Mervyn Hammond and his psychometric testing. Patrick's heartbeat increased. If Shawn was a psychopath, if he was a killer, this was going to be the news story of the year. It would overshadow every other story about celebrity crime. Bigger than Jimmy Savile or even Oscar Pistorius. If Shawn Barrett did it, a million teenage hearts would be broken.

'Shawn, I need to ask you about your whereabouts on a couple of dates. First, the evening of Wednesday, fourth of February, and, second, Saturday, seventh of February, all day and evening.'

Shawn looked blank. He turned his head towards his manager, who produced a sheet of paper.

'We knew you would ask that. On the fourth, which was two nights before OnT played Twickenham, Shawn was here, at home.'

'On your own?' Patrick asked, addressing the singer.

'Yeah.'

'Just chilling, I assume?'

Shawn cocked his head. 'I guess. I was probably playing Minecraft. That's how I relax when I'm not working.'

He really was only a kid, Patrick thought. 'What about Saturday the seventh?'

Again, Rickard flapped his piece of paper. 'Shawn was in the studio all afternoon until eight.'

'Yeah, we were recording a track for a charity album, that's right. For this place called St Mary's Children's Home.'

'Lots of witnesses to that,' Rickard said. 'Then the band went for dinner, until about ten. Even more witnesses.'

'And then I came home on my own.'

Patrick thought about it. Daniel Hamlet had been unable to give an exact time of death for Jess, but he had estimated it had been sometime during Saturday night. Which meant Shawn didn't have an alibi for either murder.

'Did anyone see you come home that night?'

'Our driver dropped me off. And . . .'

'What is it?'

Shawn flicked an anxious look towards his manager. 'I'm not supposed . . . If this gets out . . .'

Rickard walked over to the couch and leant so Shawn could whisper in his ear. Patrick clenched his fists.

'We can trust you to be discreet, can't we?' Rickard said.

'This is a murder investigation. I agreed to come here, but if you want to head to the station now . . .'

'All right, keep your hair on. Tell him, Shawn.'

The pop star looked both sheepish and proud. 'Well, when I got home I sent a few messages to this girl I've been sort of seeing on Snapchat.'

'Messages?'

He smiled wickedly, the first sign of being a red-blooded male Patrick had witnessed in the flesh. 'Yeah. You know what Snapchat is?'

'Of course.' Wendy had explained it to him the day before. 'The photos vanish almost immediately, don't they?'

'That's right. Anyway, we exchanged a few pics and then . . . she came over.'

'You mean it was like a booty call?'

Shawn looked at him blankly.

'She came over for sex?'

The lupine grin returned. 'Yeah. And she stayed all night.'

Patrick felt a terrible weariness come over him. Barrett had an alibi. And Patrick had no Plan B. 'We'll need to talk to her, get her to confirm this.'

Now Shawn looked worried. 'Her boyfriend would go mental if he knew we were seeing each other.' He named the well-known member of a girl band who was living with a Premiership footballer.

'Lana Vincent,' Patrick repeated. 'We can talk to her discreetly. If she confirms what you're saying, then . . .'

'I'm off the hook.'

Patrick nodded reluctantly. This girl-band member was bound to confirm the alibi. Shawn wasn't the killer. Carmella's trip to Dublin had been a waste of time and they were no closer to knowing who had killed Rose and Jess. He wanted to punch the wall. But while he was here, he might as well see if he could get any useful information out of his former prime suspect.

'Shawn,' he said. 'Did you ever meet Rose Sharp or Jess McMasters? Did you talk with them online? Ever Snapchat them?'

'No! Listen, Detective, I honestly never met those girls. I swear. I love my fans. I wouldn't hurt any of them.'

'Except for Roisin McGreevy in Dublin?'

'But she wanted me to do it. She liked it.' Suddenly, he looked sheepish. 'I just got carried away, that's all . . . I didn't mean to hurt her. I love women. I love my mum. If she found out about me and that girl . . . If she heard what you accused me of. Well, first of all she'd give me a good clout. And then she'd come after you.'

'He's not wrong,' said Rickard. 'Mrs Barrett is very . . . formidable.'

Patrick thought back to the exchange of messages Graham Burns had shown him. 'This incident with Roisin. It wasn't a one-off, was it? I have information about another young woman you took back to your hotel room after a concert at Wembley.'

Rickard jumped in. 'Again, Detective – Shawn is a red-blooded male. All pop stars get women throwing themselves at them. It would be more unusual if he was celibate.'

Patrick clenched his jaw. Rickard was right. This was getting him nowhere. He decided to change tack.

'If you love your fans so much, you obviously want us to catch the person who murdered them.'

'Yeah, of course.'

'Have you ever seen anyone suspicious hanging around? Anyone who seems to show an unhealthy interest in young women?'

'No, nothing like that.'

'Surely you don't think it's someone associated with the band?' Rickard said. 'Do you want to know what I reckon?'

Patrick really didn't, but let Rickard continue.

'Well, I think we're dealing with a Charles Manson type. Manson thought he heard messages in The Beatles' songs, that whole "Helter Skelter" thing. I bet it's something like that.'

Frustrated by this wasted trip, by the dead end he was staring at now it looked like Shawn Barrett was no longer a suspect, Patrick snapped, 'How could anyone, crazy or not, hear messages in an OnTarget song? The lyrics are nothing but one cliché about love after another.'

Rickard shrugged. 'Well, maybe that's what it's about. Love.'

Chapter 29
Day 9 – Winkler

Come on, then,' Winkler said, ignoring the furious beeping from the Beamer he'd just cut up on the roundabout. 'Describe your ideal woman.'

DS Gareth Batey squirmed in the passenger seat. *Maybe he's gay*, Winkler thought. He'd never heard Gareth mention a girlfriend, and he blushed so easily. He glanced at the younger man as they pulled up at a red light. Regulation haircut, no jewellery or tattoos – unlike that poser Lennon – and nothing to suggest Gareth had any kind of life outside the Force. Married to the job; no time for a partner of any kind. Winkler had pretty much ignored Gareth throughout the three or four years they'd worked together. But DS Gareth Batey, Winkler realised, could be useful. His suppressed ambition, his longing to be recognised by the powers-that-be – that was the weak spot Winkler was ready to exploit.

'What's the matter?' he said. 'Cat got your tongue?'

'No, I just . . .' Gareth laughed nervously. 'I just feel a bit uncomfortable, that's all.'

Winkler slapped the other man's knee. 'Don't worry, mate, I'm not going to report you for political incorrectness. I'm not Lennon.

It's just a bit of banter to make the journey less boring.' When Gareth didn't immediately respond, Winkler said, 'All right, let me tell you about *my* ideal woman.'

As he went on to detail the cup size and leg length and proclivities of his perfect bird, Winkler could tell that Gareth was desperate to join in. He just needed a little more coaxing.

'Let me help you. Tell me what you think about Masiello.'

'Carmella?' Gareth seemed shocked. 'But she's, er, not heterosexual.'

Winkler spluttered with laughter. 'I'm not saying your ideal woman has to actually let you shag her. I'm just trying to figure out what kind of chick you're into. I know a lot of women who like men in uniform. I might be able to put a word in for you.'

'But we're plain clothes.'

Give me strength, Winkler thought. 'So you don't like Irish-Italian redheads, then?'

Gareth blushed.

'What about blondes? Older blondes? Suzanne Laughland. Would you give her one?'

Gareth's face went from candyfloss pink to fuchsia. 'She's our DCI,' he spluttered.

'That hasn't stopped Lennon from, you know.' He whistled.

Gareth stared at him as Winkler turned onto the industrial estate where the self-storage unit was based. 'Patrick and *Suzanne?*'

'Yeah, don't tell me you haven't noticed? How else do you think he gets all the plum jobs? He makes Suzanne promise him all the cushiest assignments while he's got her bent over her desk.' Winkler was horrified to feel a twitch in his pants as he pictured this.

'But Patrick's married. And so's the guv.'

Winkler laughed, focusing on the blackheads on Gareth's nose to make his semi-retreat. 'What planet did you beam down from, Batey? Firstly, Lennon's wife's a baby-battering loony who was locked up for nearly two years. You think our esteemed colleague restricted himself to bashing the bishop while the missus was in her padded cell? And have you ever seen Laughland's husband? I haven't. That picture on her desk was probably printed off the Internet. Fake husbands dot com.'

He spotted the yellow sign that told him they'd reached their destination and swerved in front of a lorry, eliciting another angry beep, into the car park.

As he unfastened his seatbelt he leant over conspiratorially. 'Lennon's not the man you think he is. Secrets and layers, that's him. Always thinking strategically. The bloke should have been a politician. Not like me. I'm the kind of guy who's straight down the line, who says it as I see it.'

He got out of the car, smiling to himself, not waiting for Gareth's reaction.

'Right,' Winkler said, striding towards the building. 'Let's see what old Nancy left behind.'

Winkler had spoken to Nancy Marr's son, George, the previous evening. George told him he was keeping his mother's possessions in storage because he didn't have room in his little flat. Mrs Marr's house was still up for sale, but her son had been advised by the estate agent to move everything out. Winkler had already been through the old woman's possessions once, when they were still *in situ*, but he hadn't looked too closely. And now he was trying to prove that this case wasn't connected to the OnTarget murders, he'd decided it was worth another look. He'd been round all the neighbours again and nobody had seen or heard anything. A couple of the neighbours hadn't lived in the street when Nancy was murdered, and Winkler needed to follow that up, find out who had been there six months ago. But first, he was going to have a good sort through the old bird's stuff.

Or, rather, he was going to watch Gareth do it. Winkler had a horror of touching stuff that had belonged to old people. He couldn't bear the smell: boiled beef and mothballs and cat wee. The thought of their wrinkly hands fingering it gave him the heebie-jeebies. Gareth wouldn't mind. This was the sort of stuff he excelled at.

George Marr had called ahead to let the storage centre know the police were coming. Winkler flashed his badge at the stocky black bloke at reception and made his way to the room where Nancy's stuff was stored, Gareth trailing behind, checking his phone as he walked.

'Anything interesting?' Winkler asked. 'Hot date?'

'No. I've been waiting to hear back from Peter Bell about the key card that Rose Sharp's murderer used to get into the hotel room.'

Winkler slowed his step. 'And?'

'Still nothing. It's so frustrating.'

'Never mind. Sounds like you're doing a good job anyway, Gareth. Reckon you'll make an excellent DI when the time comes.'

The look of pleasure that came onto Gareth's face reminded Winkler of his mum's cat when you stroked it. Poor old Gareth didn't get stroked very often. Winkler turned away and smiled to himself.

'Well, here we are,' he said, a moment later. 'All Nancy Marr's worldly goods. Better get started.'

Nancy's possessions were collected into a dozen brown card-board boxes, with 'Small Box', 'Medium Box' or 'Big Box' stamped on the side. George had stuck a handwritten label on each one. Winkler examined them in turn. '*Kitchen stuff*'. George had no doubt taken the best knives and any pots and pans that weren't old and rusty. '*Knick-knacks*', which was written on two of the boxes. Winkler remembered that Mrs Marr had a large collection of por-celain frogs and hedgehogs, along with a number of brass statuettes

that gathered around the electric fire like little sentries. *'Keepsakes'*.
'Personal items'. *'Paperwork'*. *'Books and records'*. *'Misc.'*.

'Go through the paperwork first,' Winkler said, taking a seat while Gareth crouched on the floor and removed a lid from a Medium Box.

'What am I looking for?'

Winkler shrugged. 'Anything interesting. Something that shows she was in debt or struggling to pay her bills. Letters from friends – maybe she wrote to one of her pals to say she was worried about someone lurking around. Maybe we'll strike lucky and there'll be a diary.'

As Gareth sorted through the papers, quickly glancing at each sheet before setting it aside, Winkler ate the chicken sandwich he'd brought with him.

'Makes you think, doesn't it?' he said with his mouth full.

'What does?' So far, all Gareth had found were lots of bills (all paid, no red ones), a pension book, a number of letters from twenty or thirty years ago and Nancy's driving licence.

'Well, it's sad, to think about what gets left behind when someone dies. A load of junk, mostly. And ungrateful kids who just care about their inheritance, what there is of it. What impression did Nancy Marr make on the world? What was her legacy?'

Gareth looked up and Winkler held his eye.

'That's what's important, isn't it? Making the most of your life; making an impression. So that people remember you and care that you're not around anymore.'

Gareth nodded thoughtfully, clearly thinking about his own legacy.

'The really sad thing is that the person who Nancy Marr made the biggest impression on was the person who murdered her.'

After finding nothing among the paperwork, Gareth went through the keepsakes and then the personal items – framed family photographs, an engraved Bible, some very unattractive brooches. George had obviously appropriated any jewellery of value.

'This is a waste of time,' Gareth said, sitting back and rubbing his knees, which were dusty from the floor of the storage room.

'I agree. But we might as well have a look through the last box, eh?'

Gareth pulled the lid off the large box marked '*Misc.*'. This one contained stuff that, as far as Winkler could see, should have been sent straight to the tip. A tatty-looking cuddly rabbit; a children's book called *Chips the Magic Hamster*; an old hat; an ancient golliwog; and a teddy bear. Gareth pulled an A4 folder out of the box and some loose photos fluttered to the floor. Winkler picked one up. It had a date on the back: July 1967. Mrs Marr had her arms around a bloke with long hair and a big grin on his face. She'd been quite a looker in her day. Nice boobs.

He admired the photo as Gareth continued to look through the folder. He was lost in a reverie about the sixties, free love and hippie chicks when he heard Gareth saying, 'Boss? Boss? Look at this.'

He held up a photograph, A4 sized. It was signed, '*To Nancy. With all my best wishes, Mervyn Hammond xx*'.

Winkler jumped off his seat and snatched the photo out of Gareth's hand.

'Bloody hell,' he said.

Gareth's eyes shone with excitement. 'This is a connection to the other case. At last.'

'Mervyn bloody Hammond. What's she doing with a signed photo of him? Hey, what are you doing?'

'Phoning DI Lennon.'

Winkler snatched the phone out of Gareth's hand. 'Wait a minute. Let's think about this. Mervyn Hammond probably sends out hundreds of signed photos every year. I bet most of the people who like him are old ladies like Nancy.' He tapped the photo.

'I reckon this is a coincidence. It will just cause a distraction. And then who'll get the blame if Lennon wastes days looking at Hammond, eh? It won't be Patrick, and it sure as hell won't be me.'

Gareth's brow creased with doubt.

'On the other hand, if Hammond *has* got something to do with it, who'll get all the credit? Lennon. And while Suzanne and the press are – literally and metaphorically – sucking him off for being the big hero, do you think he'll say, "Actually, it was all down to a bright young officer called Gareth Batey"? Will he hell.'

Gareth cringed at Winkler's choice of words, but nodded. He was clearly torn. 'So what do you think we should do?'

Winkler put his arm around Gareth's shoulder. 'Tell you what, why don't you and me look into it, discreetly, and if we find any more evidence that points to Hammond, we'll hand it over to Lennon; officially tie the two operations together, but make sure everyone knows it was your hard work that gave us a break. And if we don't find anything, we won't have wasted anyone's time but our own. I mean, it's not like we have any other hot leads to pursue on this side of the investigation. Make sense?'

Gareth hesitated. 'I guess. It probably is just a coincidence.'

'I'm sure it is. But if it isn't, think how good you'll look. Solving a multiple murder while you're still a sergeant? A case involving one of the most powerful men in Britain? You'll be famous, Gareth. And there won't be anything Lennon can do to take the credit.'

Chapter 30
Day 9 – Patrick

Patrick beckoned for Carmella to follow him into the major incident room and walked up to the boards where Rose's and Jessica's pictures were displayed. He took a whiteboard eraser and rubbed out Shawn's name from the list of suspects, adding it to the column containing the names of potential witnesses.

Carmella perched on the edge of a desk. 'So his alibi checks out?' She sounded disappointed.

Patrick nodded. 'I just got off the phone with Lana Vincent. She confirms that she and Shawn spent the night together on the seventh and she also gave him an alibi for the fourth – said they were on the phone for hours that evening, when Shawn said he was home playing Minecraft. She was extremely nervous, kept asking me to reassure her about confidentiality. She's terrified of the press and her boyfriend finding out.'

Carmella rolled her eyes. 'If you can't do the time, don't do the crime.'

'They should put that in big letters on the front of the station.'

Their laughter was disproportionate to the quality of the joke, but shit, Patrick thought, he needed a laugh. His whole body was taut with tension. After the meeting with Shawn, and the realisation that their only suspect was innocent, he'd come back to the station, hiding at his desk until he felt duty-bound to go home.

He didn't want another discussion with Gill about their feelings. Even more than that, he didn't want another awkward conversation in which they *didn't* talk about their marriage. Fortunately, Gill had been asleep, and he'd slipped out early this morning before she or Bonnie woke up. He'd crept into his daughter's room, kissing her warm head, aching with guilt as he'd barely seen her since they'd moved home last weekend.

At least when they were living with his parents he'd seen a lot of Bonnie. Now, though, it was too easy to be like so many other male cops: married to the job, their kids growing up without them. He was determined not to let that happen. He just needed to crack this investigation first.

Although, of course, then there would be another. And another. And . . .

He sighed heavily and Carmella came over and rubbed his upper arm.

'So what next?' she asked.

Patrick produced his Moleskine from his pocket and opened it to the page of notes he'd made when interviewing Shawn.

'I was thinking, Shawn and Lana Vincent communicated using Snapchat. Wendy – DC Franklin – tells me that most teenagers use it. And we already know that Rose consumed data on her phone on the evening of her death, as did Jess' – this was one of the first things they had checked after Jess's murder – 'maybe they were using Snapchat.'

'To communicate with their killer?'

'Seems the perfect method for a murderer, doesn't it? A way of communicating without leaving any trace. Second only to actually chatting face to face.'

'Technology. Friend of serial killers everywhere.'

Patrick smiled faintly, wondering what police work must have been like in the days before DNA and the Internet and CCTV. He would have quite liked to have operated in a Columbo-style world. Maybe, he mused, he should get himself a grubby raincoat like the TV detective.

'Are you still with us?' Carmella asked.

'Just thinking about buying a mac.'

'I thought you preferred Windows?'

He laughed so loudly that he worried Suzanne would hear him in her office and wonder what he found so amusing. That reminded him he needed to report to her and, as much as he enjoyed seeing her, he suddenly didn't feel like laughing anymore.

Looking at him curiously, Carmella asked, 'Are Snapchat pictures actually stored anywhere?'

'Let's find out.'

He called Peter Bell on the internal phone and, a few minutes later, the cyber-crime expert joined them in the incident room.

'Before I start, any progress with our hotel key card?'

The older man smoothed down a wisp of flyaway hair. 'I emailed a list of potential hackers to Gareth Batey earlier. Apologies. I've been under the cosh.'

'OK. Well, let's forget that for the moment. What do you know about Snapchat?'

'Snapchat? Interestingly, I was just talking about this with someone in child protection.'

'Why's that?'

'Because it's a new preferred method for paedophiles to exchange images. Harder to trace than email or MMS. Or, at least, a lot of them think it is.'

'Go on.'

'Well, what Snapchat don't make clear is that the images are saved into a folder on the user's phone, and they're easy to find if you know where to look.'

'What if you don't have the phone?' Patrick asked. 'Are they stored on a server somewhere?'

Bell cleared his throat. 'According to Snapchat, they keep a log of the last two hundred images sent, but don't save the actual images. Unless the image wasn't viewed by the recipient. In that case, it remains on the company's servers for thirty days.'

Patrick thought about this. It was most likely that Rose – and Jess, if the murderer had used the same method – had viewed the messages, possibly screenshot them for posterity. And the killer had taken the phones with him.

'Hang on,' Carmella said. 'Could I log in as another user on my phone, if I knew their password, and view the images they'd received?'

'No.' Bell smiled patronisingly. 'Because they disappear within seconds of being viewed.'

'Shit.'

'But if and when we arrest someone,' Patrick said, 'we'll be able to look on their phone and, if they sent snaps to the two victims, they'll still be there. Stored in a hidden folder.'

Bell nodded. 'That's right. Unless your murderer is tech savvy.'

'We'd better hope he isn't,' Carmella said.

Patrick thanked Bell and watched him leave the room. He felt frustrated, like he was looking for a trail of breadcrumbs that had already been eaten by birds.

'We'll catch him,' Carmella said. 'He's going to slip up at some point.'

Patrick stared into space. 'Maybe. But how quickly? And who's next on his list?'

Chapter 31
Day 10 – Kai

Kai slouched over to a corner table next to a massive poster reading 'Home of the Whopper', his laptop in one hand, and a plastic tray containing a box of cheeseburger and fries in the other. He dumped the items on the table and pulled back a red slatted chair, which made a loud metallic sound as it scraped across the tiled floor.

Opening the laptop with his right hand, he shovelled fries into his mouth with his left while looking around him to make sure nobody could see the screen. With greasy fingers he tapped in the Burger King Wi-Fi password and brought up the window of the OnTarget forum. He just needed to be sure about one or two things.

The thing that Kai feared more than anything was making Jade angry. She was angry a lot – he could just about deal with that – but the terror of one day making her so mad that she dumped him gave him a sick feeling in the pit of his belly that even half a burger in one big swallow couldn't obliterate. His mates thought he was a total wuss – 'pussy-whipped', according to Ed – but he didn't care. He loved her. And if this worked out like it should, Jade would be well pleased with him. He grinned to himself through the other half of the burger. He wasn't going to let *anybody* upset his boo, no way.

He finished his meal and wiped his sleeve across his mouth before pushing the empty food box to one side. Hunched over the laptop, he laboriously typed a question with two fingers, then sat back and waited.

An answer flashed back in a minute. Kai tensed, read it silently to himself, lips moving, then relaxed and started typing again. It took less than five minutes to make the arrangements. Kai was dying to message Jade to tell her, but then decided not to, not until it was done. Then he reckoned she'd Snapchat him one of her special selfies – the kind that made him go soft and hard at the same time.

Leaving all his litter on the table, he pulled on his jacket and headed out on his mission. Pausing in the doorway under a blast of hot, stale air, he zipped up his laptop inside his jacket and smiled, a slow, smug smile.

Jade was gonna be *proper* pleased with him.

Chapter 32
Day 10 – Wendy

Wendy stood at the top of the escalators in the Rotunda, music from the PA system outside Frankie and Benny's wafting over. Frank Sinatra. Her dad's favourite. He liked that restaurant too, even if it was overpriced in his opinion. As a family they had eaten in places like this many times, before her dad had run off with the woman who was now her stepmother.

Every town had a leisure complex like this, usually on the outskirts, with a big cinema, numerous chain restaurants and a ten-pin bowling centre. Wendy was pretty damn good at bowling, even if she did say so herself, and had smiled when her new contact had sent her the picture of the bowling place at the Rotunda in Kingston.

'Meet u here at 9.30pm', the caption of the photograph had read before it vanished. She'd arrived ten minutes early to familiarise herself with the layout of the place. As she headed back down the escalator leading towards the basement bowling alley, she remembered the last time she'd played with her dad and sister. Her dad had taken her aside and told her how proud he was of her.

'What, because I can beat you at bowling?' she'd joked.

'No, you numpty. Because of what you've done with your life. I'm dead proud.'

She smiled at the memory and for the umpteenth time in recent weeks felt a pang. She missed her broken-up family. Once this case was over she was planning on taking some leave, going back to Wolves to see them.

But before that, she had a chance to make her dad even prouder. The chance to make a difference to this operation.

Now that she was familiar to most of the users of the forum, Wendy had decided it was safe to mention the murders without arousing suspicion that she was a mole. There were already lots of threads about it, discussions of the vigil that had taken place, and immediately after the deaths of both MissTargetHeart and YOLOSWAG, the site had been filled with intense, borderline-hysterical tributes to the dead girls.

MissTargetHeart helped me when I was stressing about my exams . . . She'll be singing with the Angels in Heaven now.

Me and YOLOSWAG hung out after the Wembley concert last summer. She had Shawn tattooed on her skin and on her soul. RIP SISTER!!

So, earlier that evening at her desk, Wendy had started a thread: *I haven't told anyone about this, not even my mum, but ever since what happened to those poor girls I have been terrified. I keep hoping the fact they were both OnT fans is a coincidence but what if it isn't? I have a theory about what happened to them but I'm too scared to share it on here.*

This post had sparked a flurry of responses, most of the girls demanding to know about her theory.

I can't say, Wendy wrote. *I wish I'd known them like some of you did. Then I might be able to prove my theory is right.*

The conversation went on from there, mostly going in circles. Wendy waited for Jade and some of the other regulars to join in, hitting refresh repeatedly, frustrated that no-one was taking the bait.

Then a message popped up in her private inbox, headed 'YOUR THEORY'.

It was from a user called Mockingjay365, whose profile picture was of Katniss from *The Hunger Games*, bow and arrow pointed at the camera.

I'd luv to here about ur theory, the message read.

I haven't seen you on the forum before, Wendy replied.

Don't post much, usualy just read. Im not very good at riting. Too shy.

I understand, Wendy wrote, unsure if this girl was a time-waster. *I wish I'd known Rose and Jess.*

I new them.

Really?

Yeah. We used to hang out, talk about OnT. Met them outside BBC last yeer wen OnT were on Graham Norton.

Wendy waited.

I think I no something. About an enemy they had. They were talking about it.

Wendy's pulse increased. Though the chances were Mockingjay365 was talking nonsense. She typed: *An enemy? Have you been to the police?*

No! My dad hates feds. He sez they are bent. He wd kill me if I talked to cops.

I understand. Who was this enemy?

The answer came back straight away. *I'm scared. He knows who I am. And he knows that I know him.*

You can tell me. He won't be able to read this.

There was a long, frustrating pause. Eventually, a response came. *I dunno. My dad sez that any1 can spy on u on the internet. Like wen Jennifer Lawrence's nude pics got hacked.*

Wendy supposed it made sense that a *Hunger Games* fan would be extra paranoid about Internet security after the naked selfies of that film's star had been stolen and posted online.

We cd meet? Mockingjay365 wrote. *I saw you said you was local to me – Kingston?*

It was Wendy's turn to hesitate. Was it worth it? Could this girl really know something? This talk of Jess and Rose having a common enemy was intriguing, but could be a fantasy.

Yeh. Where? she typed, playing for time and looking up from her computer. It had just gone eight. She decided she would find Patrick, ask him what she should do. That was the correct protocol. So she hurried towards his desk, disappointed to find that he wasn't there.

'Looking for Lennon?'

She turned. It was Winkler, gym bag in hand, his eyes blatantly roaming up and down her body as he waited for her response.

'Yes, I—'

'He's having a party, so Masiello let slip earlier. A surprise birthday dinner with Masiello and his mad missus and the guv.' He sniggered. '*That* should be awkward. Pretty disgraceful, though, if you ask me – having a lovely dinner party when proper cops like you and me are hard at it trying to stop a murderer.'

She didn't point out that he looked like he was heading to the gym.

'Anything I can help with?' he asked, taking a step closer so she could smell his aftershave.

'No . . . It's fine. Thanks.'

She hurried back to her computer and saw that Mockingjay365 had suggested meeting at the Rotunda. She tapped out a reply: *OK. What time? And where exactly?*

Do u hav Snapchat? came the response.

She didn't, but she could download it.

Username same as on here. Add me & Ill message you. Snapchat deleets so no1 can trak it.

And now here she was, standing outside the bowling alley waiting for another message, hopefully with a selfie of her new contact so she would be able to recognise her. At least it was warm in there – it was freezing outside, cold enough to snow, and if Mockingjay365 didn't message her in the next five minutes, she was going home, back to her flat for a hot bubble bath, a glass of wine and the next episode of *The Good Wife*. And maybe to indulge her fantasies about a certain detective inspector. She hoped he was enjoying his birthday – Valentine's Day was such an apt day for someone so sexy to be born – but couldn't help but wish she was at the dinner party. She imagined herself as Gill there with him, laughing, Patrick squeezing her knee beneath the table, forgetting about the case for a couple of hours and enjoying himself, relaxing, and after their guests were gone he would take her/Gill to bed and gently lay her down and . . .

Her phone beeped, shaking her from her fantasy. Hot shame flooded through her. What was she like, thinking about such a thing? Patrick, *DI Lennon*, was married and she was on the way to meet someone who might help her find the murderer. She needed to stop thinking about him. The sensible thing would be to ask to transfer to another team, maybe even another station. When this case was over, maybe that's what she should do, after she'd visited her folks. She would work it out later, but she was glad now she hadn't left that card on his desk as she'd intended.

She took out her phone and saw, with a mixture of relief and anxiety, that she had a new Snapchat message. It was a photo of the café inside the bowling place, with another caption. 'I'm here, waiting.'

Wendy had changed into her teenage disguise at the station: skinny jeans and a parka with a furry hood, trainers and the make-up that, she hoped, made her look ten years younger. She pushed through the double doors of the bowlplex and headed towards the café.

The noise in here was incredible. From the back came the clatter of bowling balls, the crash of scattering pins, whoops of delight and groans of disappointment. Above that came the cacophony of noise from the arcade machines that took up a large area – driving games and air hockey, machines that spat out chains of tickets that could be exchanged for cheap prizes. A woman stood feeding coins into one of those machines with a large claw, trying to win an Angry Birds toy. The place was full of teenagers and kids who, Wendy thought, should be at home in bed at this hour. There were even some toddlers running about.

But there was no sign of anyone who might be Mockingjay365. She scanned the tables in the café. Lots more teens and families scoffing burgers and soggy-looking pizzas. The smell of nachos reached her nostrils and her stomach growled, reminding her that she hadn't eaten anything since she'd had a dry egg and cress sandwich at lunchtime.

Where the hell was Mockingjay?

Right on cue, her phone beeped. She had a new Snapchat message. It was a photo of a car park. The caption read: *Im in the car park round back. My ex is in Rotunda. Dont want him to see me!!*

Wendy tutted. This was getting ridiculous now. But she walked back up the stairs to the ground floor and pushed through the double doors into the freezing air.

She strode along the pavement by the one-way system, eyeing the cars and buses moving in the same direction, wishing she was cocooned inside a warm vehicle, not out here in the bitter wind. There were plenty of people around, mostly teenagers heading in and out of the Rotunda, but as Wendy turned right towards the back of the bowlplex, the noise from the cars and people dropped away to be replaced by near-silence.

Wendy checked her phone again, then looked around her. She was standing in a residential road around the back of the Rotunda. Across the road was a car park on the ground floor of what looked like private flats. That must be where Mockingjay was waiting for her.

Wendy hesitated. It not only went against her police training but her instincts as a woman: you didn't go into dark, deserted places like this on your own. She badly wanted to talk to Mockingjay – the girl was her only potential lead – but how did she know she could trust her? She could be anyone.

She sent Mockingjay another message. *I'm outside the car park. Come out. There's no-one else here. No need to be scared.*

There was no response. Still holding her phone, Wendy made a decision. She would call DI Lennon, let him know what she was doing. He'd given her his mobile number in case she had anything important to tell him. Well, this qualified.

His phone rang five or six times before he answered.

'Boss? It's Wendy . . . Listen, I . . .'

'Oh, Wendy. Is it life or death?'

Wendy hesitated. She heard a woman's voice calling Patrick impatiently.

'I'm at the Rotunda in Kingston. I think I've made contact with—'

Again, she heard a woman calling Patrick at the other end of the phone line, saying something about a door. Wendy felt a flash of embarrassment. She shouldn't be calling him, spoiling his birthday dinner.

'I'm really sorry, Wendy. Can I call you back in thirty minutes?'

'Yes, of course. Sorry to disturb you, boss.'

'No problem. I'll talk to you later.'

'Happy birth—'

But he had hung up. While she was talking to him, a teenage boy had come out of the car park, fiddling with the waist of his low-hanging trousers, a cat-that-got-the-cream look on his face. He smirked at Wendy as he walked past her and she turned to see him swagger towards the road.

Fuck this, she thought. The car park was reasonably well lit and Wendy knew how to handle herself. She wanted to talk to Mockingjay, find out if the girl was a complete time-waster, and head home to that bubble bath and bottle of wine. She strode towards the car park and squeezed around the barrier.

'Hello?' she called.

No response.

She walked farther into the car park. Where the hell was the stupid girl? She took her phone out of her pocket again and started to tap out a message to Mockingjay.

A noise came from beside the far wall, where it was almost pitch dark. Broken glass crunching under her feet indicated that there had once been lights above her. Wendy strained to see, imagined her mum saying that if she'd eaten her carrots, she'd be able to see in the dark. She took another step forwards.

'Hello?' she said. 'Mockingjay? What are you playing at?'

A shape appeared from behind a car, moving fast and, at the same time Wendy registered that this was no teenage girl, this wasn't the person she'd been chasing, she felt a sharp, hot pain close to her heart. Then another.

And then she was falling, her palms clutching her chest, her dying mind refusing to process the facts, that the warm liquid on her hands was her own blood, that the person who had stabbed her stopped for a moment to look down at her. They had crouched and taken the phone from her hands before running away.

As her life slipped from her she was vaguely aware of another figure – brown skin, wide eyes, a teenage girl; Mockingjay? – crouching beside her, saying 'OhJesusohJesusohJesus' while Wendy tried, and failed, to ask for help. Her life didn't flash before her eyes. All she felt was disbelief, and then nothing.

PART TWO

Chapter 33
Day 10 – Carmella

Carmella and Jenny stood hand in hand outside the Lennons' front door. In their spare hands Jenny held a bunch of white roses and purple sweetpeas and Carmella a bottle of Picpoul de Pinet, the sweat from her palm making the cold bottle's condensation even more slippery.

'I'm nervous. Why am I nervous? Are we late?' Carmella said in a low voice, tucking the bottle tightly under her armpit so she could fish her phone out of her pocket and check the time – 8.25 p.m. They weren't late.

Whenever she felt tense, the scar at the side of her belly where the bullet had grazed her began to feel stretched and achy, and it was really taut now, even though it was a year on. To take her mind off it, she surveyed the small, modern house, Patrick's bronze Prius in the driveway the only feature distinguishing it from the other identical houses in the cul-de-sac.

'Why are you nervous?' Jenny grinned at her. '*I'm* not nervous, and I've never met any of these people before.'

'I think I'm just worried that Pat will freak, having us all over for dinner when he didn't know about it. It's just so not—'

'Hey,' Jenny interrupted, as a shadow loomed towards the other side of the frosted glass panel front door. She leaned across and hastily kissed Carmella on the lips. 'Happy Valentine's Day, wife,' she whispered.

'Happy' – Carmella, smiling, was about to say the same – even though they had already exchanged cards and handmade gifts when they got in from work – but when Patrick opened the door, slipping his mobile into his pocket as he did so, she changed it – 'birthday, boss!' She thrust the bottle towards him. 'Sorry it's not wrapped. Um, hello? Are you OK?'

He snapped out of the trance he was in. 'Sorry. Thank you, Carmella. I think I'd have been able to figure out what it was anyway,' he said, taking it from her. He held out his hand to Jenny. 'You must be Jenny. Lovely to meet you, I've heard so much about you.'

'Likewise,' said Jenny, shaking hands with him and handing over the flowers with a smile. Carmella had pre-warned her not to go in for the kiss on the cheek. Patrick wasn't much of a kissy person, she said – although obviously Carmella didn't see that side of him at work anyway. He just didn't strike her as very tactile. He looked very different to how he'd looked at work earlier, in a bright blue shirt that clung to his body, tucked into the sort of jeans that cost about a hundred and eighty quid. Carmella wondered if Pat had bought them, or whether Gill had.

'So, when did you find out we were all turning up?' she asked as they followed Patrick into a small hallway, squeezing past a push-chair and a small pink tricycle. Voices from the back of the house indicated that the other guests had already arrived.

'About half an hour ago.' Pat grinned ruefully. 'Gill told me she was cooking the lamb to make some shepherd's pies and that we were going out for a curry. I was getting narky with her for insisting I had a shave and put on a smarter shirt. For a curry? I should've known something was up. Let alone that she'd bought a great big leg of lamb just to mince up for shepherd's pies . . . you wouldn't guess that I'm a detective, would you?'

'I won't tell Winkler,' Carmella said.

'You'd better bloody not!' He nudged her affectionately. 'Come and meet Gill and everyone.'

This, if Carmella thought about it, was the bit that was making her nervous. Although normally fairly unshockable, she'd been very taken aback to hear Patrick's wife's message on the voicemail of her mobile a week ago, inviting her and Jenny round for Pat's birthday. Even though she had worked with Pat for over three years, she had never met his wife, and Carmella and Jenny had indulged in a fair bit of curious pillow talk about what she was like.

They both felt deeply sorry for her, of course, and for Pat – what a nightmare, to suffer so badly from post-natal psychosis that you almost kill your baby, and then end up in a secure hospital for over a year and a half!

When Carmella had confessed her dread about this event to Jenny later as they lay in bed, Jenny had laughed and kissed her and said, 'Speak for yourself – I can't wait! Your boss, his wacko wife, *his* boss – that he's clearly got the hots for – her husband, who probably has no idea . . . What could *possibly* go wrong?' She had then cackled annoyingly, until Carmella whacked her with a pillow to make her stop.

Now, Patrick took their coats and showed them through to a surprisingly spacious kitchen-diner in which Suzanne Laughland sat on a sofa with a man who Carmella recognised, from the photo on the DCI's desk, as Suzanne's husband, Simon. Another woman – Gill, obviously – stood near the counter with a sleepy toddler in her arms, swaying gently from foot to foot.

Bonnie had her thumb in her mouth and her head on her mother's shoulder. She wore an all-in-one flannelette jumpsuit thing with feet, and for a moment Carmella suddenly felt like her ovaries would explode. She and Jenny had talked about having kids, but neither of them thought the time was right; not yet. She was so busy at work, and Jenny wanted to better establish herself in her new role as deputy head in a local comp, before thinking about motherhood.

'Ah, this must be the beautiful Bonnie!' Carmella exclaimed, rushing over, beaming. 'She's *gorgeous!*' But her beam faded as Gill held up her free arm as though stopping traffic.

'Please don't, she's almost asleep!'

Bonnie's head jerked up and then slumped back down again, her eyelids drooping and her curls bouncing. Gill spoke again, in a more conciliatory tone. 'Sorry. I'm about to take her off to bed. You must be Carmella. I'm Gill.'

Carmella shook hands with her. She couldn't help feeling chastened, as if she'd committed a huge *faux pas*, which then made her annoyed, because she hadn't. Gill wasn't how she had imagined her. She was taller, bigger. Her face was pale, but she had clearly made an effort for the occasion – her long brown hair had been professionally straightened into a sleek curtain and her lips were glossy with coral lipstick. She wasn't beautiful, certainly, though nor was she plain. She had the sort of smile that lit up her whole face and transformed her.

'Pat, will you sort out drinks while I get Miss B down for the night? I won't be long; she's pretty much out for the count already.'

Simon stood up and stuck out his hand. He was shorter than his wife by about three inches, with a receding hairline and very slightly bulging eyes, but in possession of the sort of charisma that meant it was possible to overlook the physical flaws. 'Hi! I'm Simon Laughland. Where have you two come from tonight?'

Several minutes of awkward small talk ensued, about where they all lived, and what Patrick had got for his birthday – Gill had bought him tickets for The Cure in March, which impressed Carmella. She was finding it hard to tear her gaze away from Suzanne, who looked completely different to her rather buttoned-up work appearance. She was wearing a short grey silk dress, killer heels and her blonde hair was in long, loose curls down her back.

Patrick handed around a tray of something sparkling. 'Well, it *is* my birthday,' he commented, slightly sheepishly. 'The missus insisted. I'm sure a little sip or two is allowed . . .' He looked at Suzanne, who smiled at him.

'Of course!' she said, raising her glass. 'To Pat! Happy birthday.'

Carmella noticed that Suzanne hadn't waited until 'the missus' returned to do the toast.

After that, the evening progressed in the way of most dinner parties where the guests aren't already close friends: awkward and slightly stilted for the first hour, until alcohol – mostly being consumed by Jenny and Simon, with Gill sipping at a small glass – smoothed off all the scratchy edges. Loud, muffled music through the thin party wall was mingling badly with the mellow Spotify playlist that the Lennons were playing, so Patrick turned it off. For a while nobody talked shop, out of deference to the civilian attendees – Simon, it turned out, was a management consultant – until Jenny brought up the subject.

'So,' she said in Suzanne's direction, as Gill cleared away the remnants of their prawn cocktails. 'What's the latest with the big investigation? Thanks, Gill, that was delicious – I love a retro starter, me . . .'

Carmella frowned warningly at her. An expression flashed across Gill's face that suggested perhaps she thought Jenny was having a dig, although Carmella knew she wasn't.

'She's not kidding. It's your favourite sort of food, isn't it, darling?' Carmella added hastily. 'Prawn cocktail, Black Forest gateau, gammon and pineapple – you're a seventies throwback.'

'Are you any closer to finding who killed those girls?' Jenny persisted, ignoring Carmella. 'Jessica McMasters was a pupil at my school, you know. Everyone's devastated.'

'We're working flat out,' Patrick said – defensively, Carmella thought – from across the kitchen, where he was carving slices from a fragrant garlic-studded leg of lamb. 'What do you teach, Jenny?' Carmella could tell he was anxious to change the subject and she felt slightly annoyed with Jenny.

'Geography – and I'm deputy head too. So, any new leads? Carmella won't tell me anything!'

'Oh I know,' Gill interjected. 'I'm always badgering Pat to dish the dirt and he never does!'

Carmella made a face at Patrick and he grinned back at her. But Suzanne, who was completely sober, upbraided Gill. '*Dish the dirt?* We're talking about young girls being murdered here, not the gossip at the local WI!'

There was a shocked silence round the table. Gill, who had been in the middle of handing around plates of meat, froze briefly and the smile fell off her face.

'It's just a figure of speech,' she said, her voice brittle.

'Of course!' Patrick jumped to his feet and helped her pass a plate to Simon. Carmella noticed him take his e-cigarette from his shirt pocket and heave a long, desperate drag into his lungs when he turned away to fetch another serving spoon from the cutlery drawer. There was a prickly feeling in the air, like pre-storm static electricity, and her scar started itching again in recognition of it.

Suzanne didn't apologise, but, in a noticeable effort to be conciliatory, said, 'It's a pretty stressful time . . .' Her husband glared at her.

Jenny pitched in. 'I heard that Shawn Barrett's got form . . . And as for that creep Mervyn Hammond!' Then she glanced at Suzanne.

'I mean, I didn't hear any of that from Carmella, obviously, she never tells me anything either, just the kids at school, rumours, you know . . .'

Carmella felt like sinking her head into her hands. She waited for Suzanne to tear Jenny off a strip, but the boss merely smiled and said, 'It's OK, Jenny. We all talk to our other halves.'

'Pat never talks to *me*,' said Gill, overly brightly, dishing up a bowl of steaming peas. She somehow managed to make it sound simultaneously like a compliment and an accusation.

As they ate, Simon and Patrick engaging in a desultory discussion about Brighton and Hove Albion's surprisingly good recent form, someone's mobile began to buzz, just audible over the sound of scraping cutlery and the bass thumping through the walls.

They all looked around at each other.

'Whose is that?' Suzanne asked.

The women delved into handbags and Patrick slipped his hand into his back pocket.

'It's mine,' he said, extracting it and frowning at the screen. 'Sorry, it's the station, need to take it.'

He stood up and walked a little way away over to the French windows where he leaned against the glass, his back to them all.

'Lennon.'

Carmella watched him intently, her glass halfway to her lips. She suddenly had a horrible premonition – as her granny would have said, *a ghost walked over your grave* – and Patrick's reaction confirmed it. Although he was facing away from them out towards the dark garden, she saw the reflection of his face in the window and for a second, it crumpled like a child's as he listened. Then his shoulders slumped and Carmella thought he was going to fall. She leapt to her feet.

'What is it?' Her voice came out in a croak of alarm and everyone fell silent.

'Right. Thanks for letting me know,' he said faintly into the phone, clearly dazed. His hand dropped down by his side and when he turned back to the room, his face was chalky white.

'Oh God,' Suzanne said. 'Don't tell me there's another dead girl?'

Patrick couldn't speak. Carmella had never seen him looking so shocked. 'Pat?'

He sank down onto the sofa as though his legs couldn't hold him. Gill rushed over to sit by him, sliding a protective arm around his waist, but he then immediately stood up again and Gill looked crushed.

'We have to go,' he said to Suzanne and Carmella.

'Patrick, tell me *now*,' Suzanne barked, making a move towards him as though she wanted to shake him. Carmella was already on her feet, dreading his next words.

When they came, they were far worse than she could have imagined.

'There's another murder, yes . . . But – oh God, I can't believe it – it's Wendy Franklin. *Our* Wendy . . .'

Carmella swallowed into the silence, unable to prevent tears flooding her eyes. She thought of the tenacious, down-to-earth DC with her Black Country accent and slight figure; how hungry she was for success and approval; how desperate to be taken seriously. Wendy hadn't been Carmella's favourite person – keen to the point of being irritating – but it seemed inconceivable that she was gone.

'What happened?' she croaked, wiping her eyes on her napkin.

'She's been stabbed, in a private car park behind the Kingston Rotunda. One of the residents came down to get his car and found her body by the front wheel. Come on, let's get moving.'

Patrick recovered himself, grabbing his coat from the peg in the hall, but Suzanne stood. 'Pat, no. There'll be a team on it already; we'll only be in the way if we pile in.'

He faced her, coat half on, glaring. 'Try to stop me. Carmella – you coming?'

Carmella jumped up. 'Yes, boss. Sorry, Gill.' Jenny reached out a hand to her, but whether out of sympathy or restraint, Carmella wasn't sure and didn't really want to know.

'Oh for heaven's sake,' Suzanne said. 'Gill, I'm so sorry. Come on, then, you two, we'll take my car.'

The last thing Carmella saw when she glanced back over her shoulder was Simon, Gill and Jenny sitting in stunned silence at a table covered with half-full plates, meat already beginning to congeal in the gravy.

Chapter 34
Day 11 – Patrick

Patrick was sitting in his car again, his forehead resting on the steering wheel, his eyes squeezed tightly closed. He hadn't felt this terrible since the day he'd found Gill incoherent on their stairs, and Bonnie half-dead upstairs in her cot.

His team's offices were a taped-off crime scene now, so they had all been relocated to an empty office downstairs, provided with hot desks and computers to log onto the intranet to carry on with Operation Urchin while a different MIT swarmed over Wendy's workspace. Over at the Rotunda, reporters with cameras and microphones jostled together trying to keep warm in the chill dawn light, laying claim to the best pitches, waiting for someone to come out and make a statement.

Patrick had held it together all night, listening to the SIO who had been assigned the investigation into Wendy's murder, a sombre-faced DCI called Vanessa Strong, briefing the other murder investigation team.

He had held it together while DCI Strong instructed Daniel Hamlet to fast-track the post-mortem, feeling deeply relieved for the protocol that insisted a different team investigate a colleague's death. He wasn't sure he could have stomached watching Hamlet dissect poor Wendy.

He'd even held it together when Wendy's mum, Sheryl, had rung from Wolverhampton and asked for him by name because she 'knew how much Wendy had admired you, she talked about you all the time'. Through her sobs, Sheryl had brokenly repeated, 'Why? Why? How could you let this happen? She was only twenty-five! Twenty-five!'

He hadn't been able to tell her how he had let it happen, because he didn't know. All he did know was that he *had* let it happen. He hadn't stopped Wendy from going off under her own steam to meet God-knew who, or why. Hopefully he would know soon, once her mobile phone provider had sent over the records from her stolen phone, and once the lab had thoroughly gone through her computer, but he knew that even then it wouldn't make him feel any better, not in the slightest.

One of his officers was dead, and he felt utterly responsible. If he hadn't cut her off when she called him . . .

Winkler pitching up and shaking his head sadly and ostentatiously in his direction hadn't helped either, the sanctimonious bastard, Pat thought.

But the final straw, after a very long night of straws, came when Suzanne summoned him into her temporary office. As he trudged across, he saw her standing in the doorway, holding an evidence bag containing a bright pink envelope. She had changed out of the grey dress she'd been wearing last night, but her hair was still in the same long, loose curls. Patrick wondered if she had been home, or whether perhaps Simon had brought her in a change of clothes.

'What's up?' he asked, puzzled at how annoyed she looked. When he sat down, she closed the door and gestured at the evidence bag. Through the clear plastic he saw his own name handwritten on the front of the envelope.

'Would you care to explain the meaning of this?' Suzanne asked, in the sort of voice that almost made Pat wonder if she was messing with him.

'Well, I would, if I had any idea what it is,' he replied, picking it up and examining it. It wasn't sealed, and when he lifted the envelope's flap a flash of bright pink appeared. Puzzled, he pulled out a large Valentine's card – a rather tacky teddy bear clutching a bunch of roses and heart-shaped balloons. Inside there was a message: TO PAT, YOU MAKE ME MELT LIKE CHOCOLATE. BE MY VALENTINE? LOVE FROM A SECRET ADMIRER XXX

He snorted. 'Is this some kind of joke? Hardly the time or place. Why's it in an evidence bag?'

'Don't be ridiculous, Patrick, are you insane? Of course it's not a *joke*,' Suzanne snapped back at him. 'Strong's team found it in Wendy's locker.'

She paused to let the realisation sink in.

Patrick gazed speechless at the card, the words inscribed in Wendy's neat round handwriting.

'Oh no,' he said eventually, unable to prevent tears springing into his eyes. He cleared his throat noisily. 'Oh God.'

'Is there something you'd like to tell me, Patrick?'

Pat had never heard her use such a frosty voice. When he looked at her, despite the curled hair and still made-up face, she was almost unrecognisable from the relaxed woman who had sat at his dinner table just hours before, laughing and chatting . . . oh, he thought, apart from that awkward little spat she and Gill had had . . . What had that been about? Not that it mattered in the slightest now.

He shook his head. 'Absolutely not. I had no idea she felt like that towards me. If I'd known, I'd have assigned her to a different team. I'm not an idiot.'

Was it true, he asked himself, that he'd had no idea? If he was honest, he had suspected it for some time. Wendy's eagerness to please – the same bloody eagerness that had doubtless got her killed – the way her big brown eyes became more puppyish when she gazed at him . . .

He pinched the bridge of his nose to try to regain control of his expression. 'Poor kid,' he said. 'That poor kid.'

'You sure you had no idea?'

Patrick felt himself getting riled. 'The clue's in the words "secret admirer", Suzanne.'

Tension bristled in the air between them. There was silence for a few moments, broken only by the sound of an early morning cleaner banging a hoover into the corners of the corridor outside.

'OK. Rather unfortunate timing, that's all. What are you going to do now?'

Patrick ran his hand through his hair. He hated it when Suzanne was cold with him – although that was currently the least of his problems. 'I need to get out of here. I'm going to take Carmella and go and speak to that bodyguard guy, Kerry Mangan. Barrett gave me his name – sounds a bit shady. I'm not overly optimistic he'll know anything, but it's worth following up.'

Suzanne nodded. She wasn't smiling, but her voice was softer and she held his gaze. 'Right. You do that. Let DCI Strong's team figure out who Wendy was going to meet last night – you need to distance yourself from that for now, OK?'

He shook his head. 'Wendy called me last night, told me she'd made contact with . . . Well, that's as far as she got before I cut her off. But she must have meant she'd made contact with somebody connected to Operation Urchin. That's who she was going to meet. And either that person killed her, or the guy who killed Rose and Jessica found out and stopped her.'

Suzanne's expression changed straight back to icy. 'You spoke to her? Last night?'

He hung his head.

Suzanne exhaled. 'OK. Listen. You need to pass this information on to Strong. Let her deal with it. You're too emotionally involved. Let Vanessa handle that side of the investigation – and you concentrate on our two teenage victims. Unless you think it's too much for you. I could let Winkler—'

'No! No way.' He could feel his cheeks burning. 'This is my case.'

As he said this he heard a whisper of doubt. This investigation was ridiculously over-complicated, what with Patrick concentrating on the teenagers, Winkler on Nancy Marr and now Strong taking the lead with Wendy. Maybe he should step back, let Winkler take over; simplify everything.

But the way his stomach clenched as this thought raced through his head told him he could never allow that to happen.

Without a word, Patrick got up to walk out of the office. He was shaking with anger and emotion.

'Pat?' Suzanne called, just as he was going through the door.

'Yeah?' He didn't turn around.

'Thanks for your hospitality last night. Please thank Gill for a lovely dinner.'

He snorted. 'It should never have happened, not in the middle of an investigation, and you know it. Wendy might still be alive if I hadn't been too busy greeting guests to talk to her properly. But I didn't listen to her, and now she's dead.'

It was only later, leaning on a wall outside in the car park trying to gather his thoughts, that something occurred to him through the maelstrom of emotion whirling around in his head: could Suzanne be *jealous* that Wendy had had a crush on him?

He immediately dismissed the thought as ridiculous and narcissistic. Taking a few long drags of his e-cigarette, his resolution hardened. He understood the protocol, knew why the investigation into Wendy's death had to be kept separate. But he was convinced the same man had killed all three victims – and possibly Nancy Marr, though he was still unsure about that. If he had to tread on Strong's toes in order to catch that person, so be it. Justice was more important than protocol. And if he committed career suicide but found the killer, it would be worth it.

Chapter 35
Day 11 – Winkler

The Mervyn Hammond PR Agency was situated a long way from Winkler's patch, in a converted warehouse set in a quiet street between Clerkenwell and Farringdon, surrounded by media companies and Internet start-ups. Winkler hated it around here. All those fucking hipsters, with their ludicrous facial hair and ridiculous trousers. Apparently there was a café near here that sold nothing but breakfast cereal, and the morons who dwelled in these parts were happy to shell out over three quid a pop. *Three quid a* Coco *Pop*, he thought, deciding he had to get that joke into a conversation at some point.

He looked sideways at Gareth Batey, deciding the younger cop wasn't bright enough to appreciate his humour. They were parked outside the office, a little way down the road, in Winkler's white Audi. The engine ran, filling the car with warm air.

'I'm really not sure about doing this,' Gareth said, for about the tenth time. 'Shouldn't we be doing something to help catch Wendy's murderer?'

Every time Gareth mentioned what had happened to Wendy his eyes misted over, making Winkler wonder if the detective sergeant had been carrying a torch for the dead DC. Perhaps Wendy had been Gareth's ideal woman. That would be another reason for Gareth to hate Lennon. Maybe he should hint that he'd actually seen Lennon and Wendy together . . . really get his rival into trouble. The guv had been stomping round like a rhino with piles ever since that Valentine's card was found in Wendy's locker, and Winkler was pretty sure it wasn't just because one of the team had been murdered. Laughland was jealous! Of course, he felt sorry for Wendy, poor dead cow, but apart from that it was too delicious for words.

Winkler turned down the rainforest music a notch. 'Leave all that to DCI Strong's team – we're investigating Nancy Marr, remember? Though I bet Lennon won't be able to resist sticking his beak in. He's all over the shop. I reckon he's losing it.'

Gareth appeared to be suffering an internal struggle, but he pulled himself together. *That's my boy*, Winkler thought. *I'm your ally. Not that tattooed tosser.*

'So are we actually going to talk to Hammond?' Gareth asked.

'No. Not yet. I just want to watch him, see what he gets up to when he's not putting on his public face. If he doesn't seem to be up to anything, or this looks like a massive waste of time, we'll move on.'

'But you're starting to think it *could* be him?'

Winkler held his hand out flat and tilted it from side to side. 'I don't know. But trust me – if he is guilty, I'll find out. I've got the best clear-up stats in the MIT, did you know that?'

'It's not the first time you've told me, boss.'

Winkler was deliberately down-playing his suspicions about Mervyn Hammond, not wanting Gareth to think it was so important that he had to go running to Lennon about it. But since they'd found the signed photo of the PR man among Nancy's belongings, Winkler had done some digging into Hammond's background and what he'd found was interesting. Very interesting indeed.

A few years ago, Winkler had investigated – and solved, natch – the murder of a young female journalist who wrote for the now-defunct *News of the World*. That case had brought Winkler into contact with one of the newspaper's Features editors, a guy called Doug Sandwell who reminded Winkler of an emphysemic crocodile, leathery and wheezy. They should stick a picture of Sandwell on cigarette packets – the smoking rate would halve overnight.

Sandwell had retired a couple of years ago, but Winkler knew the old journo had dealt with a lot of showbiz stories at the paper, as well as a number of juicy sex scandals and exposés of corrupt politicians. Winkler also strongly suspected, from conversations he'd overheard during the murder investigation, that Sandwell had colluded in phone hacking, though it appeared that – unlike many of his fellows – he'd got away with it.

Last night, after getting home from the gym, Winkler had given Sandwell a call. After listening to the other man cough for a couple of minutes, he'd asked Sandwell what he was up to these days.

'Writing my autobiography, aren't I?' His voice crackled. 'Great fun.'

'I bet you can tell some stories, eh?'

'Oh, you bet. Trouble is, most of this stuff couldn't be published till after everyone involved is dead.'

'Really? Like what?'

'I could tell you, but then I'd have to kill you.' The older man snorted.

Twat, thought Winkler.

'So, what, is this a social call?' Sandwell asked. 'Ringing to ask me out on a date? You know I'm not that type . . . I never go out with cops.' More hissing laughter.

'I was actually wondering if you ever had any dealings with Mervyn Hammond.'

'Hammond? Fuck yeah. We used to deal with that snake all the time. Got some of our best stories from him.' He named a couple of fabricated scandals that Winkler vaguely remembered. 'What are you asking about him for?'

'Well . . . A mate of mine might be involved in a scandal himself. Hammond's representing this bird who claims to have slept with my mate, and I was hoping to find some leverage to dissuade Mervyn from selling the story.'

'A cop, is he? Someone high up?'

'Something like that.'

'Hmm. Well, since you ask . . .' Glee crept into Sandwell's voice. 'This was about ten years ago and involves a bloke called Colin Denver. He worked as a nightclub promoter, knew loads of famous people, and that was his MO. He used to tell these young girls that he could introduce them to celebs, help their careers – all that bullshit. So he'd take them to parties and then, well, you can imagine the rest.'

Winkler waited impatiently for the other man to get to the really juicy bit.

'So one of the girls came to us, wanting to expose these creeps, and it was potentially a huge story. She said she'd been to the police but couldn't get your lot to believe her.'

Winkler cringed, thinking about the bashing the police had received over the Jimmy Savile case.

Sandwell coughed. 'Two or three household names involved. A Radio 1 DJ, a TV presenter, these middle-aged scumbags who had probably been getting away with this stuff for decades. And they were all clients of Mervyn Hammond. As soon as he got wind of it, he came to us, claiming the story was bullshit, that this girl was a gold-digger and his clients would sue if we printed a word of it. Plus he'd stop giving us any more good stories. So we backed off – didn't have enough evidence. But, according to the girl, Hammond wasn't only doing it for his clients' sake. He was one of the creeps. He molested her at one of these parties.'

'I knew it,' Winkler said. And he started to get that tingle, thinking ahead to his moment of glory when he exposed Hammond and cracked this case. With the Yewtree operation, and so many celebs now rotting in prison for committing the same offences Sandwell was talking about, the climate was very different now. This young woman might be willing to talk. 'Do you remember her name?'

'Yeah.' The former journalist sniffed. 'But it won't do you any good.'

'Why not?'

'Because she topped herself, about six months after all this happened.'

'Shit.'

'Yeah. Shit. It's haunted me ever since. I know you think we journos are a bunch of heartless wolves, but I met this girl. She was fourteen, a sweet little girl who'd got sucked in by men who really are wolves. I would fucking love it if you got Hammond. Just, er, don't say you heard it from me, OK?'

Winkler wanted Hammond too. *Hammond might be a wolf,* Winkler thought, *but I'm a hunter.* And he entertained a brief fantasy in which he chased the PR man through the woods with a shotgun.

'What about this Colin Denver guy?' Winkler asked. 'What happened to him?'

'Last I heard he'd buggered off to Thailand, along with all the other nonces.'

Now, sitting next to Gareth in the car, Winkler imagined what would happen after he caught Hammond and proved he was responsible for the OnTarget murders. With Lennon in disgrace after the cock-up with Wendy, and with Winkler showing yet again that he was the best detective in south-west London – probably all of London, possibly the world – DCI Laughland would have no choice but to make him the lead detective on all future big cases. Lennon would probably be moved to traffic and he, Adrian Winkler, would be king. He'd be commissioner by the time he was fifty.

'He's coming out,' Gareth hissed.

Winkler snapped out of his daydream and saw that Gareth was correct: Mervyn Hammond had emerged through the front door of the building, another thuggish-looking bloke beside him. Hammond waited while the thug went off round the back of the building. Winkler's car had tinted windows, so he knew the PR man wouldn't be able to see inside.

Hammond had a bag of nuts in his hand, the contents of which he daintily popped into his mouth, one by one, until a gorgeous Jag Coupé pulled up and he got in. The car headed towards the end of the quiet street, purring as it passed Winkler's car.

They followed, Winkler driving.

The side street led onto busy Goswell Road. Hammond's chauffeur – assuming that was who the thuggish bloke was – indicated right, cutting across the left lane and joining the queue of traffic on the other side.

'Shit, we're going to lose him already.'

There was no sign of another break in the traffic. Hammond's Jag was being held at a red light, but the moment it changed he'd be off and would vanish at the crossroads ahead.

'Fuck it,' Winkler said, swinging out into the traffic, gambling that the oncoming car, a red Mini, would see him and brake.

The Mini did brake, but as Winkler attempted to cross the lane he stalled the car. He hurriedly turned the ignition, flushing pink, mortified that Gareth had seen him stall – the shame! – and as he fumbled to get going the Mini driver and all the cars behind beeped their horns. Hammond's car was still stuck at the red light, and Winkler stalled the car again, at the same time that the driver of the

Mini jumped out of his car and strode over, banging on the window of the Audi.

Winkler pushed the button to lower the window, flashing his badge at the irate driver. 'Police. Piss off.' The red-faced man retreated to his car.

He finally managed to get into gear, but now the traffic in the far lane was moving, and he had to wait for someone to flash him and let him across. Hammond had gone.

Chapter 36
Day 11 – Patrick

Patrick found Carmella in the canteen, staring into a mug of coffee, a half-eaten Kit Kat beside it, chocolate crumbs scattered across the Formica. There was an old stain on the table that made Patrick visualise the shape of a stricken body. He closed his eyes to clear his head of the image. His ears whistled, his stress tinnitus drilling into his brain. He plonked himself down in the seat opposite Carmella.

'We need to find out exactly who Wendy was talking to before she went to the Rotunda.'

'I'm fine, Patrick, thanks for asking. How are you doing?'

He sighed. 'I'm sorry. I'm just . . .'

'I know. Me too. What did the boss say?'

Patrick pointed at the remaining half of the chocolate bar. 'Do you mind?'

'Go ahead. I've lost my appetite. Jenny would go nuts if she knew I'd had half a Kit Kat for breakfast. Anyway . . .'

The chocolate made him feel a tiny bit better. 'Suzanne said that we need to leave the investigation into Wendy's murder up to DCI Strong and her team.'

'But we're not going to do that, are we?'

Their eyes met.

'I don't want to get you into any trouble, Carmella. This is down to me. Wendy called me just as you and Jenny were arriving at my place. I cut her off. So this is down to me. My bad, as Wendy would have said.'

Except 'my bad' wasn't a strong enough expression, was it?

'Pat, Wendy was my colleague too. Whatever you think we need to do to find her killer, I'm in. Besides, we find her murderer and we almost certainly solve our case too, right? It makes sense.'

He nodded, finishing the Kit Kat. The whistling in his ear had dropped to five or six. 'All right. The first thing we need to do is find out exactly who Wendy had communicated with over the last few days, follow the posts she made on the OnTarget forum, Twitter, et cetera. The problem is, Strong's team have her computer, and her phone was, presumably, taken by her murderer.'

'We don't need her computer to track her online activity. We only need her log-ins – her usernames and passwords. Did she give those to you?'

'Shit. No.'

'All right. Well, maybe we can figure it out.' She looked around and Patrick followed her gaze. The canteen was busy, dozens of potential witnesses, flapping ears and beady eyes. 'I'll meet you in the car park in five minutes. We'll go to mine.'

Carmella's flat was as immaculate and homely as Patrick had always imagined – the home of a couple who obviously had no children. Patrick took a seat at the small table in the living room where, he imagined, Carmella and Jenny ate dinner together while listening to tasteful music. He didn't imagine them as the types to scoff dinner in front of the TV with plates on their laps, and certainly not at a table with toddler-flung spaghetti shapes and sausages around their feet, CBeebies blaring in the background.

Carmella grabbed her laptop and sat down beside him. 'Jenny's at work. She just texted me to tell me she's got a raging hangover. Apparently, she, Gill and Suzanne's husband had a good chat after we left your party.'

'Oh God.'

Carmella chuckled. 'Don't worry. Nobody discussed how you've got the hots for the guv.'

'Carmella! I don't—'

She held up a hand. 'It's all right, Pat. I'm only teasing you. But you've gone very pink.'

He fixed his attention on the laptop screen. 'Can we concentrate on this?'

'Sure.' The smile slipped from her face and he felt yet another prick of guilt – a sensation he shook off as he watched Carmella type in the URL of the official OnTarget forum. Wendy had told Patrick she had spent most of her time on this site because, although there were plenty of others, this was the most active. Immediately, Patrick realised this was going to be like searching for the proverbial needle. There were thousands of posts, most of them seemingly nonsensical – a sea of acronyms and bouncing smileys.

'We need to know what her username was,' Carmella said. 'Otherwise we've got no chance of figuring out who she was chatting to.'

'I should have got her to tell me.'

'What about Strong's team? They must have figured it out already. Can't we ask them? We are meant to be working together, after all.'

Patrick shook his head. He knew that would be the sensible thing to do, but he was paranoid about Strong trying to take over the entire investigation, especially if he admitted to any weakness. That weakness being that, so far, they didn't have a bloody clue who had murdered Rose and Jess, despite having worked on this investigation for a week and a half.

'No. Let's try to figure it out ourselves first.'

She looked at him, then nodded. 'OK. We know Wendy went to the book signing at Waterstones – I saw her there – so maybe she was involved in one of the chats about that.'

Carmella typed 'waterstones' into the search box and two dozen forum topics appeared on screen. She sighed and began to click on each one in turn, skimming through the discussions about the event, from the build-up, with all the fizzing excitement about being in the same room as the OnT boys, through to the aftermath, with loads of links to photos of the signing, dozens of selfies with the pop stars behind a desk in the background. Patrick glanced over the photos to see if he could spot Wendy – he couldn't – but that wouldn't be helpful anyway.

'Look,' he pointed out. 'There's a number beneath each name stating how many posts they've made.'

Most of them numbered in the hundreds or thousands. Blake7 – 2,356 posts; CroydonChick – 1,398 posts; Jade – 18,467 posts.

'Good grief!' Patrick exclaimed. 'I wonder if I'd have used these forums if they'd been around when I was a teenager.'

'Yeah, in those days you had to use smoke signals, didn't you?'

Patrick smiled but wasn't in the mood for banter. 'Look, this one, ShawnsCupcake, has only posted seventy-four times.' He tapped the screen, indicating a message about the book signing: ShawnsCupcake asking who else was going to be there.

'Let's have a look at her profile,' Carmella said.

Clicking on the username took them to a new screen showing the profile of ShawnsCupcake. The profile picture was, like many of those on the forum, a photo of Shawn, giving nothing away about the real identity of the user. Again, Patrick wished dearly that he'd got more detail from Wendy about what she was doing. He hadn't realised there would be a time limit. But he still blamed himself, knew he wouldn't stop beating himself up about it until he'd found her murderer. And even then, he didn't know if he'd feel better. Because whatever happened, poor Wendy wasn't coming back. She would never achieve the potential he knew she'd had.

'ShawnsCupcake joined on the eleventh of February,' Carmella said, snapping him out of his reverie. 'Is that the date she started?'

Four days ago. 'Yes, that's right.'

The page linked to all of the discussions ShawnsCupcake had taken part in. The first was a joke about Shawn making her feel like a Haribo sweet.

'Does that sound like something Wendy would write?' Carmella asked.

'I think so.' He thought about the message in the Valentine's card. *You make me melt like chocolate.* Carmella didn't know about the card yet, but he bet it wouldn't be long before word got around the station.

'Look,' Carmella said. 'There's a discussion here about football – did you know that Carl from the band is rumoured to be buying his local team, Torquay United?'

In the discussion, most of the users were talking about how they were going to become Torquay fans, that they were going to start going to the matches, despite agreeing that most of them hated football.

ShawnsCupcake had written, *Not me! I'll be Wolves till I die. Even though I live down south in Kingston.* ☺.

Wolves. Wolverhampton Wanderers. Wendy's hometown team. And she'd lived in Kingston.

'It's definitely her,' Patrick said, sitting up straighter.

'Look at this. She started a thread about the murders: *I have a theory about what happened to them but I'm too scared to share it on here.* Fuck. Looks like she was trying to flush out anyone with information.'

'And it worked. Can we access her private messages?'

She gave him the look she used when he said something that made him sound like an old man. 'Not without her password.'

'Yeah, I knew that . . .'

'And we could sit here typing in educated guesses all day, but we're unlikely to get it right. This isn't one of those stupid films. We need to talk to Strong's team. They've got her computer – they're bound to have found all her log-ins.'

'And I'll ask Graham Burns. You know, the social media guy. He gave me the messages that Rose and Jess exchanged.'

Patrick stood up and walked away from the table, over towards the window. He looked down at the street, red buses gliding by, a cyclist weaving through the traffic.

'If it was you . . . if you were the person who'd killed Rose and Jess – assuming of course that you use the forums, which you probably do, to have found them – and you saw that, what would you do?' he asked. 'You'd want to know if this theory bore any relation to the truth.'

'Yes, and I'd private message her. Find out about this theory.'

Patrick stepped away from the window. 'The way Wendy was killed was completely different to Rose and Jess. Nancy Marr too. No sign of torture, just a swift . . . execution.' He winced, imagining the shock Wendy must have felt as the knife flashed in the darkness.

'He was trying to keep her quiet. Stop her exposing him.'

'Which suggests that Wendy actually did have a theory, and that it was close to the truth. Close enough to worry the killer, anyway. We really need to get into her private messages. Let me call Burns now.'

He had Burns's number stored on his phone. Burns picked up on the third ring and Patrick explained what he needed. 'All private messages sent and received by a user called ShawnsCupcake.'

Burns made a groaning noise. 'You know I could get in a lot of trouble for this . . .'

'A police officer was murdered and we believe it was by someone using your forum. Now, if you want the whole OnTarget website shut down, your computers impounded, while we—'

'OK, OK. I'll help.'

He ended the call and Carmella came over, touching his upper arm. 'Why don't you go home, get some rest? You look like you're about to collapse, Pat. I'll do it.'

'I don't—'

'Patrick. Boss. I insist. Go home; spend some time with Bonnie and Gill.'

As he was walking out to the car, his phone pinged. A message from Burns. That was quick.

Detective Lennon – I've found the messages . . . I'll copy everything into an email for you – give me an hour. GB.

As he put the car into gear and waited for a gap in the traffic, he had another idea. It was all very well searching the Internet for answers, but perhaps they would find the truth in the real world, where he felt most comfortable. The only problem was, to seek answers in the real world he was going to have to risk his career.

Chapter 37
Day 12 – Chloe

The roar of the engines inside the small twin-propeller plane was deafening. Chloe clung on to the wooden struts lining the interior as though at any moment she could be sucked out of the gaping opening through which the wind already howled and buffeted, trying to make itself heard over the wall of sound. She closed her eyes, as the too-big jumpsuit flapped around her legs and she already felt as though all the air had been squeezed out of her chest. Why the *fuck* had she agreed to this? Her dad's joking words from that morning came back to her:

'That would be a bit ironic, wouldn't it, love – you survive leukaemia, do a charity skydive, then peg it when your parachute doesn't—'

'*Dad!*' Chloe and Brandon had shrieked simultaneously, as her mum looked appalled.

'Sorry, love,' her dad had said, kissing her loudly on the cheek. 'It will be fine, I promise you. No-one's ever died doing a tandem skydive. I wouldn't have said it if they had. I wouldn't let you *do* it if they had.'

'You don't have to go through with it, you know, darling,' Chloe's mum had added anxiously. All four of them had been – as family tradition decreed – squeezed together in her parents' bed before breakfast, a heap of brightly coloured presents in front of the birthday girl. Her mum had already been in tears once, and kept hugging her. Her sixteenth birthday – a day that none of them had been sure would ever come, particularly not last year, when Chloe had been in a haze of morphine and terror, cursing her cancerous white blood cells and fully believing that she was going to die without ever even having a snog, let alone any sort of sexual experience.

'Of course I do!' Chloe had scoffed, although her heart was already thumping and they weren't due to leave the house for four hours. 'Can't back out now; I've raised seventeen hundred quid!'

How the hell would she feel once she was thirteen thousand feet in the sky? She'd tried to swallow the lump of fear lodged in her chest as she ripped the wrapping paper off a small present from her aunt and uncle, barely seeing the ugly necklace before putting it to one side. She had announced months ago she would do the parachute jump on her sixteenth birthday, when she'd been exhilarated with the news that her bone marrow transplant had been a success and she was on the road to recovery.

But in hindsight, it seemed like a stupid idea. A really, *really* stupid idea.

'Who's this one from?' She'd picked up a present that looked like a short length of piping, with no gift card attached.

Her parents had exchanged worried glances.

'What?'

Her mother had reached for her hand. 'We weren't sure whether to give it to you, love. It's from Jess. Angelica dropped it round yesterday saying that Jess bought it for you ages ago . . .'

Chloe's eyes had immediately flooded with tears. 'Oh my God.'

'Shall I take it away, darling?' Her mother had welled up again too.

Chloe'd shaken her head. Wiping her eyes, she'd ripped the paper off to reveal a cardboard tube. Popping the plastic top, she'd fished out its contents, giving a watery smile when she saw what it was.

'OnTarget tour poster. Cool. That's so nice of her . . . *was* so nice of her.' She'd dropped it on the bed and given a sob, covering her eyes with her forearm like the child she still felt she was.

Nine days had passed since Jess's death; six since Chloe had run away from the book signing. Looking on the OnT forums now, it was as if the murders had never happened. Everyone had moved on. And because it was too painful to think about, Chloe had – she admitted to herself with a prick of shame – tried to put it from her mind. It was the only way to cope. She needed to stop thinking about the connection between Rose and Jess (and Jade, and *her*) because she couldn't bear the shame and fear. She convinced herself that there couldn't possibly be a connection between what had happened last year and the murders. It was a crazy idea; a coincidence.

Now, in the plane, squashed together with six other terrified people plus six cool-as-cucumber instructors, Chloe was so focused on her fear of jumping that everything else felt unreal. But there was no going back now . . .

Or was there? Surely she could still say she'd changed her mind? Then Chloe thought, *Jess would have done this without wimping out.*

Chloe clearly wasn't the only one suffering from nerves. The boy next to her, who looked about nineteen, was so white he was almost yellow. She'd noticed him earlier when they were all sitting on the ground going through the landing procedure, when he'd still been looking cocky. He had a wiggly line shaved into his head, snaking all around the back and up over his other ear. You couldn't see it now because, like the rest of them, he was wearing a stupid-looking, tight-fitting helmet that looked more like a skullcap. He was kind of cute, actually – weirdly, cuter now that he looked as though he was about to either puke or pass out with fear.

She would never normally be brave enough to initiate a conversation with an older boy, but his terror suddenly reduced and compacted her own.

'Scary, isn't it?' she yelled towards him, and he made a face at her.

'To be honest, I'm shittin' meself!' he yelled back.

She moved closer to the boy's ear so she didn't have to yell so much. He smelt of sweaty fear and shower gel. 'You doing a charity jump too?'

He nodded. 'It's for the Tommy D Project. It's a foundation set up for teenagers who've lost a parent.' For a moment, the boy looked about five years old.

Chloe blushed with pity and embarrassment.

'What about you?' asked the boy, and she felt relief combined with guilt that she didn't actually have to enquire as to the details of his loss.

'I'm jumping for the Anthony Nolan Trust. I got a bone marrow transplant through them that saved my life.' Chloe thought she still couldn't say those words without sounding somehow smug.

'Cool,' said the boy, vaguely, as though he hadn't really heard.

'I had leukaemia.' She wasn't sure why she was pressing the point. Perhaps because she wanted him to know that she wouldn't jump out of a plane for any sort of trivial reason.

'Wow. That must have been . . . pretty shit.'

She nodded. 'It was. Apart from when Shawn Barrett came to visit me in hospital.'

'Who?'

Surely he couldn't be serious. 'Shawn from OnTarget?'

'Oh right – them. You don't like them, do you? They're for little kids.'

She blushed again. 'Well.' She could hardly believe the words she was about to say, especially as she realised that she meant them. 'I used to be really into them. Not so much now, though.'

Jess's face came into her head, her fervent passion for and utter loyalty to the band, and Chloe felt as though she had betrayed her. The tears that had never been far from the surface since the terrible news of Jess's death threatened again, but luckily – *if you could call it luck*, thought Chloe – her instructor tapped her on the shoulder and indicated that they should start the process of being clipped together. Her companion's instructor did the same.

'Oh gawd, it must be nearly time,' the boy shouted. He rattled at one of the big buckles on the straps that now held him to his jump partner. 'This will hold, man, won't it?' he called over his shoulder. The man behind him nodded reassuringly. *As if he'd say 'no'*, thought Chloe. She and the boy were now facing one another. 'What's your name?' she asked.

'Josh,' he said, grinning suddenly at her. He was even cuter when he smiled.

Impulsively, Chloe grabbed one of his hands. 'Good luck, Josh. See you back on the ground.'

'You too – er?'

'Chloe.'

'Yeah, you too, Chloe.'

At that moment, Chloe's phone vibrated against her hipbone. The phone was in the front pocket of her jeans, inside the massive blue romper suit they were all wearing. She knew she was supposed to have left it in the locker on the airfield with her other possessions, but she never went anywhere without her phone, so it was coming with her. *It's probably Mum, wishing me luck*, she thought as she managed to un-Velcro the lower part of the jumpsuit, fish out the iPhone and peer at the screen. She frowned in confusion as she glanced at the abbreviated message that appeared on her home screen:

Hey Chloe babe, it's Shawn here, how—

Before she could click on it to read the rest of it, her instructor tapped her shoulder again. 'We're up first – let's go!'

She hastily slid the phone back into her pocket and did up the jumpsuit with shaking hands, unable to process the words she'd seen. Her instructor guided her over to the wild blowing of the open door and she fixed the goggles firmly onto her face. Her breath was coming in great ragged gasps. No backing out now. Why did she have to be first?

The next few moments were a blur of wind and sound and adrenalin as they edged closer to the lip of the plane.

'Aaaand – GO!' yelled her instructor, and they were out before she could scream that she'd changed her mind, she wanted to be at home watching *TOWIE* in her bedroom; then they were whirling and falling into the great tumble dryer of sky and wisps of cloud and cold, cold air, up and down and round or maybe just down – she couldn't tell until she opened her eyes, then shut them again fast as they plummeted, her scream ripped out of her.

Thirty seconds later she felt a colossal jerking sensation, like being snatched upwards by a giant hand, and a huge whoosh as the parachute – thank God, thank God – opened and ballooned above them. *I'm alive*, she thought, spreading her arms wide and screaming with relief and exhilaration. *I survived!*

It was only then, in the stillness and utter calm of the descent, patchwork fields spread out beneath her, that she had another thought: *OMG, did I really just get a text from Shawn Barrett?*

Chapter 38
Day 12 – Patrick

Gill looked askance at Pat as he laced up his ancient grey Vans, the ones he usually only ever wore to do DIY or gardening in. The left one had a large dark stain on the top, where Bonnie had vomited Ribena on it some months ago.

'You're even more stubbly than usual – aren't you going to work today?'

'Of course. But I don't want anyone to know I'm at work,' he replied, raising his voice to be heard over Bonnie singing 'Let It Go', off-key, along with the DVD.

'They'll never recognise you with those shoes on,' Gill commented sarcastically.

'I'm not going to the incident room yet – I'm going back to the Rotunda first. I just can't believe that those clowns haven't managed to uncover anything at all. They've been door to door round the flats above the car park. They've been all over the Rotunda for two days now – nothing. It's ridiculous – someone must have seen something!'

Gill put a hand on his arm. 'Um . . . far be it for me to tell you how to do your job – but shouldn't you leave that to the other team?'

Pat straightened up and scowled. 'But they clearly aren't doing their job, are they? I owe it to Wendy.'

He'd called Carmella as soon as he woke up. She hadn't been able to find anything useful on the OnTarget forum yet. No strange gaps in conversations, no signs that someone had been through and deleted evidence that they'd chatted with Wendy.

'I didn't realise you were that close to her,' Gill said.

'I wasn't.' He hadn't told Gill about the Valentine's card. He was going to, but didn't know how she'd react. Would she be suspicious, think he'd led Wendy on? In the end, he'd decided not to risk it. 'But she was part of my team. And I told you about the phone call . . . I fucked up, Gill. I need to make amends.'

'As long as you don't do anything that could potentially harm your career.'

'Especially now mine's the only income we have?'

She flinched like he'd slapped her and he instantly regretted his words. How easily his resentment bubbled to the surface. He and Gill needed to talk . . . about everything. But now wasn't the time.

'I'm sorry, I didn't mean . . .'

'It's fine. I'll be back at work soon anyway.'

'I know. I have to go,' he said, gathering Bonnie up in his arms, tipping her upside down and kissing the soft podgy underside of her chin until she squirmed and giggled. 'Bye, then, monster. Be good for Mummy.'

Then he kissed Gill politely on the cheek – 'Bye, Gill. Text you later' – and let himself out of the house before he could see the expression of disappointment that he instinctively knew was on her face.

The private messages that Graham Burns had emailed Patrick – which he'd forwarded on to DCI Strong, explaining they came through a contact on Operation Urchin – had confirmed to Patrick what he suspected. Wendy had gone to the Rotunda to meet someone who'd contacted her on the OnT forum: a user called

Mockingjay365. The 365, Patrick guessed, was a reference to the OnTarget song, and the room in which Rose was murdered.

Frustratingly, Burns had only been able to find Wendy's side of the conversation. Mockingjay365 had deleted his own messages; indeed, he had deleted his entire account.

'It was set up using an anonymous Gmail account,' Burns explained. 'No real name given. I knew you would ask me about the IP address, so I already looked it up. It was set up in an Internet café in Soho.'

Patrick knew DCI Strong would ask one of her team to visit this café, but had little hope it would lead anywhere. Which was why he was doing this. Risking the fury of both DCIs: Laughland and Strong. But he didn't care. If he found Wendy's murderer, it would all be worth it.

The basement bowlplex at the Rotunda was swarming with teen-agers even though it wasn't yet noon. Patrick was momentarily perplexed by this, until he remembered it was half-term. A short, barrel-shaped security guard leaned on the railing halfway up the curving staircase leading back to the ground floor, looking as though he'd been standing there for about a week. Patrick stood next to him in silence for a moment or two, both of them surveying the alleys and café below, until the man spoke.

'Looking for someone?'

Patrick arranged his features into a sorrowful, bitter expression – without much difficulty, he realised. It was pretty much his default expression these days. But the bouncer wasn't looking at him anyway.

'Kind of.' He tried to emulate the cadences of Wendy's Black Country accent, just slightly, hoping that he didn't sound like he was channelling Noddy Holder.

The bouncer grunted uninterestedly. 'You ain't a journalist, are you?'

'No. No way.' He paused. Lying did not come naturally to him, never had – but this was for Wendy. 'I need to talk to someone about what happened in the car park round the back . . .'

The guard rolled his eyes. Patrick noticed that the man's stubble, crew cut, uniform and skin tone all seemed the same shade of grey. Perhaps it was the lighting. 'If you're a journalist, mate, you can sling your hook right now. I got a job to do here.'

'I'm not, mate, honest. Thing is – that cop – she was my sister. Wendy. My kid sister . . .'

That got his attention. For the first time he looked sharply at Patrick, taking in his stained Vans and stubble, and the beginnings of the tears that Pat found no difficulty in summoning. 'Oh. Right. Um . . . sorry to hear it. My condolences.'

Patrick scrubbed his sleeve across his face. 'Thanks,' he said in a cracked voice. 'I heard she was in here before it happened. Meeting someone, but I don't know who. The fucking police don't have a clue and I can't sit at home another day waiting for them to update me when they can't seem to pull their fingers out. I mean, someone must've seen something!'

'I feel for you . . . cock,' said the guard. Two teenage boys loped down the stairs, one of them with his arm inside the front of his jacket. '*Oi! You!* No alcohol brought in, you know the rules. Give it here!'

The boy scowled and withdrew his arm to reveal the two open beer bottles he had hidden, which he handed reluctantly over.

'If I catch you smuggling booze in one more time, you're barred, you little toerag,' the guard said.

Patrick watched the boys sulkily march down to the bowling lanes minus their contraband. 'So, were you here that night?' he asked the guard, who shook his head.

'Nah, mate. Day off. Came in yesterday morning, all bleeding hell had broke loose. Manager handing over the CCTV. Cops interviewing all the staff.'

'What about kids like those two?' Patrick jerked his head down the stairs. 'Obviously regulars, aren't they?'

The guard leaned his elbows on the rail again and gestured down. 'Cops identified one or two from the CCTV who were here when your sister come in. They've had a chat, apparently, but no-one had seen her before. Them two weren't here at the time.'

'Mind if I have a word?'

'With them? Good luck to you. They're so thick they probably don't even know their own names.'

'Could you, er, introduce me?'

Patrick had decided in advance this was the necessary level of obsequiousness. He didn't want to plough in, in case the guard or the boys realised he was a cop – 'the feds', as kids called them these days. The feds! Like they lived in downtown Detroit, not suburban south-west London . . .

The guard appraised him, then shrugged. 'If you want.' They walked down the stairs together and over to the café area, where the two boys were examining a notice on the wall, which was advertising for part-time staff here at the Rotunda. They turned and looked up suspiciously at Patrick and the guard. The taller of the two held up his hands.

'We don't want no trouble. We're just hanging out. Thinking of applying for a job here, actually.'

The guard rolled his eyes. 'Good luck with that. This gentleman here wants a word. Show me you're not both a waste of space and I might put in a word for you.'

A small, fascinated gaggle of teens had formed around them, bowling and flirting temporarily forgotten.

'This is the brother of that cop that got murdered. So do something useful for once in your lives, and help him out, eh?'

Six or seven faces gaped in fascination and horror at their proximity to tragedy.

The taller of the two boys scrunched his nose like he'd smelled something nasty. 'She was a fed. Why should we help someone catch the killer of a fucking cop?'

It took all Patrick's willpower not to grab the kid by the front of his jacket and shove him against the wall.

'Listen,' he said, addressing the boy. 'I'm not a huge fan of the police either. But Wendy wasn't just a fed, as you call them. She was a human being. She was my sister.'

He glanced around, to make sure that none of his Met colleagues were in the bowlplex, before nodding gravely.

The group of teenagers stared at him, the tall boy hanging his head, one of the girls – a very pretty blonde with a nose stud, crop top and double-denim – punching the tall one on the shoulder and hissing, 'You twat.'

'So – were any of you here the night it happened, last Saturday?' Patrick asked. 'This is Wendy. Ever seen her in here?' He took out his wallet and showed them a photo he'd printed off from Wendy's Facebook page that morning – Wendy astride a pony, looking about twelve even though the photograph's caption had been 'On Holiday in the New Forest 2013'.

'Ahhhh,' sympathised an overweight girl whose bare muffin-top oozed over the waistband of her tight stonewash jeans, a silver belly bar almost completely hidden in the overhang. 'She was ever so pretty.'

'It didn't happen in here, did it?' the girl who'd punched the fed-hater asked. 'My mum and dad won't ever let me come here again if it did.'

'No. It was round the back, opposite the bus station. But she was in here first to meet someone, so I want to know if she went there with them, or someone followed her?'

Blank faces all round.

'Did any of you see her?'

They all shook their heads.

'OK. If you weren't here on Saturday, then you probably wouldn't have. I don't think she'd been here before. How about anyone else, your mates, who might have been? That guy' – he pointed at the guard, who had drifted back to his vantage point halfway up the stairs – 'says that you all hang out here every weekend. Why weren't you here on Saturday?'

'We were,' chimed the prettier girl. 'But the cops told us she – your sister – come in about 9.15 and we've usually gone home by then. Hardly any buses after half nine out towards Molesey.'

This was where Patrick and Gill lived, and he knew this to be true. 'Do you all live on the 411 route, though? What about people who don't – do they ever stay longer?'

The group all looked at one another, then the mixed-race boy said, 'Well, yeah – the Feltham kids do, 'cos they can get the train back.'

'Who are the Feltham kids?' Patrick was dying to get his Moleskine out of his pocket.

The boy made a face. 'We don't like them. They only come here 'cos they got barred from Cineworld in Feltham.'

'Really? Were any of them here when you left on Saturday?'

The blonde girl shook her head, making her poker-straight hair whip across into the eyes of her tubby mate, who jerked back.

'Emily! That went in my eye!' The two giggled self-consciously, then rearranged their faces back into sympathetic expressions.

Emily nudged her friend. 'Wait – didn't Foxy pull on Saturday? She was snogging the face off that chav from the Kennedy, remember?'

'She left at the same time as we did, with him, didn't she, so she wouldn't have seen anything.'

The boys had started to lose interest and drift away back to their table in the café area, but it was the two girls that Patrick felt a spark of hope from.

'Foxy? Who's she?'

Emily shrugged. 'Dunno. She's always here, but we don't know her real name. She knows all the Feltham boys, so I reckon she lives over that way, or goes to their school. I only know her 'cos she lent me her mascara in the bogs once.'

'And she left with a boy around the same time as you did? I don't suppose you've got her number, do you?'

To Pat's disappointment they both shook their heads again. Anyway, he thought, it was probably nothing. There must have been loads of kids who were around that night and hadn't seen anything.

'Can I give you my number? Just in case you think of anyone else, or if Foxy shows up.'

Emily looked puzzled, as if something had just occurred to her. 'Yeah, that's weird actually.' She pointed at the poster advertising the part-time jobs. 'I thought she had an interview here today for one of them jobs. I'm sure that's what she told me.'

Hope flared again in Patrick's chest, stronger this time. He scribbled his number on the back of a sandwich receipt he found in his pocket and handed it to Emily. 'Please? I'm counting on you. I've got to find the scum who did this to Wen— my kid sister.' He made his eyes go round and watery, and was rewarded by the two girls' own eyes filling up. 'You've been really kind. Thanks so much for your time.'

Right, he thought, as he strode away, thanking the security guard on his way out. *Next stop: Tenpin Bowling's HR department.*

Chapter 39
Day 12 – Winkler

Winkler was parked outside a coffee shop on Goswell Road, with a view of the cul-de-sac on which Mervyn Hammond's office was based. He had sent Gareth to check that Hammond's Jag was there and to confirm there was only one way out of the little street. Winkler wasn't going to risk getting stuck in traffic again – he had woken up in a cold sweat last night, remembering the moment he'd stalled and everyone had started beeping at him – much smarter to wait here. Unless Hammond had a car that could transform into a helicopter, or access to a secret network of subterranean tunnels, he would have to drive past this spot.

Gareth opened the door and squeezed through the gap, being careful not to spill the coffee. Winkler took his cup and sniffed it.

'It's organic, right? Did you ask?'

'Yes. Specially imported from Guatemala. Grown by peasants. Fair trade, organic and decaffeinated.'

'Good.' This area was full of hipsters. Usually, the hairy bastards made Winkler wish they'd bring back National Service, but he could just about forgive them if it meant he could get a decent cup of something that wasn't going to poison his perfect body.

'I don't see the point of decaf coffee,' Gareth said. 'It's like—'

'A woman without a vagina?' Winkler suggested.

Gareth spat out his caramel macchiato and Winkler laughed. Over the last few days he'd found something he enjoyed even more than winding Lennon up: making outrageous statements that made politically correct DS Batey shudder and squirm.

'You know the old joke about why a woman has legs?' Winkler began. 'So she can get—'

'There he is,' Gareth said, clearly relieved that he wasn't going to have to suffer the punchline.

Hammond's silver Jag glided out of the side street and Winkler could almost hear the engine purr as it crossed the road and joined the slow-moving traffic, heading towards the crossroad.

'Right. Here we go.'

Hammond headed past the Barbican towards the Museum of London. Winkler stayed two cars back, and could see that, again, Hammond wasn't driving. It was his bodyguard, Kerry Mangan. Winkler had run a background check on Mangan already – he was thirty-eight; born and bred in Tottenham; joined the army in 1992 when he was sixteen, serving in Bosnia. He was discharged from the army after five years, though Winkler hadn't been able to find out the reason for this discharge. After leaving the army he'd worked as a nightclub bouncer for a few years before getting a job as a bodyguard – or personal security, to give the role its proper title. Mangan had left the security company that employed him five years ago to work for Mervyn Hammond's PR agency. Since then he'd been like Mervyn's shadow, and could be seen beside the PR man in most photographs of Hammond in the press, standing beside or just behind him.

Winkler wondered why Hammond felt the need to have a bodyguard. Had he received threats? Was he paranoid because of the number of people he upset with the stories he fed to the press?

Or was there a more shadowy reason? Whatever, Winkler bet that Mangan knew all of Hammond's dirty little secrets.

The Jag reached the river and turned right, driving west through town. Once they got to Hammersmith, Winkler realised they were heading towards his and Gareth's patch, past Chiswick and out on the A316.

By the time they reached Richmond it was growing dark and rush hour was beginning, the roads becoming more choked with traffic, Hammond's Jag just visible ahead, though a bus had pushed in between it and Winkler's Audi.

'Where the fuck are they going?' Winkler asked.

A few minutes later Mangan took a right at a roundabout signposted Isleworth, almost catching Winkler off guard. He turned left and saw the Jag just up ahead, following it through a series of left and right turns until, suddenly, the Jag pulled up and drove between two pillars onto the forecourt of a large white building.

Winkler pulled up in a parking space on the street and turned the car lights off.

It was a shabby-looking street, comprising mostly terraces, apart from this building. The streetlamp outside was broken, so he couldn't make out the lettering on the sign attached to the white building's front wall. He cracked the window a little, letting in freezing air, and waited till he heard Hammond's car doors shut. This was followed by men's voices, and the faint thud of a front door closing.

He got out of his car and examined the sign: 'St Mary's Children's Home.'

He lifted his head slowly to look up at the building, most of the windows illuminated, a dark figure drawing a pair of curtains as Winkler watched. Ice and heat – horror and anger – competed for supremacy in his veins. Only last week Winkler had watched a documentary about the systematic abuse of hundreds of kids in children's homes in North Wales. And many of the girls forced into prostitution, raped and abused by gangs of men in Rochdale and Rotherham, two other big news stories, had been in the care system.

Winkler thought back to his own childhood. There had been a children's home near his primary school – Winkler's mum was always telling him she'd send him to live there if he didn't behave – and several of the kids from the home had been in Winkler's class. One of the boys, a kid called Michael, had gone berserk one day, shitting his pants and wiping it on the walls, sticking a turd underneath a girl's desk. Michael always had brown stuff caked on his fingers and the other kids, including Winkler, would tease him mercilessly, though Michael was a fighter, could handle himself. Winkler's mum told him he should stay away from the boy. Thinking back now, it seemed highly likely that Michael must have been a victim of abuse.

He stalked back to the car and jumped into his seat.

'It's a children's home,' he said.

Gareth's eyes widened. 'What's Hammond doing here?'

Winkler picked up the coffee they'd bought back on Goswell Road. It was almost completely cold, but he needed something to take the bad taste out of his mouth.

'These places are like honeypots for paedophiles and child abusers,' he said.

Gareth's eyes grew even wider. 'I don't think—'

'Yeah, yeah, I know. I'm sure most of them are run by well-meaning do-gooders. But you watch the news, don't you? Every other story in the papers over the last few years has been about some child abuse scandal, from Jimmy Savile to Rochdale. They're nearly always centred on some place where kids are easy to get at: hospitals, youth clubs, care homes. Places like this.'

'But the two victims – Rose and Jess – lived at home with their families,' Gareth said, wincing. 'They didn't have any connection to the kind of places you just listed.'

'It doesn't matter,' Winkler insisted. 'Hammond is the only link between the murders of Rose, Jess and Nancy Marr. He has access to teenage girls through his work. He's never married, never had any kids of his own. He drives around with some shifty bloke who got kicked out of the army for some reason we don't know about. And now we see him visiting a children's home miles away from where he lives and works, after dark. I bet he treats this place like a drive-through McDonald's.'

Gareth looked like he was going to be sick.

'So what do you want to do now? Go in, see if we can catch him with his . . . with his pants down?'

Winkler thought about it. 'No, if we could sneak in through a window, surprise him . . . But that's not going to happen. I bet you he'll have an excuse for coming here. "Market research" or something,' he said, waggling his forefingers in quote marks. 'Wait here.'

He got out of the car and jogged into the forecourt of St Mary's, then took a couple of snaps of Hammond's car on his phone, making sure the building was clearly visible in the background.

Before getting back in the Audi and driving away, he looked up at the closed curtains and felt the bile rise in his throat as he imagined what might be going on behind them. He made a silent vow.

Hammond was going to spend the rest of his life shivering in a cell, fearing for his arse and his life. But first Winkler needed some evidence.

Either that or a confession.

Chapter 40
Day 13 – Patrick

Patrick was back in his car, sitting in the station car park yet again while he called Tenpin's head office. He didn't want anyone overhearing and asking why he was ringing them when he ought to be concentrating on Rose and Jessica. He was also taking the opportunity to charge up his e-cigarette in the car's phone charger – it had run out after only two puffs that morning, and he was dying for a nicotine fix.

After a twenty-minute wait while the director of HR tracked down all the CVs received for the current job advertised at the Kingston Rotunda, Patrick had the address of a girl with the incongruously glamorous name Chelsea Fox. He was sure she was the one he needed to talk to. Not only had she not showed up to her interview the previous day, with no reason given, but the scan of her application form said under Additional Comments:

I know Tenpin in the Rotunda really really well its my faverite place to hang out with my mates so I would totally love to work there and you wouldn't even need to show me around there ☺

Tutting at the misspelling and inappropriate font, he jotted down the address at the top of her meagre CV – it was indeed the Kennedy Estate – and rang the mobile number. Somewhat to his surprise, Chelsea answered on the first ring.

'Yeah?'

'Chelsea Fox?'

'Yeah. Who is it?'

Patrick cleared his throat. 'Ah, hello, Miss Fox. My name is . . .' He looked around the car park for inspiration, his eyes lighting on Winkler's flash car. '. . . Adrian Wilson, assistant director of HR at Tenpin Leisure Group. I'm just ringing to ask if there was some kind of mix-up regarding your interview yesterday, since we didn't hear from you – we were expecting you in our Kingston office at 2.30 p.m.'

There was a brief silence, then a feeble, artificial-sounding cough. 'Oh yeah, I'm ever so sorry, I was ill, I've got the flu, and my phone had run out of credit, so I couldn't let you know, I was going to email, but I felt too ill, I've been off school and everything . . .'

Patrick decided not to point out that it was half-term.

'Please don't worry, Miss Fox. Are you still too unwell to come in for an interview, if we reschedule for tomorrow?'

More fake coughing. 'Yeah, sorry.'

'Well, not to worry. We'll be in touch if another suitable vacancy arises. I take it you're at home tucked up in bed and keeping warm?'

'Yeah,' she said feebly.

Patrick wished her well – the flaky little mare – terminated the call and switched on the car engine. He very much doubted he'd find her tucked up in bed smelling of Vicks VapoRub, but hopefully she was at least telling the truth when she said she was currently at home.

Twenty minutes later, he was suppressing a brief shudder as the familiar towers of the Kennedy Estate rose above him. He hadn't set foot on it for over a year, since he and Carmella had tracked down two other wayward teenagers who had run away and hidden here.

His professional life seemed full of recalcitrant teens, he reflected as he got out of the car. He made a vow to do everything in his power to keep Bonnie on the straight and narrow once she hit puberty – although with her start in life, who could blame her if she did go off the rails? He was dreading the point, surely not too many years away, when she would find out that her mother had tried to kill her when she was a baby. He and Gill would have to tell her first, to prevent her from stumbling across it online or being told by a ghoulish classmate.

Then he wondered if he and Gill would even still be together in a few years' time to have that conversation. It took several deep drags on his now-charged e-cig to help shift the thought as he headed for Block B.

The estate was actually looking a lot better than it had last year. It had clearly been given, if not a makeover, a bit of much-needed TLC. There were new little shrubs dotted about the grounds, and the doors had all been painted a kind of dull green, the same shade that Patrick used to paint his Airfix models.

'Olive Drab,' he said out loud, putting the e-cig in his coat pocket.

The lobby no longer stank of piss either, which was a pleasant surprise. He pressed the door buzzer of Chelsea Fox's ground-floor flat and waited. Nobody came, but he thought he heard a movement inside, so he buzzed again.

Eventually a bolt shot back and the door opened a tiny crack. Even though it was fairly obvious that Foxy's name was a derivative of her surname, Patrick had still made a mental assumption that the girl would be sharp-faced and ginger-haired, so he couldn't help but feel surprised when instead the face, from the small portion of it he could see, belonged to a very pretty black teenager.

'Chelsea Fox?' he asked doubtfully, holding out his ID badge.

The eye widened in the gap.

'Is your mum or dad in? My name is Patrick Lennon, I'm a police officer. Nothing to worry about at all, but I just need to ask you a few questions. May I come in?'

'I live with my nan.'

'Well, is she in, then?'

'I can't let you in. She'd kill me if she knew you were here!'

Patrick moved slightly closer to the door. 'Chelsea, please. I think you can help me. You haven't done anything, so there's nothing to worry about.'

The eye filled with tears and the door shut in his face. He felt a small thrill of excitement, the knowledge that this almost certainly wasn't a wild goose chase. She knew something.

He buzzed again, and called through the door. 'Chelsea. If you don't let me in now, I'm going to have to stand out here till your nan gets back, and then she'll definitely know I was here. Come on. I just need a few minutes of your time.'

The door opened again, slightly wider but on a chain.

'You don't look like a cop.'

He held his badge closer to the crack. 'A few minutes,' he repeated, and finally Chelsea let him in.

They stood in the narrow hallway and Patrick took in the girl standing next to him. She had a sweet face, huge brown eyes under a wide forehead, although her cheeks were spotty and she had the puppy fat of a twelve-year-old. Anyone less like a 'Foxy' he couldn't imagine.

'Is there somewhere we can sit down?' he asked, and she led him through to a small living room, claustrophobically warm. Two plump black cats sat curled up, one at each end of a much-clawed sofa, like two cushions. Cat hair covered every surface, making Pat want to sneeze, but apart from that the room was immaculately tidy. There was a door off either side of the room – one open and one closed – and through the open one Patrick saw a familiar sight: the four chis-elled youths from OnTarget staring at him from a poster on the wall. *Could mean nothing at all*, he thought. *Most teens have at least one.*

'Just you and your nan, is it?' He settled himself in a large flow-ery armchair next to the television, and Chelsea plonked herself reluctantly in between the two cats. She nodded miserably, her eyes flicking to a photograph on the mantelpiece above the gas fire. It was of a beaming couple in swimsuits holding hands on a beach. The woman was curvy and gorgeous, and Patrick found himself hoping that this was how Chelsea – 'Foxy' – would one day look, once she grew out of the acne and awkwardness. 'Your mum and dad?'

'They were killed two days after that photo was taken. Boating accident in Jamaica when they went home to visit my dad's mum.'

'I'm so sorry. How old were you?'

'Four. Been living here ever since.'

Poor kid, thought Patrick. *What people go through.* He took out his Moleskine. 'I understand you didn't turn up for a job interview you were supposed to have yesterday at the bowling alley in Kings-ton? Would you mind telling me why not?'

Chelsea immediately looked away, her mouth twisting in shock. 'Is that why you're here?' she said, stroking one of the cats so hard that it wriggled away and stalked off into her bedroom. 'It's only a poxy Saturday job! I was ill.'

'What's wrong?' Patrick asked kindly. 'Are you better now?' He waited for the fake cough again, but Chelsea just stared at the carpet.

'Chelsea?'

'Women's troubles,' she said stubbornly.

'Shame. That would've been a nice job for you, wouldn't it? I hear that you hang out at the Rotunda a lot anyway?'

'How do you know?'

They seemed to be playing a game of Question Tennis, he thought, batting them back and forth without many answers.

'I've been asking around, trying to find out who was there on Saturday night when Wendy was killed. She was a colleague of mine. You heard about it, right?'

Tears welled in Chelsea's eyes again.

'You were there that night, weren't you, Chelsea?' he prompted gently. 'Some of your friends said you were. They said you left with a boy.'

Chelsea sank her head into her hands. She seemed to have lost the ability to speak.

'Was that your boyfriend?'

'I'm not allowed boyfriends,' she whispered, pulling her sleeve down over her hand and wiping her eyes with it.

'Really? But you're sixteen, aren't you?'

She nodded. 'Almost seventeen. In April.'

'That doesn't seem too young to have a boyfriend.'

'My nan says I am. She says I'm not allowed until I finish A levels in case it interferes with my schoolwork . . . What's the time?'

Her eyes were fearfully darting towards the door.

Patrick pulled out his phone and looked at the screen. 'Ten past two.'

'Oh my days.' She jumped up and ran over to the window. 'She'll be back at quarter to three! You can't be here!'

'Chelsea, that's over half an hour away. Please don't worry.' *Bloody hell*, Patrick thought. *She's petrified of her.* 'Come on, sit down. Why are you so scared of your nan coming back?'

She started to cry in earnest this time. 'I want to help, I do, but I wasn't supposed to be there, and if she finds out about the car park, then she'll kick me out like she did before and I'll have to go into one of them homeless shelters and it'll be even worse than living here with her, otherwise I'd have gone myself ages ago—'

Patrick straightened up, every hair on his body standing to attention. 'The car park? Chelsea, what do you know about the car park? Tell me!'

The girl was almost hysterical. Patrick got up and found a plastic beaker upturned on the draining board in the kitchen. He filled it with water and took it in to her, with a clean tissue from his pocket.

Crouching down next to her, he handed her the water and the tissue.

'You were there, weren't you? In the car park? Is that why you didn't go to your interview yesterday, because you were too scared by what you saw?'

'What if she finds out?' the girl wailed.

'Were you doing something you shouldn't have been doing? Drugs? I don't care if you were.'

'NO! I don't do that shit.' Her outrage seemed to help her gather herself. She sniffed mightily, then dabbed under her eyes with the tissue – although, Patrick thought, she'd have been a lot better off wiping her runny nose. Something clicked into place.

'You were with that boy, weren't you? It's OK,' he reiterated. 'You aren't in trouble, not with us. We just need to know.'

'Nan will kill me!'

Patrick knelt beside her, his knees cracking loudly. 'She won't need to know. You're sixteen. It's confidential, I promise you.' Especially because he wasn't here officially, though Chelsea didn't need to know that.

She looked up at him then, her face a pulpy mess of snot, smeared make-up and tears.

'I saw it happen,' she whispered.

Patrick stopped breathing altogether. The only sound in the room was the gentle purring of the cat.

'Go on.'

'Me and – do I have to give his name? I don't want to.'

The boy's name would be useful. Another potential witness. But he knew if he insisted Chelsea would clam up again. 'That's OK – you and the boy, you were there . . . where?'

'In the corner of the car park, although he'd gone by then. I just needed a minute to . . . get myself together again. It was dark in that corner and nobody else was there, not when we arrived. We just wanted to be on our own. We, er, you know . . .' Chelsea's voice was strangled with embarrassment.

'Were having sex?'

She nodded, mortified. 'Promise you won't tell Nan!'

'I won't. It doesn't matter. All that matters is what you saw.'

She took a sip of the water, her hand shaking. 'We, um, did it, quite fast, then he had to go otherwise he'd miss his bus.' Patrick had a flash of Bonnie telling this sordid tale in a decade and a half and shuddered. 'I didn't want to run with him, I hate running, so I told him to go without me. Anyway I was a bit – emotional. It was my first time. It wasn't how I thought it would be.'

Poor kid, Patrick thought again. Her first experience of sex was a shag in a freezing dark car park, the experience topped off by her partner legging it and leaving her to witness a murder. *Wendy's* murder.

'I was about to leave and then I saw this girl come in – well, I thought she was a girl, I didn't know then that she was a cop. She looked well young, too young to drive, so I thought it was weird she was there. She walked over to the far side – it was dark over there too, the lights were out – and next thing this man comes running in and they didn't even speak or anything, he just stabs her and runs away and she's lying on the floor and there's blood everywhere and I sort of run over and her eyes were open, but then they closed and I could see that she was gone and I did mean to call 999, honest I did, but my phone was dead and I was really scared and I felt sick, so I—'

She collapsed into fresh sobs.

'Ran away?' Patrick supplied. He was feeling a bit emotional himself, at the knowledge that he was talking to the last person who had ever seen Wendy alive.

'I ran away and went home and heard it on the news and haven't been out since. I never want to go there again. I never want to see Josh again – not that he's called me anyway. He was only after a shag . . . Nan doesn't know I go out at night. She cleans in a hotel every weekend till 11 p.m. I'm supposed to be here. I thought if I got a job at the Rotunda, then I'd still be able to hang out there and see my mates, but I don't want it now . . .'

Josh. So that was his name, thought Patrick. They'd need to speak to him too, although it sounded like he had gone before either Wendy or her assailant arrived. Chelsea was still gabbling, so he put a hand on her arm to stop her.

'Chelsea, this is the most important bit: what did he look like, the man who stabbed her? Did you recognise him, from the bowling alley, maybe?'

Shoulders heaving, she puffed out her cheeks and squinched her eyes closed. Then she shook her head.

'He was tallish. Medium size. White. Brown or black short hair. That's all I can remember.'

'Age?'

She shrugged. 'Couldn't tell. He had a big coat on.'

'What sort of coat?'

Another shrug, then another panicked glance at the door. Patrick stood up. He knew he couldn't push her too much when she was this anxious. He also knew that, now Chelsea had revealed how much she'd seen, there was no way he could keep this from Strong and her team. He was going to be in deep shit for coming here, but right now he didn't care.

'OK. I don't want to get you into trouble, so I'm going to go now. Chelsea, thank you, I can't tell you how helpful you're being.

I'm going to need you to phone the police station in Wimbledon and ask to speak to someone called DCI Vanessa Strong. She's heading up the investigation into Wendy's death and this is vital information. Your nan need not know, I promise.'

'Will I have to go to court?'

Patrick hesitated. 'You might. But not for ages, and we can hide your identity. We have to catch this guy, Chelsea, before he does it to someone else.'

She nodded reluctantly. 'I knew I'd have to tell someone eventually,' she said. Now the storm was over, she seemed almost relieved.

'It was a horrible thing to have witnessed. We can put you in touch with Victim Support, get you some counselling,' he said, standing up to leave. He scribbled the MIT's main number onto the back of one of his business cards and handed it to her. 'Promise me you'll call DCI Strong?'

'Yeah,' she said. 'I will.'

Just as they were leaving the sitting room, his eye caught the OnTarget poster again.

'You're a fan of OnT?'

Chelsea made a face. 'I used to be, I guess. Not so much now.'

'Not so keen on their latest albums?'

'I don't listen to their albums, never have.'

Patrick raised his eyebrows. 'No? Why do you like them, then, because they're . . . ?' He had to think about whether to say 'cute' or 'hot', and it came out as a mixture of both: 'cot'. He covered it up as best he could, but she gave a tiny smile. She was pretty when she smiled.

'I like reading the OnT fanfic on StoryPad. I write a lot of it, but I haven't had the nerve to put any of it on there yet.'

StoryPad. It rang a bell with Patrick – who was it at the station who had been talking about that site? It was Martin, he thought, in one of the early briefings following Rose's murder.

A thought occurred to him, although it seemed like clutching at straws. 'Do you ever go on the OnTarget forums?'

She opened the front door, peering swiftly out into the corridor to make sure her nan wasn't coming. 'Nah. Had a look, but they're all really cliquey and bitchy. Not my scene. But I like the stories.'

'When you had a look, I don't suppose you came across two girls called MissTargetHeart or YOLOSWAG?'

Chelsea frowned. 'Don't remember them from the forums, but it kind of rings a bell . . . oh, I know! I'm sure I read a story by them. Yeah, that's it! There was this really good story that got thousands of votes, written by them, I'm sure.' Her face brightened at the knowledge that she was being helpful. *Sweet girl*, Patrick thought, feeling sorry for her again.

'Thousands of votes?'

'On StoryPad.' She seemed to stop herself from adding *Duh!* 'People vote for the best stories. I remember it 'cos it was written by a group of users, which is, like, quite unusual. There was MissTargetHeart, YOLOSWAG and two others, I think. I thought it was ever so good . . . but what's that got to do with what I saw?'

Patrick did up the zip on his coat and stepped out of the flat, turning to face her. 'I don't know. Nothing, possibly. Or everything.'

Thanking her again, and resisting the urge to give her a kiss on her plump cheek, Patrick walked away, his head full of all the new information he had received. The two teenage murder victims had collaborated on a piece of writing. Finally, a firm link between them.

But who were the other authors of that story?

And were they in danger too?

Chapter 41
Day 13 – Kai

Kai regarded Jade, who was leaning her forehead against the industrial-sized drinks fridge in Mervyn Hammond's kitchen to try to cool down. She looked unbelievably hot – in both senses – in the tight black skirt, white blouse and weird little frilly white thing on her head that the temp agency had made her wear for the occasion. Her hair was scraped back off her face and she had not, to her rage, been allowed to wear more than the bare minimum of make-up.

They were both taking advantage of the fact that the chef – a scary-looking tattooed geezer – had gone for a ten-minute break and Mervyn's housekeeper, an excitable Thai woman, was AWOL too.

'It's not fair!' Jade grumbled. 'Why should that tall slag get to serve OnT's drinks, when *I* want to!'

She was referring to the fact that their agency boss had reiterated, in no uncertain terms, that Jade, Kai and the other temp staff were not permitted to talk to or even look at the boys in OnT, who had their own private waitress – an incredible-looking six-foot Somalian girl with skin like milk chocolate who was gliding around them smiling serenely and discreetly, waiting on them hand and foot. Jade was only allowed to serve the lesser mortals, and Kai only allowed to collect and wash the glasses.

'Babe, you're in the same frickin' *room* as them! Ain't that enough? And all them other slebs – did you see him off *Match of the Day* in there, talking to whatserface from *The One Show*? It's dead exciting!'

Jade softened, happy again. 'Yeah, bae, you're right, how incredible is this? We're really here. Aren't you proud of me for getting us the jobs? I just gave a mini-burger to Nicoletta, you know, that model that Blake's nobbing! But I tell you what, I'm gonna fill up Shawn's glass tonight if it kills me. I'll do it when the dragon isn't looking.'

She hugged herself with joy. Kai secretly hoped she would spill red wine all down fucking Shawn Barrett's front and get kicked out. But it was kind of cool to be there, he'd thought when they arrived. Jade had been directly approached on the forum by someone saying that the agency were looking for temp staff for a 'special event' and there was a rumour that OnT were involved. The rumour had turned out to be true.

But he and Jade had hardly seen one another for more than a few moments since before the party started – Kai was buried in clouds of steam, constantly loading and unloading the dishwasher. Cool or not, he was teetering on the edge of a pretty bad mood, despite his enthusiastic comments, and the steam was making his acne itch and burn. He was only allowed out of the kitchen and into the party itself whenever the clean glasses ran out and he had to go and collect empties, and every time he'd been in there, Jade was beaming and blushing and totally obviously being ogled by the pervy host, Mervyn Hammond, as she filled up the guests' glasses, sticking out her massive boobies the whole time. Hammond's bodyguard couldn't take his eyes off her either, Kai noticed. His heart sank in despair – the guy looked like Ross Kemp while he, Kai, had to do about nine million chin-ups before he got any noticeable muscle definition in his biceps. He'd worked hard at it, and his torso was getting there – although there was nothing he could do about the fact that he looked like a fucking Oompa Loompa from the waist down. How could he compete?

The party planner, a.k.a. the dragon, their supervisor for the evening – an anorexic old lady of at least forty-five dripping in diamonds, in a hideous long purple dress that exposed her wrinkly old cleavage and bony shoulder blades – burst into the kitchen, waving a thin arm at them. 'Come on! Stop standing around looking gormless, it's at least an hour until your break! You' – she pointed at Kai – 'get out there and collect some more glasses, there are no clean ones, and you, Jane, take the beef satay out of the oven, now!'

'It's *Jade*,' muttered Jade under her breath as she donned oven gloves and removed the tray of food. It was the first time in her whole life she had opened an oven door, and she only knew to use the oven gloves because she'd seen the chef do it earlier.

Once the dragon had swept out again, Kai scurried over to try to give Jade a quick snog, but she brushed him off impatiently. 'Don't, Kai, I just put on more lip gloss. Got to hand round this beefy shit – hey, maybe this is my chance! The dragon said I can't serve drinks to Shawn and the boys, but she didn't say nothing about beef on sticks!'

She was gone, leaving Kai hot and frustrated. He picked up an empty plastic basket and followed her back into the party. Gainful employment was not something that either of them had very much experience of, and it was turning out to be surprisingly hard work. He was not enjoying the dirty looks all the B-list celebs were giving him as he noisily stacked glasses into the basket. Not enjoying that creep Hammond and his meathead bodyguard staring at Jade's tits. Not enjoying seeing Jade practically soak her pants every time she caught a glimpse of one of the OnT twats among the crush of bodies in Hammond's massive living room.

Kai was becoming increasingly worried that Jade was going to leave him for someone more glamorous – probably not Shawn Barrett, though. Kai wasn't so deluded that he thought Jade stood a chance with any of OnTarget. But that bodyguard . . . Jade wouldn't be able to resist an offer of going out with him, Kai knew. It would give her a chance to hobnob with OnT and Hammond, and other people like that record company twat talking to Hammond now – the one with the hairy waistcoat and tweed baggy trousers even though the guy was, like, twenty-five.

His bad mood increasing, Kai picked up the full basket of glasses and pushed his way back towards the kitchen, accidentally on purpose barging a sharp corner of it into the tweedy guy's arse.

'Oi, watch it, idiot,' the guy said, glaring at him.

'Sorry, sir,' Kai said, baring his teeth in a smile. *Not sorry, arsehole.* Why had he let Jade talk him into this? They were only earning six quid an hour, and most of that would go on a taxi home – no public transport out here in the Surrey countryside.

He craned his neck to look for Jade and his heart sank. She was talking to Hammond's bodyguard, giggling and jiggling her boobs, leaning close to him and flirting for England. Every part of him wanted to stride over there and wipe the smile off the minder's ugly face. But Kai knew he should never pick on anyone bigger than him, so he turned away, clenching his fists, reminding himself that Jade loved him. After everything he'd done for her, she owed him a lifetime of love, not to mention eternal access to those amazing boobs.

He went back into the kitchen and made himself feel better by picking his nose and wiping it on an hors d'oeuvre.

Things did not improve over the next hour. The chef came back in and shouted at him for not washing up the dirty platters fast enough. The dragon shouted at him when she caught him doing a bit of minesweeping – swigging the dregs from a couple of the glasses as he loaded them into the dishwasher. *Jade* shouted at him when he accused her of fancying the bodyguard: 'Oh for fuck's sake, Kai, give it a rest! I can't help it if blokes stare at me, can I?' Her mood seemed to have plummeted too, since some of the party guests, including OnTarget, had gone over to the leisure area of the house for a swim.

They were allowed a fifteen-minute break at 10 p.m. and Jade dragged him outside to see if they could see anything through the steamed-up glass of the pool room – 'Let's try and take some photos on our phones, omigod, maybe they're skinny-dipping, can you imagine how much *The Sun* would pay for a photo of OnT naked? We'd never have to work again!'

Kai had already decided that after tonight he was never going to work again, but he didn't tell Jade that. He followed Jade over to the pool house.

They had signed confidentiality agreements as part of their contracts for the night, but neither of them understood what that meant. Kai was relieved that there was no chance of seeing anything through the window – he'd started obsessing about the size of his willy. OnT were all bound to have massive great pop star wangers, and he didn't want Jade to start making comparisons . . .

'We'd better get back to the house, or the dragon will sack us,' he said, as Jade was putting away her phone. It beeped with a message and when she looked at it, she gasped and jumped as though the phone had given her an electric shock.

'What, bae?'

Her shoulders were rigid. She shook her head and stared at the screen again. Then, out of the blue, she vomited neatly into a lavender bush by the pool.

'Jade! Are you sick?' He rushed over to her. Puking always made her cry – she was practically phobic about anything to do with sick. But to his amazement, when she straightened up she had the biggest smile on her face that he had ever seen, even bigger than when she got them the jobs tonight at this party. Then she started to laugh hysterically, cackling as though she'd lost it.

'*What?*'

But she wouldn't tell him. She tucked her phone back into her bra, still laughing and doing a little dance and basically looking as though she was about to explode with glee.

'Did one of them footballers give you some drugs, or what?' he demanded. She looked totally high. He felt even more pissed off. Suddenly, he was sure he knew: she'd had a text from that bodyguard twat!

'You gave him your number, didn't you!' he yelled at her.

'Who?' she said innocently, not even bothering to conceal her happiness.

'Oh, screw you, Jade,' he said, and stalked back inside to carry on with the dishwashing. He'd have gone home right then, but until he got his cash at the end of the night, he had no way to do so.

Part of him felt a sick little thrill at telling Jade to screw herself; he'd never dared do anything like that before, but suddenly he felt that he, Kai Topper, had a limit, and she had just pushed him right over it. He'd done stuff before that he shouldn't have, but usually only because other people – often Jade herself – wanted him to do it. This time he was going to do something that *he* wanted to do. Screw the lot of them, the posh record company twats, the snooty celebs who thought they were better than everyone else – and as for that bodyguard! He was going to fuck them up tonight, good and proper. What he was going to do would get someone into so much trouble . . .

The next time the chef went outside for a fag, Kai slipped into the cloakroom and retrieved his backpack from under a bench. He unzipped it, reached down to the bottom and felt his fingers close around what he wanted. Pulling it out, he smiled to himself.

Nobody was going to walk over Kai Topper, not anymore.

Chapter 42
Day 14 – Winkler

Winkler pulled up in the lane outside Mervyn Hammond's Surrey home, got out of the car and immediately stepped in a puddle up to his ankle. He cursed aloud, the calming effects of his rainforest CD blown away in an instant. Goddamn fucking countryside; if he could pave over this shithole . . . He took a deep breath.

Cold, stinging rain lashed down on him, soaking his hair. As he walked towards the gate, his sock squelching inside his shoe, he ran a hand across his scalp, icy fingers searching out skin. Last night, he'd had his head between Francesca's thighs, wondering if she'd ever come, when she'd said, 'You've got a little bald spot.'

He had sat upright. 'What?'

'It's cute. I like it.'

He had immediately got up and run over to the mirror, trying to see the bald spot. He loved his hair, so much so that when he'd left his ex-wife her final words to him were, 'I wish you baldness.' Now it looked as if the witch's curse was coming true.

He hadn't been able to perform after Francesca's words. She'd tried to get him back in the mood before eventually leaving in a huff. Winkler had found a hand mirror and located the offending patch. His dad was as bald as Kojak, but Winkler Junior had always believed that he took after his mum's side of the family: hirsute and manly. But this was it. The beginning of the end. He spent the rest of the evening looking up hair re-growth products on Google.

So he was in a foul mood this morning. And Mervyn Hammond was going to take the full brunt of his bad temper if he wasn't one hundred per fucking cent cooperative. Over the past twenty-four hours, Winkler had become increasingly convinced that Hammond was, if not the killer, definitely involved. He had the access to the young fans and would easily be able to persuade them to meet with him by making promises these desperate girls wouldn't be able to resist. He had, Winkler knew, paid off a young girl who'd been molested by Shawn Barrett, which made Winkler wonder if this Irish girl hadn't told them everything – if Mervyn's involvement went beyond bribery and corruption.

There was the signed photograph of Mervyn among Nancy Marr's belongings – the only connection between the old woman and OnTarget anyone had been able to find. Finally, there was Hammond's mysterious after-dark visit to the children's home in Isleworth. Hammond liked young girls. Winkler's guess was that Hammond had molested Rose and Jessica, and they had threatened to expose him. Or perhaps he hadn't done anything to them directly but they had found out about him. Hammond was so furious that before killing them he had tortured them.

He pressed the buzzer by the gates and a female voice came smoothly through the intercom. A housekeeper or PA, Winkler guessed.

'Police,' he said firmly. 'I need to have a word with Mr Hammond.'

After a long pause, there was a beep and the double gate swung slowly open. Winkler decided to leave his car out there and walked through, finding himself on a path that led through an immaculately landscaped garden, cone-shaped little pine trees and everything, up to a grand house – one of those Huf houses that were popping up around Surrey. Ridiculous – a house that came in kit form and still cost a couple of mill? It was impressive, though, he had to admit, with its glass frontage and chalet roof.

He passed a kidney-shaped pond, gold and white koi darting beneath the surface, and considered propelling a juicy globule of phlegm into the water. He was so going to enjoy taking Mervyn Hammond down.

Winkler reached the house, walking past a white van parked close to the entrance, to find a middle-aged Asian woman in a white apron – yep, the housekeeper – standing in the doorway. Several black bin bags lay at her feet. He flashed his badge at her.

'Mr Hammond in his shed,' she said. *Not long off the boat, this one*, Winkler thought. 'I call him and he say please go there.'

She pointed towards a large brick building across the garden. A shed! It was bigger than the house Winkler grew up in; it was in fact a converted barn, by the look of it. Winkler was about to walk towards it when he had a thought.

'How long have you worked for Mr Hammond?' he asked, using his most authoritative police voice, wanting her to believe she'd be in trouble if she didn't cooperate. If she didn't answer, he might have to use the magic word: immigration. That always worked.

The woman, whom Winkler was pretty sure was Thai, shuffled so half her body was concealed behind the door. Frightened. Maybe Hammond threatened her. Beat her. *Don't worry*, Winkler wanted to say. *I'm here to take the bad man away.*

'Two year,' the housekeeper replied.

'Is he a good man to work for?'

She nodded vigorously. *Too* vigorously.

'I bet he has lots of parties, eh? Lots of clearing up for you to do.'

She nodded again, smiling tentatively. 'Yes, many party.'

'Famous people, yes? Celebrities?'

The housekeeper's eyes darted about like the koi had done. She leaned forwards, her eyes like saucers, voice dropping to an awestruck whisper. 'Yes. I meet *Harry Potter*.'

'Really? Nice kid. Any other . . . kids come here?'

The woman cocked her head.

'You know, like, young girls. Teenage girls.'

She grinned again and nodded enthusiastically. 'Yes, yes, many young girl. Pretty girls.'

I bet, Winkler thought. He caught movement behind the housekeeper – a woman dragging a vacuum cleaner across the hallway – and took a second look at the bin bags.

'Was there a party here last night?'

'Yes. Big party! We clean up now. Many people sick from drink.'

He tried to get a better look, but she moved her body to block his view.

'Who was here? Anyone exciting?'

She opened her mouth to answer, then appeared to change her mind, probably realising she'd already said too much. Possibly because he hadn't been able to control his face when she said 'pretty girls'. He decided not to push it.

He nodded at the woman and said, 'Thanks. You've been very helpful.'

She wore a bemused expression as he strode off across the damp grass towards the 'shed'. It was raining even more heavily now and by the time he got there water was dripping into his eyes. He was thankful he'd had the good sense to slip the signed photo, which was tucked inside his coat, into a laminate sleeve. He banged on the door.

'Come in.'

Winkler wasn't sure what he expected to find inside the converted barn, but he'd have been less surprised if he'd found a dozen bodies hanging from the rafters.

The entire space was filled with model trains. Not just trains: an entire landscape, with rolling hills and valleys, bridges and tunnels; miniature houses and churches; tiny plastic sheep grazing in a field; people the size of thumbnails waving from a station. And, gliding on tracks around this landscape, replica steam trains, gleaming black and green engines hauling cargo and passengers, round and round, pausing at signals before emitting a whistle and chugging away again.

Mervyn Hammond stood at a control deck on the far side of this display, his mop of black hair falling into his face as he fiddled with levers and rotated dials. He glanced up as Winkler approached but didn't stop playing with his giant train set.

Winkler noted that Hammond didn't seem surprised to see him.

'Mr Hammond,' he said. 'I want to ask you about—'

'Magnificent, isn't it?' Hammond said. 'You know, when I was a kid my granddad used to take me to the station at Crewe to watch the trains. I used to dream of being a train driver. That was all I wanted to do.' He chuckled to himself. 'My granddad would turn in his grave if he knew what I do these days. But he could barely afford to buy me a single wooden engine to play with. If he saw this . . .' He stretched out his arms to indicate his miniature kingdom and Winkler was rendered speechless.

But he thought to himself: *train sets. Toys. What does he do, use this to lure kids to his house? Is he into boys too?* His paedo radar wasn't just tingling now, it was going berserk.

Hammond stepped away from the control panel, the fervour in his eyes dimming a little. 'How can I help you? Detective . . . ?'

'DI Adrian Winkler.'

'A colleague of DI Lennon's? Don't tell me he's sent you to ask more questions about Shawn Barrett?'

Winkler shook his head. Beside him, an engine whizzed by dragging half a dozen passenger carriages behind it. The constant circular motion of the toys was making him feel queasy. And there was a cold, squelching sensation in his left shoe. *I'm going to get sodding flu,* he thought. And it was all this creep's fault.

'This isn't about Shawn Barrett,' he said, taking a step towards Hammond and pulling himself up to his full height. 'It's about you.'

Hammond adopted a puzzled expression. 'Me?'

'Yes, Mervyn. Hope you don't mind if I call you Mervyn.'

'What are you—?'

Winkler interrupted him, producing the signed photo from inside his damp coat and holding it in front of Hammond's face. 'Do you recognise this?'

'Well, yes. It's a photograph of me.'

'A *signed* photograph of you. Send many of these out, do you, Mervyn?'

Hammond was looking at him as if he were talking in riddles. 'No. Hardly any. But I appear in the media quite a lot, so I get the occasional request for a signed photo. Why are you—?'

'Recognise the name Nancy Marr, Mervyn?'

In the moment before Hammond answered, his eyes shifted up and to the right. This was a sure sign that the PR man was about to tell a lie. Winkler held his breath.

'No. I've never heard of her.'

He was lying. Definitely lying.

'So you don't remember sending, or giving, her this signed photo?'

'No. Detective, I don't send the photos out myself. Do you really think I'd have time to do that? I signed a small stock of pictures and if a request comes in to the office, my PA sends them out.'

'Really?'

Winkler had spent much of the past twenty-four hours trying to work out why Hammond had killed the old woman and he was sure he'd figured it out. Somehow, Mrs Marr had discovered the truth about Hammond. Maybe Mervyn had assaulted or threatened a girl Mrs Marr knew. She had threatened to expose him. Blackmailed him, perhaps. So he'd murdered her to keep her quiet.

And perhaps he'd left the signed photo as a kind of calling card . . . ? Unlikely – but not impossible. Winkler would work out the details later.

Right now, he didn't have enough to arrest Hammond. He could get him to come to the station again, but he strongly suspected this time Hammond would lawyer-up – an extremely expensive lawyer – and wriggle off the hook, then go crying to the papers about police harassment and how the cops were wasting their time on him when there was a murderer of teenage girls on the loose. Winkler knew there was no way the guv would allow them to touch Hammond without something rock solid. Winkler needed more . . . something to justify getting a search warrant for this place and Mervyn's office, to seize his computer. He needed a girl to make a complaint about this pervert. An accusation.

He looked around, checking there were no CCTV cameras pointing at him, that it was just him and Mervyn. It was time to crank things up a little, get Mervyn to start worrying.

He walked over to the model train set and caught hold of one of the engines as it trundled past, snatching it up. The carriages it was pulling fell away and landed on the ground with a clatter.

Mervyn rushed over. 'What the hell?'

Winkler stepped into his path, holding up the green and black locomotive. The letters LNER were stamped on its side.

'Put that down,' Hammond demanded.

'Worth a fortune, is it?' Winkler held it higher, his arm fully outstretched. 'Would be a real shame if I dropped it.'

Hammond tried to grab at it, but Winkler pushed him away. Winkler was delighted to see that the PR man's face had turned as red as the carriages that had fallen to the floor. 'That was my granddad's,' Hammond said.

'Ah. What a shame. Was your dear old granddad a kiddie fiddler too? Is that how it started? Granddad climbing into your bed at night, asking for a special cuddle?'

Hammond stared at him. 'You're sick. Who's your superior officer? I'm going to call him right now . . .' He pulled his phone out of his pocket.

'Him? Sexist too, as well as a sexual predator. How many have there been, eh? Over the years?'

Hammond had gone so red now, breath coming out of him in quick, shallow gasps, that Winkler was slightly concerned the other man was going to have a heart attack. He didn't want him to die before he faced justice. He lowered the train and gently placed it back on the track.

At that moment, Hammond's mobile rang in his palm, making him jump. He stared at the screen, clearly debating whether to take it, but it must have been important because he lifted it to his ear and said, 'Mervyn Hammond. Oh . . . Good morning, your Excellency . . .'

Winkler's phone started ringing too. He checked the display: Gareth. He backed away towards the door, pointing at a spot below his eye and then at Hammond. Winkler felt satisfied. Hammond would definitely make some kind of move now. He would wonder how Winkler knew about him, move to further cover his tracks. *Cover his train tracks*, Winkler thought, sniggering. He really was a comedy genius.

He answered his phone as he walked towards the house. 'Yeah?'

'Boss, it's DS Batey. We've had a call . . . You're going to find this interesting.' Gareth sounded excited.

'Go on.'

'Someone called Crime Stoppers anonymously. You're not going to believe this, but they mentioned Hammond, said they were at a party at his house last night and saw some teenage girls' clothes in one of the bedrooms. Including a pair of pink knickers with the word "LUCKY" printed on them.'

Winkler stopped dead. 'What?'

'I know. Rose Sharp's underwear.'

Winkler's heart was thumping like a full-size train thundering along the tracks. 'Did this caller give any more details? Leave a name?'

'No, like I said, it was anonymous.'

'And who else knows about this call? Lennon?'

'Not yet, no. The referral just came over – I picked it up and called you right away.'

Winkler raised his eyes to the heavens and mouthed 'thank you'. 'OK. Great. Keep it that way for the moment. I'll call you back.'

He ended the call and jogged back towards the house, watching several Asian women emerge carrying bin bags that they dropped beside the white van he'd noticed earlier.

He broke into a sprint, glancing over his shoulder to see if Hammond had emerged from the barn yet. He must still be on his call to 'his Excellency', whoever that was.

As he reached the house, the Thai housekeeper emerged through the front door to join the three other women, an expression of alarm crossing her face when she saw Winkler running towards her.

'I need everyone to stop,' he said. 'Listen to me.'

Four pairs of eyes stared at him.

'Did any of you find any clothes, women's clothes, when you were cleaning up?'

The women all started talking at once. He held up a hand. 'Please. One at a time.'

One of the women, another East Asian, about twenty-one, Winkler guessed, said in a whisper, 'I find knicker.'

Winkler thought he was going to have a heart attack. It was lucky he was so fit.

'Where? Show me.'

The four women all started rummaging through the bin bags, untying them and sticking their gloved hands inside. Winkler looked over his shoulder. Hammond still hadn't appeared.

'Come on, come on,' he urged.

'I can't find,' the young Asian woman said.

'Oh for fuck's sake.'

He pushed her aside and grabbed the bin bag she had been rummaging through, tipping it out onto the path. Beer bottles, screwed-up napkins, food waste, cigarette ends, a couple of used condoms. But nothing pink. He did the same with the next bag, and the next, the women gawping at the horrific mess that spilled onto the edge of the lawn, all their hard work undone.

'Where the fuck are they?' Winkler snapped.

There was one bin bag left. He untied it and tipped its contents onto the pile of trash.

And there they were.

'Gloves,' he demanded. 'Now.'

The housekeeper peeled off her transparent gloves and handed them to him. He slipped them on and crouched down, imagining himself being carried around the station, aloft on the shoulders of his colleagues, everyone chanting his name.

He held up the garment, pinching the knickers lightly between finger and thumb, and a thrill of excitement coursed through him.

'Gotcha,' he said.

Chapter 43
Day 14 – Chloe

Even though two days had passed since her birthday parachute jump, Chloe was still finding it difficult to process the maelstrom of emotions and adrenalin that had little dispelled in the aftermath. The goggle marks had long faded from around her eyes, her cheeks were no longer reddened from the freezing cold descent, and it felt as though she'd dreamed the whole thing. Then she would experience another flutter of excitement and the sheer joy of being alive – only to find guilt thudding down on top of her, that she shouldn't feel that way, not after Jess's murder.

And then there was this other, new thing, more exciting than everything else put together – more than the parachute jump; way more than her sixteenth birthday; more than the cute nervous guy from the plane asking for her number – an actual message from Shawn Barrett.

Shawn Barrett texted me, she thought, a smile curling irresistibly up at the corners of her lips. *Me!*

She felt a punch of shame and guilt in her gut – only recently she had felt embarrassed by her love of OnTarget, had thought herself too grown-up for them. Thank God Shawn would never know her traitorous thoughts.

As she sat at the breakfast table in her pyjamas half-heartedly eating a bowl of Special K, her mum noticed how distracted she was.

'Still thinking about the jump, Rog? I'm so proud of you, you know. I couldn't have done that, not in a million years. You've been so brave . . .'

Her mother's eyes suddenly filled with tears. She switched off the radio, reached across the table and took Chloe's hand between her own, her voice thick.

'We don't get that much time together on our own, do we? I just wanted to say that the other day was incredible. There's always so much going on here, and I feel like I'm constantly nagging you and Brandon about something or other—'

'You are,' Chloe confirmed, prompting a tearful laugh.

'So anyway. I just wanted to say that it was amazing to take you to the jump, just the two of us, and watch you floating down to earth with that massive grin plastered all over your face, and to know you've recovered, that you're well again, I can't tell you . . .'

She was openly sobbing now, and Chloe gave a self-deprecating sort of huff, although, annoyingly, her own eyes had filled up too.

'Oh God, Chloe, when I thought we were going to lose you, I just couldn't bear it. I really couldn't. The relief that you're OK!'

'Yeah, I'm fairly relieved too,' said Chloe. She examined her mother's profile, still attractive – although she really ought to pluck that one long hair she never noticed growing out of the mole by her left ear, and she was getting wrinkles in her neck. Chloe wondered what her mum had been like as a teenager. What she herself would be like as an adult, as a mother.

'I'm glad you're my mum,' she said impulsively, leaning over her cereal bowl to kiss her, which prompted another sob before her mum blew her nose and straightened up.

'Sorry, darling, I'm just being over-emotional. You just turned sixteen, and jumped out of a plane – how could I not be! Either that or I'm getting the menopause.'

She switched the radio back on, indicating that the chat was over, and started clearing up the breakfast things.

Chloe slid her phone out of her dressing gown pocket. She re-read the message – a PM sent from the OnTarget forum – for about the thirtieth time since she'd got it.

She still couldn't believe it. She was dying to tell her mum, or Jess – how jealous would Jess have been! Another visceral pang of guilt shot through her, a little spear of actual pain in her belly. Jess was probably lying in a stainless steel drawer in a mortuary, like on *CSI Miami*.

Hey Chloe! It's Shawn Barrett here. I've got something TOP SECRET I want to ask you about.

Even though Chloe was almost paralysed by the sheer excitement of getting a message from Shawn, she also found it too good to be true. She had watched *Catfish*. She knew all about people posing as others online.

Sorry Shawn, she wrote back. *But how do I know it's really you?*
The reply came back almost immediately.

Remember when I came to see you in hospital, when you had cancer? I asked you what your favourite OnT song was. You said that you tell everyone it's Forever Together but actually you like Small Victory better.

'Small Victory' was a bonus track on OnT's first album and generally considered a bit cringe. But it was true! It was her favourite. And she had never told anyone that except Shawn.

OMG! she replied. *It IS you!!!*

Yeah, it's me all right. TOP SECRET yeah, but I'm funding a new kids' cancer charity and want YOU to be my main girl, cos we go back, right? Can we meet up to discuss? Want you + me to be filmed, I'll hand you the massive cheque, it'll be on the news and that. But seriously, babe, please tell no-one, not even ur best mate or family. Need to know I have ur absolute discretion. DM me back and let me know if your up for it! Hope so! X ps., and I'm glad you're better now.

He hadn't used the correct version of 'you're', Chloe couldn't help thinking. But that was OK. He didn't need to be academically clever. He'd told her in the hospital not to let her studies slip like he had, and she was determined not to, retaking a whole academic year. That had been so tough. She ought to be doing her own GCSEs now, but as it was, she had another whole year to go . . . ugh.

Anyway, what did that matter now? In the car on the way back from the jump, her fingers trembling, she had typed a message, finding it hard to believe that she was sending words that his fingertips would touch on his own phone screen . . . his long slim fingers with their heavy silver rings, the same fingers that had stroked her fringe in hospital.

Hi Shawn! she typed. *I'd love to. Half-term ATM so I can meet anytime – just say when and where! I'm so excited!!!! Xxxxxx*

Chloe hesitated, then deleted all but the biggest of the kisses. Shawn needed to know that she was a mature woman, not some stupid little fan.

She couldn't wait to see him. After all the suffering she'd been through, all the bad luck and the pain of her losing her friend, this was just the tonic she needed. The jump had been the start. From this point on, she was going to embrace life. She wasn't going to be afraid of anything or anyone.

Chapter 44
Day 14 – Patrick

As soon as Patrick entered the station, he detected something new in the atmosphere, a charge of excitement – the kind that sizzled in the corridors, the incident rooms and offices whenever a big case had been cracked, a suspect arrested and charged. He felt immediately wary. What was going on? Martin and Gareth were chatting by the vending machine, big grins on their faces. Gareth looked over and gave Patrick a look he couldn't read, somehow mixing satisfaction, embarrassment and, what else? It looked like pity.

Patrick strode past them and headed straight towards Suzanne's office.

He had been up half the night trawling through the StoryPad website, following his visit to Chelsea Fox's flat and the revelation that Rose and Jess had collaborated on a piece of fiction on that site. It hadn't taken long to find a few solo stories written by Rose (MissTargetHeart) and Jess (YOLOSWAG), all of which featured members of OnTarget in clichéd romantic scenarios. Patrick didn't get much time to read fiction these days – in fact, the last novel he'd read had been Camus' *The Outsider* when he was eighteen – but he recognised bad writing when he saw it, and the girls' stories managed to combine purple prose with cringeworthy poetry. None of the stories contained any clues, as far as he could tell; nothing that told him anything at all about Rose's and Jess's lives.

More crucially, and frustratingly, he couldn't find any stories that Rose and Jess wrote together; nor were there any stories that either of them had written with other people. He had combed through the comments on Rose's and Jess's stories, but most of the 'reviews' were one or two words long. Convinced there must be something on the site that would help him, refusing to accept that this was another dead end, he spent the next few hours reading through fan fiction, finding himself drawn into a world where OnTarget were like the gods in Greek and Roman myths, mixing with mortal girls who were almost always flame-haired, milky-skinned virgins who found themselves swept into a world of excitement, danger and blood-sucking. It was amazing how often Shawn was depicted as a vampire overlord in these tales. What was it with young women and the undead?

This morning Gill had woken him up at 10 a.m. He'd fallen asleep at his desk at home and as soon as she shook him awake and he saw the time, he ran into the shower, shouting at her for not waking him earlier, then regretting it. As he soaped himself he castigated himself for being such a bastard to her recently. She was trying, really trying, and his response was to be grumpy, withdrawn and passive-aggressive.

'You need to make a decision,' she said when he emerged from the shower. She stood in the bathroom doorway, arms folded, trembling with the courage it took to say these words. 'Because we can't go on like this, Patrick. If you want me to leave, if you can't ever forgive me, you need to say.'

Then she had walked away, tears in her eyes, leaving him feeling wretched – but as confused as ever.

He followed her into the kitchen, where he found her standing by the sink, gazing out of the window. He went up and hugged her, feeling her respond, tentatively at first, before putting her arms fully around him and squeezing him, pulling him against her with a rare display of strength. He was still hot and a little damp from the shower and, emotionally charged from the scene in the bathroom, he found himself becoming aroused. Gill noticed it and pushed herself against him, tilting her face and kissing him.

'Where's Bonnie?' he whispered into her mouth.

'Watching *Ben and Holly* in the living room.'

'How long does an episode last?'

'About ten minutes.'

'Plenty of time.'

He took her by the wrist and pulled her gently out of the kitchen and into the utility room, shutting the door behind him. Gill's eyes widened as he lifted her onto the washing machine, no more words exchanged as she unbuckled his belt and he reached beneath her skirt and pulled down her knickers, tossing them onto the floor, kissing her hard as she shuffled forwards a few inches so he could push into her. He felt himself heading straight towards orgasm. He tried to slow down, but she urged him on, biting his lip and pulling at his hair as he thrust into her, his wife, the taste and feel and smell of her so familiar but so strange, almost forgotten, and as he came he gasped her name, his face pressed against her neck.

'Mummy, where are you?'

He stared into Gill's eyes and they both laughed before Gill called out, 'I'll be one minute, sweetheart. I'm just helping Daddy with something.'

They rearranged their clothes, smiling but not speaking, until Patrick said, 'I'm sorry. About before.'

'It's OK. But we do need to talk.'

'I know. I promise. It's just . . . this case, I have so little time.'

275

She placed a hand on his chest. 'I understand. And I'm sorry too.'

She left the room and came back carrying Bonnie.

'Let's arrange a date night,' he said. 'As soon as this investigation is over or slows down. I'll get my mum to babysit. OK?'

He'd left them both with a kiss, and now here he was, two hours late, heading towards Suzanne's office, wondering if perhaps that date night might arrive sooner than he'd thought. If the investigation had ended without him.

He knocked on Suzanne's door and was called in, surprised to find her with the chief superintendent, Gordon Stretton, who wore the same kind of smile Gareth and Martin had displayed. Stretton was a large man in his fifties, with thick hair and – according to gossip – thin skin. He stood beside Suzanne's desk. She was smiling too, but a little more warily.

'Guv,' Patrick said, nodding at Stretton.

For the second time that morning, Patrick found himself on the receiving end of a look he couldn't quite read. In retrospect, he would remember it as the look a football manager gives their former star striker just before telling them they're going to spend the foreseeable future on the subs bench.

'Patrick,' Stretton said. 'I was just congratulating DCI Laughland. Seems she has one or two excellent DIs under her command. Or one, anyway.'

Patrick bristled. What did that mean? He looked at Suzanne, but she was shuffling some papers and avoiding his eye.

'See you for a celebratory drink later, Suzanne?' Stretton said, pushing past Patrick and heading out.

As soon as Stretton shut the door behind him, Patrick said, 'What the hell's going on?'

'It's Winkler. He's arrested someone for the murders of Rose and Jess. Wendy's killer too, I expect, but Adrian is talking to him first, then Strong is going to interview him about Wendy's death.'

'Hang on. Interview who?'

'Mervyn Hammond.'

Patrick blinked. 'What? *Hammond?* That's . . .'

'An item of Rose's clothing was found at Hammond's house.'

'By Winkler?'

'Yes, following an anonymous call. Winkler was already there, questioning Mr Hammond.'

Patrick listened with increasing disbelief as Suzanne relayed the story Winkler had told her that morning, after turning up at the station with Mervyn Hammond handcuffed in the back of his car.

Winkler and Gareth Batey had found a photograph of Hammond among Nancy Marr's possessions. Winkler had unearthed rumours about Hammond and young girls, followed him and seen him visit a children's home after hours. Finally, he'd discovered Rose's 'LUCKY' knickers in a bin bag on Hammond's property.

'Hammond's got no alibi for any of the murders. Not that he's telling us about anyway. When Winkler brought him in, Hammond started shouting about how he was going to make sure Winkler and I were on the front of every paper between here and Timbuktu for threatening and intimidating an innocent man. Since his lawyer arrived he's gone quiet, started saying "no comment" to every question.'

Patrick's mind raced. Hammond? Could it be him? He thought back to his own interview with the PR man. He found Mervyn deeply repellent, arrogant and slimy – but a serial murderer?

'Stretton was acting like we've definitely got our man,' Patrick said.

'Yes. Well, this underwear.'

'Which seems very convenient. An anonymous tip-off?'

'Exactly. I can already hear Hammond's lawyer in court. If it even gets that far. We need more, Patrick. I want you to join the interview. See if you can get Hammond to start talking. And be careful, OK? I really have no desire to see my name on the front page of *The Sun*.'

Chapter 45
Day 14 – Patrick

Suzanne knocked on the door of interview room one and beckoned for Winkler to come out. He pushed himself slowly up from his seat and loped out of the room. Before the door shut, Patrick caught a glimpse of Hammond sitting beside his lawyer – a red-headed woman whom Patrick didn't recognise. Hammond had his trademark bag of nuts open in front of him and was staring into space, seemingly deep in thought. If you could hear a mind whirring, Hammond's would be as loud as a helicopter.

'How's it going?' Suzanne asked.

'He's still saying "no comment" to everything, on the grounds that he may incriminate himself. But I'm going to crack him. Don't worry. We've got almost a whole day before we need to charge him. I've already caught him out lying, a ton of times. He looks up and to the right when I ask him anything tricky, which, as we all know, is a clear indicator that he's fabricating instead of remembering.'

Winkler sounded so smug that Patrick couldn't help snorting. 'You're kidding! You'd be laughed out of court if you use *that* as evidence!'

'I want Patrick to join the interview,' Suzanne said.

'No way!'

Patrick was tempted to say 'Yes way', but resisted, even though the horror on Winkler's face had brightened his mood considerably.

'Patrick has interviewed Mr Hammond before and I believe he was very communicative then.'

'Highly,' said Patrick.

'Yeah, well, Lennon gets on well with people who hurt kids.'

Suzanne stepped between them before Patrick could punch Winkler in the face. 'Adrian. That is uncalled for. Patrick is going to lead this interview from now on—'

'*Lead?*' Winkler's voice rose an octave.

'—and if you make one more comment like that you'll be looking at a transfer to traffic before the week is out. Do you understand?'

Winkler glared like a toddler who'd been told to share his precious sweets with his sibling. 'This was my arrest, though, don't forget that. I don't want *him* getting all the credit.'

Suzanne hissed at him. 'For fuck's sake, we are a team. Do you understand that? I've a good mind to pull you out of this interview now and send Carmella in with Patrick instead.'

'Good idea,' said Patrick. 'Where is Carmella?'

'In interview room three, taking a statement from Hammond's housekeeper, Miss Wattana.'

Winkler had gone purple. 'You . . . You can't—'

Suzanne pointed a manicured finger at him. 'I won't do that. Yet. But I want a word with you after this interview. Just get Hammond to talk. Both of you.'

She turned and marched away, leaving both Patrick and Winkler looking after her. Patrick opened his mouth to say something conciliatory to Winkler, to try to make peace before they went into the interview room. If they didn't put up a united front, this interview was doomed. But before he could speak, Winkler pushed open the door and went inside, giving Patrick no choice but to follow him.

———

Winkler threw himself down into the chair farthest from the wall, leaving Patrick to sit down in the 'driving' seat, beside the tape recorder.

'Bringing in the good cop now, are we?' Hammond said, smirking as Winkler glared at him. 'Detective Lennon, have you met my lawyer, Cassandra Oliver?'

The red-headed woman reached across the table and shook Patrick's hand. Her grip was cold, but she was an attractive woman in her late forties, with green eyes and pale skin. Her name was familiar and Patrick had the feeling she'd been involved in several celebrity trials. No doubt she was ludicrously expensive.

He switched on the recorder and told the machine the time and date and who was present. Hammond watched him expectantly.

'Mr Hammond, as you know, you are being questioned regarding the unlawful killings of Rose Sharp and Jessica McMasters. Can you tell me where you were between the hours of 7 p.m. and 11 p.m. on Thursday, fifth of February, and Saturday, seventh of February?'

'Your "bad cop" colleague has already asked me these questions,' Hammond snapped.

'But I believe you didn't give him an answer.'

Hammond sat back in his chair.

'Mr Hammond, can you answer my question?'

'What question was that?'

Patrick sighed and was about to go through the process of repeating his words when the PR man said, 'Oh for goodness' sake, I don't have an alibi for either of those dates, nor when the policewoman was murdered. They happen to be the only three evenings this month when I wasn't either working, at a social engagement or at the gym.'

'What a coincidence,' muttered Winkler, so quietly that the tape machine wouldn't pick it up. Raising his voice, he said to Patrick, 'He's got no alibi for Nancy Marr's murder either.'

Patrick nodded. They didn't know exactly when Mrs Marr had been killed, but he assumed Winkler had ascertained that Mervyn had not been out of the country or otherwise engaged for the entire period they were looking at.

'So where were you on the dates I mentioned?' Patrick asked, still using his politest tone.

'I was at home. On my own. I am allowed to relax occasionally, you know.'

'What were you doing?'

Hammond looked directly at Winkler. 'I was playing with my train set, as your colleague would no doubt put it.'

Patrick blinked. 'Train set?'

Mervyn popped a nut into his mouth and chewed. 'It's my hobby. I collect and build model railways. I have an incredibly busy life, and it's how I relax. Unfortunately, it's something I do on my own. So no, nobody can corroborate my "story".' He waggled his fingers.

'What about your housekeeper? Did she see you?'

'She doesn't work during the evenings unless we have a function. I'm not a slave-driver.'

'You have a bodyguard, don't you? Kerry, er . . .'

'Mangan. Yes. But he doesn't work when I'm at home on my own. I don't expect thugs to come into my home and attack me or my property.' He looked pointedly at Winkler and Patrick thought, *Oh God, what did Winkler do now?*

Cassandra Oliver spoke up. 'I think we've established that my client does not have an alibi for the times you're interested in. That doesn't mean he murdered anyone. And these allegations that Detective Winkler mentioned before you joined the interview, Detective Lennon, are pure malicious hearsay, lies from a former tabloid journalist with a grudge against my client.'

'What about the underwear?' Winkler said, unable to keep quiet any longer. 'How do you explain that?'

He reached beneath the table and produced an evidence bag containing the pink knickers that had been found on Mervyn's property. It was the first time Patrick had laid eyes on them, and seeing them now, slightly crumpled inside the transparent bag, caused a wave of sadness to hit him. He would never forget the way Sally Sharp's face had folded in on itself as she'd told him what Rose had been wearing the night she was killed.

He took a deep breath. 'Mr Hammond, this item of clothing was found inside a bin bag at your house. Do you deny that?'

Hammond shrugged, a gesture that Patrick reported verbally to the tape recorder.

'How do you explain its presence on your property?'

Hammond leaned forwards. 'I can't explain it. There was a party at my house last night. Dozens of guests, waiting staff, cleaners in this morning. This underwear must belong to one of them.'

'Are you aware that Rose Sharp was believed to have been wearing an item of underwear matching these the night she was murdered?'

'Only because your colleague told me.'

The lawyer spoke up again. 'Primark knickers. There must be hundreds, thousands of young women walking around London right now wearing the exact same pair. Have these been DNA tested already?'

Patrick looked at Winkler, who said, 'Not yet.' Patrick suppressed a sigh. Evidence like this would normally be sent straight to the lab for testing, but he guessed Winkler had decided the impact of presenting them in the interview took precedence.

Cassandra Oliver raised her palms. 'Then you don't even know if they were Rose Sharp's. This is ridiculous. You should release my client right—'

Winkler cut her off. 'When we do test them, which we will immediately after this interview, I am sure they will match Rose Sharp's DNA. We received information—'

'An anonymous tip-off.'

'Information that Rose Sharp's underwear could be found at your house, Mr Hammond. I then undertook a search after questioning your cleaning staff who reported finding the item I was looking for. What were they doing at your house?'

'Like I said,' Hammond replied. 'They must have belonged to one of the party guests. I can only assume that somebody sneaked off to one of the bathrooms or bedrooms and got carried away. It all did get, *ahem*, slightly out of control towards the end. Some people were totally off their heads, skinny-dipping, shouting – actually I wondered if someone had spiked the drinks. The rational explanation is that some daft bint had a shag and was too out of it to put her knickers back on.'

'Only if they don't contain Rose's DNA.'

'And if they do – why, if I killed this poor girl, would I leave her underwear lying around at my house?'

It was a good question, Patrick thought, and one that Winkler had no answer to. Something else occurred to him as he watched Hammond pick up another nut.

'Mr Hammond – are you right-handed or left?'

Hammond scowled. 'Well, I don't see what that's got to do with anything – but I'm left-handed.'

Cassandra Oliver leaned forwards. 'If this underwear did indeed belong to the victim, it seems clear what's happened,' she said. 'My client has been framed. Somebody planted it at his house and called you anonymously. It doesn't take a genius to work that out.' She looked pointedly at Winkler.

Patrick paused, thinking about what to do next. He was tempted to suspend the interview, get the underwear sent for DNA testing, but Suzanne had instructed them to get Hammond to talk, and so far he had said nothing useful.

'Let's move on,' he said. He decided to take a risk, to try to get things moving. 'Mr Hammond, do you have a sexual interest in underage girls?'

Mervyn Hammond's expression was one of pure outrage. 'No, I do not!' He thumped the desk. 'How dare you?'

Winkler sneered. 'What were you doing visiting St Mary's Children's Home last Monday night?'

For the first time, Hammond's air of superiority wobbled. 'What?' he asked.

'You were seen,' Winkler went on, 'entering St Mary's Children's Home in Isleworth at 18.49 that evening. What were you doing there?'

'No comment,' replied Mervyn.

This was interesting, Patrick thought.

'Have you interviewed the staff of this children's home?' asked Oliver.

'There's a pair of officers on their way now,' Winkler replied.

'Why did you go there?' Patrick asked before Winkler could say anything else.

'No comment.'

'I don't understand what this has to do with your murder investigation,' Oliver interjected.

'We believe,' Winkler said, 'that it shows a pattern of behaviour, that Mr Hammond here enjoys the company of schoolgirls.'

'This is preposterous,' Hammond said, spluttering.

'Then why won't you tell us the purpose of your visit?' Patrick asked.

'Because it's none of your fucking business, that's why.'

Patrick sat back. Could Hammond actually be guilty? They knew he was sleazy. He had paid off Roisin McGreevy after Shawn Barrett hurt her. No doubt that wasn't the only occasion he'd had to help shut someone up. Patrick also knew that Hammond had represented a rock star who had been shacked up with a fifteen-year-old girl in the eighties, helping this ageing rocker win public sympathy by portraying the girl as a gold-digging hussy who lied about her age.

So Hammond had shown little moral fibre when it came to the issue of underage sex. Also, he had no alibi. He definitely had the access to teenage girls. It would be easy for him to promise that he would introduce them to members of OnTarget, get them tickets to concerts and signed merchandise, or deliver messages to the boys. Now he was refusing to answer a simple question about this children's home, was flustered, his usually cool demeanour heating up.

'So you're not willing to tell us why you visited St Mary's?' Patrick asked.

Hammond folded his arms. 'No.'

'OK. I'm suspending this interview. The time is 12.25.'

The two detectives walked to Suzanne's office, not speaking to one another. As soon as they got inside the office, Winkler said, 'He's lying, and he's guilty. We need to get authorisation for a full search of his house, his office, his cars—'

'Hold on,' Suzanne said. 'Patrick? What do you think?'

'I don't know for sure.' He ignored Winkler's puff of exasperation. 'But what I do know is that Adrian's almost certainly got one thing wrong.'

'What?' Winkler squared up to him.

'Your theory about him lying because of the direction his eyes are going is, frankly, bullshit.'

Winkler blustered with outrage. 'It's not! It's widely known that if a suspect looks up to the right, he's lying, because he's creating a visual construct, not a remembered one . . .'

Patrick resisted the temptation to roll his own eyes. 'Yes – perhaps. A *right-handed* person. Hammond's left-handed, as he just confirmed. Which means that the process is likely reversed. When he's remembering, he looks to the right, and if he's making stuff up, he'd look left.'

Winkler looked mortified and Patrick allowed himself a small moment of triumphal one-upmanship.

Suzanne interjected. 'Can we stick to actual facts, please? It's certainly suspicious that he won't answer any questions about the children's home. Who's gone to talk to them?'

'Gareth Batey's headed down there.'

'And is Carmella still in with the housekeeper?'

'No. She's writing up the statement now. But Miss Wattana stated that she's never witnessed any teenage girls at Hammond's house except when there's been a party. Carmella said that Miss Wattana actually laughed when she was asked if she knew anything about Hammond's sexual preferences. She said, and I quote, "He only like trains."'

'Yeah. Lying or not, he's still a weirdo,' Winkler said. 'We need to search his house.'

Patrick put up a hand, refusing to get drawn into an argument with Winkler. 'I think we're looking at this all wrong.'

'What do you mean?' Suzanne asked. She had taken a seat behind her desk and in that moment the sun broke through the clouds outside, brightening the room, catching Suzanne's hair. *She's beautiful* . . . Patrick immediately stamped on the thought.

'This case, it's not about sex. Don't forget, none of the victims, Rose, Jessica, Nancy Marr or Wendy, assuming she was killed by the same person, were sexually assaulted. There was no sign of any sexual activity at all. Winkler here is following a trail based on his belief that Hammond is a paedophile. But that doesn't fit with the murders.'

'No,' Winkler said. 'My belief is that Hammond is a paedophile, that all of the victims found out, and he killed them to shut them up, to stop his secret getting out.'

'And that theory could still work,' Suzanne said, 'if Hammond isn't a sexual predator. There could be other reasons he needed to keep Rose, Jessica and Nancy Marr quiet. Some other criminal activity. Drugs, for example. Maybe he deals drugs, sells them to OnTarget's fans, to the kids or staff at the children's home.'

'Maybe,' both Patrick and Winkler said at the same time.

Suzanne frowned suddenly. 'Well, whatever it is, we need to decide what to do with Hammond. Patrick?'

'We don't have enough to charge him.'

'Bullshit,' said Winkler.

'No, we don't. Not without a DNA test on the underwear. If we charge Mervyn and then they turn out to belong to someone else . . .' He didn't need to finish the sentence. 'Let's see what Gareth comes back with from St Mary's and get the underwear through the lab ASAP. How quickly can they do it if we ask them to make it priority one?'

Suzanne looked at the ceiling. 'I'd have to ask Stretton to twist some arms, try to get it done overnight.'

'And in the meantime, we hold Hammond. If the DNA matches Rose, if the children's home can't give us a good reason why he was there, then we can search his property. But if we go in now, tear his place apart without even knowing who those knickers belong to, we'll all be famous. The dumbest police since the Keystone Kops. With you, Winkler, as the dumbest of them all.'

Chapter 46
Day 14 – Patrick

P atrick loitered outside Suzanne's office for a moment, watching Winkler stomp off towards the custody suite. Usually, it would give him great pleasure to piss Winkler off, but Patrick wasn't feeling joyful right now, just satisfied that they had bought a little time. He needed to talk to Carmella. Because while they waited for the DNA results, there was another line of inquiry he was desperate to follow.

Carmella wasn't at her desk, so he headed towards the canteen, hoping he would find her there again. As he turned into the corridor that led to the canteen, he saw Gareth Batey walking towards him.

Gareth stopped in his tracks when he saw Patrick.

'Gareth.'

'Boss.'

'A word, please.' He gestured towards an empty meeting room and the detective sergeant followed him inside.

Before Patrick could speak, Gareth said, 'I need to report back to Winkler.'

'Your new best mate.'

Gareth's face as usual turned a shade of pastel pink. He was clearly having to work hard to maintain eye contact. 'I need to report back to him. I've just been to—'

'St Mary's Children's Home. Yes, I know. I'm leading this investigation, remember? And I've just been interviewing Mervyn Hammond. Tell me what you found out.'

Gareth hesitated. 'But . . . Winkler told me to speak to him first. I mean, it was him and me who saw Hammond go in that place. Me and Winkler who've been tailing him. Adrian said you'd step in and try to take all the credit as soon as we got our man.' Gareth's eyes glinted in the artificial light, damp from the emotion it took to give this speech.

'For fuck's sake. Can't you see? Winkler's using you.'

'No! He's the only one who recognises my potential. You treat me like the canine unit treat their dogs. Loyal, useful but dumb.'

Patrick took a step back, shocked at the turn this conversation had taken. Gareth was visibly shaking now and Patrick was reminded of an argument with Gill, when she accused him of being uncaring, of taking her for granted. At home, he always admitted that Gill had a point. But here? What had he done to make the young DS feel like this? He tried to think back, was going to suggest that they arrange a meeting to talk about it – a necessary evil of being a manager, a higher rank, the kind of touchy-feely stuff he instinctively shied away from – when Gareth said, 'Winkler's a better detective than you.'

A flash of anger propelled Patrick towards the younger man, until their faces were just inches apart.

'Say that again.'

'You heard me.'

Patrick pulled himself up to his full height. But what happened next surprised him. Instead of reaching boiling point, the anger in his veins drained away as he realised how ridiculous this was. It wasn't really like an argument with Gill; it was like being at school.

Patrick walked away and sat down, inviting Gareth to do the same.

Gareth stared at him, breathing hard, nostrils flaring.

'Come on, Gareth, take a seat.'

To Patrick's relief, the other man did as he was asked. He sat stiffly, his back straight, but he appeared to be calming down.

'We can talk about this later, OK? When emotions aren't running so high.'

Gareth nodded reluctantly. Now he appeared embarrassed.

'Tell me what happened at the children's home. What did they say about Mervyn Hammond's visit?'

'Nothing.'

'Come on, Gareth . . .'

'No, I mean they wouldn't say anything. The manager refused to talk about it, and the staff were obviously hiding from me. All the kids were at school, so I couldn't talk to them.'

'Really? That's very . . .'

'Suspicious.' Gareth had relaxed a little now, his body less rigid. 'What have they got to hide?'

Before he could reply, Patrick saw Carmella walk past the room. He stood up.

'All right. Let's arrange a meeting, just you and me. I'll talk to you later. I need to talk to Carmella.'

'OK. Boss.'

'Good man.'

Patrick hurried out of the room, calling to Carmella. As he hurried up to her, Gareth came out of the room and walked off in the opposite direction.

'What's up with your man?' Carmella asked.

'Gareth?'

'Yeah. He looks like you just told him you don't want to go out with him anymore.'

Patrick sighed. 'Come on, I'll update you on the way to the car.'

'Where are we going?'

'What would you say if I told you we're going to talk to someone about erotically charged teenage fantasies involving boy-band members . . . and vampires?'

'That I want a transfer?'

He smiled. 'Come on.'

StoryPad's British office was based in a converted warehouse close to Silicon Roundabout, where many of the UK's Internet start-ups are based. Mervyn Hammond's office wasn't far from here, nor was Global Sounds Music. This investigation had drawn Patrick close to a world of glamour he'd once dreamed of living in. But now he'd seen what it was really like, he half-hoped the next murder investigation would start somewhere at the other end of the glamour spectrum, like the Kennedy Estate or an old folks' home.

Patrick filled Carmella in on what he'd learned from Chelsea Fox, that she believed Jess and Rose had collaborated on a piece of fiction on StoryPad.

'It's the only link between them that we've been able to establish so far – assuming Chelsea isn't mistaken.'

'But there's no connection to Nancy Marr through StoryPad?'

'Hmm. I don't think she's quite their target market. But I spoke to one of Strong's team who confirmed that StoryPad was in Wendy's browser history, that she'd been looking at it in the days before she was killed.'

Carmella was checking out the website on her phone as Patrick drove. 'I remember Martin mentioning it in one of the briefings, but, apart from that, I've never heard of it.'

'Nor had I. But it's incredibly popular among teenagers, especially girls. According to the "about" page on StoryPad, they've got over thirty million users, and there are something like ninety million stories on there. It's pretty straightforward, really. Users can post pieces, either short stories or whole novels, which are divided up into chapters, and other users can read and comment on them. I guess the users compete to get as many reads as possible because then they get ranked higher, which leads to more reads. It's like a big popularity contest. Plus, of course, it gives these girls an outlet for their creativity.'

'I used to write poems, but I never wanted anyone to read them,' Carmella said. 'Ugh – cringe.'

'Same with me and lyrics.'

'Really? Were they any good?'

'No, they were shit. But this is the Instagram generation, isn't it? They share everything and they all want to be famous.'

'You're sounding like a grumpy old man again.'

They reached their destination and pulled up in a courtyard outside the old warehouse. 'It goes without saying,' Patrick said, 'that the most popular category on the site is fan fiction, and stories featuring OnTarget make up about fifty per cent of that. I looked through some of it last night. My God, some of it is almost pornographic. They call it "shipping", short for "relationshipping", and imagine these . . . trysts between members of the band.'

'And between band members and their fans?'

'Yes.'

'And the vampires?'

'Oh, in a lot of the stories, Shawn and Blake and co happen to be immortal blood-suckers with a thirst for the blood of virgins.'

'Well, I know what *I'll* be reading tonight.'

They walked towards the front door. 'I'm guessing you weren't able to find anything that Rose and Jess had co-written?'

'No. Either it's buried so deep that I missed it or it was deleted.' He paused for a moment, fixing his strategy in his mind. 'It might be nothing. But if I'm right and Mervyn Hammond does turn out to be another false lead, this is all we've got.'

Chapter 47
Day 14 – Kai

Kai had only slept for two hours in the previous twenty-four since the party at Mervyn Hammond's house – which was extra-annoying, because he was truly worn out. Never again, he thought, would he be persuaded to dress up in a stupid bow tie and an apron so long that it had come down to his shins, making his legs look even shorter, working his arse off for six quid an hour. Slave labour, that's what it was! Not to mention the ingratitude of everyone involved. As far as he was concerned, it totally had *not* been worth it just for the sake of being in the same room as OnTarget and all those other D-list celebs. Hell, he got to be in the same room as OnTarget at the book signing just days before, and all that had involved was queuing in Piccadilly for an hour or two. The only thing that really made the whole thing worthwhile was what he'd left at the house. Now that *had* been funny.

His hands were still bright red and chapped from loading and unloading the dishwasher, and once he'd forked out for a solo cab home – that took two hours to arrive – he only had £23 wages left. He had assumed that he and Jade would be splitting the cab fare, but oh no, she had 'sorted herself out', as she'd informed him at the end of the party, the chill in her voice almost frightening. She had refused to tell him how she was getting home – but he could guess. That frigging bodyguard, doubtless.

Since then he had rung her numerous times, and been round to her house twice, but her phone just rang out, then went to voicemail, and nobody had come to the door despite him leaning his finger on the bell for ages. He remembered Jade telling him that her mum, Alison, was going away for a couple of days. He'd been excited at the prospect of having Jade and her small council house to himself for a while, without having to make small talk with Alison, who scared him, with her wrinkly lips from decades of sucking on fags and God knows what else, and her enormous arse. Jade hated her too, although she pretended that they were 'bezzies' when she wanted to ponce twenty quid off her.

Now, with a pang, Kai realised that Jade might well be taking advantage of her mum's absence by temporarily shacking up with Kerry the bodyguard. The thought of it gave him such pain that he felt murderously angry. If there had been a kitten nearby, he'd have twisted its head right off, no question.

Shame he couldn't do the same to Kerry. *As if.*

'Where are you, bae?' he cried in an anguished voice, addressing the bathroom mirror in his house and noticing another new crop of zits as he did so. Kerry the frigging bodyguard didn't have zits.

A sudden inspiration occurred, and he slapped the side of his head at his stupidity in not remembering before: the tracking app!

A couple of weeks back they had both installed a phone-tracking app on their phones so that if they got separated at the OnTarget gig at Twickenham, they'd be able to find each other by identifying where the other one's phone was. Jade had once got really upset when she lost him in Guildford Spectrum, and he'd been well pleased at his resourcefulness when he found and installed the app. She had twined her arm around his neck and cooed into his ear what a genius he was, and how much she loved him . . . Mind you, he thought, she wouldn't be so chuffed with him if she knew what he'd done afterwards, when he'd told her he was un-installing the app so that she needn't worry about him keeping tabs on her. Instead, he'd slid the app into a folder on Jade's iPhone screen, buried among a load of other apps she never, ever used. The folder was labelled 'Health', so she'd never notice that the phone-tracking app was in there.

Holding his breath, he clicked on to the app on his own phone. A green pulsing circle on a map indicated that Kai's phone had found Jade's.

Kai punched the air and zoomed in on the map. To his puzzlement – and then anger – Jade appeared to be very close to the Thames, near Hampton Court, in a place called Platt's Eyot. It looked like there was a little wood nearby and he immediately imagined her leaning against a tree with the bodyguard, her legs purple with cold and her skirt up around her waist.

Fuck him, thought Kai, sliding a carving knife out of the knife drawer in the kitchen – making sure his mum, who was watching afternoon telly in the next room, didn't hear him – then grabbing his parka and calling out a goodbye on his way past the living room.

He could get the train from Wimbledon to Hampton Court, he knew; he'd seen the station stops. On the map, the river and wood didn't seem very far from the station. He didn't even hurry, particularly – with the app working, there was no rush. He'd be able to find her. And when he did, the bodyguard's muscles would be of no use to him. All the muscles in the world couldn't stop you from getting stabbed in the back, could they?

Chapter 48
Day 14 – Patrick

Patrick and Carmella sat in one of StoryPad's meeting rooms, all of which were named after famous writers. This was the Orwell room and Patrick wondered if the CCTV camera that pointed at them from the ceiling was functional or a wry joke.

After initial reluctance, mutterings about privacy and confidentiality, and lots of whispered conversations between various members of staff, a young woman called Dawn Latuske had ushered Patrick and Carmella into this room and sat down with them, placing an iPad on the desk. Latuske was a black woman in her late twenties with trendy, thick-framed glasses.

'I could come back with a court order—' Patrick began, but Latuske stopped him.

'It's OK, Detective. We're going to cooperate. The thought that two of our users have been murdered, that more might be in danger . . .' She shuddered. Patrick had used the line about others being in danger to prompt StoryPad's staff to help. 'We've been in touch with Seattle and they've given us the go-ahead. So . . .'

She pressed a few buttons and a screen flickered to life at one end of the room. Patrick realised that the iPad was connected to the screen so they could see what Dawn was doing as she flicked and scrolled.

'This is MissTargetHeart profile.'

'Rose,' said Patrick.

'Yes, sorry. Rose. And this is Jess's.' The girls' profile pages appeared side by side on the screen. 'This shows a full list of the stories both girls submitted or contributed to, including any that were deleted. I'm basically showing you an admin view. Nothing is ever fully deleted – it stays on the back end until it's a year old, at which point it gets archived. But this is everything both girls wrote over the last year.' She flicked down the page. 'There weren't many – a dozen or so each. We can also see all their comments on other people's stories, but there are hundreds, if not thousands, of those.'

'We might come back to that later,' Patrick said.

Latuske nodded, then pushed her glasses back onto the bridge of her nose. 'I think this is what you're interested in. A story that both Rose and Jess wrote.'

She clicked on a link, bringing the story up on the screen. Patrick felt that tingle – the one that made him love this job. Chelsea Fox hadn't been wrong. This was it – the link.

The story was called *Fresh Blood* and according to the stats Patrick could see on screen it had been read 343,524 times and had thousands of comments.

'I remember this story,' Dawn said. 'It was really popular last autumn, I think. It would have been featured on the homepage at one point. I didn't realise it had been deleted.'

Patrick couldn't make out all of the text on the screen. 'Is it about OnTarget?'

Dawn laughed. 'Yes. Well, Shawn and Blake. They're vampire princes . . .'

Patrick and Carmella exchanged a look.

300

'. . . who both fall in love with a mortal girl called Ella. It's quite . . . fruity, as I recall.'

'Hang on,' said Patrick, spotting something. 'The authors' names . . .'

He stood up and moved closer to the screen, wondering if he needed glasses.

'Therearefourco-authors,'hesaid.'MissTargetHeart,YOLOSWAG, F-U-Cancer and Jade.'

'That's right,' said Dawn.

He turned to her. 'Can you give me the real names of the other two users?'

'I don't know.'

He slammed his palms down on the table. 'Dawn. These girls could be the next targets of a serial killer. I need to know their names.'

Dawn Latuske swallowed visibly. He could see the war going on in her head: job versus conscience.

In the end, she switched off the screen, tapped her iPad a few times and said, 'I need to use the loo.'

She got up, leaving the meeting room, the iPad still on the table. Carmella grabbed it.

'Here we go. Jade Pilkington and Chloe Hedges. We've got their addresses, dates of birth and email addresses.' Patrick took out his Moleskine to note the details down, but Carmella took a photo of the iPad screen using her iPhone.

Patrick put his notepad away, feeling hopelessly old-fashioned.

'Chloe Hedges,' Carmella said. 'How come I know that name?'

'I . . . Oh shit – she was Jess's best friend. Gareth interviewed her. Right, let's head back to yours, pick up your car and you go to Jade's address while I head to Chloe's.'

Chapter 49
Day 14 – Chloe

Chloe's stomach was fizzing with excitement. Even though they hadn't confirmed a date and time yet, she felt as though the imminent meeting with Shawn Barrett had been dropped into the puddle of her insides, like the lurid Vitamin C tablets in water that her mum forced her to drink every morning. It was a secret that was hers and Shawn's alone and she hugged it to herself with glee, feeling so grown-up to have been entrusted – by one of the most famous people in the country – with such a responsible and glamorous task. They had exchanged a dozen or so messages on the private message board of the forum over the past twenty-four hours, to the point that it had almost become normal to see his name pop up in her inbox. *Almost.* Their conversation had developed from Shawn's first, slightly formal request into a more chatty tone. She might, if she allowed herself, even believe that Shawn was flirting with her.

It was too exciting for words.

Last night, she had been telling Shawn how lucky she felt to be alive, after the cancer, and that had made her think about Rose and Jess, and her idea about what had happened to them, the connection

that had led to their deaths. Before she could chicken out she had
sent Shawn a message:

*You know those girls that were murdered? Rose and Jess. I knew them
on StoryPad, co-wrote a story with them along with another friend.
I've been thinking: what if it's got something to do with their deaths?*

A reply had come back ten minutes later.
Why would it, babes?
She wrote back. *I don't know. But . . . we did something . . .*
She needed to tell someone, after all this time keeping it secret,
hiding her shame over what she and the other girls had caused to
happen. She let it all out now, spilling the secret that only she and
Jade, and possibly Kai, knew about. The terrible thing they'd done.
She'd wanted to ask Kai about it the other day, when he came to see
her to get Jade's UV nail lamp back, but he'd been acting like such a
dick that she changed her mind. Kai was making out that he was
a massive hero, that Jade was going to think he was the bee's knees for
getting the lamp back. All Jade had needed to do was ask. Instead,
her dozy boyfriend had messaged her via the forum and arranged to
come to her house to pick the lamp up. Chloe guessed Jade simply
didn't want to see her, because of what had happened before.

When she'd finished writing to Shawn she sat back, sweating,
wondering if she'd done the wrong thing. She was pretty sure Shawn
would understand. That he would believe her when she said she had
no idea it would all get so out of hand. But what if he didn't? What
if it made him hate her? She waited for five excruciating minutes
before a reply came back.

It wasn't your fault, he wrote. *How could you have known that
would happen?*

She exhaled with relief.

Do you think I should tell the police?

Another long pause while he typed.

Why don't you leave it to me? I met the chief detective on the case. Let me talk to him, see what he thinks. I'll put in a good word for you.

She had tears in her eyes now. He was such a good person. So lovely.

Thank you ☺ she wrote.

No probs, babes. So . . . ready to meet up? How does this afternoon sound?

She didn't hesitate. *Perfect,* she wrote. *I can't wait!!*

⌣

She called goodbye to her mum, saying that she was going out shopping with a friend, and let herself out of the house before her mother noticed the amount of make-up she was wearing, and that she had on platform shoes that weren't strictly suitable for shopping. Trembling with excitement, she pulled out her phone and double-checked the instructions. A car would pick her up outside the newsagent's round the corner at 4 p.m. – obviously Shawn didn't want to arouse suspicion by having the car pick her up from home. It was 3.57 p.m.

This was really happening! As she let herself out of the front gate, her face entirely overtaken by a massive grin, she turned to see her little brother upstairs, gazing curiously out through his bedroom window at her. When he caught her eye he made a horrible face at her, squishing his nose against the glass and pressing his splayed fingers up on either side of his face. She laughed, louder than she normally would have done – a welcome release of the bubble and fizz of adrenalin – and he looked suitably gratified.

Bless him, she thought. *He's all right really, for a kid brother.*

Life felt great.

She couldn't help entertaining a fantasy that Shawn fancied her and that this was just an elaborate ruse for him to get to know her. They'd keep their relationship secret for a while – how long? A few months, probably, because after all she was only just sixteen. God, though, better make it longer. The OnT fans would rip off her head if they found out she was going out with Shawn. Come to that, she thought, they'd probably rip her head off right now if they knew where she was going.

Not that *she* knew where they were going either. Shawn had said it was best that way, in case his messages were being hacked and the press turned up.

If they got married, it would probably be best that they move abroad, to some massive estate on a cliff somewhere hot. Of course, Shawn would be away a lot, but that would be all right – OnT had so much security whenever they went anywhere, she and Shawn would be safe if they were together, and of course he'd want her to come on tour with them . . . And the money! She'd be so rich that she could buy her mum and dad a really nice house. Maybe even next to where she and Shawn were going to live. They always said they wanted to retire somewhere hot.

But, of course, the money was only an added bonus. She'd marry Shawn in a heartbeat even if he was penniless.

As she walked towards the main road, feeling as though her feet were floating above the pavement, she saw the car waiting for her. A black Audi A4 – she only recognised it because Shawn had told her this was what it would be, and she'd Google-imaged it. She wouldn't have had a clue what they looked like otherwise.

Even though she already knew it wouldn't be Shawn himself behind the wheel, her bowels clenched with nerves when she saw it. Any vestiges of fear that this was some sort of elaborate wind-up vanished, replaced instead with a different fear: that Shawn would be disappointed in her somehow; think her too young or too naïve.

She had to remind herself that this wasn't a date. She was getting carried away with all the excitement. This was for charity.

It was still real, though. She was still going to meet Shawn Barrett, and then she'd be in the papers with him, maybe on TV. Who knew what might come of it?

The tinted passenger window slid down when she drew level with the car.

'Hi, Chloe, jump in,' said the driver, leaning across and smiling at her. He was clean-shaven with a nice smile, black shades, a dark suit and chauffeur's hat. Chloe couldn't help feeling very slightly put out, though, that he hadn't leapt out to open the back door for her. Weren't chauffeurs meant to do that? Maybe they only did that for VIPs.

She bent down and looked in. 'Should I get in the front?'

'You do that,' said the driver, winking at her.

Chloe pulled open the heavy door and climbed in, grinning uncontrollably.

'Hi. Oh my God, I'm so excited to see Shawn again.'

The driver checked his rearview mirror and pulled the car away from the kerb. 'He's excited to see you too. Great to meet you, Chloe. I'm Pete, Shawn's driver.'

'Hello, Pete,' said Chloe solemnly. 'Can I take a photo of you? I'm thinking I might write a blog about this after, you know, about the whole day.' She pulled her phone out of her Paul's Boutique handbag, but Pete put a hand up in a 'stop' gesture.

'Whoah, hold on! Sorry, but I'm not allowed to have my photo taken. You know how it is – strict company policy. It's to do with security for the boys – if people recognise me, then the boys might get hassled even more by the paparazzi and the fans, who'd realise that if they saw me, Shawn and the others would likely be nearby . . .'

'Oh I see,' said Chloe, feeling foolish. 'Sorry. I didn't think.' Blushing, she put her phone back into her bag.

'No problem at all,' Pete said, slowing down at a zebra crossing as a small hunched lady tottered across.

'Where am I meeting Shawn?' she asked, trying not to sound too eager. 'Is it far?'

He shook his head. 'Not far at all – just down the road in fact. It's a private venue near Sunbury. It's tricky to find somewhere that Shawn won't be mobbed, so his manager hired it out for you and him.'

'Cool,' Chloe said, although she felt slightly perplexed. It all sounded a bit vague.

Pete shrugged. 'I know, strange, right? These pop stars have some funny ideas! Shawn's really into symbolism. He thinks it would be memorable for you to meet him in the shell grotto of this place, because—'

'Oh! I know!' Chloe interrupted. 'Because that's where the picture on the cover of *Twilight Kisses* was taken!'

Pete laughed. 'He knew you'd know.'

'Wow,' Chloe breathed. 'That's *so* cool!' Although she hoped that once they'd met, there'd be a chance of some hot chocolate somewhere. It was a cold February afternoon, on the way to getting dark already, and she was only wearing a thin denim jacket and black jeans; no gloves or coat because Shawn hadn't mentioned they'd be outdoors. She'd assumed the meeting would take place in an office, or a private room of a pub perhaps; even – she'd hoped – at his apartment. That grotto looked pretty chilly, even from the photo on the album sleeve.

'How will I find it?'

'Don't worry,' said Pete. 'I'll show you.'

Chapter 50
Day 14 – 4 p.m. – Patrick

When Patrick knocked at the door of Chloe Hedges' bungalow, it was opened by a boy of about seven or eight, the age where new front teeth have just come through and still look disproportionately enormous to the rest of the child.

'Are you a politician?' the boy asked.

'No. I'm a detective,' Pat replied, and the boy gaped at him.

'Mu-um!' he yelled, without turning away. 'There's a policeman here!'

'All right, Brandon, you don't need to tell the whole street,' came an answering voice.

Mrs Hedges came to the door. She was a tired-looking slim lady, probably in her forties but who looked a lot older, perhaps from exposure to the elements. Her skin was weather-beaten and wrinkled. But she had a lovely smile, which she hesitantly bestowed on Patrick as he introduced himself. They shook hands.

'Hello. I'm Rebecca Hedges. Would you like a cup of tea? Brandon, go and make the detective a tea. Milk? Sugar? Is this about Jessica McMasters? My daughter's already given a statement, as you probably know.'

She ushered him inside and looked pointedly at his feet as he confirmed that a tea with milk would be lovely. Patrick looked down at them too, momentarily puzzled. Then light dawned as he noticed that she wore slippers, and Brandon was in his socks. 'Shall I take off my shoes?'

There was that smile again. 'If you wouldn't mind . . . we just had the carpets cleaned. Thanks. Come through.'

He slipped off his brogues and followed her into the front room. It felt oddly intimate, being in a stranger's house in just his socks – which, he noticed, were odd ones. He sat down where she indicated, next to a big ginger cat on the sofa. 'I'm just following up a new lead in Jessica's murder investigation, Mrs Hedges, and I wanted a quick word with Chloe.'

Rebecca Hedges looked pained. 'I'm ever so sorry, Detective Lennon, but she's gone out shopping at the Bentall Centre in Kingston with a friend. You just missed her. I'll give her a call and ask what time she'll be back.'

'Who has she gone with?' Patrick looked at the photographs around the room, mostly school portraits of the two kids at different ages, in different coloured school jumpers; Brandon with baby teeth, then no front teeth, then the massive ones in the latest photo.

'Someone called Pareesa. I don't know her,' Rebecca confessed, pulling a mobile out of her cardigan pocket and holding it to her ear. 'She's been hanging out with some new girls from school, since Jessica died. It had a big effect on her, as you can imagine . . . No answer. It's gone straight to voicemail . . . Chloe, darling, it's Mum – give me a call back as soon as you get this message, would you? See you soon, don't be late. Love you . . .'

'Must have been a hell of a shock for her, Jess's death. Has she been struggling?' Patrick asked sympathetically, and Rebecca looked almost sheepish as she put her phone away again.

'Well,' she said. 'That's the thing. I mean, yes, obviously she has in some ways. She gets a bit tearful at times. But I think in other ways it's been a real wake-up call for her. She turned sixteen the other day and did a charity parachute jump! We're so proud of her. It's like she's decided to embrace life, and just go for it. Today she was on a real high, just getting ready to go out shopping with her mates. She's a great girl. And she deserves to look forward to life, after what she went through last year . . .'

She looked expectantly at Pat.

'What was that?'

'Oh, sorry, I thought you'd know. She nearly died, of leukaemia, you see. She was ill for a year, but she's fine now.'

Brandon came slowly back into the room carrying the sort of cup of tea that Patrick, once he'd tasted it, realised only an eight-year-old could make – tepid, unboiled dishwater. He thanked the boy and left it undrunk on the floor by the arm of the sofa. Brandon disappeared again, looking pleased with himself.

'Mrs Hedges, what I really wanted to ask Chloe – or you – was if she knew a girl called Rose Sharp?'

Rebecca's eyes opened wide. 'The other girl that was killed,' she stated flatly, panic edging in her voice. 'Why are you asking that?'

'Did Chloe know her?'

Rebecca sank her head into her arms, then looked up fearfully. 'You think Chloe's in danger, don't you? I'm going to ring her again. Let me ring her . . .'

'Mrs Hedges, please, there's no immediate cause for concern. I'm following up on a lead, and I need to know.'

She had the phone in her hand again, but didn't lift it to her ear, just twirled it miserably between her fingers.

'I don't think she ever met her, no. But she and Jess went to the vigil for her, after the OnTarget concert at Twickenham. And I think they might have spoken on the – what do you call those websites where they chat about bands and stuff?'

'Forums?'

'Yes, that's it. Forums.'

'OK. And have you ever heard of a website called StoryPad? A lot of teenagers use it, particularly, it seems, OnTarget fans. They write stories about the band members.'

Pat's own phone vibrated with a text, and he pulled it out of his coat pocket. The text was from Carmella:

ON MY WAY TO JADE PILKINGTON'S. BTW – PRESS HAVE GOT WIND OF HAMMOND'S ARREST. BRACE YOURSELF!

He sighed and put it away again.

Rebecca frowned. 'I don't know about that. Chloe loves writing stories, though. She got an A* in her last English test. I think she may have put some up online, yes, although I don't know which website.' She stood up, pressed the phone's keyboard, and paced around the room listening, her slippers gently flip-flopping. 'Still nothing. I'm getting worried. Should I be worried? I can't believe I haven't been more worried before, I mean, obviously, two young girls murdered around here and Chloe was friends with one and knew of the other one, I should never have let her go out on her own – but she's not on her own, she's with her friends – but is she? Maybe she isn't! Oh my God, I need to ring my husband, get him to go and find her in Kingston. It's not safe . . .'

The woman was becoming more and more distressed, so Patrick stood up too. 'Mrs Hedges, please. We have just arrested someone for the murders of both Rose and Jessica, so it's highly unlikely that Chloe is in any danger.'

Mrs Hedges sank back into an armchair. 'Oh thank heavens. I'm so sorry, Detective. You must think I'm a terrible parent, letting her go out when I didn't know you'd arrested someone. Who is it?'

At that exact moment, Patrick's eye fell on a framed photograph that he hadn't spotted before, tucked away in the corner of a built-in bookcase. It was of a girl, Chloe, he assumed, lying in a hospital bed hooked up to drips and monitors, deathly pale but with the biggest beam on her face. Flanking her, one on each side of the bed, were two men, each holding one of her hands. One was Shawn Barrett and the other one Mervyn Hammond.

He made an involuntary noise in his throat. Walking over to pick it up, he answered her question with another. 'When was this taken?'

Mrs Hedges smiled fondly. 'Last April, when she was undergoing her final chemo session. They were amazing, those two – and the other guys from the record company who made it happen for her. I honestly think that it got her through it, that visit.' She turned serious again and repeated her question. 'Who is it that you've arrested?'

Patrick knew that he shouldn't tell her. But – in the light of the photo he was holding, and the fact that it would be all over the papers in the morning – he had to let her know.

'Well. I'm sorry to tell you, and I shouldn't really – but you'll hear it on the news soon anyway – it's actually him.' He pointed at the photograph. 'Mervyn Hammond.'

Rebecca's face drained of every last bit of colour and she flopped against the back of the chair. 'That's impossible!'

Patrick sat back down again too, still holding the photo. 'We're questioning him about both murders, and another one, of an older lady.'

Her reaction surprised and worried him. She looked as though she had just been informed that her son, Brandon, was the serial killer.

She shook her head. 'No. There's no way!'

'What makes you say that, Mrs Hedges?'

'That man,' she said, pointing a shaky finger at the photograph on Pat's lap, 'is a *saint*. A *saint*, do you hear me? I would trust him with my daughter's life! Do you have any idea how much charity work he does?'

Patrick resisted the urge to cough out the words *Jimmy Savile*. He found it difficult to reconcile the image of the smug, nut-munching attitudinal cynic that he'd found Hammond to be with anything approaching 'a saint'. And yet – first impressions, and all. PR people were notoriously good at projecting only the image they wished to project and, despite Winkler's convictions, it just didn't all add up.

Rebecca continued to sing Mervyn Hammond's praises for several minutes more. She seemed torn between relief that she didn't need to worry about Chloe being temporarily incommunicado anymore and genuine distress at the news about Hammond. Patrick cut her off as politely as he could, standing up and asking her to ring him the moment that she got in touch with Chloe. He dressed it up in a request to ask Chloe about StoryPad – but he still couldn't shift a sense of unease that she was currently AWOL, arrest or no arrest.

Carmella rang him in the car as he was driving away.

'Chloe Hedges wasn't in,' he said. 'Her mum seemed devastated at the news that Hammond's been arrested.' He briefly told her about Mervyn's secret charity work. 'She said – and I quote – "That man's a saint."'

He heard Carmella snort down the phone. 'Jade wasn't home either. Nobody was in – a neighbour told me Jade's mum was away visiting her sister. The neighbour, a Mrs Sherry Downs, saw Jade being dropped home at 3 a.m. the night before. We don't know what time she went out again.'

'I don't like this,' Patrick said, increasing his speed so he was just above the limit. 'Mrs Hedges says Chloe's gone shopping, but she's not answering her phone either.'

'Probably doesn't want to be bothered by her mum.'

'Maybe. But I'm going to phone the Bentall Centre in Kingston, ask them to put out an announcement over the tannoy, ask her to call home.'

'I hope you don't do that to Bonnie when she's a teenager,' Carmella said.

'Huh. After this case, when Bonnie's a teenager I'm never going to let her out of my sight. Did Mrs Downs say anything else about Jade?'

'I was about to get to that. She said she was woken up, like I said, at about three by the sound of a car door slamming outside and loads of shrieking and laughing, so she looked out of the window and saw Jade coming through the front gate. She said she banged on the window to give Jade a hard time about waking up the whole street, and Jade was all excited. She called up to her to say she'd been to a party working as a waitress, that all of OnTarget were there, and Mervyn Hammond's bodyguard had given her a lift home. Mrs Downs had assumed she was drunk, until Jade said she'd been working. Mrs Downs thought that was unusual – she'd never known Jade to have a job before. She also said she'd never seen Jade so happy and excited.'

'Jade was at Hammond's party.' That was *very* interesting.

'Yep. Are you thinking what I'm thinking?'

'Call Gareth. Let's find out everything we can about this bodyguard, assuming Gareth hasn't gone off somewhere in a massive sulk. And I'm going to call Suzanne. I'm getting a bad feeling about Chloe and Jade. A very bad feeling.'

Chapter 51
Day 14 – Chloe

Shawn Barrett's chauffeur, Pete, pulled off the road and drove down a small path, parking up outside huge iron gates in a tall, old-looking wall. He jumped out and deftly undid the padlock that held the chain together, opened the gates, drove in – then got out and re-locked the padlock.

'We've got this place booked out, but they're very security conscious,' he commented as he got back behind the wheel. 'It's empty at the moment, but the developers were still really keen that nobody knew Shawn was coming.'

'Oh,' Chloe said, wondering why, in that case, there were no security guards to be seen. She wasn't really sure what a 'developer' was either. Pete parked the car at the end of a long driveway, in front of an enormous house, all turrets and fancy stonework. Its front door was up a sweeping flight of stone steps, and Chloe looked longingly through the car window at it – even if it was closed, it was a place that would have a toilet! – as Pete walked round to open the door for her. That was more like a chauffeur should behave, she thought. He was carrying a black backpack that she hadn't noticed before.

'Could I nip in and use the loo before I meet Shawn?' she asked shyly. Nerves were starting to get the better of her and she was desperate for a wee.

He looked at his watch. 'Hmm. Sorry, love, time's a bit tight. We need to get on, really. He's a busy man. He just texted me to say he's out there already and it's cold!'

Chloe felt the disapproval in his voice. 'Oh yes. Sorry. Sorry. I don't want to take up much of his time.' Again, she wondered why the symbolism meant so much to Shawn that he'd want to meet her in a freezing cold grotto in the middle of February, in the dark. And she hadn't seen Pete reading any texts . . . She looked sideways at him.

'One other thing,' he said, as she climbed out of the front seat. He held out his hand, palm up. 'You're going to need to leave your phone in the car. Shawn's got a strict rule about that, in case anyone tries to sneak a photo.'

'Oh.' Chloe's prickles of unease increased. 'I'll turn it off, I promise.'

Pete shook his head. 'Just leave it here, love, it'll be fine. Look, I'll put it in the glove compartment. It'll be completely safe.'

She reluctantly handed it over, noticing that her heart rate had rocketed. Perhaps it was just excitement at being about to meet Shawn.

Was she about to meet Shawn?

Pete locked the phone into the car and hoisted the backpack onto his shoulder. That was bothering her too. Where had that come from and what was in it?

'What's in there?' she asked.

He glared at her, not friendly anymore. 'Stuff for Shawn. None of your business. Come on, then, we haven't got all day.'

Chloe suddenly thought she was going to be sick. Her teeth chattering, she followed him as he walked away from the house, down a gravel path that curved away behind some tall forbidding trees in the house's grounds. It was very cold, and getting dark. There was no sound anywhere apart from a distant rumble of traffic and then the sudden shrill bark of a fox.

Was it a fox? Her ears must be playing tricks on her, she thought. It sounded like a *girl* crying.

She forced herself to remember Shawn's sweet messages on the forum. She was just being silly, going overboard on the 'stranger-danger' paranoia.

But something did not feel right. *Always trust your instincts, Chloe*, she heard her mother whisper.

Crunching along the gravel path in almost complete darkness behind Pete, Chloe dithered. For some reason she could not get the image out of her head of Rose Sharp, plump and freckled in the blown-up school photograph propped on the table at the vigil, nor of the wrapped-up poster in a tube that Jess had got her for her birthday. She imagined Jess's fingers struggling with Sellotape as she put the garish gift wrap around it, the fingers that only days later were stilled forever, stripped of the cheap H&M gilt rings that were now probably in an evidence bag somewhere.

She stopped. Pete noticed, and turned.

'Uh, sorry,' she began, clutching her handbag closer to herself. 'Bit of a nightmare, but I'm not feeling very well. I think I'm going to have to go home and meet Shawn another time. Can you apologise to him for me? You don't have to give me a lift home or anything, just give me my phone back, and I'll find my own way . . .'

The expression on his face was like nothing Chloe had ever seen before. He looked furious. 'You can't do that. Shawn's gone to a lot of effort over this. He's expecting you.'

Tears rushed into Chloe's eyes. She hated making people cross and upset, and the thought of pissing off Shawn Barrett was

unbearable. 'I know, but' – she never normally used her leukaemia as an excuse, apart from to get out of tidying her room, but it
was all she could think of – 'I'm sure he'd understand. He knows
that I was really ill last year, he visited me in hospital, and I'm still
not right . . .'

Pete put down the black backpack and walked up to her so that
his face was mere inches away from hers. In the gloom, his eyes
looked huge and black, demonic.

Oh shit, thought Chloe. The fox shriek came again, louder this
time, and it spurred her into action. She turned to run, but his left
arm had shot out and grabbed her biceps, squeezing it tight. She
tried to shake it off, staring down at it in horror and pain, which
made her not notice his right fist – until it connected with her collarbone in a sickening pistol-crack that sent agony flooding around
her chest, up her neck and cascading down all her ribs.

She passed out.

When she awoke, the first thing she was aware of was being in a very
cold and dark place, leaning against a wall that seemed to have been
wallpapered with sharp stones that stuck into her back. The fox was
still shrieking. It sounded so loud now that she thought it must be
in there with her.

She opened her eyes to try to see it and threw up all over herself,
causing the already sharp pain in her shoulder to intensify and
amplify, so intense that she saw it as scarlet ribbons in her vision
lighting up the darkness. She tried to lift a hand to wipe her mouth,
but found she couldn't – her arms were handcuffed together behind
her body. She tried to move her legs, but they were bound together
with what looked like rope.

Chloe groaned, in too much pain to properly cry out. She was a moron. Of course Pete wasn't Shawn's chauffeur. Of course it hadn't really been Shawn Barrett messaging her . . . Oh God.

'I'm going to die,' she whispered.

Then, to her complete shock, the fox cry stopped and the fox spoke to her, a voice coming out of the darkness. 'I thought you were already dead.'

She was hallucinating; she must be. This was some kind of horrific nightmare. But the stones sticking into her back and head and the pain in her chest told her that she couldn't be.

She wailed, peering into the thick black air, trying to see the source of the voice. 'Who are you? You're a fox!'

The voice came back, more thickly. 'I ain't no fox, what are you on about? My name's Jade, and he's got me locked up in here too.'

'Jade? Not Jade as in Jade and Kai?'

There was a faint snort. 'Don't talk to me about that twat.'

'Oh my God, Jade, it's me, Chloe Hedges. F-U-Cancer. Where the fuck are we? What's going on? I came to meet Shawn.'

'Oh, babe, so did I! I got a text at this party last night. Shawn was there and he said he'd seen me and thought I was gorgeous. Asked me to meet him at this place down on the Thames called Platt's Eyot. Shawn, I mean the bloke pretending to be him, said he had a houseboat and was going to meet me there.'

How stupid and naïve, Chloe thought, then stopped herself. She had been just as stupid, hadn't she? They had both allowed their desperation, the years of fantasy about meeting Shawn, to blind them to danger. Exactly the same thing must have happened to Rose and Jess.

Jade's words tumbled out. 'So I was, like, waiting there, on the edge of the car park, looking around coz there was no sign of him and the whole place was deserted coz it was pissing down with rain, and I got my phone out to Snapchat who I thought was Shawn and *he* came up behind me and grabbed me, stuck a knife in my back and told me if I cried out, I was dead.'

Chloe could hear Jade panting, seemingly drained by the memory and the torrent of words.

'It's only just struck me, but I'm sure I've seen him before,' Chloe said. 'There's something familiar about him.'

Jade didn't respond. What did it matter, anyway? He had them now, and all that mattered was whether he let them live. Or if they would die here.

'You handcuffed too?' Chloe asked.

'Yeah, and my feet are tied to some weird sort of stone bench thing. I can't move. My legs have gone dead. Everything's numb.' Jade started to cry again.

'I think I know why we're here. Why he chose us, and Rose and Jess.'

'What? Why?'

'The StoryPad thing. It has to be that. It's the only thing that connects the four of us.'

'Oh shit oh shit oh shit.' Chloe could almost hear Jade's brain whirring in the darkness. 'That's why he brought us *here*.'

'What?'

'I never told you, did I?' Jade said. 'The day . . . the day it happened.' She began to cry. 'I had no idea. If I'd known she . . .' Jade's voice broke apart and she dissolved into sobs.

'We'll die of hypothermia if he leaves us here all night,' Chloe said when Jade was finally silent. Already her voice was coming out all funny with cold – her mouth wasn't working properly.

'Oh God, why did I do it?' Her voice tailed off and the fox wail returned. Chloe wanted to know exactly what Jade had done, but for now it was far more important to attempt to get out of here.

'Shhh, Jade, listen. I heard you crying back from where he parked his car. There's a road not far away. If we both scream, someone might hear us.'

More sniffing. 'I've already tried. Nobody came.'

'Yeah, but there's two of us now. We need to get out of here before he gets back. Let's try it – after three: one, two, three . . .'

Chloe filled her lungs, although it was absolute agony on her busted collarbone, and the two of them lifted their heads and screamed as loudly as they could, the sound filling the small, freezing grotto, bouncing off the shells and – Chloe prayed – through the gaps in the boarded-up windows and the weird arched doorway, out over the trees to the road.

They screamed and screamed until their voices cracked and sputtered to nothing, like a gust of wind blowing a candle flame back to darkness.

When they stopped screaming, a man's voice came out of the ringing silence – *his* voice. 'Are we quite finished?'

Chloe's heart somersaulted in her broken chest. Jade screamed again.

She heard someone moving towards her. He had been here, in the darkness, all along.

Chapter 52
Day 14 – Patrick

Patrick and Carmella had arranged to meet at her flat, which was close to Chloe's address, and were now together in Patrick's car. As usual, Carmella looked as fresh as a newly bathed baby; her red curls in individually spaced, smooth spirals; her skin dewy-clear. Patrick had no idea how she did it. His skin felt prickly and sticky; his lower back aching from sitting in the car; his tinnitus whistling feedback in his ears; and his throat sore from constantly puffing on his e-cig. *I'm falling apart*, he thought.

'Have you managed to get through to Gareth about Hammond's bodyguard?' he asked.

'Not yet. He wasn't answering.' She produced her phone. 'You think he's our man?'

'I don't know. Have we encountered him?' Patrick felt the need to consult his Moleskine, but it was back at the office.

Carmella had her phone to her ear, waiting for Gareth to answer. 'I think he was there when we went to Global Sounds Music, waiting in reception . . . Hello, Gareth? You all right? Listen, what's Mervyn Hammond's bodyguard called? . . . Kerry Mangan. What do you know about him?'

Patrick half-listened, while trying to puzzle everything out at the same time. Mervyn had insisted he'd been set up, that the 'LUCKY' knickers had been planted at his house. The DNA result wasn't back yet, but that didn't matter. If, God forbid, Chloe and Jade had been abducted, then obviously Mervyn, who had been in police company all day, couldn't be responsible. There was a chance he was connected, was orchestrating everything, but after what Chloe's mother had said, Lennon had discounted him pretty much entirely – though he was glad they were still holding him. Hammond had shifted from number one suspect to their most important witness.

Because if the underwear had been planted at Mervyn's house, it must have been put there by somebody who'd been at the party. The same man who'd called the next morning and left the anonymous tip. They knew for certain that Mangan had been at the party, and had given Jade a lift home. Had he arranged to meet her again later?

Was he the killer?

Whoever it was, they now had a probable motive to explain why the killer had taken the girls' clothes from the two crime scenes. He had been saving them to plant on some other poor sucker. That poor sucker being Mervyn.

Carmella ended the call. 'Mangan was with Hammond when they visited the children's home. And while Gareth was talking, I remembered something Roisin told me in Ireland. She said something about Mervyn's bodyguard being there, giving her dirty looks while Mervyn was persuading her to keep quiet. I'm pretty sure he was there at the signing at Waterstones too. I have this memory of him looking over at me and Wendy when I was talking to her . . .'

'We need to get a photo to Chelsea Fox,' Patrick said.

Carmella nodded. 'Gareth told me that Mangan is ex-army, but was discharged back in the nineties for reasons Winkler was unable to ascertain. Let me ring Gareth back, see if he can get a photo now.'

'Get an address first. We'll go to Mangan's now, assuming we can get his address. Then tell Gareth to get round to Chelsea Fox's, show her Mangan's photo.'

Adrenalin surged beneath Patrick's skin. But running alongside the excitement, the conviction that they were close, so close, was a deep, horrible fear. Jess had been missing for twenty-four hours before her body was found, suggesting that the killer liked to play with his victims like a cat with a mouse.

Jade could already be dead. Possibly Chloe Hedges too – he'd instructed Rebecca to ring him the second she turned up, and there had been no call.

The alternative, Patrick thought with a shudder, was even worse. Both girls could be suffering torture, right now, begging not for their lives but to die. For the pain to end.

Chapter 53
Day 14 – Patrick

Halfway to Kerry Mangan's place, the address of which Gareth had sent them within minutes of talking to Carmella, Patrick noticed the petrol light flashing in his car, reminding him that he'd been meaning to fill up for the past two days. The dashboard informed him he had five miles left till the tank was empty. He banged the steering wheel with his fist. For fuck's sake. Normally, this would have drawn a quip from Carmella, but she was as tense as he was; her knee bouncing up and down; swearing at the traffic; leaning out of the window at one point and aiming a stream of insults in her thickest Irish accent at a portly man who was blocking the road with his white van. She didn't look quite so fresh anymore.

'Which one of us will have a heart attack first, do you think?' Patrick asked, as they turned into the street in Surbiton where Mangan lived.

Carmella didn't reply. She was too busy gawping at the scene halfway down the street.

'Who the hell's that?' she asked, unbuckling her seat belt as Patrick did something he'd never done before: bumper parking the car, shoving a tiny Fiat a foot forward so he could squeeze into a space.

A mixed-race teenager was hammering on the front door of a Victorian terraced house, before stepping back and yelling up at the first-floor window. 'Jade! I know you're in there with *him*, bae! Come out, you fucking slag, I love you.'

'Police!' Carmella shouted and the boy turned his stricken face towards them, his mouth dropping open. Tears streaked his spotty cheeks and his fists were red from where he'd been thumping the door.

Patrick ran towards the teenager and for a moment he thought the kid was going to do a runner, that they were going to have to chase him. But then he heard a window open above them and they all looked up.

A muscular man with cropped hair – Patrick remembered him from the reception area at Global Sounds – leaned out and called down, 'Are you the police? You got here quick – I only just put the phone down.'

'Are you Kerry Mangan?' Patrick asked, but the man's reply was drowned out by the boy screeching, 'Where's Jade? She's in there with you, isn't she? Jade! Come out! I love you!'

'This little twat thinks I've got his bird in here.' Mangan laughed.

We've got it wrong, Patrick thought with a lurch in his gut, peering up at the bodyguard, at the mixture of irritation and amusement on his face. Got it wrong again.

'Shut up, you,' he said to the boy, who was immediately cowed. He muttered something about Mangan being a 'homewrecker', then hung his head.

'What's your name?' Patrick demanded. 'And how do you know Jade?'

'She's my girlfriend,' the boy said meekly.

'And your name?'

'Kai Topper.'

'*Is* Jade Pilkington in there?' Carmella asked, calling up to Mangan.

'What, that OnTarget nut? You must be fucking kidding.'

'He's lying,' Topper said.

'Can you let us in?' Patrick asked.

Mangan pointed at Kai Topper. 'As long as you keep that dickhead away from me.'

Some bodyguard, Patrick thought. He turned to the teenager. 'Kai, I think you need to cool down, all right? Let's put you in the back of our car for a minute while we have a word with Mr Mangan.'

'Are you arresting me? I ain't done nothing!'

'We just want you to cool down, OK? Come on . . .'

He escorted Topper along the road to the car, put him in the back seat and locked the doors so he couldn't get out.

Kerry Mangan was waiting on his doorstep when Patrick got back to the house, talking to Carmella. Mangan was unshaven and wrapped in a navy towelling dressing gown, with bare feet. 'I was in the bath when I suddenly heard someone banging on the door and yelling.' He yawned. 'Stupid prat. Why the hell does he think his bird would be here? Come in and see for yourself.'

They followed Mangan up a staircase and into his flat. He led them into the living room. It was all very tastefully decorated, if somewhat uninspired, framed prints from Ikea above furniture from the same store.

'Mind if I take a look around?' Patrick asked.

'What, you really think she might be here?'

'We just need to check.'

Mangan shrugged. 'Fine. Whatever. But it's a bit messy. Like I said, I just jumped out the bath. I've been asleep all day, had a late one last night.'

Patrick left Mangan with Carmella – he heard her start to make small talk about a framed photo of Mangan in Dublin – and went into the little kitchen first, then the bathroom. The bath was still filled with water and the choppy remains of bubbles. A plastic eye mask hung from the tap and a paperback novel lay face down on the toilet lid.

Next he checked the spare room, which was piled high with junk, before going into the bedroom. A double bed with a crumpled duvet, piles of clothes on the floor. He checked the wardrobes and under the bed, feeling foolish. As he was about to leave the room, he noticed a framed photo on the bedside table. Kerry Mangan and a good-looking tanned man, their cheeks pressed together, beaming at the camera.

'Satisfied I'm not hiding any teenage girls?' Mangan asked as Patrick re-entered the living room. The bodyguard was seated in an armchair, Carmella on the sofa opposite. Patrick took a seat beside her.

'Jade Pilkington is missing,' he said. 'We're extremely concerned about her well-being. Do you have any idea where she might be?'

'Shit, you think . . . ? Like those other poor girls? Fuck.' He pulled his dressing gown tightly around him. 'I gave her a lift home from this party Mervyn had at his place last night. She said her boyfriend was doing her head in and asked me if I was heading back into town. I don't normally give lifts to girls I don't know, by the way. But the party got so wild towards the end, everyone was off their tits all of a sudden – not me, 'cos I was driving, obviously. I felt a bit worried about her, so I offered to drive her back. She'd already said she lived quite close to me.'

'Did anything happen between you?' Carmella asked.

Mangan laughed. 'What, you mean, did I bring her back here and shag her? I don't think my boyfriend would like that very much.'

'Oh,' said Carmella. Patrick couldn't help but smile, and wished he'd had a chance to tell Carmella about the photo in the bedroom.

'Is that why you were discharged from the army?' Patrick asked.

Mangan's expression darkened. 'Yeah. They still did that in the nineties. I had to, like, hide it when I first joined up, but they found out, the fuckers. That's one of the reasons Mervyn took me on . . . When I applied for the job at his company I told him the truth about why I was discharged and he was furious, said it was a disgrace.'

Something struck Patrick. Mervyn Hammond had never been married. He lived the life of a bachelor. 'Is Mervyn gay too?'

'Nah. I thought he was, at first. Thought he was in the closet, like a lot of blokes of his generation. But he doesn't seem to be interested in men or women. He's one of them asexuals. All he's interested in is his business and his model railways.'

Patrick wanted to get back onto the subject of Jade, but there was something he needed to know first. 'Kerry, why did you and Mervyn visit St Mary's Children's Home the other night?'

'Hasn't he told you? I guess he wouldn't. He doesn't like anyone to know about it. Very private, is Mervyn.'

Patrick nodded. This chimed with what Chloe Hedges' mum had told them about his work helping kids with cancer.

'He helps them with their fundraising. Plus he works with the kids, gives them inspirational talks about never letting themselves be handicapped by their background, their start in life. He tells them they can achieve anything if they put their minds to it. He's great at that stuff. I'm always telling him he should go public, put his talents to wider use, but he won't.'

'Why does Mervyn need a bodyguard?' Carmella asked.

Mangan grinned. 'He doesn't really. It's all for show. Good for his image, you know, makes him look important. Plus I think he likes my company. He might act like he's the king of the world half the time, but I reckon he's lonely really. Christ, don't tell him I told you that.'

'We won't.' Patrick felt slightly ashamed. First, Rebecca Hedges had told them about Mervyn's work with children, and now this. They had got him all wrong – although it was understandable with the image Hammond projected of himself. Patrick couldn't decide if the public relations man was brilliant or terrible at doing his own personal PR, but it reminded him of a lesson this job had taught him over the years: never take anyone at face value. Everybody has secrets, and not all secrets are bad.

'Let's get back to Jade,' Patrick said. 'Where did you drop her? At home?'

'Yeah. It was about three by the time we got there. I was knackered, but she kept me awake on the way home babbling on about someone who'd messaged her.'

Patrick leaned forwards. 'Did she say who?'

Mangan twigged to the importance of what Patrick was asking. 'Shit. I wasn't really listening, to be honest. She was going on and on about how "someone amazing" had told her he'd seen her and wanted to meet her. It was like she wanted me to ask her who this amazing person was, but I wasn't that interested. I just wanted to get home.'

'Do you remember if she said when she'd got the message?'

'I'm pretty sure it was at the party.'

'And the person who sent the message was at the party too?'

'I think so. God, I'm sorry, hang on.' He propped his chin on his fist, thinking hard. 'Yeah, I'm sure she did. She said something like, "Maybe he liked me in my waitress uniform," and started giggling.'

'But she definitely didn't give you a name?'

'No.'

'Not Shawn Barrett?'

Mangan's eyes widened. 'You don't think it's him, do you? I thought you questioned him already.'

'I think it's someone pretending to be Shawn.'

Someone who was at the party. The same person who'd planted the evidence to frame Mervyn.

They thanked Mangan and headed back to the car. Patrick had almost forgotten that Kai Topper was on the back seat, looking like a dog who'd been locked in by a thoughtless owner. Patrick slid into the driver's seat, Carmella climbing in next to him, and turned round to talk to Topper.

'She's not there,' Patrick said.

'Are you sure?' His eyes were bloodshot and watery and Patrick was sure he'd been crying again. Did he realise how much danger his girlfriend was in?

'We're going to take you back to the station,' he said. 'We— For fuck's sake!'

Topper had produced a knife from his inside pocket. Patrick immediately dived between the seats, grabbing the boy's wrist and twisting his arm. Topper cried out and the knife fell onto the car seat. Patrick snatched it up. Carmella had already exited the car and yanked the door beside Topper open, handcuffs at the ready.

'I wasn't going to stab you!' Topper blurted. 'I just thought I'd better tell you I had it.'

'Got any more concealed weapons?'

'No. I swear.'

'What were you doing, Kai? Planning to stab Kerry Mangan?'

Topper's eyes fell. 'I wouldn't have actually done it. But he's a hard man, a bodyguard. I thought he might attack me. I just . . . I just want to find Jade.'

As he spoke, Carmella searched him and cuffed his hands behind his back, just in case.

'You're going to tell us everything you know, Kai,' Patrick said. 'If you do, I'll think about letting you off with a caution. Understand?'

The boy refused to meet his eye. 'Yeah.'

'Good. And in the meantime, you know what I want you to do?'

'What?' The boy's voice was a squeak.

'I want you to shut the fuck up.'

Chapter 54
Day 14 – Patrick

The incident room was packed full of bodies, every pair of eyes focused on Patrick as he paced up and down in front of the whiteboard. Photos of Chloe Hedges and Jade Pilkington had been pinned up beside the pictures of Jessica and Rose, plus the smaller one of Nancy Marr. Patrick stopped pacing and raised a hand, the whole room falling silent, including Winkler, who was skulking in the corner. Gareth was there too, refusing to meet Patrick's eye, and Suzanne, standing upright by the door with her arms crossed, one foot tapping anxiously. It was 7.30 p.m. but nobody wanted to go home. Patrick knew this team would stay here all night if they were needed.

'I'll keep this brief,' Patrick said. 'But I want everybody up to speed with what's going on. The first thing to say is that, contrary to rumour, we do not believe Mervyn Hammond is guilty of the murders – not least because he's been here all day and, before that, DI Winkler was with him.'

Several heads turned towards Winkler, who pretended to be examining something beneath his fingernails. Fifteen minutes earlier, Winkler had called Sandwell, the journalist who accused Hammond of molesting a teenage girl years before. Hearing that Hammond was in custody, Sandwell had panicked at the thought of testifying in court and admitted to making the whole thing up, trying to settle old scores.

'However, we are keeping Hammond at the station for the time being as we believe he holds important information and we don't want to lose track of him. We also have Jade Pilkington's boyfriend, Kai Topper, here for an interview.'

He turned to the whiteboard.

'Here's what we know at the moment: Jade Pilkington got a lift home from Hammond's party last night and was dropped off just after 3 a.m. At noon, Topper went round to her house, but she wasn't in. Luckily for us, Topper had an app linking his and Jade's phones, so he could trace where she was.'

'Creepy little fucker,' said Winkler.

'The phone signal told him Jade was at a place called Platt's Eyot. He went there and looked round, but there was no sign of Jade or her phone, and the signal had gone, like the phone had been turned off. He then assumed she must have hooked up with Kerry Mangan after the party and headed round there, having looked up his address online.' Patrick paused for a moment. Most people were shocked to discover how easy it was to find home addresses on the Web. 'But Mangan hasn't seen Jade since he dropped her home at 3 a.m. I've sent a couple of uniforms to this Platt's Eyot place to look for the missing phone.

'Chloe Hedges went out at around 4 p.m.,' Patrick went on. 'She told her mum that she was going to meet a friend and that they were planning to go shopping in Kingston later. We've contacted the friend, Pareesa, who tells us she had no plans to meet up with Chloe and, in fact, hasn't heard from her for a few days. We called the Bentall Centre in Kingston who put out a tannoy announcement that got no response, and I'm going to ask one of you to go down there to review CCTV footage, though we don't believe she ever went there. We are trying to pinpoint the location of Chloe's phone, but it appears to be switched off.'

He paused and surveyed the room, ensuring that everyone was listening.

'Here's why we believe Chloe and Jade are in danger, why they may have been targeted and haven't just gone off somewhere, either together or separately: we discovered that Rose and Jessica were the co-authors of a piece of fiction on a website called StoryPad.'

Martin Hale nodded as Patrick said this.

'There were two other co-authors: Chloe and Jade. We don't know what it is about this story that has made them the target of the killer – we're going to talk to Kai Topper about this shortly.'

Winkler finally piped up. 'You reckon someone killed them because of a *story*? What's it about?'

Patrick counted to three under his breath before replying. *Stay calm. Don't let him rile you.*

'It's about OnTarget. Carmella and I have read parts of it, but it doesn't appear to contain any clues – certainly not clear ones. StoryPad have provided us with a huge number of comments that were made about the story by other users and we'll need a couple of you to go through these. Though we're hoping Topper will be able to save us the trouble. We've also spoken to Strong's team who have confirmed that Wendy had been looking at StoryPad shortly before she left the station and headed to the Rotunda. My belief is that she discovered something that put her in danger – that she made contact with the killer.'

There was an audible puff of breath from half the officers in the room. Patrick thought he could feel a draught.

'Finally, we all know that somebody called the station this morning informing us that we would find Rose's underwear at Hammond's house, which led to his arrest. We believe that this caller planted this evidence during the party last night and made contact with Jade at the same time. Given everything that has happened today, it's likely that this was a diversionary tactic – intended to distract us today while they went after Chloe and Jade.'

He gestured at the photos of the two missing girls, drawing every pair of eyes in the room to the pictures.

'I want you all to be aware that we don't have much time. The man who murdered Rose and Jess did not keep them alive for long. And during the time he did have them, he tortured them. Chloe and Jade may already be dead. And if they're not dead yet . . .' He let his words hang in the air.

'I've got a theory,' said Winkler.

Patrick suppressed a groan. 'Let's have it, then.'

'What if Chloe and Jade are the killers? They murdered the other two girls. Jade planted the knickers at Hammond's gaff last night. All this stuff about her getting a mysterious message is bullshit. They've got scared and done a runner.'

Patrick had already thought of this. 'Chloe has a solid alibi for the time of all of the murders. And Kai Topper says Jade was at her house with him, with her mum downstairs, when Rose and Wendy were murdered. We can't get hold of Jade's mother at the moment to corroborate this, but we believe him.'

'And how does the old lady fit in?' Winkler asked. 'She writing stuff about OnTarget too?' He laughed and looked round for others to join in. Nobody glanced at him.

'We don't know that yet. But we're going to find out. And we're going to find these girls.'

'Dead or alive,' said Winkler. Before Patrick could respond, he added, 'Right, I'd better go and talk to Hammond, find out who else was at this party last night.'

'No way.'

Patrick turned his head. It was Suzanne. She took a step towards Winkler, a fierce expression making the other detective visibly shrink away. 'Everybody else can leave the room now. But don't leave the station. You'd better call your partners and spouses: tell them not to wait up.'

The rest of the officers filed out, leaving Patrick, Suzanne, Winkler and Carmella, whose arm Suzanne had caught as she went to exit the room.

Suzanne addressed Winkler again. 'I've already spoken to Mr Hammond and he's willing to help us.'

'Great.' Winkler looked relieved.

'But only if you apologise to him.'

'What?'

'He told me about your behaviour at his house. What you did to his personal property. I've persuaded him not to make a complaint against you by offering my own time. I'm going to talk to the children at St Mary's and the other children's homes where he volunteers, help Mervyn out by talking to them about a career in the police force. A good cause, and one I'm happy to help with. But he also wants a personal apology from you.'

'But—'

She jabbed a finger at him. 'Not just an apology, Adrian. He wants you to grovel. Now get out there and do it.'

As Winkler slunk from the room, Patrick was almost able to raise a smile.

'Carmella, after Winkler's begged for Mervyn's forgiveness I want you to go in and get the details of who was at the party.'

'And I'm going to talk to Kai Topper,' Patrick said. He rolled his eyes. 'Hopefully he'll have stopped crying by now.'

Topper had indeed ceased his blubbing. He sat in interview room three, twisting a can of Coke in circles, fidgeting and chewing his grubby fingernails. As soon as Patrick entered the room he looked up hopefully. 'Have you found her?'

'I'm afraid not.' Patrick took the seat opposite Kai.

He had already asked the boy if he had any idea where Jade might have gone, if there were places where his girlfriend hung out, friends she might be with. Topper had simply repeated that he was sure Jade had gone off with another bloke. 'They're probably doing it right now.' He'd sniffed, but he sounded less sure.

'Kai,' Patrick said now, 'I need to ask you some more questions about Jade, OK?'

'Yeah, I guess.'

'Kai. It's vitally important that you tell me the truth, that you don't try to protect Jade or yourself. All we care about is find-ing Jade. If there's anything she did that might have got her into trouble, we don't care about that right now.'

Topper gawped at him. 'What do you mean? You think she's in trouble? What kind of trouble?'

Patrick knew there was only one way to ensure Topper told him any uncomfortable truths, assuming he genuinely cared for Jade and hadn't been spilling crocodile tears. 'We think Jade might be in danger, Kai.'

To guarantee the full impact of this he opened his Moleskine and wrote 'DANGER' in block capitals at the top of a fresh page, then underlined it twice, making sure Kai could see it.

'Oh my days.'

'But if you tell me everything you know, we can find her. Stop her coming to any harm. OK?'

The boy nodded eagerly.

'Firstly, how come you two ended up working at Mervyn Hammond's party? Do you know him or something?'

Kai shook his head. 'Nah, man. Jade got us the jobs with some temp agency. It was the first time we'd worked for him.'

'Bit of a coincidence, wasn't it, that the first job you got was working at a party that Jade's idols were at?'

'Not really. She got told to apply, by someone on the forum, like, a tip-off that the band would be there. She wouldn't have done it otherwise. She hates working.'

'And how was it?'

Kai shrugged. 'Boring. Shit money. The guests were horrible, dead rude to me—' He stopped abruptly, slapping his forehead. 'Shit!'

'What?'

The boy swallowed hard. 'I did something.'

'What? What did you do?'

'I think it's my fault, if someone's got Jade.'

'How come?' Patrick held his breath, trying to sound nonchalant.

'Oh man.'

'Tell us, Kai.'

He looked up at Patrick with eyes like a cowed puppy. 'It wasn't my gear, so you can't nick me for dealing! I swear to God I, er, *found* it, under a railway bridge couple weeks ago, someone must've dropped it . . .'

'Drugs? What's that got to do with Jade? What sort of drugs?'

'It was a bottle of liquid acid. In one of them ziplock bags. I don't do acid, and I didn't want to sell it 'cos I ain't no dealer . . . I'd put it in me backpack and forgot about it . . . until that night.'

'What did you do, Kai?'

In a tiny little voice, Kai said, 'It was near the end of the party. I got fed up with them all being ungrateful twats. Jade was in a right strop with me, flirting like mad with that Kerry and all. So I thought it might be funny if they all got off their tits, specially him – but that didn't work, did it, 'cos he was driving, so he didn't drink the punch . . .'

'You *spiked the punch*?' Pat shook his head. *Stupid idiot.* 'How much did you put in it?'

Kai shrugged. 'It was a small bottle. Big bowl, though. Are you gonna nick me?'

Tears filled his eyes again and he held out his wrists, inviting Patrick to handcuff him.

'Nick me. Go on, I deserve it. I reckon someone got so high that he followed Jade home and has done something to her. I thought it was that Mangan bloke, but it must have been someone else . . .' He dissolved into sobs again.

Patrick feared the interview was getting out of control. He handed Kai a tissue and the boy scrubbed at his face.

'Kai, I don't think that's the case. We know that Kerry drove her home. It's hardly likely that someone else followed them, is it? If anyone was that high, there's no way they'd have been capable of that. I'm not going to nick you, not right now. It was a dangerous and, frankly, moronic thing to do, but we need to concentrate on finding Jade. So – let's go back a bit. Who was it on the forums who told Jade to apply for the job?'

Kai shrugged. 'No idea.'

Patrick sighed. It would have been too good to be true, if Kai could have given him a name.

'OK. Let's talk about something else. What do you know about Jade and StoryPad? Specifically a story she wrote called *Fresh Blood*.'

Topper went pale, sitting back in his chair. His reaction was worse than when he'd confessed to spiking the punch and Patrick suddenly had a horrible feeling that he was going to have to ratchet up the 'Jade's in danger' stuff.

'What are you asking about that for?'

'We know that Jade was one of four co-authors of that story. Two of them are dead, Kai. The fourth, Chloe Hedges, is also missing.'

'Chloe? What, F-U-Cancer? I only saw her the other day. She had this UV nail thing of Jade's and I went round to get it back. She's a nice girl.'

'A good friend of Jade's?'

Kai tipped his head from side to side. 'They fell out, didn't they? After that . . . *Fresh Blood* thing.'

Patrick wanted to grab Kai and shake the story out of him, wished he could lift off the top of his skull and pluck the answers out of his brain, rather than having to drag them out of him like this.

'Tell me from the beginning, Kai.'

'All right. Like you said, there was four of them: Jade, Chloe, MissTargetHeart and YOLOSWAG.'

'Rose and Jess.'

'Yeah. Jade didn't really know them in real life, not properly. She'd met them at some OnT gigs and sort of became mates with Chloe. We went to Rose's vigil, but I don't think Jade ever really knew her. She wasn't that cut up when Rose got killed, anyway.'

'So they were mainly online friends . . .'

'Yeah. Jade's on the OnT forum all the time. It does my head in, to be honest. But she met the others on there and I think they started chatting about StoryPad and all the OnT fan fiction on there. Jade had written a few things, same as the others had. But Jade thought most of the stuff on there was pretty shit and suggested that they team up to write something really, like, epic.'

'Go on.'

'Well, that's what they did. I barely saw her for a couple of weeks because she was spending all her time, when she wasn't at school, writing. Jade's really imaginative. She came up with most of the story, I think. But Chloe was better at writing it down. I don't think the other two did that much. Just wrote the odd bit here and there. Jade was always moaning about how them two didn't contribute enough, you know?'

'And the story became popular?'

'Yeah, it was well popular. Thousands and thousands of hits, and loads of comments too. Most of them were, like, really gushing about how great it was, the best OnT story ever. Jade was in ever such a good mood. That was when we first, you know, did it.' He blushed. 'But then her mood totally changed.'

'Why was that?'

'Because some girl started slating it. Leaving loads and loads of negative comments, saying the story was shit, that it was a rip-off of *Twilight* and that the writers had got Shawn and the other OnT boys all wrong. Jade was fuming, said this girl was a jealous bitch, a troll, and that she was going to get revenge, teach her a lesson.'

He was twisting the Coke can around again, faster and faster.

'And what happened after that, Kai?'

The boy looked up at him.

'It was war. All-out fucking war.'

Chapter 55
Day 14 – Chloe

I think we're going to have to go somewhere more . . . *spacious,*' said the man calling himself Pete, once Chloe and Jade had stopped screaming. 'Right old racket you two are making. My ears are ringing. Should have gagged you both. Although nobody will ever hear you out here. I'm not worried about that. I just need a bit more space for what I've got in mind.'

He sounded so calm, almost chatty, as though he was sitting next to them at an OnTarget gig, rather than in the dark in a spiky cold grotto. The sound of his disembodied voice so close to them made Chloe wet herself, and just for a moment the warmth of the urine soaking the crotch of her jeans was comforting. *I want my mum,* she thought, too frightened even to sob. *I want my mum.*

Jade was whimpering now from across the grotto. Chloe wished she could comfort her, and be comforted, but her hands were tied – and she was far too terrified to make any sort of move.

'Right, let's go, then, you silly little tarts.' The girls heard the sound of him jumping up and clapping his hands together, like a primary school teacher trying to galvanise a crocodile of kids into action. 'It's getting too dark now. I won't be able to see what I'm doing out here' – his voice suddenly changed, deepened – 'and that would never do, would it? What would be the fun in *that*?'

Jade burst out crying again. 'Please, let us go! Why are you doing this? We haven't done anything to you!'

There was a long pause, then the click of a cigarette lighter. A wavering flame appeared in the dark grotto, and Chloe gulped as she saw the man's face, his eyes two black hollow circles like a skull's. He moved towards Jade and held the flame under her chin.

'*You!*' Jade gasped, frantically shaking her head to try to escape the fire. So Jade did know him, Chloe thought. She tried to pay more attention to his appearance – he was youngish, tallish, good bone structure and long slim fingers. He did not look the type to be doing this.

'Haven't. Done. Anything. To. *Me*?' he repeated slowly, menace dripping from his voice. 'Well, that's where you'll find you're wrong. You two, and the two other stupid little girls. You know exactly what you've done to me. What you did to *her*.'

'We didn't mean it!' Jade cried. 'How were we supposed to know—'

He thrust the lighter upwards so that the flame licked at the soft underside of Jade's chin. Chloe shuddered and looked away as the smell of burning skin and hair filled the air, and Jade kept violently shaking her head from side to side, trying to get away but not being able to with her hands and feet tied, screaming and crying. The man held the flame steady for what seemed to Chloe like an eternity until she thought she was going to faint. Was it her turn next?

'Stop, please stop!' howled Jade, and finally the man moved the flame away. He crouched down and lifted the glass cover off an oil lamp on the floor of the grotto, touching the lighter to the wick, then replacing the cover. More light flickered around the grotto and

Chloe took in Jade's distraught face, screwed up in agony and panic. Even in the dim shadowy light she could see the huge blister that had formed on Jade's chin.

The man opened his black backpack and took out a horrible curved, serrated knife.

So this is how it's going to end, Chloe thought, shrinking back against the shell wall. She'd survived leukaemia, chemotherapy, jumping out of an aeroplane – but she'd fallen for this psycho's lies, had believed he was Shawn. She wondered briefly how he had known about her conversation with Shawn when she was in hospital, but there was no time to mull it over now. Not when she was about to be sliced up and killed.

Sorry, Mum and Dad and Brandon, she whispered. *I'm really sorry.*

But Pete – or whatever his name really was – did not kill them. Instead he cut the ropes that bound their feet, leaving their hands tied. 'I'm not going to gag you,' he said. 'As you've already discovered, nobody can hear you out here. But if either of you makes a noise, I will cut you. I will cut your pretty little faces. I might even cut out your tongues . . .'

Chloe realised she was hyperventilating. She staggered to her knees, and then to her feet. Perhaps if he was taking them somewhere, somebody would see. Somebody would come. *Please God, let someone come,* she prayed.

This just couldn't be happening.

'Stop that fucking noise,' he said harshly to Jade when she too had managed to stand up. He backhanded her hard across her face, making her fall against the grotto wall. Then he took out a third pair of handcuffs from the backpack, linking the two girls together so they were tied back to back. Chloe felt for Jade's fingers and gave them a squeeze, but the burn and then the slap seemed to have put

Jade into a trance. She had fallen completely silent, and only the heaving of her back and ribs against Chloe's own back indicated that she was even breathing.

The man calling himself Pete put away the knife and picked up the backpack and the oil lamp.

'Let's go,' he said, cautiously opening the grotto door. It was now almost as dark in the wooded grounds as it had been inside the shell place. He pushed them through and they had to do an awkward kind of sidestep in order to both be able to move in a forward direction, rather than one of them having to walk back-wards. They moved in silence along the path under the trees, and Chloe wondered if they were getting back into the car – but when they reached the dark façade of the big house she'd seen earlier, she realised that this was their destination. The building was enormous – a once-grand ivy-covered edifice with towers and turrets and fancy woodwork on the front of it.

Pete prodded them round the back to a large conservatory. One of the panels on the glass double doors was broken, and he put his hand through the hole, deftly twisting the handle from the inside. *He must have been here earlier*, Chloe thought – there was evidence that it had been boarded up, but now the boards across the door were lying on the ground next to it.

The inside of the house felt even colder than the grotto had done, if that were possible. Glass crunched under their feet as he led them through the conservatory, down a long tiled corridor and through a door that led into some kind of massive room – *A ballroom?* Chloe wondered, until she saw the stage. No – it was a little theatre, the seats long gone. There was no furniture anywhere – the place looked as though it had been abandoned for years.

Nobody will find us here, Chloe thought in despair. She squeezed Jade's fingers again, more for her own benefit than Jade's, although she had started to feel weirdly calm. The man came over and undid the handcuffs connecting them; then he held up the lamp and studied their faces.

'One at a time?' he mused, as though talking to himself. 'Or both together?'

He tipped his head to one side and Chloe thought again how weird that he looked so normal.

'One at a time,' he decided out loud. He pointed at Jade. 'More fun that way. You first.'

Jade began to shake and whimper again. Pete dragged them both to the side of the stage and expertly clipped Chloe's cuffs to a pipe running up the wall in the wings, behind the thick, dusty old stage curtain.

'I'll be back for you in a bit,' he hissed in Chloe's face, then turned to Jade. 'It's your moment in the limelight,' he said, smiling a terrible smile at her before marching her back into the centre of the stage.

Chloe couldn't look. She bent her head and averted her eyes, but could not prevent herself hearing the heavy thud as Jade's body was pushed to the floor.

And then the screaming started.

Chapter 56
Day 14 – Patrick

Patrick emerged from interview room three, rubbing his stubble and thinking about the story he'd just heard, at the same moment that Carmella opened the door of room one to let Mervyn Hammond and his lawyer out.

'Mr Hammond has given us a full list of his party guests and the details of the company who provided the catering service,' Carmella said.

'I hope you catch him,' said Mervyn. 'This business is terrible for OnTarget's PR.' He strode off down the corridor, already talking on his phone, Cassandra Oliver hurrying to keep up with him.

'He can't help himself, can he?' said Patrick, amazed that Mervyn couldn't drop the bad-guy act even now.

'I kind of like him now, though,' said Carmella, shrugging. 'And at least we've got the list.' She held up several sheets of A4 paper. 'He could actually remember everyone who was there. I guess that's one of the reasons he's so good at what he does.'

'Any names jump out at you?'

'It looks like the guest list for the BRIT Awards,' she replied.

They went into interview room one. Patrick needed space and quiet to talk to Carmella, and to pass on what he'd heard from Kai Topper, who was still in the other interview room, just in case they needed to ask him anything else.

Patrick scrutinised the list, each of the names printed by Hammond in cramped block capitals. As Carmella had said, it looked like a who's who of the British music industry, many names that he recognised – mostly veteran rock stars – but more that meant nothing to him. Shawn Barrett's name was there, along with Lana Vincent, the woman he'd been secretly sleeping with. Several of the people they'd met at Global Sounds Music were on there too, plus a section headed 'STAFF' under which Mervyn had written Kerry Mangan's name along with his housekeeper and the name of the catering company that had temporarily employed Jade and Kai.

'Pop stars; magazine editors; record company people; actors; a couple of football players . . .' Carmella laughed. 'Hammond asked me if I'd ever thought about a career in the media. Said he could make me famous.'

'He used that one on me too.'

'Suddenly I don't feel special anymore. I told him I'm happy doing this. He called me a mug.'

'But you still like him?'

She shrugged again. 'I like people with hidden depths. Not sure why I get along so well with you . . .'

'Ha ha.' He frowned suddenly, aware of the ticking clock. 'I need to tell you what Kai said. Actually, we should get Suzanne in here – she needs to hear this too.'

Patrick decided to tell the story standing up, pacing. It helped him think. As he spoke he looked down at the faces of the two women staring up at him. Carmella, who he would take a bullet for. And Suzanne . . . How did he feel about Suzanne now? When he was in the same room as her he felt more alive; more aware of his body; the blood pumping in his veins; the hairs standing on end on his arms. She cast other people into shadow. But it wasn't a feeling he enjoyed – or wouldn't allow himself to enjoy. When he left her company he felt simultaneously saddened and relieved.

He had no idea if she felt anything like this when she was with him. Sometimes he caught her gazing at him when she didn't know he was looking, and she would turn her face away quickly. Right now she was all business: drawn with worry; a little tic beneath her right eye. He felt the urge to reach out, touch her face. But it could never happen. They could never touch. And the realisation blew through him like a cold draught, a stiff wind slamming a door shut.

He recounted the first part of what Kai Topper had told him about StoryPad.

'Then, he said, war broke out. The person who was leaving all the negative comments on Jade and co's story had written her own OnTarget fanfic. It was far less popular than *Fresh Blood* – that's the story written by Jade, Chloe, Rose and Jess.'

'Boy bands and vampires,' Carmella said.

'I see.' Suzanne shook her head almost imperceptibly.

'You can guess what happened next,' Patrick went on. 'Jade and friends started to slate this other person's stories, leaving loads of scathing reviews, encouraging other users to join in, to laugh at her writing. This made the other person retaliate and do the same on *Fresh Blood*. Kai said Jade was pretty sure this "troll" was setting up loads of sock-puppet accounts, as he called them, in order to leave bad reviews. Then it got even worse. It spilled over onto the official OnTarget forum, where this other user also had an account. Everything Jade and her friends posted got slated, and they did the same back. Kai says that it was mainly Jade and Jess, that Chloe and MissTargetHeart, as he calls Rose, wanted to let it go.'

'But they didn't?' Suzanne asked.

'Far from it. According to Kai, Jade became obsessed with this troll, decided to see if she could find out their real identity. So she started trawling back through the troll's old posts until she found one in which her nemesis had posted a link to her Tumblr account. The Tumblr account had a link to this girl's blog—'

'It was a girl?' Carmella looked disappointed. 'I was hoping—'

'That it was our killer? No. Let me tell you the rest. The blog linked to the girl's Facebook page. Now Jade knew her real name: Melanie Haggis. And the Facebook page and blog had photos of Melanie on them that she hadn't protected. Our charming friend in room three says that Melanie was a "real minger". He reckons she was in her mid-twenties, too old to be on the OnT forums or StoryPad, according to him. And Jade decided to go nuclear.'

Both women were holding their breath.

'She set up a fake Facebook profile in Melanie Haggis's name, filled it with all of these cruel status updates about how she'd just eaten seventeen Mars Bars and used the last one to masturbate with; stuff about fancying really "sad" people like David Cameron; some really cruel things too. Statuses saying that she'd been molested by her uncle and felt guilty because she enjoyed it. How she'd had sex with a German shepherd and was worried she was going to have babies who were half puppy. Sick shit. Jade got all these photos of morbidly obese women too and Photoshopped Melanie's head onto them. Once she'd set this all up, she shared the link to the Facebook page on the OnTarget forum.'

Carmella gasped. 'Oh my God.'

'Apparently the whole forum went mental, everyone on there wading in and giving Melanie Haggis abuse. It got shared on Twitter, Tumblr, everywhere.'

He was pacing faster now, back and forth across the room.

'At first, Melanie tried to fight back, to respond to the posts. But then she went quiet. Disappeared. Kai didn't want to tell me the last bit, but he said that Jade sent Melanie a private message, saying she was going to send her boyfriend round to rape her, that she knew where she lived. He swears it was an idle threat, that he didn't know about it until after Jade had sent the message. Anyway, Melanie didn't respond.'

'Because . . .'

Patrick could see that Carmella had guessed it.

He nodded. 'She killed herself.'

The room was silent for a few seconds. 'How,' Carmella asked, 'did Jade and Kai know she'd committed suicide?'

'It was in the local paper, apparently. Just a small piece, following the coroner's report. She took an overdose. According to Kai, Chloe's nan reads the paper front to back and mentioned it to Chloe because it said she was a big OnTarget fan in the report. Chloe then told the other girls and they were mortified. Even Jade felt bad about it, according to Kai. Although it sounds like she was more worried she was going to get the blame, that people were going to find out. So she deleted the fake Facebook page and all the posts she'd written about Melanie, getting the others to do the same. Kai says the others blamed Jade and they had a massive falling-out. Chloe and Jess were "real life" friends, so they stayed mates, but Jade never communicated with the others again, except to send Kai round to Chloe's to get back some UV nail thing she'd borrowed. They even deleted their *Fresh Blood* story.'

'And now two of them are dead,' Carmella said.

Patrick pointed at Mervyn Hammond's list. 'Melanie Haggis and the party. Find the connection, and we find the killer.'

Patrick left the interview room to find Martin Hale, giving him Melanie Haggis's name and asking him to find out everything he could about her. Then he headed for the incident room, followed by Carmella and Suzanne.

He pinned Mervyn's list to the wall, studying it again, willing a name to jump out at him. Everyone on it was being run through the database. If there was time, if Chloe and Jade weren't currently missing, they would bring in everybody who'd been at the party, ask them if they knew Melanie, if they'd seen or heard anything. He could imagine the furore in the press if they did this, the obstacles that would be thrown into their path. It had been hard enough interviewing a single boy-band member.

He studied each of the four girls' photographs in turn: Rose, Jess, Chloe, Jade. Gazing at them, with Topper's story ringing in his ears, Patrick felt certain he knew the motive for the murders now. Vengeance. But who? Who had sought bloody revenge against the girls who unwittingly drove Melanie Haggis to suicide?

'It's Hammond.'

He turned. Winkler had entered the room, Gareth just behind him. Winkler had a look of triumph on his face.

'What are you talking about?' Patrick asked.

'This Haggis girl – she used to live at St Mary's Children's Home. You telling me that's a coincidence?'

'But Mervyn was in custody all day.'

'He must have an accomplice.'

Patrick opened his mouth to argue, then shut it. Could Winkler be right?

'There's more, boss,' said Gareth. 'Melanie Haggis's address. She lived in Wimbledon – on the same street as Nancy Marr.'

That was the final piece of proof. The murders had to be connected to Melanie. But Mervyn? Had he fooled them? Was his list incomplete, all names present apart from Mervyn's secret accomplice?

He snatched up his jacket and headed towards the door.

'Where are you going?' Winkler demanded.

'St Mary's.'

———————

Patrick hammered on the door of St Mary's Children's Home, Carmella standing beside him. It was 9.30 p.m. and he was trying not to panic. What were the chances that Jade and Chloe were still alive? They needed to get in here and get the information they needed fast.

A middle-aged man with a grey beard opened the door and Patrick immediately flashed his badge at him and said, 'Police. Are you the manager?'

'I'm the deputy. The manager's not—'

Patrick cut him off, stepping past him into the entrance hall, Carmella following. It reminded Patrick of the reception area of a clinic or, indeed, a police station: uncomfortable seating; low tables piled high with leaflets; posters on the wall offering advice or guidance. He wondered where all the kids were. As he thought this a skinny teenage girl with copper hair wandered into the room, spied Patrick and Carmella, and slipped away, vanishing like a ghost.

The bearded man shut the door behind them and turned, his eyes wide. He reminded Patrick of a hamster, with his chubby cheeks and furry face. 'What's your name?' Patrick demanded.

'Simon Fletcher.'

'How long have you worked here, Mr Fletcher?' Patrick knew that if he asked questions rapidly like this, in his most authoritative tone, he would get speedy, honest answers.

'Five years.'

'I need to speak to someone who was here a decade ago.'

Fletcher hesitated.

'Come on!'

'Fran Dangerfield. She's one of our senior care workers. She's here now, but—'

'Get her,' Patrick said. 'And tell her we're investigating a murder and abduction. This is life or death, Mr Fletcher.'

'You'd better come to my office.'

On the way up to the office, Patrick and Carmella passed a communal room, where several teenagers of both genders were watching TV and chatting loudly. They reached the office – more official posters on the walls, plus lots of photos of groups of teens – and Fletcher scurried away to fetch Fran Dangerfield.

'I didn't know places like this still existed,' Carmella said after a while.

'They're still necessary, unfortunately.'

A woman in her late fifties had entered the office. She had short plum-tinted hair and the air of someone who had seen a lot and didn't take any nonsense.

'Some kids aren't able to go into foster homes because of the terrible situations they faced at home. Or they have very difficult behavioural issues. We exist for the minority of children who can't fit into family life.'

Patrick nodded, remembering the skinny redhead downstairs, the kids watching TV and chatting boisterously. What had they been through? Imagining it made his heart ache.

'What's this all about?' Dangerfield asked. 'We had one of your blokes here this morning, asking ridiculous questions.'

'About Mervyn Hammond? This may or may not be related to that.'

Patrick remembered what Kerry Mangan had told them about Mervyn's visits to St Mary's. Could Kerry have been lying? A chill ran through his blood as he imagined one possible scenario: that Kerry was Mervyn's accomplice, or even working on his own, and that Topper had been right.

'What do you mean?' Fletcher, who had re-entered the room, asked.

'We know that Hammond helps out here, gives motivational speeches and so on to the children, and that he wants this to remain confidential.'

Neither Fletcher nor Dangerfield responded verbally, though he could see in their eyes that this was right.

'We actually want to ask you about a former resident here: Melanie Haggis.'

'What about her?' Dangerfield asked, crossing her arms over her heavy bosom.

'You remember her?'

'I do.'

'And are you aware that Ms Haggis died last year?'

Dangerfield's hand went to her mouth. 'Oh. No, I didn't know that. How awful. What happened?'

Patrick met her eye.

'She committed suicide.'

Dangerfield almost fell into a chair. For someone who had clearly dealt with hundreds of kids, who must be hardened to some degree, she appeared surprisingly upset.

'That poor girl.' Her eyes were shining. 'I guess she was, what, twenty-six?'

'That's right.'

Fletcher looked on as Dangerfield gathered herself. 'She was a lovely girl, but . . . damaged. Like so many of the children here. Her mum and stepdad, they . . . well. Do you need to know all these details?'

'Not necessarily. Did Melanie meet Mervyn Hammond?'

'I think . . . I guess so. She would have been here when he first started visiting us. Why are you asking that?' She had recovered a little from the blow of hearing about Melanie's death. 'Simon said you are investigating a murder, not a suicide. Oh my God, do you think somebody murdered Melanie, made it look like she'd killed herself? Not *Mervyn Hammond*?'

'Mervyn is a good man,' Fletcher said. 'A great man.'

Carmella spoke up. 'Was there any deeper connection between Melanie and Mervyn that you know of?'

'No. To be honest, Mervyn has always seemed more interested in helping boys – and no, not for sexual reasons, before you make insinuations. There have been one or two boys who Mervyn helped after they left: gave them a hand finding a job, for example.' She made an amused noise in her throat. 'Actually, one of those boys was Melanie's boyfriend.'

Patrick stepped towards her.

'Mervyn helped Melanie's boyfriend?' Was *that* the connection? 'What was his name?'

But Dangerfield appeared to be lost in a memory. 'You know, even though Melanie had a lot of serious issues – emotional problems, difficulties with trust and authority, you name it – I always thought she'd be OK, that no harm would befall her. We all used to talk about it.'

'Why?' Patrick asked.

'Because of her great protector. The boyfriend I mentioned. They were only fourteen, fifteen, but they were obsessed with each other. It was a bit of a mismatch intellectually, but I think he liked the fact that she was vulnerable, and that she saw him as some kind of hero. He thrived on it, on the way she worshipped him. If anyone did the slightest thing against Melanie, he would be there, protecting her. It caused a lot of issues because he often went too far.' She frowned as she remembered more details. 'There was a girl who Mel had a big falling-out with, typical teenage-girl stuff. But then Mel went running to Graham to tell him and the next thing we knew, this girl's room had been trashed, her teddy bear's head ripped off, pet goldfish nailed to the wall . . . God, I'd forgotten about that.'

Patrick and Carmella both stared at her.

'What did you say her boyfriend's name was?' Patrick asked.

'Graham,' Dangerfield replied. 'Graham Burns. Like I said, Mervyn helped find him a job. I think he works with that band now, OnTarget, and . . . What is it? What did I say?'

Patrick was already on his phone, calling Suzanne. Graham Burns. The social media manager at Global Sounds.

He was the killer.

Chapter 57
Day 14 – 10 p.m. – Chloe

C hloe slid down the pipe she was attached to, her legs unable to bear the weight of her – or, rather, the weight of Jade's screaming. It felt as though the sound of it was pressing down on her head, filling her eyes and nose and mouth as well as her ears – quick-drying cement that she would never escape.

She couldn't even put her fingers in her ears to block it out because her hands were tied to the pipe behind her back. The smell of Friendship drifted over to her as if Jade had screamed it out of her own mouth.

Chloe squeezed her eyes tightly closed and told herself to think of the worst, most painful, frightening, horrible things that had ever happened to her:

Chemotherapy.
Lumbar punctures.
That terrifying moment right before jumping out of the plane.
The guilt. The guilt.
Stem cell transplant.
That time that Brandon shut her hand in the car door.

Pete punching me in the chest.

Finding out that Melanie Haggis, the girl we tormented online, following Jade's lead like a pack of crazed dogs, had killed herself.

But none of it, nothing, nothing, nothing was, ever had been, or ever could be worse than this.

She forced herself not to look, to peek out between the stage flats like she was waiting in the wings – well, she *was* waiting in the wings, wasn't she? Waiting for it to be her turn, for him to carve her up with that horrific knife, as if she was in some nightmarish play and she had to wait for her cue for it to be her turn in the spotlight . . .

This just couldn't be happening.

She had remembered, now, where she recognised him from. The hospital. He had been there the day Shawn had come to visit her. He'd been lurking in the background, standing just behind Mervyn Hammond. He'd looked different back then, with a trendy beard, but now it made sense how he'd known what she'd spoken to Shawn about, telling him her favourite song.

Don't look, Chloe, don't look, Rog; no, not Rog, don't say Rog, because it was too painful to think of her dad's nickname for her then, because to think of that was to think of her mum and dad and how they'd been through so much with her, days and weeks and months of sitting by her hospital bed, for it to end like this with her stupidity and vanity, naked and cut up and killed like Rose and Jess . . . and soon Jade.

But somehow, unbidden, her eyes flicked open and up, just for a split second, but in that one split second what she saw made her vomit all over herself again, retching uselessly, sick and tears mingling with the piss and shit until she thought there was nothing left inside her except terror.

Jade looked like a toppled store mannequin, her limbs rigid in that split second, with *him* crouched over her, the knife blade glinting in the light of the oil lamp as he cut her, like her dad making Sunday roast when he would put cuts all over a leg of lamb to stick garlic cloves under the skin of it.

Amid the screaming, the man ranted at Jade, told her how he'd found Melanie's suicide note written on the back of a poster, a poster that had been attached to the gate here. From his screeched words and Jade's begging, Chloe made out something about how Jade had contacted Melanie telling her she'd won a competition to meet the band here at this hotel, but when Melanie turned up she'd found the place derelict, the poster containing a Photoshopped image of OnT laughing at her, 'LOSER' written above her head. Chloe guessed all this was in the suicide note.

It had been the final straw.

Chloe shuddered and gagged again. She couldn't scream. She couldn't help Jade. All she could do was wait for it to be her turn, and pray that it would be over quickly.

She shut her eyes again, kept them closed.

After a few more minutes there was no more screaming, then a *hmphhhmph* sort of noise and Chloe could hear the man breathing loudly.

Silence. Stillness. Just the scent of Friendship hanging in the air like a poisonous gas, mixing with the smell of her fear.

———

Then, out of the silence, a dragging sound. Jade being moved.

Heavy footsteps across the stage, coming towards her.

Eyes still closed, Chloe started to shake and hyperventilate. *Our Father who art in Heaven hallowed be Thy Name, forgive me, Lord, I'm sorry for everything I did wrong especially for the mean things I said about Melanie I didn't mean them, look after MumandDadandBrandon I'm sorry I'm sorry I'm—*

The man, stinking of Friendship, crouched down behind her and unlocked her handcuffs.

'Get up. And take your clothes off. It's your turn.'

Chapter 58
Day 14 – Patrick

We need to find where he's taken Chloe and Jade.'

Back at the station, Patrick had pulled Carmella, Suzanne and Gareth into the incident room. Irritatingly, Winkler was there again, looking like someone who'd just swallowed a mouthful of sick.

Fran Dangerfield had filled in more details about Graham and Melanie, which Patrick now recounted.

'Melanie was taken into care when she was eight, after they discovered what her mother and stepfather had been doing to her. Graham went into care when he was a toddler because his mum, a single mother, neglected him. Apparently they'd both been floating around the care system for years before they ended up at St Mary's when they were teenagers.' He explained what Dangerfield had said about how Melanie wasn't able to cope with family life.

'What about Graham?' Suzanne asked.

'Same, but for different reasons. He was too much of a handful for anyone to cope with. Always running off, stealing, being cruel. Dangerfield told me that on the surface he came across as an intelligent, normal boy. But if anyone crossed him . . . They thought he was heading for a life of crime until he met Melanie.'

'Romeo and Juliet,' said Carmella, with irony.

'Inseparable, besotted, uninterested in anyone apart from each other, apparently. And Graham became Mel's protector, the person who fought off the bullies.'

'And killed their goldfish,' added Carmella.

Patrick went on. 'I guess they are used to seeing what we might think of as psychotic behaviour there. Remember, these kids, all of them, have been through a lot. These are the boys and girls who can't adapt to family life.'

'But he seems so normal now,' Gareth said. 'So . . . nice.'

'Don't they always.' Winkler sniffed.

'Apparently, Mervyn Hammond took Graham under his wing, mentored him. Encouraged him to go to college, helped him get a job after that.'

'And what about Melanie?' Suzanne asked.

'We don't know much. Left St Mary's when she was sixteen and went straight onto benefits. She had various part-time jobs over the years but nothing long-term. It appears she led a very boring life.'

'Maybe Graham was supporting her, helping her out,' Carmella said. 'I wonder why they didn't live together. Get married. If theirs really was a great love affair.'

'Probably didn't fit with his image anymore,' Winkler said. 'He was moving in starry circles; she was stuck in a council flat. He drank flat whites; she preferred a nice cup of tea.'

In his own crude way, Winkler was probably right. Patrick had been wondering why Graham hadn't known about the bullying of Melanie on the forums, why he hadn't put a stop to it. Why hadn't she told him about it? Perhaps it had something to do with what Winkler had said. The two of them lived in different worlds now. Melanie could have kept her online activities secret from her friend. He, however, was meant to police the OnT forums, to stop bullying. Why had he failed so spectacularly?

'They must have been in contact still,' Patrick said. 'We know that for a fact. Because Graham found Melanie's body.'

While Patrick and Carmella were at St Mary's, Gareth had tracked down the officer – PC Sarah Chance – who had filed the incident report when Melanie's body was found. Sarah told Gareth that Melanie was discovered by her friend Graham Burns, who had said there was no suicide note and that he had no idea why Melanie had killed herself.

'The flat was full of OnTarget merchandise,' Sarah Chance had said. 'Posters, dolls, T-shirts, newspaper and magazine cuttings all over the walls. Seemed a bit weird that a woman in her mid-twenties was so obsessed with a boy band, but the friend said she was very immature, trapped emotionally in her early teens. She had problems forming attachments with new people. That's why she didn't have a job. I got the impression she sat at home all day on the Internet.'

No suicide note. It would have been easy, Patrick thought, for Graham to pocket the suicide note, especially if it revealed the reason for Melanie's suicide, and he came up with his plan for revenge on the spot. Easy, too, for him, with his top-level access to the official OnT forum, to delete all the posts in which his first love fought with her persecutors. So no-one would know the link between the four girls he planned to kill – apart from the girls themselves, and Kai Topper. If only Topper had come forward sooner – but the boy was clearly too stupid to have realised what was going on.

What about Chloe and Jade? Didn't they realise they were in danger after their fellow co-authors were murdered? How could they have been so naïve? It was another question he hoped to ask soon. If it wasn't already too late.

The final piece of the puzzle was how Nancy Marr fitted in. All they knew so far was that she'd lived three doors down from Melanie Haggis's small council flat.

It was far more important to find where Graham was at that moment. His phone was off, so they couldn't get a trace on it. They would need to figure it out.

Patrick placed a laptop on the desk in the centre of the room and gestured for everyone to gather round.

'We know,' he said, 'that the first two murder scenes were connected to OnTarget. Jessica was killed at Rocket Man Studios, here.' He had already brought up Google Maps and pointed at the location of the disused studio on the map. 'That place was used to shoot an OnT video. And Wendy told me that "Room 365" is an OnTarget song. Rose was found in room 365 of the Travel Inn, here.'

He typed in the address and pointed to the location.

'We know Burns isn't at home.' Two uniformed officers had already been round to check. All the lights were off and the neighbours said they hadn't seen him or his car all day. 'He hasn't taken them to Melanie's old flat either. Somebody else lives there now. It has to be somewhere connected to OnTarget, like the others. Somewhere symbolic.'

All of the faces around him were blank.

'If only Wendy were here,' Carmella said quietly.

'Hang on,' said Winkler. 'Didn't that teenage twit have an app that traced Jade's phone? Where was it?'

Occasionally, Patrick thought, Winkler could surprise him. 'Yes. He traced it here.' He typed Platt's Eyot into Google Maps. The uniforms he'd sent to the Eyot had found the phone in the undergrowth, lying among wet leaves. It was dead, water damaged, and wouldn't switch on. Patrick guessed it had survived just long enough for Kai to trace it. Now it was a useless lump of plastic. 'If

Jade met Graham here, the chances are he didn't take her far. We need an OnTarget expert.'

'Don't look at me,' said Winkler.

'Hattie Parsons,' Patrick said, calling her and putting her on speaker.

She answered on the second ring. 'Detective Lennon,' she said in a flirty voice. 'I was wondering if you'd call me again.'

Winkler guffawed.

'Are you near a computer?' Patrick asked.

'Right in front of one. Why?'

He told her to open maps and to look up Platt's Eyot. 'Are you there?'

'Yep. Well, I'm looking at the map. What's—?'

'I need to know if there are any locations near there that have any connection to OnTarget. Somewhere referenced in one of their songs. A place where a video was shot. The house where one of them grew up, or where they met, or where Shawn lost his virginity. Anything.'

She laughed. 'I think Shawn popped his cherry in a park in Stoke.'

'Hattie. This is serious. Please.'

'OK. Sorry . . . Let me think.'

'You should zoom out, look at all the locations around Platt's Eyot; be systematic.'

'All right.' There was a protracted silence at the other end of the line. Then: 'Yeah. That old hotel . . . Sunbury Lock Manor.'

'Did the band stay there?'

'Maybe. Sunbury Lock Manor is dead posh – or, rather, it was. It's shut down now – I think some other hotel chain is planning to refurbish it at some point – but the band shot the cover of *Twilight Kisses* there, in this amazing shell grotto they've got in the grounds.'

'And that's the only place you can think of that's nearby?'

'Yeah. Why—?'

He hung up.

'Sunbury Lock Manor,' he said, fingers flickering over the keyboard to get the address. 'Let's go.'

———⌣———

Patrick put on the blues and twos all the way to Sunbury, switching them off as they neared the derelict building, not wanting to alert Graham who might be listening out for sirens. Carmella sat beside him, rubbing the side of her belly, subconsciously remembering what had happened at the end of their last big case. Suzanne was back at the station organising the armed response unit, getting uniforms in place, but Patrick had been unable to wait. They needed to get here as quickly as possible, so Suzanne had given him permission to scout ahead.

He killed the lights and pulled up outside the hotel gates, which were chained up – but with, he noticed, a new and shiny padlock. Beyond the gates, the building sat among rolling lawns, the grass now overgrown, piles of rubbish lying in heaps where someone had been fly-tipping. Patrick realised now that he had driven by here before. In daylight, the place looked like a typical English stately home – the former home of a long-dead earl or duke. But in the darkness its abandonment lent it a creepy air, like a haunted house, a place where schoolboys would dare each other to spend the night.

He got out of the car and went up to the gate, rattled it. Carmella came up behind him.

'It's been shut for three years,' she said. She'd looked it up on the way over. 'Useless management ran it into the ground – and then there was a near-fatal food-poisoning case that proved the final straw. It says on Wikipedia that Shawn Barrett was rumoured to be buying the building, after falling in love with it during a photo shoot. But it never happened.'

'We need to get in there,' Patrick said, examining the surrounding walls, trying to work out how easy it would be to climb over. He would need Carmella to give him a leg up, but it was possible.

'No, Patrick. We need to wait.'

'He could be killing them right now.'

'In which case, we're already too late,' she said.

'But what if they're still alive?' he said. 'What if we wait, get in there and discover that they were murdered while we were standing here following fucking protocol?'

'Pat . . . there must be loads of other places associated with the band. What if we're wasting time here when he's got them somewhere else . . . ?'

But he was walking off along the side of the wall, trying to find a way in, anxiety making his voice sharper than he intended.

'What do you propose we do, Carmella? Just walk away, and find out later they're in there?'

'No . . . but—'

'Give me a leg up – now.'

'Let me call and see how far away back-up is—'

'That's an order.'

Carmella knew better than to continue to question him. She crouched and held out her cupped hands so he could step onto them and hoist himself up to grab hold of the top of the brick wall. She pushed and he pulled, heaving and panting until he was on the wall, looking down at his colleague. Without another word, he was over, and running. Tucked in a clearing between the trees was a small car park – empty, apart from one solitary vehicle: a new black Audi A4 with tinted windows.

'Shit!'

They were definitely in there.

———— ⌣ ————

Halfway across the lawn he realised he'd left his phone charging in the car. But he wasn't turning back now. He had no weapon, but he didn't care. He had to reach Chloe and Jade. He could hear Wendy's voice in his ear as the building loomed up from the darkness, framed by moonlight. *Go on, boss,* she urged. *Go on, Patrick.*

He reached the hotel. Of course, the front doors were shut, locked. He could smash a window with one of the earthen pots that lay scattered around, but he didn't want Graham to know he was coming, in case it made him panic and kill the girls, if he hadn't already.

Patrick stepped back, searching for another entrance. The front door was framed by two Roman pillars and a porch, surrounded by thick ivy that had proliferated out of control, thick and dense, making him think, bizarrely yet appositely, of Graham's beard. A window just above the door had been smashed, presumably by vandals, jagged shards of glass clinging to the frame like monstrous teeth. If he could reach it, get onto the top of the porch . . .

A scream came from inside, quickly followed by a girl's voice begging, '*No!*'

He snaked his fingers through the thick ivy, finding a wooden trellis beneath. He tugged at it – it seemed to be attached securely. Placing one foot against the trellis, he pulled himself up, arm muscles flexing, then found purchase with his other foot. The trellis dug into his fingers, but the pain was unimportant. He heard Wendy's voice again, urging him on, telling him to save the girls, to stop the man who had killed her. There was a bitter, metallic taste in his mouth – the flavour of hatred. He used it to propel him, to give him strength as he pulled against the trellis, straining his biceps, scaling the ivy and throwing himself sideways, landing on top of the porch on his belly.

He lay there for a moment, the wind knocked out of him, then pushed himself up, the sudden movement almost making him lose balance. After pulling off his jacket, he used it to knock away the shards that clung to the edges of the window, then ducked through, lowering himself until he felt solid ground beneath him.

He stood panting in a pitch-black hallway. It smelled damp, of bird shit and dust. Treading quietly, he headed towards the staircase that curved down to the lower floor.

This, now, was the entrance hall. He hadn't heard another scream since he'd entered the building and he had a terrible feeling that he was too late.

A pair of double doors stood shut at the end of the hallway, and Patrick realised that a line of light flickered beneath them. He took long, quiet strides towards the doors, braced himself and pushed them open.

It took him a moment to focus, to take in what he was seeing. It was a large old theatre, wooden chairs scattered about, with a stage at the opposite end of the space. An oil lamp flickered on the stage, two figures silhouetted against a tatty, crimson curtain, one standing, one lying on the stage floor. The standing figure – Graham, now without his beard – stood frozen, a curved, serrated knife visible in one hand.

The other figure screamed.

'Police!' Patrick shouted, breaking into a run.

Graham ran too, retreating towards the back of the stage, slipping behind the curtain and out of sight. Patrick reached the stage and looked down at the girl lying there, staring up at him, her eyes glassy with shock. It was Chloe Hedges. She was naked apart from a pair of knickers, her wrists cuffed above her head. Blood trickled across her ribcage in two, no, three places. Little cuts. But, thank God, it seemed Graham had only just started. The scent of Friendship, the OnTarget perfume, hung in the air and Patrick knew Graham would have squirted it into each cut, one by one, drawing out the torture, the pain.

He needed to find Graham but was torn. He couldn't leave Chloe here like this. He looked around for a key to the cuffs but couldn't see one, so he gently laid his jacket over the girl to cover her as much as he could.

'Where's Jade?' he said softly.

Chloe tried to speak, but nothing came out. Instead, her eyes shifted to the left and Patrick's mouth went dry as he saw what she was indicating.

Jade Pilkington lay on her back at the edge of the stage. She was completely naked, her body covered with hundreds of cuts, the skin around them shiny where Graham had sprayed them with Friendship. Her eyes were open and he knew before he tried to take her pulse that she was dead. Strangled like Rose and Jess.

'I'll be back,' he said in his most gentle tone to Chloe. 'More police are on their way. Just close your eyes, I won't be long, and you're safe now, sweetheart.'

He hurried to the back of the stage and into the backstage area. It was pitch black here, so he ran back and was about to take the oil lamp but realised he would be leaving Chloe in darkness. He couldn't do it.

He swore to himself. Graham was gone.

Chapter 59
Day 15 – Patrick

Carmella dropped a copy of *The Mirror* on Patrick's desk. 'Thought you might want to see this.'

The headline yelled 'KILLER ON THE LOOSE' above a photograph of Graham Burns, a serious profile shot grabbed from the Global Sounds website. The sub-heading read '*Cops Let On Target Murderer Escape After 3rd Teen Slaying*'.

'You're on page three,' Carmella said.

'Take it away from me. Please.'

'We're going to find him, Patrick.' She laid a hand on his shoulder and he wondered if she could feel how tense he was. 'If it wasn't for you, Chloe Hedges would be dead. You stopped him.'

'But I was too late to save Jade, wasn't I?'

It was 2 p.m. Kai Topper had already been on the TV news that morning, sobbing on camera and telling the whole world the story he'd shared with Patrick the previous evening. Except in this new version, Jade had been rewritten as an angelic figure, begging the other girls not to get involved in the StoryPad war. He made Rose and Jess, who couldn't contradict the tale, out to be the ringleaders. Mrs Pilkington was on TV too, weeping copiously about her little girl. Patrick had been forcing down breakfast at home, unable to tear his eyes from the screen as Jade's mum turned to look, it seemed, straight at him. 'If the police had been quicker . . .'

Gill had sat beside him and put her arms around him, telling him not to beat himself up, that he was still a hero, that he'd done everything he could. It was becoming the theme of the day. Suzanne had said something similar, without calling him a hero, and even Winkler had nodded at him when he'd come in, probably feeling guilty about his own role in the affair.

Chloe Hedges was in hospital now, being monitored. Her injuries were superficial, but she was still in shock, barely able to speak about what had happened. They'd need to interview her as soon as possible, find out what Graham had said to her, if he'd given her any clues about where he might have gone, though that seemed highly unlikely. All she'd said so far was that she thought she'd been meeting Shawn, that the man she knew as Pete had used the OnTarget forum and then Snapchat to communicate with her.

They had surveillance teams watching Graham's flat, Melanie's old address and the Global Sounds office. His social media was being monitored as was his phone, which hadn't been used for twenty-four hours. Airports and seaports were on alert, and Graham's photo was all over the media, including a mock-up of him without his beard. The whole country was looking for him, but he had vanished – on foot, because his Audi, which was now being combed for evidence, had been left behind at the hotel.

'I shouldn't have stopped to check Chloe was OK. Should have pursued Graham before I helped his victims.'

Carmella shook her head. 'But that's what it's all about, Pat. The victims. That's why we do this, isn't it? You did the right thing.'

He wasn't so sure.

Gareth poked his head into the office. 'Boss, DCI Laughland wants to see you.'

Patrick got up. His body felt heavy, his arm muscles aching from when he'd climbed the ivy. He was tired, so tired. He trudged down the corridor to Suzanne's office feeling like he was wearing antique diver's boots. Just before he got there, he heard footsteps hurrying up behind him. He turned to see Gareth again.

'Boss. I wanted to apologise . . . for the other day, you know, our argument. I was being a baby.'

Patrick patted him on the shoulder. 'It's fine, Gareth. Just remember who your friends are in future. OK? And I'm sorry too, I was out of order. Let's put it down to the pressure of the case, shall we?'

Gareth nodded gratefully. Patrick grinned at him, turning away to knock at Suzanne's office door.

'Hi, Patrick.' Her voice was soft, but she looked as weary as he felt. 'Come in, close the door.' She gestured for him to sit. 'I've just had a call from Mervyn Hammond.'

'Don't tell me, he's offering to do our PR.' Suzanne was in the papers too.

She dragged out a smile. 'No. He wants to talk to you, though.'

'What about?'

'He says he has information that will help us find Graham, but he wants you to go there, to his house.'

Patrick heaved himself up, his knees cracking as he stood.

'Hammond's *still* trying to call the shots? This had better not be a waste of time,' he muttered as he left.

In the car on the way to Hammond's, Patrick thought over the investigation, about everything they knew.

They had shown Graham's picture – *sans* beard – to Chelsea Fox, who confirmed he was indeed the man she'd seen stab

Wendy. And Strong's team had finally managed to find traces of a conversation between Wendy and someone called Mockingjay365 arranging the meeting at the Rotunda. The exchange had taken place on the OnTarget official forum. Mockingjay was obviously Graham who, with his top-level access, had been able to delete the private messages from the forum, although they had remained on the server.

They had also taken Graham's photo to the Travel Inn. The manager, Heidi Shillingham, recognised him immediately, with his trendy clothes and stupid socks. He had stayed at the hotel a week before the murder, had even stayed in Room 365, under Melanie's surname: Graham Haggis. Peter Bell surmised that Graham must have got his key card cloned, using the same kind of machine fraudsters use to duplicate credit cards, while he was staying at the hotel, so the magnetic strip contained the correct code to let him back into the room a week later.

What else? An officer had been to the street where both Melanie Haggis and Nancy Marr lived and canvassed the neighbours. The old chap who lived in one of the houses between the two women told them that Nancy and Melanie were friendly, that Nancy was always popping round to see the younger woman because she worried about her and thought she needed looking after.

Patrick had his own theory about what had happened. Perhaps Nancy had popped round one day to see Melanie, perhaps concerned because she hadn't seen her for a day or two, and discovered the suicide scene. She had called Graham – Patrick guessed Melanie had talked to the old lady about her great love and best friend – who had rushed round. Somehow, Graham had found out why his friend had killed herself. Had there been a suicide note, naming the girls Melanie blamed? Had the note asked Graham to take revenge on them? If there had been a note, and Nancy had seen it, it made a sick kind of sense that Graham had decided to kill Nancy to keep her quiet before embarking on his trail of vengeance. Why torture Nancy, though? She must have made him angry. Perhaps he blamed her in some way, thought Nancy should have been keeping an eye on Melanie. Or perhaps he'd just been practising on her, the sick fuck, working out how he was going to get revenge on the younger girls.

The neighbour, the old chap, had told them one more interesting fact. Melanie was not only obsessed with OnTarget, she collected signed photos from celebrities. Among her collection was a picture signed by Mervyn Hammond. 'She gave it to Mrs Marr,' said the old man. 'I don't think Nancy really wanted it, thought Mervyn Hammond was a creep, but Melanie insisted. She said she knew him, that he was friends with her boyfriend.'

Patrick was close to Hammond's house now and would ask him about this. As he got nearer he felt a stirring of hope. Hammond worked with Graham. Patrick was still suspicious that Mervyn was going to pitch to him, tell him he needed a PR man, but maybe Hammond really did have some useful information, something that would help them locate Graham.

He would soon find out.

He thought back to his second meeting with Burns, when he had come into the station to show Patrick the private messages between Rose and Jess. It had been a clever move. Graham must have fabricated those messages, knowing that it would strengthen Patrick's suspicions about Shawn. A diversionary tactic, a trick he had later repeated to put Mervyn in the frame. At the time, Patrick had thought Burns was faintly ludicrous, a comical character. Did he dress the way he did to deflect attention away from his true nature? Or was he simply dressing to fit in with the media world? Psychopaths were good at that – camouflaging themselves, acting and looking like the people around them. Burns had fooled him, too, with the private messages from Mockingjay365. Burns had written those messages, had passed them on, no doubt edited so they didn't give anything away.

He cursed aloud. Burns had fooled him. Finding him, ensuring he faced justice, was now a matter of personal pride.

Chapter 60
Day 15 – Patrick

Patrick parked outside Mervyn's house and pressed the buzzer. The gates clicked open and Hammond's voice crackled, very faintly, over the intercom: 'I'm in the old barn.'

It was a miserable afternoon – the air cold and damp, the kind of weather that penetrates the skin and seeps through to the soul. Patrick headed towards the barn and knocked on the barn door. Mervyn called, 'Come in.'

The light was poor in the barn, gloomy, filled with shadows. There was a distinctive smell in the room: petrol. Patrick clocked the model railway that filled almost all the floor space, three locomotives gliding slowly around the network of tracks, the little houses. There was something off about the display and it took Patrick a moment to notice what it was. All of the tiny figures – the passengers at the plastic stations, the conductors and guards and engineers, the trainspotters – were lying down.

'Mr Hammond?' he called.

'I'm round here.'

Something was very wrong here. Patrick walked slowly around the edge of the model railway, noticing a small group of plastic female figures, four of them, lying at the edge of the display. They had been doused with red paint, like they were lying in a pool of blood. And another female figure stood close to them, gazing down on them.

Patrick stepped around the corner and froze.

Hammond was tied to a chair, his hands cuffed behind his back, ankles tied with rope to the legs of the wooden chair. He was dripping wet and, sniffing, Patrick realised immediately that the liquid that soaked Hammond's clothes and hair was not water.

It was the petrol he'd smelled when he'd entered the barn.

Hammond looked up at Patrick, a desperate look on his face. He was pale, shivering, suddenly appearing twenty years older, an old, frightened man. 'You need to do what he says,' Hammond whispered.

Graham stepped out of the shadows. In his hand he held a large box of matches, the kind used by chefs.

'Do you have a weapon?' Graham asked in a calm voice. He was dishevelled, his hair sticking up in tufts, stubble darkening his face. He looked like he'd slept rough and Patrick guessed he'd walked all the way out here, knowing the police would be looking for his car.

Patrick shook his head. 'No, Graham. Why don't you put down the matches? Then we can talk.'

A small smile. 'No, we're going to talk anyway.' He coughed. 'You think I'm a murderer, don't you?'

Patrick didn't respond. He waited.

Graham pointed a finger at him and Patrick noticed that it was shaking, his body betraying his nerves, the tension. 'I'm not a murderer. Not a criminal. I killed those girls, sure, but it was justice.'

'Because of Melanie,' Patrick said gently.

'Yes! Those bitches . . . those fucking little bitches murdered *her*.'

'She killed herself, Graham. I understand how hurt you must have been. Your friend.'

'She was more than my friend! She was my soulmate' – he laughed crazily – 'my whole *world*. I promised her that I'd always protect her.'

'You didn't do a very good job, did you?' Mervyn said.

Graham swung around, pulling a match from the box. Mervyn shrank away. 'It wasn't my fault. She didn't . . . She never told me what was happening.'

Guilt. That was what was driving this, Patrick realised. Graham knew he should have been aware of what was happening on the forum that he managed. He wondered if there was more to it, if Melanie had only been into OnTarget because her boyfriend worked for them.

'It was those little bitches' fault,' Graham hissed, turning back to Patrick. 'The things they said about her . . . She was so sensitive, so vulnerable. She couldn't take it. She was a beautiful person. I looked out for her at St Mary's. And afterwards, I always kept in touch with her, helped her, even when . . . even though we couldn't be together anymore.'

'Why not?' Patrick asked in a soft voice. 'Why couldn't you be together?'

'Because she didn't want me anymore. She wanted them. Those fucking . . .' He breathed deeply. 'OnTarget. She retreated into a fantasy world, thought that Shawn and the others were in love with her, that they were going to save her. Suddenly, I wasn't good enough anymore. I stopped going to see her for a while. It all seemed so cruel. It was me who got her into OnTarget. Me who was supposed to run the forums she was so interested in, that she spent all her time on. I didn't look at any of her posts on the forum for weeks because it made me feel too sick, knowing she was on there talking about her new great loves.'

Patrick was surprised. After talking to the staff at St Mary's he had assumed that the love between Graham and Melanie had been one-way: the boy who longed to be wanted loving the attention he got from the vulnerable girl who worshipped him. But it seemed that Graham loved Melanie too. It made sense. Graham had been abandoned, thrown into the care system. He had been vulnerable too.

But that didn't mean Patrick felt sympathy for him.

'You tried to frame Shawn, didn't you?' Patrick said. 'Asked Hattie to tell me about him and that Irish girl.'

Graham didn't reply. He just smiled slyly.

'And then you tried to frame Mervyn, leaving the underwear at his house, calling us.'

Another smile.

Burns still hadn't told Patrick what he wanted and why he had brought him here.

'Let's talk,' Patrick said. 'Tell me how I can help you.'

Graham gathered himself, but still held the match between his trembling fingers. 'I want the true story made public,' he said. 'My side of the story. Melanie's story. I need him to call his friends in the press, make it happen. I want a full interview, front pages, my words with no censorship. I want the world to know that Melanie – the real Melanie, the one who loved me – was pure and innocent, and that I was only granting her dying wish: retribution against the bitches who killed her. Justice. Melanie's soul is in torment right now. I can *feel* it. I thought that the only way Mel could find bliss in death would be for her tormentors to suffer and die. But if that can't happen, if one of them lives, then the only way to stop her suffering is to make sure the world knows the truth.'

'I can do that,' Mervyn said. 'Just give me my phone back and I'll call the editor of *The Sun* right now.'

'But why do you want me here?' Patrick asked, having a horrible feeling he knew what Graham was going to say.

'You're going to vouch for me, back up my story. Speak to the journalists, tell them I'm not guilty of any crime. You need to tell them I did *the right thing*.' He shouted the final words, his face contorted. 'And you need to arrest Chloe Hedges for murder.'

Patrick kept his voice even, neutral. 'I can't do that, Graham.'

Graham took a step towards Hammond and placed the head of the match against the side of the box.

Hammond struggled on the chair, rocking from side to side, almost tipping it over. Patrick moved towards Graham slowly. Could he grab him before he struck the match? It was too risky. Better to talk. It seemed pretty clear that Graham hadn't thought this through. Not unless he planned to keep them here all day and night until he saw a copy of the next morning's newspaper. And how was Patrick supposed to arrest Chloe, while he was stuck in a barn full of petrol?

'Graham,' he said in a soothing tone. 'We can get you help. Maybe . . . maybe we can help organise a memorial for Melanie. Set up a foundation in her name against Internet bullying. Whatever you want. But Chloe Hedges is innocent, just like Melanie was. And what about Nancy Marr? You killed her too, didn't you?'

Graham's eyes flashed. Did he think he'd got away with that one?

'What happened, Graham? Did she find Melanie's body? And the suicide note?'

The other man clenched his jaw.

'And you decided on the spot to kill Nancy because you didn't want anyone to know why Melanie had committed suicide, so you could get revenge without anyone seeing the connection between the victims?'

Graham's silence told Patrick his theory was correct.

'And you practised your torture method on her . . .'

'She told me it was my fault!' Graham yelled. 'That I should have been keeping an eye on Melanie, should have known what was going on. She was an interfering old bitch, just like all the interfering bitches at St Mary's!' Spittle sprayed from his lips. 'I'm sick of this!' he roared and it was as if something snapped in his head, the final thread of self-control. He loomed towards Mervyn.

'Don't do this, you're my son!' Mervyn yelled.

Graham stopped, the unstruck match only inches from Mervyn's skin. Patrick was terrified the petrol fumes would ignite. He couldn't wait. While Graham was momentarily distracted, Patrick launched himself at him, knocking him down, both of them falling to the ground, which was slick with petrol. Graham jumped to his feet and as Patrick tried to stand he slipped and fell to his knees. Graham stepped forwards and kicked Patrick in the face, the explosion of pain sending him reeling.

'You're lying,' Graham said, producing another match from the box. 'Always lying. It's what you do for a living.'

Patrick sat up. His clothes and hands were covered with petrol. Graham was holding the match but was shaking so hard now that he couldn't strike it, cursing and muttering with frustration while Hammond begged him not to do it.

Patrick needed to get Graham away from Mervyn.

He stood up. 'Your girlfriend deserved to die,' he said.

Graham's head whipped round towards Patrick, mouth opening, eyes flashing with shock.

'She bullied those girls – Chloe and Jade and Rose and Jess. She got what was coming to her.'

'Don't. Say. That.'

'I'll say what I like, Graham. I don't give a toss if you turn Mervyn here into a human flambé. He's a scumbag. Go ahead, torch him. Do the world a favour. But after you do I'm going to tell the whole world what Melanie was really like – a girl in her twenties who was obsessed with a fucking boy band. An ugly, weird freak.'

'Shut up!' Graham screamed, running at Patrick, who side-stepped, leaving a leg trailing so Graham tripped and fell hard to the floor. As he pushed himself up, Patrick moved past him towards the door, drawing Graham farther away from Mervyn. The PR man was out of sight now, around the edge of the model railway, but Patrick could hear him sobbing.

'I bet all that stuff on her Facebook page was true. About how she liked shagging dogs . . .'

Graham threw himself at Patrick, his face twisted with fury, and Patrick braced himself, ready to fight. But then Graham stopped.

'No,' he said. 'I know what you're doing.'

He smiled like he was oh so clever and pulled another match from the box, turning to walk back towards Mervyn.

He struck the match.

The flame shot up his petrol-soaked arm. Patrick jumped away from him and Graham screamed, pulling open his jacket, popping the buttons and throwing it to the floor just as the flames rippled across the entire garment, consuming it. Patrick held his breath, convinced the fire would spread, that he and Graham had left a trail of petrol droplets across the floor. But the jacket blazed in isolation, for the moment at least. Patrick looked around frantically and spotted a bottle of mineral water on the model railway's control panel. Snatching it up, he doused the remaining flames.

Graham was making a terrible noise, breaths coming quick and shallow. He held up his arm, his face contorted with agony. The fire had eaten through the sleeve before he'd torn off the jacket and his arm was black and pink. Patrick could smell burning meat.

'Help me. Please.'

Patrick grabbed hold of Graham's other arm and yanked him towards the exit, pulling him out into the open air. But Graham broke free. Patrick chased after him, but realising Graham was heading towards the fish pond, he slowed to a walk.

There was a part of Patrick, a dark part, that wished Graham Burns's whole body had been wet with petrol, not just his arm, that the flames had engulfed him. That Graham had died in unspeakable pain, his punishment for what he'd done, the torture he'd inflicted on those girls, the lives he'd ended prematurely, including Wendy's.

Especially Wendy's.

Instead, Graham would go to prison, or a secure hospital, the kind of place they sent the criminally insane, and he would probably spend the rest of his life there, living and breathing, fed and looked after. Graham talked about justice, but the justice he believed in was an eye for an eye. Not justice, but vengeance.

We're better than that, Patrick thought as he strode after Graham, watched him plunge his arm into the cold water of the carp pond, up to the elbow. Graham lay still on his front, his arm hanging in the water, his cheek against the concrete. His face appeared to glisten with tears, but perhaps it was only water from the pond.

Patrick took out his phone and called Carmella.

'We've got him,' he said. 'I need back-up and an ambulance.' He sniffed the arm of his jacket, could feel the petrol soaking through to his skin. 'And a change of clothes.'

He sat on the damp lawn, realising he ought to go back and release Mervyn, but he wasn't going to let Graham out of his sight this time. He took his e-cigarette out of his jacket pocket and took a long drag, watching Graham and feeling thankful that he didn't smoke real cigarettes anymore.

Epilogue

It was the third encore, 'Boys Don't Cry', and Patrick sneaked a look at his wife, standing beside him, mouthing the words along with the singer on stage. She looked about eighteen, with her long hair tied back and minimal make-up, the heat and excitement giving her cheeks a pink flush.

'My God,' he shouted in her ear. 'I haven't seen you smile like that for years!'

In reply, she slipped an arm around his waist and hugged him. He'd almost forgotten how much of a Cure fan she was too, how that was the first thing that had bonded them all those years ago when they met.

It had been in the function room of a pub down by the river in Hammersmith, a mutual friend's thirtieth birthday party. Pat had turned up not knowing anyone except the birthday girl's fiancé, and he'd been on the verge of going home again when suddenly 'Just Like Heaven' came on over the PA and Gill, sitting at a table nearby with a bunch of mates, had started to sing along, her lips moving in perfect synch with every syllable and phrase.

Patrick hadn't wanted to go home again after that. And when he did, eventually, it was with Gill on his arm, and they'd been almost inseparable from that point on. Until . . .

Well, no need to think about that. Not tonight, he thought, with Bonnie safe on a sleepover with his mum and dad, a nice three-pint beer buzz on, his wife's arm around his waist and his idol, Robert Smith, on stage.

It had been a tough month, one of the toughest, especially Wendy's funeral last week. Patrick and Suzanne had driven up to Wolverhampton together to represent the MIT, their faces rigid with the effort of not displaying the emotion they felt, surrounded by Wendy's weeping family and friends. It seemed unthinkable that Wendy was no longer on the planet, her chirpy presence and eager voice gone forever – particularly because Pat felt so responsible. Suzanne had been great – quietly supportive, surreptitiously putting a hand on his arm during the funeral when she felt that he was about to lose it – and he had been grateful to her.

He'd been anxious about spending so much time with her that day, just the two of them, but the gravitas of the situation had instantly and utterly expunged any hint of romance. Suzanne had been warm and kind, but, to both their unspoken surprise, there hadn't been a trace of flirtation or any of their prior longing glances. Perhaps Wendy's death was the stopper that had crammed that particular genie firmly back in its bottle before it escaped altogether.

It was a relief. Patrick hadn't realised how much added pressure it had been putting on him, the possibility of something happening between him and Suzanne, and the inevitable night-marish ramifications of it. *Keep it simple, stupid*, he muttered to himself. That would be his mantra from now on. 'Simple' was the simplicity of the family unit, the absence of choice, the embrace of commitment. Him and Gill and Bonnie; that was all that mattered.

At least that's what he'd thought until Suzanne texted him half-way through the gig. He pulled out his phone and surreptitiously read the message:

HOPE YOU'RE LOVING THE GIG. YOU DESERVE A BIT OF FUN! MISS YOU. SX

Miss you? He deleted the text without replying, but he could not delete the feeling that it left inside his head and in his heart. She had never said anything so overt to him before, and he felt a flash of anger at her choosing to do so now.

He would still 'keep it simple', he decided – but those few words on his phone's screen made him aware of how difficult it would continue to be. You couldn't just switch off your feelings for someone, no matter what the circumstances were.

He tried to look at the positives. At least he still had a family, a career, his life – unlike Wendy, who had nothing and who'd been killed for nothing.

Patrick felt again the sting of how senseless her death had been. DI Strong's team, working with the Global Sounds IT department, had traced a deleted conversation between Wendy and Graham, posing as a user called Mockingjay365. Graham had clearly been worried that Wendy had found out something that would get him arrested, but in reality Wendy's theory didn't exist. Graham had had no reason, even following his own twisted logic, to kill her.

It was a sickening waste. And Patrick would always feel partially responsible.

The final triumphant guitar chord of 'Boys Don't Cry' rang out and the band bowed and smiled through the cheers.

The house lights came up and the crowd started shuffling out, streaming down stairs and through the venue's reception, ready to do battle with the knock-off merchandise sellers and overcrowded Tube trains.

'Best birthday present ever!' Pat said as they pushed through to the exit. 'Thanks, angel, I loved it.'

'I could tell!' Gill laughed, and kissed his cheek. 'So did I.'

They were almost at the door when someone caught Patrick's arm. 'Mate!' said a man. The man was young, muscular and very familiar-looking, although Patrick couldn't place him. The fact that he wore mirror shades and a huge woollen fashion-victim cap didn't help.

Patrick and Gill stopped, jostled on all sides by the departing crowd. 'Yes?' Patrick said suspiciously.

The man lowered his shades and flashed a smile at him. 'It's me – Shawn.'

Gill made a strange sound in her throat and started subconsciously fiddling with her hair. She'd recognised him before even Patrick had.

'Shawn *Barrett,*' he hissed. 'Sorry about the shades, but you know . . .'

Patrick raised his eyebrows. Shawn Barrett. He remembered then that Shawn was a Cure fan too, via his grandfather. *His grandfather, for fuck's sake!* he thought.

'Quick word?' Shawn dragged them to one side of the reception area. It was astonishing that nobody seemed to recognise him at all, but he guessed it was because most of the audience here were at least twenty years older than Shawn's 'target' market.

'This is my wife, Gill,' Patrick said, grinning at Gill's starstruck face as Shawn shook her hand. She wasn't remotely a fan of OnTarget, but Shawn Barrett was a very good-looking bloke.

'Awesome gig, wasn't it?' Shawn said, pulling at a tuft of facial hair under his lower lip. 'Anyway, mate, just wanted to say good job, like, for catching Graham Burns and getting Mervyn off the hook. He can seem like a right twat, but he's got a heart of gold, that one. And as for Burns, fucking hell, what a number. Doing that shit to those poor girls. Unbelievable! If I'd had any idea what he was like . . .'

Patrick couldn't help but remember Carmella's account of little Roisin McGreevy and how Shawn Barrett had ruined her life. And how 'heart of gold' Mervyn Hammond had had no qualms about buying her silence.

Still, he thought. Nothing was ever straightforward, was it? He had a brief flash of memory of Suzanne in the park, in her running gear . . . Fifty shades of grey, indeed. Wasn't everything, where morals were concerned?

'Hey, is it true?' Shawn whispered. 'That Mervyn is Graham's dad?'

'You shouldn't believe everything you read in the papers,' Patrick replied.

'Ha!' Shawn grinned his famous grin.

But it was true. Mervyn Hammond was Graham Burns's father. After the ambulance had turned up and taken Graham away, under police escort, Patrick had gone back into the barn and released Mervyn, who sat shivering and snivelling on the chair. Patrick had a feeling Mervyn would never be the same after this.

'It's true, what I told him,' Hammond had said as Patrick struggled with the wet rope that bound Mervyn to the chair. 'He is my son. It was a long time ago, when I was just starting out and did the PR for this little club in the East End. I've never been, ah, a very sexual person.'

Patrick had wondered if he really wanted to hear this, but nodded for Hammond to continue.

'But Sandy, that was her name, she had this magnetic quality. A seductive quality. We did it once, in a dressing room, thirty seconds of fumbling, and three months later she told me she was pregnant. I'm ashamed to say that I freaked out. I really didn't want kids, and Sandy had a reputation . . . I accused her of lying, said she couldn't know who the dad was because she slept around so much. She went away and I forgot all about it.' He cleared his throat. 'Made myself forget about it.'

'But Graham ended up in the care system?' Patrick had asked.

'Yeah. But I didn't find out about that for years. It was about ten years later, when I was starting to get pretty successful. I bumped into an old mate from the club who asked me if I'd heard about what happened to Sandy. He said she'd had the baby but hadn't been able to cope, was still going out, taking drugs, sleeping around . . . leaving her son at home alone. Social services had intervened and taken the baby into care.'

Patrick had removed the rope, freeing Mervyn, but he remained in the same position, his head hanging low.

'I knew the baby would be, what, nine or ten by this point. And I started to wonder . . . was he my son? My own dad had just died and I was feeling vulnerable, thinking about family and the meaning of life, all that shit.' He laughed without humour. 'So I decided to track down Sandy's little boy, spoke to some social workers . . . greased a few palms. And there he was, at St Mary's. They told me he had a lot of behavioural issues, that they hadn't been able to place him in long-term foster care or find anyone to adopt him because he was too difficult.'

Mervyn had pushed himself to his feet, bones and joints cracking. He'd drifted over to his model railway, watched the locomotives running round the track, a faraway look in his eye.

'I still didn't know if he was my son . . . until I saw him. The second I laid eyes on him, I knew. He was my flesh and blood. But . . . I didn't have room for a kid in my life. I was so busy, travelling here, there and everywhere, working sixteen-hour days, seven days a week. I thought he was better off where he was. The solution, I thought, was for me to start visiting St Mary's, under the guise of a mentor, helping coach the troubled kids. I mean, I still do it now. I enjoy it. It makes me feel like I'm atoning for my past mistakes, for all the bad stuff I've done.'

Patrick had nodded.

'But I kept a close eye on Graham. Him and his little girlfriend, Melanie. They were inseparable, you know. If anyone did anything to hurt her . . . well.'

'He'd hurt them?'

'I never knew what he did. But whatever it was, the person who'd upset Melanie never went near her again.' Hammond had fiddled with the controls of his train set. 'I didn't even know he was still in touch with her, after they left St Mary's. I thought she was off the scene. Because I took him out of that world, got him jobs, helped him – like an invisible, guiding hand. A guardian angel. That's what I thought anyway.'

Mervyn had looked like he was on the verge of passing out.

'Funnily enough, I mentioned Melanie to Graham the other day, asked him if he was still in touch with "that weird girl" he used to be so crazy about. He snapped at me, said she wasn't weird. But I didn't think anything of it.'

'When was this?'

Mervyn had gone quiet and Patrick had thought he'd slipped into shock. But then he'd said, 'Monday. The day before the party.'

At that point, more paramedics had arrived and taken Mervyn out to an ambulance and to hospital to be checked over. Patrick had stood in the converted barn for a while. He expected this would all come out at the trial. Mervyn Hammond's career would be ruined. And Patrick wasn't sure how he felt about that. He thought about Mervyn mentioning Melanie to Graham. Was that why Graham had chosen to frame Mervyn, because he was angry about him calling Melanie weird? Patrick had wondered why Graham had left more than a week between targeting Rose and Jess and then Chloe and Jade. This was something he intended to ask Graham, but his guess was that Graham had been scared after the police visited Global Sounds, decided to lie low. Maybe Mervyn had stirred up Graham's anger again, prompting him to finish what he'd started sooner rather than later.

An examination of Graham's phone had answered the final question. As Peter Bell had predicted, a cache of photos Graham had sent to the girls through Snapchat had been stored in a folder on the phone. They knew exactly how he'd lured them to their deaths. The evidence against Burns was rock solid. Even if he had the best lawyer in the world, he was going to prison probably for the rest of his life.

'So what are you boys up to these days?' he asked Shawn now. 'New album in the pipeline?'

Shawn looked surprised. 'Haven't you heard?' He sounded slightly outraged. 'OnT have split up. This thing with Burns was, like, the final straw, but I've been thinking about going solo for quite a while, you know, be a real musician. No more of that manu-factured shite.'

'Oh right,' Patrick said politely, declining to add that he'd been rather too busy attending court as a witness for the prosecution of a serial killer to have noticed that Britain's favourite boy band had gone their separate ways.

'Speaking of real musicians, I'm just on my way backstage now to meet Bob and the lads,' Shawn said casually. 'I remember you mentioned you're a fan. Want to tag along? I can get you a couple of these, no bother.' He stuck out his hand to show off his Access All Areas wristband.

Gill's eyes opened wide as saucers. Patrick smiled at her, then looked back at Shawn Barrett; little more than a kid with muscles, really, he thought. A very rich kid with muscles.

'Very kind of you,' he said. 'I'm tempted – but to be honest we need to get home. Send him my best, though, won't you?'

———

'Are you insane?' Gill asked him once they were on the train, surrounded by hot, excited middle-aged people in Cure T-shirts. 'I thought you'd have sold your mother for a chance to meet Robert Smith. We don't even have to get back for a babysitter!'

Patrick looked pensive. 'Yeah, a few years ago maybe. But you know what they say – never meet your idols.'

He saw the girls then in his mind's eye: Rose, Jessica, Jade, Wendy . . . and Chloe Hedges, at least home now with her family. Thank God one of them was. *The blissfully dead*. It was a phrase from 'Lullaby', the song the band had opened their set with, and it chased itself around his head.

He hoped that they were; that such a thing was possible.

Letter from the Authors

Dear Reader

Thanks for reading *The Blissfully Dead*. It goes without saying that we hope you enjoyed it and would love to hear your thoughts about it. Our email address is markandlouise@me.com or you can message us through our Facebook page: www.facebook.com /vossandedwards.

In this letter we're going to tell you a little about the inspiration behind this book and also how we write together. Please be aware that this letter may contain some spoilers, so please don't read it if you haven't already finished the book.

The initial idea for this book came from a TV documentary called *Crazy About One Direction*, which was shown on Channel 4 in the UK in 2013. In this documentary, a number of teenage fans of the titular boy band demonstrated their extreme love for their idols and revealed the rivalry and jealousy that can spring up when emotions are high and hormones are running riot. One interesting thread of the documentary focused on fan fiction and 'shipping', the creation of stories in which members of the band are engaged in a love affair.

The documentary itself was illuminating, but the reaction of One Direction's fans was even more fascinating. Twitter exploded with outrage and horror, the girls who appeared on the programme were vilified and, bizarrely, thousands of fans began to tweet claims that a number of 'shippers' were so distraught they had committed suicide. These claims were false, but it demonstrated how fandom and social media can collide to create what can only be described as hysteria.

We are both big music lovers and first bonded over our love of The Cure (whose song 'Lullaby' gave this novel its title). Also, Louise used to work in the music industry. We knew writing a novel set in that world would be fun.

As we started to write *The Blissfully Dead*, and to think about the relationship between fans and celebrities, our thoughts turned to the Operation Yewtree investigations of the last few years. For non-UK readers, these investigations exposed a number of high-profile pop stars, DJs and TV personalities when women came forward to claim that they had been sexually assaulted as teenagers by these famous men decades ago. In most cases, they had been afraid to accuse them at the time – or had done so and been ignored or ridiculed. As we write, some formerly much-loved stars are now in prison, their pasts exposed, their reputations destroyed.

We should point out that all of the characters in *The Blissfully Dead* are fictional and not based on any real people, but some of the cases referred to in the book, including Ian Watkins, the former singer with Lostprophets, are factual. OnTarget are not based on

One Direction but are a composite of all the manufactured bands who have inspired devotion over the years.

So how did we write it? This is the question we get asked more than any other: exactly how do two people go about writing a novel together? We live several hundred miles apart (that's not too bad; we wrote our first novel with one of us in London, the other in Tokyo) and don't meet up very often. But when we start, we get together and discuss the basic plot of the book and create a chapter plan.

We follow the 'driving in the dark' method of writing, where you can only see a certain distance ahead. So our initial chapter plan might cover the first ten chapters. We divide them up and get going. One of us writes a chapter and sends it to the other. That person edits it and makes comments, then sends it back. When we are both happy with the chapter it goes into a master document.

Our books nearly always have multiple narrators, so we each choose characters to write, though we take turns to write from our main character's point of view. There are certain types of scene that suit us best. For example, Mark usually writes action scenes and Louise tends to write more emotional chapters. But we mix these up more than we used to. We're not saying who writes the sex scenes . . .

During the writing of the novel we meet several times to discuss the plot and when we finally reach the end, we both go through and produce a huge list of points to be addressed. But co-writing is much easier than writing a novel solo because you get instant feedback and somebody to bounce ideas off. We highly recommend it – as long as you find the right person. It's no lie to say that over the course of six novels together we have never argued. We imagine that married couples who co-write books have far more heated discussions than we've ever had!

The Blissfully Dead is the second novel to feature DI Patrick Lennon, following *From the Cradle*. We have lots more adventures planned for Lennon and we hope that you'll be there to find out what challenge he faces next . . . and whether Winkler will ever turn out to have any redeeming qualities.

Best wishes
Louise and Mark

P.S. If you want to be the first to find out about our new books, special deals, etc., you can join our email list at www.vossandedwards .com/newsletter.

Acknowledgements

A number of people generously helped with research for this book, including Elizabeth Haynes, Simon Alcock, Chris Phillips, Elaine Burtenshaw and (for Dublin-based information) Alice Brady. As always, any procedural inaccuracies are ours.

Thanks to everyone who helped us make this book better, including our editor Katie Green, our agent Sam Copeland and Sara Edwards who read an early draft and helped with research into the foster care system. Thank you too to Gracie Voss for helping with the teen speak!

A big thank you to everyone at Thomas & Mercer, especially Emilie Marneur, for her passion and enthusiasm, and to the rest of the T&M team, especially Sana Chebaro, Neil Hart and Eoin Purcell.

Finally, we want to thank our readers on facebook.com /vossandedwards who are not at all like the fans in this book – though they can be as enthusiastic! Some names in this book were provided by members of that group, including Cassandra Oliver and

Sandra Mangan, whose surname we borrowed. We would also like to thank Tracy Fenton and all the members of THE Book Group on Facebook for being such fun and keeping Mark's ego in check.

About the Authors

Photo © 2014 Mark Earthy

Mark Edwards and Louise Voss are the co-authors of psychological thrillers *Killing Cupid* and *Forward Slash* and two medical thrillers, *Catch Your Death* and *All Fall Down*, as well as *From the Cradle*, the first in the DI Patrick Lennon series.

They met in 1999 after Mark appeared on a BBC documentary about aspiring writers. They were the first British 'indie' writers to reach number one on the Kindle chart and have sold over 650,000 books, including Mark's solo novel, *The Magpies*.

Louise lives in Surrey with her daughter, and Mark lives in Wolverhampton with his wife and their children. Mark and Louise love hearing from readers and can be contacted via markandlouise@me .com or on www.facebook.com/vossandedwards. They blog regularly on www.vossandedwards.com.

Download a Free Short Story by Voss & Edwards

One Shot

A new short story featuring DI Lennon's partner, DS Carmella Masiello.

When a man is killed during a dispute with his next-door neighbour, DS Masiello has to prove that it was murder – or let a killer walk free . . .

Get it now by visiting www.vossandedwards.com/oneshot